S0-BDM-272

Praise for Jay Lake's *Mainspring*

"*Mainspring* is a nonstop adventure yarn that's the equal of anything from Fritz Leiber or Robert E. Howard, with a premise that's so mind-bendingly weird that it'll have you giggling in public. The idea is that the universe is a giant, magnificent clockwork, the planets themselves on gears whose teeth are visible in the night sky. A humble apprentice is catapulted into adventure when an angel charges him with a quest to save the world from ruin when its mainspring winds down. There's zeppelin battles, demented theology, and lots and lots of clocky, mechanical goodness here. This is blasphemy at its finest."

—BoingBoing.com

"The world is a giant clockwork mechanism powered by hidden gears and moving along a track through the sky. When the Archangel Gabriel visits apprentice clockmaker Hethor, instructing him to take the Key Perilous and use it to rewind the Mainspring of Earth lest the world come to an end, Hethor embarks on a journey that takes him to unexplored lands and sets him against many in high places who believe him to be deluded or heretical. Lake's first trade hardcover novel presents an original and intriguing vision of an alternate Earth during its period of Enlightenment. As Hethor and his companions find their faith in the Divine Clockmaker both challenged and justified, so, too, do they discover the humanity that both blesses and curses them in a mechanistic world. All but the smallest libraries should consider this for their SF or speculative fiction collections. Highly recommended."

—*Library Journal*

"Could *Mainspring* be the opening canto of a metaphysical magnum opus in the vein of Wolfe? Yes, very plausibly. The language is lyrical and perfectly calibrated; the symbolism is profound; the intelligent mystification is just at the appropriate level. With this novel, Jay Lake has ascended from journeyman to master; let the masterwork now unfold."

—*Locus*

"Lake envisions the universe as an enormous clockwork, put in motion by God, complete with gears and a mainspring hidden at Earth's center, in his intriguing first trade hardcover novel, a fantasy set in the magic-tinged late nineteenth century. . . . Lake demonstrates his enormously fertile imagination in this unusual book."

—*Publishers Weekly*

"*Mainspring* is a grand and glorious adventure, an epic journey of imagination the likes of which I haven't often seen. . . . A breathlessly exciting tale that takes the best old-school storytelling and the most vivid contemporary world-building sensibilities and spot-welds them together. Think Edgar Rice Burroughs or Philip José Farmer meets China Miéville or Ian R. MacLeod by way of religious allegory. *Mainspring* is always gripping and often dazzling in its vision."

—*SFReviews.net*

"Theological steampunk set in a mechanical universe— the debut novel from a noted short-story writer . . . Good elements—intriguing alternate history, solid characters, briskly moving plot."

—*Kirkus Reviews*

"A fascinating take on the God-as-clockmaker theory, this is a compellingly readable coming-of-age story. . . . Superb world-building and an original take on an old idea."

—*Romantic Times BOOKreviews*

"From the sweeping mechanisms of his clockwork world, down to the subtle movements of his characters, all drawn with a clockmaker's eye, Lake gives us a story both grand and intimate, smart and savvy . . . and a whole lot of fun to boot."

—Hal Duncan, author of *Vellum*

"As if Edgar Rice Burroughs had collaborated with Adam Roberts, or as if Robert Louis Stevenson had partnered with Gene Wolfe, Jay Lake, in his new novel *Mainspring,* delivers a mad, brave, compellingly readable tale of an alternate universe where the gear-stuffed Earth literally rolls through the Heavens on a brass track, and one commonplace but bold and noble-hearted young man— apprentice horologist Hethor Jacques—finds himself nominated by an angel to set right the faltering orrery.

"Tendentious politicians compare our Creation to a watch found in the jungle, implying a Maker. Lake, with the artist's instincts for narrative and character over dogma, takes this conceit and runs with it in postmodern fashion toward a conclusion both shattering and redemptive. Lucent, tactile, deeply inhabited, the world of Hethor Jacques is a marvelous subcreation stuffed full of miracles, both cosmic and domestic. In Hethor's world, one can hear the midnight meshing of mystical gears. I imagine they sound somewhat like the subliminal hum of this book."

—Paul Di Filippo, author of *The Steampunk Trilogy*

MAINSPRING

JAY LAKE

A TOM DOHERTY ASSOCIATES BOOK • NEW YORK

NOTE: If you purchased this book without a cover, you should be aware that this book is stolen property. It was reported as "unsold and destroyed" to the publisher, and neither the author nor the publisher has received any payment for this "stripped book."

This is a work of fiction. All of the characters, organizations, and events portrayed in this novel are either products of the author's imagination or are used fictitiously.

MAINSPRING

Copyright © 2007 by Joseph E. Lake Jr.

All rights reserved, including the right to reproduce this book, or portions thereof, in any form.

Edited by Beth Meacham

A Tor Book
Published by Tom Doherty Associates, LLC
175 Fifth Avenue
New York, NY 10010

www.tor-forge.com

Tor® is a registered trademark of Tom Doherty Associates, LLC.

ISBN-13: 978-0-7653-5636-9
ISBN-10: 0-7653-5636-8

First Edition: June 2007
First Mass Market Edition: May 2008

Printed in the United States of America

0 9 8 7 6 5 4 3 2 1

For Kristine Kathryn Rusch,
Dean Wesley Smith,
and Loren Coleman,
who made me do it in the first place,
in a place called Lincoln City

ACKNOWLEDGMENTS

This book would not have been possible without the kind assistance of many people, including Kelly Buehler and Daniel Spector, Sarah Bryant, Michael Curry, Rose Fox, Tami Gierloff, Anna Hawley, Robin Hill, Carolyn Lachance, Ken Scholes, my entire LiveJournal community, and many others I have doubtless neglected to name. I also want to recognize the Brooklyn Post Office here in Portland, Oregon, as well as the Fireside Coffee Lodge and Lowell's Print-Inn for all their help and support. Special thanks go to Jennifer Jackson, Beth Meacham, and Deanna Hoak. Any errors and omissions are entirely my own.

ONE

THE ANGEL gleamed in the light of Hethor's reading candle bright as any brasswork automaton. The young man clutched his threadbare coverlet in the irrational hope that the quilted cotton scraps could shield him from whatever power had invaded his attic room. Trembling, he closed his eyes.

His master, the clockmaker Franklin Bodean, had taught Hethor to listen to the mechanisms of their work. But he'd found that he could listen to life, too. Hethor heard first and always his own breathing, even now heavy and slow despite his burgeoning sense of fear.

The old house on New Haven's King George III Street creaked as it always did. A horse clopped past outside, buggy wheels rattling along with the echo of hooves on cobbles. Great steam-driven foghorns echoed over Long Island Sound. The new electrick lamps lighting the street outside hissed and popped. Underneath the noises of the city lay the ticking of Master Bodean's clocks, and under that, if he listened very hard, the rattle of the world's turning.

But there was no one in the room with him. No one else drew breath; no floorboard creaked. No strange smells either. Merely his own familiar sweat, the hot-tallow scent of his candle, the oils of the house—wood and machine—and a ribbon of salt air from the nearby sea.

Was this a dream?

"I am alone." He said it as something between a prayer and the kind of spell he used to try to cast in the summer woods when he was a boy—calling on Indian lore and God's word and dark magic from the Southern Earth and the timeless power of stone walls and spreading oaks.

Finally Hethor opened his eyes.

The angel was still there.

It no longer seemed made of brasswork. Rather, it looked almost human, save for the height, tall as his ceiling at the attic's peak, close to seven feet. The great wings crowded the angel's back to sweep close across its body like a cloak, feathers white as a swan. Its skin was pale as Hethor's own, but the face was narrow, shaped like the nib of a fountain pen, with a pointed chin and gleaming black eyes. The lines and planes of the angel's visage were sheer masterwork, finer than the statues of saints in the great churches of New Haven.

Hethor held his breath, afraid to even share the air with such perfection. No dream, this, but perhaps yet a nightmare.

The angel smiled. For the first time it appeared to be more than a statue. "Greetings, Hethor Jacques."

With voice came breath, though the angel's scent was still that of a statue—cold marble and damp stone. Or perhaps old metal, like a well-made clock.

Hethor dropped his grip on the blanket to grab the chain around his neck and traced the wheel-and-gear of Christ's horofixion. "G-g-greetings . . . ," he stammered. "And welcome." Though that last was a lie, he felt he must say it.

"I am Gabriel," said the angel, "come to charge you with a duty."

"Duty." Hethor sucked air between his teeth and lips,

finally filling aching lungs with breath he had not even realized he had been holding in the strangeness of the moment. "My life is filled with duty, sir." Duty to Master Bodean, to his studies at New Haven Latin Grammar School, to his late parents and the church and the crown.

The angel appeared to ignore Hethor's statement. "The Key Perilous is lost."

Key Perilous? Hethor had never heard of it. "I . . ."

"The Mainspring of the world winds down," the angel continued. "Only a man, created in the image of the Tetragrammaton, can set it right. Only you, Hethor."

Hethor's fists clenched so tight he felt the tendons stand out. His pulse hissed in his ears. This was a trick, a trap, some fiendish silliness dreamt up by Bodean's dreadful sons and their Yale friends. "There are no angels. Not anymore."

Gabriel extended a fist toward Hethor, nearing the apprentice in his bed without seeming to move. The angel's wings parted to reveal a body of marbled perfection clothed in a state of nature. The angel twisted its hand palm up and opened its fingers.

A tiny feather lay there. It was not much larger than the goose down from Hethor's often-patched pillow. The angel pursed its lips, blew a breath that sparkled like shooting stars in a summer sky, then vanished. A thunderclap nearly deafened Hethor. As he shook his head to clear the noise, he heard all the bells of the house and shop below him ringing, clanging, banging—hundreds of clocks chiming heaven's hour at once.

Master Bodean's sleep-muddled curses rose through the floor as the tiny feather circled where the angel had stood.

Hethor scooped it up, cutting his right palm in the process. As he struggled left-handed into his breeches, he looked at what he had caught.

The feather was solid silver, with razored edges. It gleamed in the candlelight. The cut on his palm was in the shape of a key.

"Hethor!" bellowed Master Bodean from below. "Are yer alive up there, boy?"

"Coming, sir," Hethor yelled back. Setting the feather on his writing desk, he stepped into his boots—two sizes too small—grabbed his coat, which was a size too small, and raced out the little door and down the attic stairs.

IT TOOK more than an hour to settle all the clocks in Master Bodean's workshop. Some had sounded out the sum of the hours—the holy number twelve—then resumed their ticking slumber. Others, especially the smaller, more delicate mechanisms, had been possessed of a nervous tinkling that could only be dampened by careful attention with rubber mallets and soft chamois. Hethor and Master Bodean moved from clock to clock, ministering to their brass and copper hearts, right through the chiming of eleven o'clock of the evening.

Finally they stood in the workroom. Both were exhausted from the hour and the work. Master Bodean, redfaced and round-bodied in his nightshirt and gray cable-knit sweater, nodded to Hethor. "Good work, boy." He was always a fair man, even in meting out punishments.

"Thank you, sir." Hethor glanced around the workroom. All was in comforting and familiar order. A tiny furnace, newly powered by electricks. Casting slugs. Tools, ranging from hammers almost too small to see to vises large enough to crack a man's head. And parts in their bins; springs and gears and escapements, all the myriad incarnations of brass, steel, and movement jewels.

It seemed as if the angel Gabriel—archangel? Hethor suddenly wondered—had risen from the genius loci of this workshop. He had felt a sense of deliberation, precision, even power, from his visitor that reminded him of the greatest and slowest of clocks.

"Yer all right, boy?" Bodean asked, interrupting

Hethor's reverie. "You're ordinarily a bit more talkish than this."

Hethor found himself unwilling to mention the angel. Bodean would have thought him mad, for one thing. The very idea sounded horrendously self-important. He needed to sort his own thoughts, try to understand what had taken place. "I . . . it was the lightning, Master. It frightened me."

"Lightning, eh? Some bolt that must've been. Never seen a storm set all the clocks a-chiming before." Bodean shook his head. "Lightning and more than lightning. One of the good Lord's mysteries, I'll warrant." He walked over to his locked cupboards and pulled a set of keys from a pocket in his nightshirt. He took down a small pewter flask and two tumblers. "Sounds like you need a little lightning of your own, boy." Golden liquid splashed into each glass. "This'll help you sleep."

Hethor had never tasted anything stronger than table wine. The whiskey, or whatever it was, had no attraction for him. Yet here was Master Bodean, holding out the little glass, smiling. Hethor took it and sniffed. He almost choked on the sharp scent alone.

"This is true lightning," said Master Bodean with a broken-toothed grin. He tipped the glass to his lips and drank it all in one quick swallow.

Hethor tried to imitate Bodean. It was like drinking fire. The whiskey went down, barely. He had to cup his hand over his lips to keep from coughing some of it out. It tasted like he imagined lamp oil might taste—foul and sharp and strange.

Laughing, Master Bodean slapped Hethor's back, which only made the choking worse. "Never fear, lad, this will all seem less than a dream to yer in the morning."

Hethor stumbled to bed to lie hot and thick-skulled under his blanket waiting for sleep. He barely heard the clatter of sidereal midnight echoing through the skies, never heard the clocks of the house strike the twelfth hour. Cotton-mouthed and woolly-headed, he dreamt all night of keys and feathers and clocks with steel teeth.

MORNING BROUGHT sunlight, a headache, and the realization that he was going to be late for his studies at New Haven Latin. Hethor scrambled into his good trousers and his second-best shirt while he tried to shake the clouds out of his mind. Though he kept no clock in his attic room, Hethor always knew the time. He would be late for Master Sullivan's maths class. Knowing Master Sullivan, the door would be locked and Hethor would be forced to seek Headmaster Brownlee's indulgence.

As a mere apprentice, that was dangerous. No one would think to question Brownlee throwing a boy of Hethor's low standing out of school, even in his final year. Only Master Bodean's goodwill and the last of the money from Hethor's late father had kept him enrolled until the age of sixteen.

Hethor shrugged into his corduroy coat—yet another Bodean family hand-me-down. Boots gripped by his fingertips, he was just about to hurl himself out the door and down the stairs when something caught his eye. It was the little silver feather, glinting on his writing desk.

The previous night came back to him in a collapsing rush: the angel Gabriel and the feather and the clocks and the Key Perilous.

Duty.

He was not mad; he had not dreamed. But he needed to understand before he could explain it to Master Bodean or anyone else.

Hethor dropped the boots, stepped into them, swept up the feather, and clattered down the stairs. New Haven Latin lay fifteen minutes' walk south and east of Bodean's Finer Clocks, Repairs and Special Commissions Welcome. Instead, Hethor headed along King George III Street and left on Elm Street. West, toward

Yale University and deeper into Headmaster Brownlee's bad books.

The angel's visit had been too real to ignore.

MASTER BODEAN'S eldest son, Pryce, read divinity at the Berkeley School at Yale. Of Bodean's three boys, Pryce had spent the least time tormenting Hethor since he had moved into the Bodean attic at the age of eleven. In point of fact, Pryce had spent the least time paying any attention to Hethor whatsoever. On the few occasions when they had spoken, Pryce had been the most considerate, if not exactly kind.

Hethor hoped his master's eldest would grant him some counsel, out of loyalty to his father. Or possibly sheer Christian virtue if nothing else.

Pryce pursued most of his studies in Yale's Fayerweather Hall. Hethor set his course for the university, figuring on locating the building when he got there. The morning was fine, beeches and elms along Elm Street in bloom, flowerbeds beneath them bright with the colors of spring. The air tasted of May, while the dust of dozens of varietals of bloom tickled his nose. The brass ring of the Earth's orbital track glinted bright in the cloudless sky, its curve making horns that arced across the blue. There were few enough people out that the day almost seemed to belong to him. Electrick trolleys that he had never had enough money to ride rattled by every so often. A few horsemen passed as well, but otherwise the street was as quiet as the morning of Creation. Not even the nannies were out with their charges yet. The morning dew hadn't quite burned off, lending damp potential to the day.

The campus itself surprised Hethor. Having come to New Haven only for his apprenticeship to Master Bodean—a seven-day-a-week affair, save for school and church—he'd never had the opportunity to simply wander the streets. Rushing about on his master's errands, head down and feet pounding, Hethor didn't know much of the city except as a limited collection of well-traveled routes.

Yale insinuated itself in the heart of New Haven as though the university were a vital organ in its own right. First a building here or there—a church, a students' rooming house—each marked by a discreet sign or a college coat of arms. Then suddenly wide-lawned parks and a bloom of towering red brick buildings with white trim. His own New Haven Latin school was but a pale imitation of these great precincts of learning.

He found Fayerweather Hall by virtue of nearly running into a signpost that announced the Berkeley Oval. Fayerweather was one of five such buildings standing on a circled drive just off Elm Street.

Hethor gripped his bookstrap tight and ascended the worn marble steps. With luck, Pryce Bodean would be somewhere within. With more luck, Pryce would agree to see Hethor. With the greatest luck of all, Hethor might be able to slip back into his own school without being suspended or worse.

THE ELDERLY porter was almost kind to Hethor, making him wait inside a dusty room occupied mostly by wide-headed brushes intended for the cleaning of sidewalks. Hethor didn't mind. He stared out a grubby window set in an odd corner of the building's front and rubbed the silver feather between his fingers, careful to avoid the sharp edges.

Elm Street was still slow and quiet. Here within the confines of Fayerweather Hall, Hethor felt a kind of peace.

Almost.

The porter came back, rattling the door as he opened it. "Mister Bodean will see you in the receiving room," the old man said, balanced on the edge between dignity and pomposity.

"Thank you."

Together they walked across a hall that gleamed with the labor of generations of charwomen. The porter held open a door eight feet tall and four feet wide.

No one had ever held a door for Hethor before.

The receiving room contained two tables, with chairs on each side, surrounded by book-lined walls. Tall, narrow windows faced trees outside. Pryce Bodean stood behind the second table, by his build and features a short, thin copy of his father. Where Master Franklin Bodean was ruddy with thick dark hair fading to silver, Pryce was pale, green-eyed, his sandy hair already growing sparse— his late mother's coloration.

Hethor had known Mistress Bodean for less than a year before a stroke took first her speech, then her life.

"Have you an errand from my father?" Pryce asked in a clear, thoughtful voice, as if he were even now practicing to preach. "Porter Andrew implied that this was so."

"No, sir," Hethor said slowly. He had to be careful, lest Pryce simply have him thrown out, then send a message to Master Bodean that Hethor was skylarking instead of studying. "I am in sore need of advice."

"An apprentice takes his guidance from his master." Pryce allowed a measured tone of exasperation into his cadenced speech. "Surely my father can aid you in whatever petty concerns you have found to occupy your idle mind."

"Not in this, sir." Hethor found his words rushing out of him despite his resolve to be careful, not to mention his rekindling dislike of Master Bodean's sons. "This is a problem of . . . of the divine."

"The divine?" Pryce grew scornful. "Hah. Enough that you seem to be incompetent to work at my father's affairs, now you are also getting above yourself. What would a mere apprentice know of divinity? Have you even been to services of late, boy?"

"Not as often as I should, no sir." Hethor stared at his morning-damp boots. They had probably first been

Pryce's, he realized, trying not to think about the trouble he was digging into even now. But where else could he go for the sort of advice he needed?

Pryce sighed, just as mannered and exaggerated as his voice. "Our Savior gave his life on Pilate's gear-and-wheel for this? A clockmaker's apprentice who cannot maintain the simplest of Christian obligations, then cheats on his duties to go wandering through the city. I should write you up, boy, but it would break my father's foolish old heart. Now what is it that you want?"

Hethor almost held back, thinking to excuse himself. It was clear that Pryce would not take him seriously. But he had come this far. He didn't think he could back out of the interview now—better to try for the truth and hope that Pryce understood, than slip into the disgrace toward which his master's son would so cheerfully shove him. Hethor laid the silver feather on the table. Blood still darkened its sharp edges. "This is a surety, Mister Bodean, of a . . . message I have received. Concerning the Key Perilous."

Pryce reached out, touched the feather with a finger. "And what, precisely, do you think the Key Perilous is, young apprentice Hethor?" His voice was deliberate, slow.

Hethor noticed Pryce was no longer insulting him with every word. "I'm sure I don't know, sir," he said quietly, praying silently to Gabriel and God that coming here had not been a mistake. Would the scales now fall from Pryce's eyes? Maybe the seriousness of Hethor's question was dawning on Master Bodean's eldest.

Picking the feather up, Pryce stared at Hethor. The green gaze seemed to deepen as some balance of impatience and consideration struggled within. Finally, like they were being forced out, the words slowly came.

"It's a legend, boy. Silly, magical nonsense from the Southern Earth, like the Philosopher's Stone or the Sangreal. People look at God's Creation, His tracks and gears high in the sky, and they believe that there must be a role for themselves in influencing the progress of the stars and planets. People who believe in things like the Key Perilous, in ancient secrets and lost knowledge, those people can be dangerously unbalanced. Whoever put the notion of the Key Perilous in your head is no friend of yours, Hethor. No friend at all."

"*He* gave me that," Hethor said. Pryce was trying to talk Hethor out of his own epiphany. "An angel came to me in darkness, told me to seek the Key Perilous, and gave me that feather as proof of his words. Have you ever seen its like?"

"Hethor, any jeweler's apprentice could cast this from a simple mold. I've no doubt you yourself could, if my father kept such tools about his workshop." Pryce sighed. "Angels no more touch the lives of ordinary boys than do kings and princes. Less so, for kings and princes walk the Northern Earth, while angels are just metaphors for God's divine agency within His Creation."

"The angel was real," Hethor insisted, still trying to rally Pryce to his cause. He was losing, though; he knew it. And Pryce held the feather. "Despite what you say. No metaphor at all. Gabriel was as real as anything I've ever seen." More real, in a way.

Edging past the end of the table where Hethor stood, Pryce walked to the door of the receiving room. "Go on about your business, Hethor. I'll have Porter Andrew write you a note that you were here at my behest. It may spare you some trouble."

"My feather . . ."

"I'll return it to my father." Pryce shook his head. "I don't suppose you've actually stolen it from him, as you wouldn't have the backbone to show it to me if you did, but an apprentice has no business with such a thing in his possession."

The door clicked shut.

Despite his sixteen years, tears of anger and frustration stung Hethor's eyes. There was nothing more to do or say. As an apprentice, he was bound to his master almost as tightly as any slave. Unlike a slave, when Master Bodean chose to elevate Hethor to journeyman, he would have considerably more freedom, perhaps be on his way to true independence. But for now, he was as powerless as any woman or child.

And he'd just been turned out like an errant brat. Without even Gabriel's tiniest feather to show for his visitation.

Hethor turned his right hand to look at the cut the feather had made the night before. Where he expected a thin scab, or perhaps an angry red line, there was only the faint key-shaped scar.

"By the gears of Heaven," he muttered, "what does this *mean*?"

Porter Andrew handed Hethor a sealed note on his way out. Hethor scuffed back down the steps toward Elm Street, wondering what he was to say to Headmaster Brownlee, when he saw a signpost pointing toward the Divinity School library.

Libraries had books, with illustrated plates. Surely in all of history someone had captured an image of Gabriel.

He could find some proof of his story. Proof for himself, at the least. At any rate, it was another path toward an answer.

"MY MASTER has sent me to find details of paintings of Gabriel, the Angel of the Annunciation," Hethor said to the library porter. He waved the note from Porter Andrew, backside out in case the porter recognized the handwriting. He knew he appeared of no consequence— a narrow-chested, sandy-haired boy of medium height, no different from half the young men in New Haven. Only the subterfuge of the note protected him.

"Who did you say your master was?" The library porter was a young man with wide-spaced eyes and a face that tended toward vagueness.

"Master Bodean the horologist."

The porter's expression narrowed, so Hethor hastily amended himself. "Clockmaker. My master is a clockmaker."

"Horo . . . horo . . . what's a clockmaker need to look at pictures for?"

Good question. The library porter was not as vague as he seemed. "Ah, well, we have a painted clockface we are repairing. There has been some damage to the brushwork. Master wants a reference to give to the artist who will be doing the restoration."

The porter thought that over for a moment. "Very well, go in and speak to Librarian Childress. You will find her at a black desk through the second set of arches."

Her? "Thank you, sir."

"I'm not a sir," grumbled the porter with injured pride. "I *work* for my keep."

Hethor grinned, hopped his way through a little bow, and scuttled inside.

LIBRARIAN CHILDRESS was indeed through the second set of arches, two pointed vaults of granite that soared over a black-and-white marbled floor showing stylized representations of the twelve stations of the horofix, one for each chiming of the hour. She was also indeed a woman, behind a tall desk that resembled a priest's lectern, her graying hair pinned back so severely that it might have been painted on her scalp.

Hethor knew little about girls and less about women, but he guessed Librarian Childress to be older even than Master Bodean. The skin of her face was lined. Tiny wrinkles folded tight around her deep brown eyes. Her lips were thin and bloodless. For all that, there was something compelling about her. He might have paused a moment to discreetly watch her had they passed on the street.

"I will assume," said Librarian Childress, "that you told some sufficiently creative story to the porter to find your way in here, rather than clambering through an open window like a petty thief." Her tone was as cold and pointed as her expression.

"Ah . . ." Hethor felt even more foolish than usual.

"Yale students are for the most part not quite so young as you." She sniffed. "Even our prodigies do not ordinarily wear work boots," she went on. "Especially so stained and scuffed. You also carry three secondary texts on mathematics and geometry. Texts that any student here at Berkeley Divinity School would either have long dispensed with, if he were a Rational Humanist, or never have come near in the first instance, if he were a Spiritualist."

"No, ma'am," Hethor said.

"No?" She leaned forward. "No, you are neither a Rationalist nor a Spiritualist. No, you are not a Yale student. Or no, you are not a petty thief."

He wanted to sink to the floor and crawl away. "No . . ." Hethor found his resolve. "I have a question."

"Then ask. As it happens, I can spare a few moments for an enterprising young apprentice such as yourself."

Hethor felt like he'd just participated in an entire conversation that had never actually been spoken aloud. "How do you *do* that?"

"I look at what my eyes find before them, not what my mind expects to see. Now what is your question?"

"I need to see pictures of the angel Gabriel."

"Archangel," Librarian Childress corrected. "Perhaps you should be at the College of Fine Arts. This is the Divinity Library."

"Please, ma'am, I was lucky to even get here. I don't expect I'll be allowed to come back."

She sighed, then vanished briefly behind her desk before reappearing at the floor level. Librarian Childress was thin, and perhaps as tall as Hethor's chin, but somehow she seemed much bigger. She wore an ankle-length black dress that communicated absolutely nothing about the shape of her body. "Come into the reading room, young man."

"Don't you want to know my name?" he asked, following her to a set of double doors carved with scenes from the life of some saint.

"No. Because then I can say I've never heard of you when trouble comes. Trouble does follow you, does it not?"

They walked into a room lined with tall shelves. Three windows at the far end admitted sunlight. It smelled of dust and paper and leather—the very scents of education and learning.

"No!" Hethor exclaimed. "I mean . . . well, maybe. Now. But I'm new to it."

She laughed. Her severe voice loosened like a brook running through the woods of Hethor's childhood. "A boy freshly grown to manhood? New to trouble? You've led a terribly straitened existence, my apprentice friend."

In that moment he decided that perhaps this woman *was* his friend. Or at least, she could be. "Maybe so, ma'am."

They stood in front of an enormous table, overlain by a sheet of glass. Yellowed maps were pressed beneath like ancient butterflies from other lands. Librarian Childress patted the tabletop. "Wait here, please."

Hethor watched her walk away. The heels of her leather boots echoed on the marble floors. He stood a while—five, then ten minutes—wondering if she'd gone for the library porter, or even worse, the New Haven bobbies. Had she forgotten him? Abandoned him? Even in her brief, sharp-witted observations, Librarian Childress had treated him with more dignity than Pryce Bodean ever had.

She reappeared, pushing a little cart laden with several large books bound in various shades of calfskin.

"Art," she announced, "so righteous that it must be locked within covers and hidden from the mass of men."

The first book hit the table with a resounding thud. Hethor read the cover, *Religious Images of the Latest English Century*, before Librarian Childress slammed it open.

"Look through here," she said sharply, then reached for the next book. Pausing, "You *can* read, yes? Those aren't someone else's schoolbooks you're carrying for a disguise?"

"Yes, ma'am. English, Latin, and some little French. I can recognize certain Chinese marks as well."

"All the great languages of Northern Earth. A studious apprentice indeed." The librarian sounded to Hethor as if she approved. The next book slammed down on the table with another resounding thud. "And here are the Italians."

Hethor began to flip through the first book, the Englishmen. It was filled with pictures of men, animals, and angels, reproduced in engravings, some of which had been tinted various colors in imitation of the original oils or watercolors.

"This one!" he shouted. It was a picture of an angel leaning over some roses to speak to the Virgin Mary. The Earth's brass tracks soared into the sky behind it.

"Shh," said Librarian Childress. "This is a library. At what are you looking?"

"Dante Gabriel Rossetti." Even the name seemed significant, albeit out of place in a book of Englishmen. "This angel."

"Archangel. What about it?" Her voice was kind.

He had already spilled his secret to Pryce. There seemed little point in hiding from this woman, who might know enough to help him. "It came to me," said Hethor, miserable. "Last night."

She reached up to stroke his cheek. "You poor, poor boy. What on Northern Earth did it want?"

Something in the way she asked the question tore away the last vestiges of his sense of secrecy. "The Key Perilous. I'm to find the Key Perilous. The world's gone wrong, and I've been chosen to fix it." His breath caught in his throat.

Librarian Childress' hand covered her mouth, her eyes wide. "Goodness. Such a burden. How did you know it was the Archangel Gabriel?"

That she did not laugh, or call him mad, was an immense relief. "It told me." Hethor nodded at the engraving. "This is the angel I saw."

Childress began flipping through the Italian book. "There are other pictures of Gabriel. Many others. Let us look some more." She turned a few pages, then glanced up at him again. "I believe that you mean what you say, but what you remember may not be the truth. The Key Perilous is legendary, in several senses of the word."

"It's real," said Hethor. "What happened, I mean. Gabriel gave me a silver feather."

"Where is that feather now?"

"Pryce Bodean took it from me. Said I didn't deserve to have it, all but accused me of stealing it."

She looked at Hethor's boots, a slow, pointed stare that was hard to miss. "One might be excused for wondering why an apprentice would be carrying silver, especially if one were a Rational Humanist such as Mister Bodean. He does not miss much in his search for a hard-edged kind of truth."

"So what do I do? I need to understand my mission."

"If this is true, you will need help." She stopped, one hand resting on the Italian book, and gave him a long, careful look, like a greengrocer with a questionable load of lettuce. "But if this is not true, if you are just a foolish boy, taken with fever or a bout of imagination, I would be more the fool to help you."

Somehow Hethor was sure that she knew something. She knew what he needed to do. How could he convince her of the truth of what had happened?

The scar. Of course. He opened the palm of his right hand and held it out to her. "Here is the scar from the feather. Its edges were sharp as a sword, ma'am."

Librarian Childress took his fingers in her own and studied the scar. "This is old, and in the shape of a key."

"It healed overnight. I don't know why it is in the shape of a key." Hethor felt like a fool, but he kept trying. "A sign, ma'am. A miracle, that I need to understand."

"A reminder, perhaps?" She smiled at him, genuine humor in her face for the first time. "Listen, boy. Her Majesty's viceroy in Boston currently has a court mystic in residence, a self-styled sorcerer called William of Ghent. It may be possible to convince him that your visitation was real. If William believes you, then you may receive help, or at least advice, from the viceroy and his court."

Hethor withdrew his hand from her touch, closing his fist. "Do you believe me?"

"I believe that you are telling the truth as you see it," said Librarian Childress carefully.

"But you want to see the silver feather. As proof."

She nodded. "As proof. As will William. Without the feather for examination and analysis, your scar is interesting, but no more."

"I don't know how to get my feather back from Pryce."

"I do." Librarian Childress smiled. "Leave that to me."

EATING A LIGHT lunch of cucumber sandwiches and tea with Librarian Childress in the staff room somewhere deep in the Divinity Library, Hethor realized that he had lost any chance of reclaiming that school day at New Haven Latin. He wasn't sure how much he cared. Gabriel's message was becoming more and more real to him as the hours went by, even in the absence of the feather. Or perhaps because of that absence. Hethor realized that his faith alone should have been sufficient—he was growing ashamed of having asked for a token.

"How is it," he asked around a mouthful of unfamiliar white bread, "that you work here? I thought only men were permitted at Yale."

She gave him a sour look, which quickly left her face. "Women were put on this Earth by God to bear children. Just ask any man. Intelligent women are here to have intelligent sons, and otherwise keep their mouths shut. Let us just assume I wasn't interested in having any intelligent sons."

"But how did—"

"Let us also assume that your mother apparently wasn't interested in having any intelligent sons either."

Hethor subsided, chewing on a mouthful of cucumber and pale bread. After a few moments, he swallowed. "I'm sorry, ma'am."

She surprised him by saying "Thank you."

A little silver bell above the door jingled. Hethor glanced up to see a whole series of bells, with pull strings vanishing into the walls.

"They're tuned," said Librarian Childress. "Each note has a different meaning. Now follow me, please."

She led him back to the reading room and pointed up a ladder that ran on rails along the largest bank of shelves. "See the alcove up there? Climb into it and behave as though you were a statue. If you lean against the paneling at the back wall, you will be invisible to anyone in the room down here."

Feeling strangely excited, Hethor climbed. The alcove was dusty, littered with mouse droppings and shards of wood. It smelled of mildew. Somehow it was comforting to know that even Yale had mice, though the thought of the little creatures near all these books worried him.

He sat back, seeing only the shelf across the room from him and part of the windows to his right, now letting in the light of the afternoon. After a moment, the door squeaked open. Had she shut it on her way out, while he was climbing?

The librarian's voice echoed from below. Her tones were formal. "Thank you for coming to see me on such short notice, Mister Bodean."

"It is my pleasure, ma'am." Pryce was less certain and haughty in his manner with her, Hethor noted with glee. "Ah . . . your note indicated that you were acting on behalf of Dean Holliday?"

"Yes. He has been investigating a rumored series of, well, apparitions here in New Haven. I have been charged with certain aspects of that work, in order to insulate the office of the dean from small-minded accusations."

"Such as we Rational Humanists might levy?" Pryce's voice reeked with false good humor.

"Precisely." She paused, diplomatically perhaps. "I have heard that something of potential importance was delivered to you today by a tradesman. A sort of minor . . . token."

Hethor was struck by how Librarian Childress' speech was slipping from her usual tart precision to the sort of self-important puffery that characterized the diction of the students. Hethor wondered if Pryce knew he was being mocked.

"I'm sure I don't know wh—"

Childress' words cut across Pryce's like a lash, in her sharp librarian voice this time. "What you don't know would overfill this room, Mister Bodean, but please do not pretend ignorance. My sources are good, much better than yours. I need to examine this token. If it is your property, I will be pleased to return it to you."

"I am in possession of such, ah, a trifle," said Pryce. He sounded angry. "It b-belongs to my father, Master Bodean the Clockmaker. I am in the process of returning it to him."

Hethor's ears burned; his face felt hot. Pryce had just told Librarian Childress that Hethor was a thief, the sort of apprentice who would steal from his master. He wanted to shout his innocence, leap from the alcove and defend his honor. But being seen to lurk in shadows in order to overhear conversations would only confirm whatever miserable opinion Pryce Bodean already had of him.

"In that case," said Librarian Childress, "I shall be certain to return it to him, with a full explanation."

"That won't be . . ." Pryce stopped. Hethor heard him take a deep breath. "Very well, madam. Since this is of service to Dean Holliday, I will raise no more objections." There was a clink as something small and metallic hit the glass tabletop; then a chair slid back. "I trust it will come back to me—rather, my father—soon enough. If that is all, I will bid you good day."

"Good day, Mister Bodean. Your services will not go unremarked."

"I should hope not."

A door clicked. Hethor held himself still in the alcove, listening to Librarian Childress hum quietly. A minute or so later, there was a discreet double rap on the door of the reading room, though no one entered.

"You may come down now," said the librarian. "He has departed."

Hethor stepped out onto the ladder, stopping to brush off his clothes before climbing down. Once on the floor, he went straight to the table.

The silver feather sat on the glass. It was still edged with his blood.

"*Libra Malachi,*" said Childress. "And do sit, please."

"The Book of Malachi?" Hethor translated as he pulled his chair in with a scrape.

"Perhaps more accurately, the Book of Messengers. In the sense of angels. From the Hebrew *malakh,* the messenger angels."

"Gabriel," said Hethor.

"Correct." Librarian Childress looked grim, though a smile quirked at the corners of her mouth. Her fingers traced the pattern of the horofix across her chest. "The messenger angel who brought news of our Brass Christ to Mary."

"And what about this book?"

"I would have to research the exact dates, but *Libra Malachi* tells us that the silver feather is a token that has been seen before. Presented to various generals, saints, and kings at critical junctures throughout history. Most recently, long after the writing of the book, to Lord Raglan in the Crimea just before he ordered the Light Brigade to charge the Chinese guns. By an angel claiming to be Michael."

"Claiming?" Hethor wondered at her choice of words.

Librarian Childress smiled. "You should have been a student. But that does not matter. You have been given a mission. Or at least an opportunity. What you do with it . . . well, that is up to you."

"So you believe me?"

"I believed you before," she said. "Enough to confront your master's son on your behalf. With this feather, others might believe you. Some few folk can see the patterns that underlie all of Creation. Someone like William of Ghent, who would know just by examining this feather that it is of angelic origin. Not all magic lives south of the Equatorial Wall."

Hethor stared at the tabletop, willing the world to be sensible, simpler. No wish of his would change the deeds of God or His angels, however. "I came to you for knowledge," he said slowly. "Seeking to understand from books what has really happened." He looked up to meet the librarian's gleaming dark eyes. "I shall do as you have advised, take this feather and go to Boston, to the viceroy's court and seek William of Ghent. But first I must ask my master for permission to make the journey." Hethor could only imagine what Master Bodean would have to say.

"And if your master forbids you?"

Hethor shifted in his seat, uncomfortable. "I am an apprentice sworn and bound. If he forbids me, well . . . He owns not my corporeal person, but my time, labor, and the value of my training. To leave him unbidden, even to come here, is a form of theft. I could get the lash."

"The Key Perilous may be legendary," warned Librarian Childress, "but if it *is* real, its secrets lie close to the heart of the world."

"And so I will risk the lash."

She just stared at him for a moment. "We each are responsible for our own souls, my friend."

"Before God," said Hethor. He made the sign of the horofix, an old reflex he rarely recalled anymore.

"Exactly. And before our own consciences. Which judge is the harsher is something only you can know.

But . . . I will pray for you. As will librarians across the Northern Earth."

Hethor rose from his chair, took his feather from her hand, then bowed to Librarian Childress. "Thank you, ma'am. You have helped me understand some of what lies upon my thoughts."

She stood in turn. "Listen. There are those who may help you. People who care about such things. I will pass word along. If you think you might be among them, ask after the albino toucan." She touched one of his elbows, then pulled Hethor into a hug, her gray hair beneath his chin. It was the first time anyone had really touched him since he was eleven, just for the sake of contact rather than to drag or beat him. Tears clouded his eyes for the second time that day. They stung his cheeks and made his face hot all over again.

Gathering his pride, Hethor strode out past the library porter into the New Haven afternoon. Turning left onto Elm Street to head back to Master Bodean's workshop, he thought he saw Faubus Bodean, Pryce's tall middle brother. But Faubus wasn't in the Divinity School. He studied architecture.

The silver feather felt hot in Hethor's hand and the afternoon streets were crowded, but the spring sky remained clear with a lovely breeze. He headed home, briefly managing to forget about angels and keys and albino toucans and divine will.

HETHOR PASSED a pair of bobbies walking the other way on King George III Street. The sight of the policemen made him nervous, reminding him of how he had violated the terms of his apprenticeship. Walking toward Bodean's Finer Clocks, he noticed a horse tied in front of the store, as well as a taximeter cabriolet—one of the new electrick horseless carriages that had recently begun driving about New Haven.

Customers?

Or trouble?

It didn't matter. Hethor owed Master Bodean an explanation of today's absence. He further hoped to beg Bodean's goodwill for a journey to Boston. He tried not to think about how improbable his own story would sound were someone else to tell it to him.

Hethor almost went around back to the stableyard, but looking at the horse and the cabriolet out front, he stepped to the front door. The cabriolet's driver nodded at Hethor and touched his cap. Heartened, Hethor set his hand to the latch and walked into Master Bodean's showroom.

Faubus Bodean grabbed the collar of Hethor's coat, the old corduroy tearing under his fingers as Bodean's son swung Hethor against the inside of the shop door. Hethor slammed into the wood with a booming rattle of the frame. The impact knocked the wind right out of him. Faubus hitched up the collar, yanking the coat upward until Hethor was forced to stand on his toes, which were wedged painfully downward inside his boots.

"Thief," Faubus hissed, so close his breath was hot on Hethor's face, scented with a bloom of ale. Then, looking over his shoulder, "Father, the family's traitor is here."

Hethor looked over Faubus' shoulder at Master Franklin Bodean and Mister Pryce Bodean, father and son, staring back at him. Master Bodean appeared sorrowful, while Pryce's face danced somewhere between suppressed glee and an attempt at somber pity.

"Well," said Master Bodean, "and how was school today, lad? You're a mite late on returning."

The question, so ordinary, was eerie in this situation. Hethor gulped, gasping over his tight collar where Faubus still held him high. "I never . . . went . . . sir . . ."

"So and you're not lying as well, I see," Bodean said.

"Not yet," muttered Faubus, once more glaring into Hethor's eyes.

"No . . . sir . . . I don't . . . lie. . . ."

"And you went over to Yale college, without my permission."

"Yes . . ."

"To see my son."

Hethor nodded, gasping hard for air now.

"Let's have it, then."

Faubus dropped Hethor hard onto his heels, then slapped him, hard. "You heard Father. Where is it?"

Hethor rubbed his throat for a moment. "What?"

"The silver feather you stole from my son," said Master Bodean.

"What!?" Hethor's face burned yet again, his head hot and full as if he would rupture or have a fit. "That's *my* feather, and he knows it!"

"See?" said Pryce quietly to his father. "I told you he was cracked."

"And where'd you come by the feather?" Master Bodean asked.

"I . . ." Words failed Hethor for a moment; then he summoned his courage. "The Archangel Gabriel gave it to me, last night. Before the clocks began to chime."

Pryce and Faubus both laughed. Master Bodean just looked sad. "And you didn't think to tell me this wondrous thing?"

Hethor stared at his boots. "No, I didn't."

"I'll not be believing such a tale, Hethor. I can't fathom what would move you to rob my son, you being such a good apprentice and all, but angels from the sky handing out jewelry ain't in it."

"It's not like that!" The tears were on his cheeks now, hot fountains of pride, even as his head filled with peppery snot. "He took it from me, and the librarian made him—"

Another slap from Faubus silenced Hethor. "Give it up, thief, or I'll slit your clothes, and you, finding it."

"She can tell you," Hethor protested.

"A woman," said Pryce, laughing. "*And* a clerk? No sensible man would take the word of such a person in a matter of this importance. They must have been in league."

Hethor tried once more, staring at Master Bodean. "I'm telling you—"

Faubus slapped him again, then twisted Hethor's right arm behind his back. "Give it now, if you have it," hissed his tormentor, "or you'll be very sorry indeed."

Shaking, Hethor pulled the feather from his pocket with his free hand.

Faubus snatched it away. "Here it is, Father, proof of his thievery." He showed the feather to Master Bodean. "Shall I call back the bobbies and have this scoundrel thrown in the stockade?"

"No . . . ," said Master Bodean slowly. He was looking at Pryce, and the gleam in his oldest son's eye. "I'll just be turning the lad out. 'S punishment enough. You two go on, now."

"Father . . . ," said Pryce, touching the old man's arm. "Are you sure?"

"The boy's desperate." Faubus shot another glare at Hethor. "He could try anything."

"He'll be gone within the hour," said Master Bodean. "And with no fight. Right, boy?"

Hethor nodded, miserable, shaking now in the wake of his anger and his shame.

"Go, sons," snapped Master Bodean.

They filed out, Pryce smirking, Faubus with a sideways shove that sent Hethor staggering. Outside the taximeter cabriolet ground into gear and wheezed off, followed a moment later by the clopping of the horse's hooves.

Hethor stared at Master Bodean, who stared back. They stood in silence, surrounded by the ticking of the clocks, an endless mechanical wave brushing against a brass shore.

"'T'would have saved much trouble if you'd shown me the feather last night," said Master Bodean quietly. "I'm too old to raise up another 'prentice."

"It wasn't hi—," Hethor began hotly, but Master Bodean put his hand up, palm forward.

"I know it wasn't what Pryce said. I don't know the

exact truth, but you see, boy, it don't matter. My son's a man of learning, soon to take the cloth, and he's family before that. I *have* to take his word over yours on both counts. Not even with some female librarian testifying against him, neither. If he'd come to me private, without dragging Faubus into it, I might have talked around the thing to the truth. But I can't be branding my eldest son a liar in front of his brother. Even if I know he is lying."

"What about me?" Hethor cried. "I'm no liar. The angel *did* come to me, with a message, and left me that feather as token. The message will not be trusted without the token."

Master Bodean looked sadder. "You speak to me of trust? You, who didn't trust me enough to tell me about this wonderful message, and the token besides?"

"I . . . I didn't comprehend it." Hethor stared at his boots again. "I still don't. But once I understood more, I came home to beg your leave to go to Boston and see the viceroy."

"You got your wish, boy," said Master Bodean. "You've all the leave in the world now. I won't have you whipped or nothing. Your father's money was good enough."

"I need to go upstairs and—," Hethor said, but Bodean interrupted him.

"I won't have you in my house. There's nothing up there that don't belong to me anyway. As I'm a generous man, you can keep the clothes you're wearing, though Pryce will shout me down for that, too."

"Oh." Feeling stupid, Hethor set down the books.

"Listen, boy," said Bodean, even quieter. He shuffled across the room, looking older than ever before. "If you'd come into your journeyman rank, and done well, as we both know you would've, you could have taken over the shop as master when I laid down my tools. Now my sons will have the shop free and clear, to lease or sell. My money will be theirs instead of yours, you see. There's lots of reasons things happen in this world. You never thought *why* I didn't ever send you down to Yale on an errand, did you? Keeping yer away from their greed was a big part of that."

He hugged Hethor, who stood stiff, resisting the affection.

Bodean whispered in his ear. "Take your message to Boston, and Godspeed to you. What I've put in your coat pocket, it's what's left of your father's money. But you must leave now. I'll warrant the boys have set someone to watch the shop."

Without a word, Hethor turned and walked out the door. Hugging his coat tight, he trudged along King George III Street, heading for the north side of New Haven and the turnpike to Boston. With a little money in his pocket, if it was enough, he might afford a train, or at least a seat on a wagon.

Two blocks down, Faubus stepped out of an alley with a pair of toughs who tripped Hethor to the stones of the sidewalk. Rifling through Hethor's pockets, Faubus found a roll of paper money, tied with a string. "Pryce was right; you *are* a thief, even robbing an old man on the way out the door," he hissed. "If I ever see you again, I will kill you." He kicked Hethor twice in the ribs before walking away.

Hethor just lay against the wall a while, counting cobbles. Eventually a young woman in a Salvation Army uniform knelt beside him and asked if he needed help.

"No, ma'am," he said, pulling himself up. "I must go to Boston."

"'Tis a slow step you walk, lying on the curb," she answered with a small, pretty smile.

"And a long trip, by the grace of God." Pondering the miracles of the heavens, Hethor limped into the evening shadows, even as the rising thread of Earth's brass track gleamed high in the darkening sky.

TWO

HETHOR HAD made it just outside the New Haven city line the first night before dropping to sleep in a damp bed of reeds beneath a rickety bridge. The second day had brought him to Cheshire, following the turnpike. This morning, after sleeping in a chestnut tree, he'd been offered a ride by an old man with a wagon full of May's first turnips.

"Hundred and thirty-some miles from New Haven to Boston, as the boots walk," said the farmer, who had not offered Hethor his name. He clucked to his team and twitched the reins. The pair of horses nickered, but they kept moving at their deliberate pace. The wagon rolled along an old country road, eternal New England stone walls following the right-of-way before shooting off at angles into the trees as the road rose and fell over ridgelines and little rocky valleys to ford muddy, sighing streams.

"As the tired boots walk, sir." On this wagon Hethor wasn't moving much faster than he had been afoot. At least now he was seated, resting his aching soles. A hamper between the driver's feet held some promise as well, after two days of gnawing on grass and the three robin's eggs he had been able to scavenge.

He would be damned before he would steal food, even to stave off the sour stitch in his gut. Not after the way Master Bodean's sons had run him out of New Haven for a thief. Thanks to them, he'd lost everything he had ever thought to have. Livelihood, a roof over his head, such family as Master Bodean had been to him.

The injustice of it gnawed at him.

"I'll be a-selling this crop to a man in Hartford," said the farmer. "Reach there tonight, I reckon. Price is worth the distance. Gum darned if I know why they can't grow they own turnips up in Hartford."

"Can't say as I have an idea either," Hethor said politely, attempting not to let his irritation at circumstance into his voice. He flexed his feet within his boots, trying to decide if he could pull the blasted things off without too much effort. He'd need them again all too soon, he was certain.

The wagon rolled along with a quiet leisurely progress. After some while, the farmer stirred himself to speak again. "Feller could take a railway train, these days."

"Yes, a fellow could." Hethor realized the boots weren't coming off. Even if he got them free, Hethor was afraid his feet would swell so much he'd never get the boots back on.

Another little while, another flick of the reins. "Trains cost money."

Hethor sighed. He couldn't very well pretend to be something he was not. "I'm broke, sir. Had some money, got robbed. I must get to Boston, though I expect the hurry's mostly in my head."

"Heh." The farmer gave Hethor a wide smile. "Well said. Any man's hurry is mostly in his head. But hurry or no, I can see that you're no tramp. Not with them boots and that coat. Too little wear on 'em. Yet the coat collar's stretched out and tore at the seams. Someone took a hard hand to you."

Hethor rubbed his cheeks. The tears of rage, shame,

frustration, whatever, all seemed burned out of him. "You could say so."

"Reckon I can share my lunch out with yer, if you've a mind."

"I have nothing to offer." *Too quick,* Hethor thought.

Another while, another flick. "Tell me a story. One I h'ain't heard before. Nothing about cows or farms or Her Imperial Majesty's tax collectors."

Hethor thought back to his Classical literature classes, cleared his throat, and launched into a loose interpretation of Book Nine of Homer's *Iliad*.

HOMER, SOPHOCLES, and the *Aeneid* of Virgil got them to Hartford that evening, with a lunch of cold fried chicken and some good brown bread. The old man twitched the wagon into a marshalling yard behind a wholesale vict-ualler's where a dozen more old men waited. Shouting lads unloaded some wagons, while others lined up by the stables, their teams unhitched and led off for the night.

"You're a right good talker, young Hethor," said the farmer, whose name had finally been revealed as Thomas Mudge. "Practically a preacher. The boys over there, they've got a little feed laid on tonight in the meadow be-hind the yard here. You can join us and talk for your sup-per. I wouldn't mind if you'd tell some of them Greekie tales again."

"Thank you, sir, but I must get on."

"Get on where? In the dark? You'll fall into a ditch. And I know you h'ain't got no coin for hot food nor a warm bed. I'll show you around to the boys; might be some feller or another's got an empty wagon heading to-ward Storrs or Westford on the morning, be glad of the company. If'n he gets to knowing you tonight. Mean-while, you can help those young lads with my turnips."

An evening of alarming corn liquor and warm roast turkey went a long way toward restoring Hethor's bruised faith in human nature. He listened to tall tales about foreign lands and the heathen magics of the Southern Earth. He told some of his own from history and the Classics, and fell under the spell of drink and firelight and the evening breeze.

Late in the night, when it was his turn to talk again, Hethor stood up with a stoneware jug in his hand. The moon was so close to new as to be little more than a nail paring in the sky, and even the stars seemed to have retreated to their rest. Four or five of the old men were snoring under blankets, for though they had a little cabin to sleep in, the night was pleasant and the fire was warm. The rest still listened, bleary-eyed.

"Had me a visit," Hethor said. His lips stumbled over the words. "Angel came down from Heaven."

"How ol' wash she?" laughed one of the men, but another elbowed him in the ribs.

"No woman angel, I reckon. Taller than any of us, with feathers white as a swan's. Eyes like a stone. Told me to go . . . go . . . find a key. A dangerous key. So I'm off, now, to see the viceroy. Give him the word."

"I've got a word or two for the visheroy myshelf," said the heckler, laughing again.

"This a fireside tale, boy?" asked Mudge, who was still awake. "Or one of them old classy stories?"

"Real thing, sir, I swear it." Hethor swallowed a burp. "I swear by the brass heavens." He added on impulse: "And the albino toucan."

Mudge was a beat too slow in responding, giving Hethor a sharp glance. "Boy knows how to move turnips," he told the rest of the men, as though that were the highest of praise. "And how to tell a story besides. Voice like an angel." He smiled sidelong at Hethor. "I'll stand good for him. Who's going east and north tomorrow?"

"Pierre Le Roy ish," said the heckler.

"Le Roy'll take our boy, then," Mudge announced. "And find him help on to Boston."

"To Boston!" They all drank.

"To Boston!" said Hethor, waving his stoneware jug

before he collapsed in a widening circle that seemed to grow as big as the Northern Earth.

THE NEXT morning consisted mostly of a series of bleary-eyed grunts exchanged between Hethor and Le Roy. Even Le Roy's mules seemed to be recovering from the corn liquor. Hethor's head felt like it had spent too much time inside Master Bodean's grandfather clock, being beaten by the sweep of the huge pendulum. His mouth had definitely hosted a small battalion of chickens, while his gut was sour as a June apple.

Le Roy's wagon lurched along the turnpike, Le Roy snoring at the reins. Hethor felt inclined to do the same. He couldn't find a way to sit that let him sleep, though, and the waking world intruded. Every sound was a magnified version of its normal self. Bees buzzing in pasturage, cattle grumbling over water and hay along the pike, every squeak and rattle of the bed of Le Roy's wagon—it was a symphony written by an idiot.

Hethor rubbed his eyes clear and stared south. That way, beyond hills and miles, lay Long Island Sound and the great Atlantic Ocean. Mathematics and common sense alike told him he could never see the Equatorial Wall from here in Connecticut. Though it was a hundred miles high, the Wall wasn't visible past about seventeen degrees of latitude—along Jamaica's south coast for example.

Yet Hethor could swear that in the rising morning light he saw brass glittering low in the southern sky to match Earth's brass tracks arching upward through the heavens.

He stared, rubbing his eyes again and looking over the low, close horizon. He listened past the idiot symphony, trying to hear the clicking of the world.

"It's one of them mirror-ages," said Le Roy suddenly. "Preacher man explained it to me oncet. The air, it gets like to a mirror, and shows you that what's far away. Like how the fields look like they got water on 'em on a hot summer day."

"No magic then," said Hethor, vaguely disappointed. He traced the horofix across his chest anyway.

They rattled on in silence. Hethor thought about Gabriel and God, the Tetragrammaton. God in His infinite wisdom had made the world so, hung Earth in the sky on the tracks of her orbit around the lamp of the sun, then left it alone, for man to find his way. After man's fall into sin and error, God had sent His son to be the Brass Christ, redeeming man by showing the way to correct thought and deed.

Hethor knew there were heresies, folk who claimed that Christ had come to wind the Mainspring of the world again, and even that He was neither the first nor the last. Others said the world was built by greater men, just as men built fences and sheds for their livestock. As a clockmaker's apprentice, he was in a sense party to those heresies, for the very keeping of time was seen by the most strictly religious as a challenge to the brasswork of the heavens. Measuring God's work was held by some to be a questioning of the divine.

Still and all, life in New Haven had always seemed safely removed from the legendary realities of biblical tradition.

Until Gabriel had come to Hethor's room to lay a duty on him.

So what did he believe? In God?

Certainly.

Proof of the divine was incontrovertible, found in every aspect of Creation. It was hard even for heretics to argue with a sky full of brass, of a design so evidently driven by keen intelligence and vast power.

As for piety, well . . . Pryce Bodean was pious, and probably someday to be a leader of the church. Hethor had full example of what Pryce's Christian compassion had bought.

He sighed, closed his eyes, and listened to the sounds of the world. God, or Gabriel, would find him soon enough if either of them wanted him. Le Roy's mules fussed their way into Hethor's uneasy daylight dreams.

LUNCH WAS cold turkey. Hethor ate slowly. Hunger warred with a general malaise. Le Roy offered him corn liquor as well, which he refused with an uneasy lurch of the stomach. The old farmer munched and drank his way through their rest stop in a copse of alders as placidly as either of his mules, while Hethor tried not to think at all.

The afternoon passed quickly enough. The wagon jarred Hethor out of his hangover in slow steps. Le Roy had nothing to say, which suited Hethor just fine, until they rolled into Storrs in the evening starlight. White clapboard buildings gleamed among towering elms that bordered streets as well cobbled as any New Haven boulevard. Storrs was a city that carried itself with pride.

Le Roy clucked the mules to a halt just outside the town center, laid down the reins, and shifted in his seat to face Hethor. "You sure you're set on a-seein' the viceroy in Boston, boy?"

"Yes, sir." Was Le Roy about to run him off?

"They's a certain cut of man welcome at court in Boston. You got the city about you, boy, but still and all you ain't their kind."

He hadn't been their kind in New Haven, either. Faubus had known no better, but Pryce . . . well, Pryce was a different matter.

Le Roy cleared his throat. "They's folks there who judge a man by his shoes afore they ever look to see if he's got truth in his eyes. Old Mudge, he saw truth in your eyes, boy, but in Boston they ain't going to get past the mud on your boots."

"I am who I am," said Hethor. The archangel Gabriel had granted him a mission, perhaps the most important mission in Northern Earth. He had to keep moving. "I've only got my story to tell."

Le Roy's voice was suddenly thick, driven by passion, or perhaps anger. "Mudge bade me tell you this, for the sake of the white bird and them what set you on this road: If you give up on the viceroy, there's a man drinks at Anthony's on Pier Four in Boston when he's in port. Goes by name of Malgus. Might tell your story to him, boy. He might even listen. And now, off with you."

Hethor hopped down from the wagon's bench seat. "I thought you were to send me on to Boston," he said uncertainly.

"And if you wait here, I shall." The old farmer was just a silhouette now, looming above Hethor as the sweat-stinking mules chuffed in the darkness. "Someone will be along presently to take you further. Won't do to show you around the livery where I'm headed right now. Farewell, boy."

As Le Roy drove away, Hethor realized he'd never given the old man his name, nor as far as he knew had Mudge done so. It felt strange to hide who he was from someone who had shown him kindness. Hethor's life had never been about fear before.

Had it become so now?

He was not sorry that the archangel Gabriel had chosen him, but this was a hard road. In a few short days his world had already come to ruin. He sat on the edge of a boardwalk and tried to remember his father. Only the sad, defeated face of Franklin Bodean would come to mind, as his master had looked when turning Hethor out.

LE ROY'S "presently" turned into the better part of two hours. Hethor's sense of time was always with him, always accurate. Several times he considered simply walking away, following the road east and north, but the long, slow prospect made his feet ache even more. Hethor chose to continue waiting. His journey so far had been difficult, but not nearly so bad as it might have been. The hand of Librarian Childress had reached far, perhaps.

He sent a silent prayer of thanks to God, Gabriel, and the secret company of librarians.

The old moon was nearly gone, and gave little enough light. Eventually a wagon—an odd, oblong thing shiny even in the dark of the evening—came for him. As it stopped, smelling of sawdust and polishing oils, Hethor realized his next conveyance was a hearse straight from the manufactory.

"Come on, then," said a boy, voice piping high. "If you're old Le Roy's friend in need of a ride, here's your coach-and-four."

It was more of a coach-and-two, but Hethor smiled at the joke. "Never been on one of these," he said apologetically, pulling himself up the iron step to the driver's bench. It smelled of leather, but crinkled when he sat.

"I should hope you haven't," said the boy. "Most people make this journey only once. Mind the newsprint, now. Protects the seat. She's newly built, and I'm to deliver her to Foxboro over Massachusetts way two days hence."

That was when Hethor realized that the boy was a young woman. Not from her voice, nor her clothes, which were lumpy and boyish enough as far he could tell in the dark, but something in her smell and the way she sat with the reins in hand, knees too close together and leaning forward not quite the right way.

A *girl*. There weren't any girls in Hethor's life, not at Master Bodean's, not at New Haven Latin. And here he was alone in the dark. . . . What was he supposed to do? Hethor could feel his face flushing hot and red, and was profoundly glad of the shadows.

"I . . . I . . ." He was lost for words.

"Don't worry. Don't scratch up the lacquer or the brightwork and you'll be fine. Le Roy slipped me a pound note for your vittles on the way, so you'll eat in style. English pound at that, not one of our American pounds."

Le Roy slipped her a *pound note*? Hidden eyes *were* watching him. Librarian Childress had given him an unexpected gift, with the password of the albino toucan. It had called forth great favor by the fire in Hartford. Who were these people, farmers and librarians and—apparently—a coach girl?

"I'm Darby, by the way."

Her voice was nice. Once he knew it wasn't a boy's voice, it didn't sound sissy any more. She was a girl . . . the kind of person a boy could spoon with if he was very lucky. She might even be . . .

That vague, pleasant line of thought broke off as his common sense awoke. Darby, a girl, was driving! Hethor wanted to grab the reins from her, save the two of them from hurtling into the nearest ditch as always happened when some man was foolish enough to let a woman take to the road. But part of him remembered the cool competence of Librarian Childress.

Who seemed to be watching over him even now, in the form of Darby's English pound note.

Perhaps he was as wrong about women as Pryce and Faubus had been about him. Except that women *were* flighty, hysterical, unreliable—they had their monthlies. Every boy was warned of that, in whispered rumor if not in the classroom. It was simple biology, not an artifice of society like the snobbery that had condemned Hethor in the eyes of Pryce.

The same snobbery that would likely condemn him in the presence of the viceroy as well, Hethor thought with glum persistence.

"Would you like me to drive?" he finally said, his voice somewhere between a squeak and a gasp. His face was still hot.

"Are you a drover? I only do this a few times a month."

Hethor wanted to say, "No, but I'm a man," but he couldn't quite find the courage. "I . . . I thought you might like some help is all."

"Why? If you're half as potted as old Le Roy, you're in no condition to drive a settee, let alone a wagon."

He gave up. The night was crisp and cool, and after a while Hethor found himself talking about spring loading

and escapements, and how the wheel train drove the mea-
surement of time so precisely that one could not discover
the errors without special instruments and training. It was
something safe and neutral that Darby seemed to find interesting. He was even able to forget she was a girl,
mostly, and not think about what there might be under her
shapeless pea coat.

She stopped for the night, offering him the hearse's
box to sleep in, but the prospect of lying where the dead
would soon travel unnerved Hethor. "I'll sleep up here on
the bench, thank you."

"Suit yourself." Darby shrugged, now visible in the
starlight, still looking boyish. She grinned, her teeth
gleaming, and climbed off the driver's seat and headed
for the box.

Hethor sat a while. His pants were suddenly tight and
uncomfortable, and he was embarrassed and hot all at
once. He wondered what he should have said or done differently. When sleep found him, he was chased by vague
dreams of looming women with fire in their eyes.

THE NEXT day was another round of quiet chatter, with
stops for stew and bread. Darby was content not to push
the horses, a mismatched team of an old gray and a
young, frisky roan. They talked about spring plantings
and the virtues of cobbled streets as compared to brick,
and why ships carry more than one clock aboard, and
who the viceroy was likely to appoint as the next gover-
nor of Connecticut. Every time the sway of the hearse
brought their forearms brushing together, Hethor felt his
face flush again. He worked very hard on forgetting that
this was the first time in his life he'd been alone with a
girl . . . well, a young woman.

In the late morning, insects droned in the trees as the
day shaped up hot. Hethor stared at the damselflies dart-
ing below the railings of a little bridge as the hearse
crossed. Darby's conversation had lapsed a while. Hethor

kept stealing glances at her profile—gray eyes, snub nose, wisps of brown hair under her cap.

She drove well. Much better than he would have, though that was hard to admit. She knew her way along the roads. She was pleasant, funny—might have made as good a friend as a boy could have.

That was when Hethor finally blurted out what had been bothering him all along. "But . . . but . . . you're a girl!"

It came out sounding like an accusation of heresy.

Darby twitched the reins, slowing the horses to a halt, then turned to look at him. Her eyes were narrow under her flat cap. "Not that my nature's any business of yours, but what of it?"

He felt like an idiot—clearly, she was driving, with no trouble at all. One of Master Bodean's sons could have explained it much better, with all the rigor and might of Yale logic, and probably the majesty of the law on his side as well. But for Hethor, the problem was so obvious, so self-evident, he wasn't even sure how to put it into words. Everyone knew that women couldn't be trusted with such responsibilities. Nor could men be trusted with a woman running free among them. "It . . . women . . . you're alone. You're not supposed to be driving the roads."

"I'm not alone," she said reasonably. "I'm with you. I'll ride Daisy back and lead Dapple, probably make it in one long day. Besides, most people think I'm a boy, and don't look twice at me. So why do you care?"

"There's an order to the world," muttered Hethor darkly, his face and groin hot all over again. She was making him sweat now. That made him angry.

"Yes, and that order is that I'm driving this hearse and you're not, which means you can get out and walk if I tell you to."

"What about your parents?"

"Mum and Da' build the hearses, along with three hired men. They can't take the time to make a delivery, and they don't have to pay me to do it because I'm family."

Somehow Hethor doubted it was that simple, but he tried to let loose of his objections. "World's a strange place," he managed, "and rarely fair."

"All the more so if you're a woman, which is why I'm just as happy to pass as a boy. I'll thank you not to say more."

As the afternoon wound on, their chatter continued, while avoiding the girl question. Hethor noticed Darby took corners a little faster, bumped into him a little more. That night she invited him into the hearse with her, to spoon a bit.

"You're a nice enough boy." Her smile glinted in the moonlight, lips parting wide in a way that made his breath catch. "Come on, we can keep warm."

"I . . ." This woman kept driving him to silence. Hethor's penis felt huge, distorted, like it would drag him to the ground. He was sure she could see it straining at his pants. Why wasn't she laughing at him? "I, no!" he said, sweat pouring down his face. "I'm already too warm!" His voice was loud and clumsy.

Then Darby did laugh, but softly. It seemed she meant to be kind. "Suit yourself." She crawled inside the hearse and tugged the door shut behind her.

Hethor sank down under a willow tree nearby, loosening the buttons on his fly, though he was careful not to touch himself. That way lay sin and madness, everyone knew.

So why was he so desperate to get closer to her?

When sleep came, it was hot and troubled. When Hethor woke later, he had to find a stream bank far from the hearse to wash his shame out of his linens. They talked very little the next morning.

TWO MORE days of travel, including another hand-off in Foxboro to a taciturn Italian man bringing early greens into Boston, got Hethor to the Boston Common. There were no more mentions of albino toucans, but Hethor still saw the influence of the white bird. "Court Street," was the only thing the last drover said to him, waving generally to the east.

He was amazed to have arrived in good order.

On the Common, Hethor found himself surrounded by horse chestnuts and elms and half a dozen more sorts of trees he didn't recognize. Men and women wandered together. Families were out taking the air with hampers of food, children screeching by the ponds. He'd never been away from the Connecticut coast before, and the journey here hadn't felt quite real. Standing on the grass of the Common, staring at the brick walkways and the spring-green trees, made him terribly homesick.

"Viceroy," said Hethor to himself and the chattering squirrels. "I must find the viceroy." He walked to the east end of the Common, then followed Tremont Street until it met Court Street. Boston was not so different from New Haven. Bigger perhaps, but with the same gas lamps and electrick cabriolets and shouting teamsters forcing their wagons through traffic. There would be more airships looming over the nearby harbor than those that called at New Haven, of that he had no doubt. Government was here, which meant the Royal Navy.

Court Street ran east from the Common, so he followed that until he came to a brick building that had to be what he was seeking. The building's center was three stories tall, topped with a clock set within a cupola, and a lion and a unicorn rampant on brick insets to each side of the clock. Two-story brick and marbled wings extended to each side away from what was clearly, even to Hethor's untrained eye, the original facade. Little round windows below the animal figures were set about an ordinary double-hung window, and below that a balcony that had the look of something used to read proclamations, or perhaps to declare public punishments. A Union Jack flew over the clock, while the blue-on-white stars of Her Imperial Majesty's New England colonies flew to one side, and an unfamiliar yellow-and-red banner flew to the other. The sigil of the viceroy, Hethor supposed. He hoped it meant that the man was in residence now.

Doubt gnawed at his heart in the face of his goal. Should he go to Anthony's tap room on Pier Four and seek out this Malgus first? Hethor had no assurance that the viceroy would not simply laugh him away, or even worse, make an example of an upstart Colonial countryman.

There was no way for Hethor to know. Master Bodean had not been a political creature, preferring to stick to his clocks and pay his assessments and let the Crown get on with the business of ruling. As a result, Hethor had inherited no politics from his master, other than the politics of business—charge cash up front, pay slow against your own credit, never sell for less than you bought plus a solid margin.

He advanced slowly up the marble steps that led to a surprisingly low door beneath the balcony. A small brass plate read MASSACHUSETTS HOUSE. Inside was cool and dark, almost damp. Two soldiers stood there in the gray wool uniforms of the New England colonial militia, each with a carbine over his shoulder. They looked bored. A circular marble desk was ensconced before a double flight of stairs, with galleries leading left and right to the wings.

Hethor stood in front of the desk. An enormous register, even larger than Librarian Childress' books of artistic engravings, lay open on the counter. Sharp copperplate script displayed the comings and goings of men of power. A thin man, face pinched tight above a dark suit and an almost clerical stiff collar, gave Hethor a fishy-eyed stare from behind the armor of his book.

"Servant's entrance is on Chatham Street." The thin man's voice was as reedy as his looks. "I'll thank you not to muddy His Lordship's front hall."

"I'm here to see His Lordship," said Hethor slowly. He was trusting inspiration to come, but his trust appeared to have been misplaced.

"One of the Specials, hmm?"

"Special. Well, er . . . yes."

"Password?"

Password? "Uh . . . albino toucan."

"Hmm . . ." The thin man pulled a small notebook from his coat pocket and flipped through it. "I see." He looked up, past Hethor. "Sar'n't Ellis. Please be so kind as to detain this . . . individual . . . for questioning. He claims to be a Special. I expect Mister Phelps will wish to see him whether or not that is true."

"Alrightie." The burly Sergeant Ellis grabbed Hethor's arm none too gently. "Come on, then."

"I suggest the Blue Room," said the thin man helpfully.

"I knows me business," Ellis grumbled before leading Hethor around the desk to a stairway heading down beneath the marble risers.

"But I need to see the viceroy," Hethor protested as Ellis tugged him through the door.

"Oh, and you will." Ellis chuckled.

Belowstairs, the hallway was vaulted brick, as if it had been tunneled rather than built. Rooms opened on each side, much like Hethor imagined a dungeon to be, but when Ellis gently pushed Hethor into one, the room proved to contain only two settees and a desk, and a small, dirty window up near the ceiling that admitted a minor ration of the morning's light.

"I'd stay out of the desk," Ellis growled. "Mister Phelps don't like people in his drawers. Bar's on your right."

Then the door was shut, and with a clear, clanking thud, locked.

Not knowing what else to do, Hethor looked around the room. This place was vaulted, too, he realized with a glance at the ceiling. It stank of salt and mold—the sweat of both men and bricks. The bar was a small cabinet pushed against the wall; it proved to contain three cut-crystal tumblers in need of a cleaning, half a bottle of lemon squash, and a tin of biscuits. He wiped one of the tumblers on the tail of his shirt, poured out a glass of squash, and opened the tin.

If this was a prison, it was a strange prison. Yet the door was locked.

Ignoring the desk, Hethor sat on one of the settees.

The window was too high and too small for him to fit through. Besides which, it had the ironwork on the outside. The door's hinges were out in the hallway. He could starve in this room if no one came.

Hethor closed his eyes and listened to the world.

First and always there was his own breathing, and the snick-snick of his pulse in his ears audible as his head leaned against the couch cushion. Hethor listened past that, to the rattle of cart wheels in the street outside the dingy window and the faint murmur of voices from elsewhere in the bricked basement. Perhaps someone in the hall. He listened past that, to the very faint groan of the foundation's stones bearing up under the heavy building above, and the even fainter rattle of the world's turning.

Only this time the rattling of the world—always the least of sounds, like a mouse in the forest—seemed louder, easier to find. Almost like it was coming toward him. Eyes still closed, Hethor listened to it click and whir, like the greatest of clocks, the sound filling him up until he realized that what he heard was the key in the lock of the little brick room.

His head jerked up with a start.

A small man with a huge head, his body so diminutive as to be almost a grotesque, stood in front of Hethor. This man wore tradesman's garb not much better than Hethor's, though cleaner and more free of wrinkles. His eyes were clear blue, almost the color of ice, and his hair a crinkling red-brown.

"I am Mister Phelps," the newcomer announced, "and Lord William suggested I come see you this evening."

Hethor looked down to notice the crystal tumbler shattered on the floor. The lemon squash was no more than a sticky spot around it. How long had he been sitting here, listening to the world? Hours. A trance, perhaps. "William," he said, feeling as stupid as if he had been roused from sleep. "Of Ghent. The so-called sorcerer?"

"Or perhaps William the tile setter's boy," said Phelps softly. "I see I have caught you unawares."

"No, no, I . . . my apologies." Hethor made as if to stand, then realized that would set him quite a bit taller than Phelps. He wound up sitting again with his hand half stuck out in abortive greeting. "I'm here to see the viceroy." *What had happened to him?* Caught up in listening to the world and forgot where he was and what he was about.

Phelps ignored the hand. "So I understand." The small man hitched himself up onto the desk, sitting so that his swinging heels banged against the pediment. "Mister Cannon at the entry hall says you claimed to be a Special upon your arrival, mentioning a certain white bird. Sadly, Sergeant Ellis thought you were an imposter when I sought him out in a tavern for a second opinion."

"I'm sorry, sir," said Hethor. *Albino toucan.* "I don't know what a Special is."

"Heh." Phelps looked thoughtful. "I thought you might not. Let's just say that Specials are men, and very occasionally women, who aid me in my discreet services to the viceroy. Some matters of governance are best not put in the hands of younger sons of powerful lords sent over here from Mother England to wait out their various disgraces." Phelps' eyes positively glinted. "Have you spoken in confidence to any women recently, young Master Hethor?"

"I . . . how did you know my name?"

"My Specials," said Phelps. "At least one of whom took you very seriously indeed. The message came to me, along with you, though your story as it was passed to my ears would bring laughter to the lips of any Rational Humanist who heard it. And I might add Rational Humanism is quite the fashion this season in the viceroy's court. They talk far more of the Clockmakers than they do of God."

"I am a clockmaker's apprentice," Hethor said. "And I have something to tell the viceroy." He picked his next words carefully. There would be no more chances after Phelps, Hethor knew that with a certainty. "It is a critical matter."

"Tell me," said Phelps, his voice soft but urgent. "I am the viceroy's ears in many things. Sometimes his hands. Even more rarely, his voice."

He had no other choices. Not in a locked room in the basement of Massachusetts House. And this was, after all, the path upon which Librarian Childress had set him.

So Hethor recounted his tale of the visitation from the archangel Gabriel. Under further questioning, he told of the steps he took, from Pryce Bodean to the library and being turned out, on to the journey to Boston.

"A DIFFERENT man might have begged forgiveness," Phelps said, pouring the last of the lemon squash into another tumbler.

"I did no wrong," Hethor insisted. Telling his tale had raised his anger all over again. The tiny room, dark now except for a candle Phelps had taken from the desk, seemed hot and close as it had not earlier in the day.

"Wrong is most often in the mouth of the accuser." Phelps sipped the squash, made a face. "Were you to call His Lordship a liar, you would be lucky only to be whipped out of hand. Were His Lordship to call you a liar, you would be lucky only to be whipped out of hand. The material facts are not at issue."

"As I have learned," Hethor muttered darkly, wishing a terrible fate on Pryce Bodean. "I had a duty."

"And so your falling out set you on the road here." Phelps waved his arm, taking in the little room. "Closer to the viceroy in miles, perhaps, but for the moment bereft of your freedom. I must put a question to you, Master Hethor."

"Just Hethor. I am master to no man. What do you wish to know?"

"I for one find you sincere. You clearly believe your story as you tell it. That being said, I am not prepared at this moment to judge the objective truth of your tale on its own merits, but I will offer you a choice. Would you prefer to take the story to the viceroy as you are, roughshod and uncultured? Or would you prefer to recount it again to an amanuensis, take some coaching in deportment and manners, and have one or another pliant gentleman of the court deliver your report in a few weeks' time, with you decorously under that gentleman's apparent sponsorship?"

The very thought of being puffed and powdered and paraded about made Hethor's skin crawl. Pryce and Faubus had communicated to him a newfound allergy to gentlemen and all their works. Besides, Gabriel's visit and the archangel's warning about the Key Perilous were *his* story to tell.

"I must do it myself," Hethor said, "and trust to the viceroy's wisdom to see through my unsophisticated veneer."

"Unsophisticated veneer indeed," said Phelps with a small smile. "He will see a rustic countryman and not hear any words at all, I am afraid. Nonetheless, it is your story. And I seem to have made it your choice as to how to tell it. His Lordship hears petitions and appeals in morning session several days per week. You shall be presented as soon as practical."

"I can see that these small rooms are for the telling of stories," said Hethor, finding unexpected courage. "Which you or your Specials must routinely relay to the viceroy. Why will you not simply relay my own story in the usual manner?"

"Because, unlike most stories I hear in these small rooms," said Phelps, his smile growing sad, "I believe yours. If the story were mine to tell, the angel would have come to me."

LATER THAT evening, a man entered the room with a little cart. He was dark-skinned, though by his clothes neither slave nor servant. "Mister Phelps said you was please to stay here until someone came for you," the newcomer said in a deep, singsongy West Indian accent. His voice put Hethor in mind of how a tree might talk. When the man left, he did not relock the door.

Hethor examined the cart. On top were a pair of covered dishes, one of which under inspection proved to be cod and pease porridge—dinner, he presumed, though almost cold—while the other was a dish of boiled eggs, onions, and a pale cheese shot through with blue veins. On the lower ledge of the cart was a washbasin and a chamber pot, along with a ewer of fresh water, a clothes brush and a rag.

Master Bodean, like most of New Haven, had enjoyed running water. Apparently the viceroy's basement guests did not.

"Thank you," Hethor told the walls, only half in jest. It would not surprise him in the least if Mister Phelps could hear his every word either directly or through the reports of one of his Specials.

Taking advantage of the last light of Phelps' candle before it guttered out, Hethor brushed his coat and trousers as clean as he could. He used the rag and water to take some of the grime off his face and hands. Then, mindful of the old farmer's comment about judging a man by his boots, he spent the rest of his effort on his footwear. After that he ate sparingly of the cod, never a great favorite. The pease porridge helped to offset the cod's lip-curling saltiness. Finally he lay down on the settee to rest. Hethor was afraid of sleep tonight, afraid of the clicking trance that had claimed the long hours of his day, but fear or no fear his body surrendered to the soft cushions and the oddly scented darkness of the room.

He slept, dreaming mostly of cod and candles and a fire that burned high in the sky.

"OUT, MON!" It was the West Indian, rousing Hethor from his sleep. "His Lordship will see you but very shortly."

Only half awake, Hethor stuffed an egg and an onion in his coat pocket, crammed some cheese into his mouth, and pulled on his boots. The cheese was unexpectedly sharp and thick. He had trouble swallowing as he followed the dark-skinned man down the brick corridor, farther from the entranceway, then up a narrow stair.

Hethor had the cheese more or less jammed down to a hard lump in the bottom of his chest when the West Indian stopped him in a coat closet. The ceiling angled to the floor, bespeaking a rising stair just above them. A dim electrick light flickered orange immediately over the wooden door that led out. The wall behind them snicked shut, the door to the downward stair now become only paneling.

"You will be silent, mon, until you are spoken to." The West Indian flicked cheese crumbles from Hethor's shirt-front and coat. "This is a hearing, not formal court. Do not be amusing, mon. I especially advise you to keep one eye on Mister Phelps and heed his signals. And for the love of God, don't lie about anything in front of that nasty Lord William."

Then Hethor was in a hallway full of wigged and powdered men dressed in a fashion that would have been wildly strange on any street in New England—either the latest mode from London, or far out of date; Hethor had no way to know which. The gentlemen of the court wore silk brocade coats in the colors of brilliant tropical flowers opened over ruffled shirts and wide sashes, while flared pants dropped to high, polished boots of exotic leathers.

The West Indian had not come with him, instead tugging the closet door shut after shoving Hethor into the hall. Hethor perforce followed the flow of peacock men into a larger room, two stories high, lined with classic white columns. Incense burned, assaulting his nostrils, presumably there to cover other, baser scents. One side of the room—the south?—had tall windows cranked open, the panes set with colored glass. Multichromatic freckles of filtered morning light stretched at a steep angle across the room from them. The opposing side sported alcoves reflecting the shapes of the windows, each populated with statuary.

Hethor wondered if some of Phelps' Specials lurked behind the statues.

Except for all the finery and the colored glass, the room seemed a large version of any New England town meeting hall or church. There were some other small differences—chairs instead of pews, no lectern at the dais at the far end—but this room was New England as Hethor knew his home, conforming to deep tradition and the inertia of place.

Despite the sense of familiarity, he had no idea where to go. The gentlemen of the court swirled in an intricate pavane known only to them, finding seats arranged by some sympathetic magic of status and rank and function. Hethor was suddenly left standing alone on the worn red carpet between the two arrays of chairs. No one ever bothered to glance at him. This was more disconcerting than if everyone had been staring.

Hethor looked at the head of the room, where four more soldiers in gray New England uniforms stood at the back wall with carbines in their hands. They were in turn flanked, two to a side, by British regulars in lobster-red coats over dark green wool. Which must be hotter than blazes in this well-warmed room, he realized.

Phelps walked onto the dais from a side door. The little man was dressed in a rainbow of silk—pink, blue, chartreuse, and half a dozen more colors besides—punctuated by fountains of lace, and an enormous matching hat. The effect made him look like a gamecock dyed for Easter, communicating an absolute lack of dignity.

"The Honorable Lieutenant-General Lord Devon de Courtenay," Phelps bawled in a voice that would have served him well in music hall comedy, "Knight Grand Cross of Saint Michael and Saint George, Order of the Wabash, by appointment of Her Imperial Majesty Queen

Victoria now Viceroy of New England and the American Possessions, Protector of Canada and Warden of the Western Frontiers, sitting *en banc* to hear the prayers and appeals of Her Imperial Majesty's people."

All the peacock gentlemen stood in a rustle of silk and a cough of rheumy lungs as a man in a simple white uniform strode in behind Phelps. A red-and-blue star hung on a ribbon, while his chest was crossed with an enormous vermilion sash. A worn silver sword dangled over glossy polished cavalry boots. His unadorned appearance made every other gentleman of the court a pompous liar by their very dress.

Everyone but Hethor, who began to wish mightily he had taken Phelps' other choice and allowed himself to be pomaded into anonymity.

The viceroy took his place on a mahogany chair that was so simple as to be a shouted understatement. As one, the peacock gentlemen sat with another rustle and cough, leaving Hethor once more standing like a muddy stick in a field of roses.

Turning a bright smile on Hethor, the viceroy narrowed his eyes as another man, taller than any in the room, with ice-blue eyes and red-brown hair over features similar enough to place him kin to Phelps, slipped in at the back of the dais. Hethor realized that this must be the sorcerer William of Ghent. The advisor affected clerical garb, a black cassock with a high collar, but he walked like a king.

And he stood *behind* the viceroy, unremarked. Even Hethor could see that was a position of tremendous trust and power.

Bright smile glittering and fixed, the viceroy pointed at Hethor. "Major domo, who disturbs the order of my morning hearing?"

"One Hethor Jacques," bawled Phelps, "an apprentice of the Loyal Order of Horologists and Timekeepers, come from New Haven on his own recognizance to seek counsel from His Lordship."

"Ah," said His Lordship. After a moment he cocked a finger over his shoulder.

William of Ghent stepped forward to have a whispered conversation with the viceroy. Still none of the peacock gentlemen would look at Hethor. He did not exist for them.

Hethor was almost relieved to see two of the redcoats at the back of the dais giving him hard-eyed glares. He had to suppress a manic desire to wave at them. At least he wasn't invisible.

"We shall indulge the apprentice horologist," the viceroy announced. "You may instruct him to proceed."

"Apprentice Jacques, you will speak your piece," bawled Phelps.

At that, all the peacock gentlemen turned their heads to look at Hethor. Now he existed, if only under the stares of a hundred dandies.

"Your Lordship," Hethor said slowly, resisting the urge to blurt out Librarian Childress' pass phrase, "six nights ago I received a visitation from the archangel Gabriel." Careful, he told himself. He would never make a more important speech. "God's messenger warning me of a grave danger to us all. It is my duty as an Imperial subject and a loyal New Englander to pass that message on to your ears, that you might best determine how to respond to the warning."

The viceroy cocked his head slightly while William of Ghent whispered again in his ear. Phelps stood like a statue, not meeting Hethor's eye. At some signal invisible to Hethor the peacock gentlemen began to titter. It was as if he were indeed surrounded by birds, in a court of birds, before a bird emperor.

"I . . ." Hethor faltered. "I was told . . . to seek the Key Perilous. To find a way . . . a danger, sir. Sire. Sir."

The tittering turned to full-throated laughter around him. Hethor would have expected no less had he dropped his trousers, or suddenly turned into a Chinaman.

The viceroy leaned forward. Silence fell as soon as he

opened his mouth. "Fascinating," he said. "And men such as you are permitted to walk the streets without a keeper?"

The laughter returned.

Hethor stood in the middle of the room, dappled in colored sunlight, while the viceroy's court roared out their amusement and contempt, until someone took his arm to tug him away. Phelps finally met Hethor's eye. The little man only shook his head with an almost imperceptible motion.

Hethor's last view of the room as Sergeant Ellis led him away was of William of Ghent, a cold smile on his lips, nodding in counterpoint to Phelps.

HE SAT alone in one of Phelps' interview rooms. The street outside rumbled with traffic, indifferent to Hethor's plight.

This time there was no food, no drink, no pretense of liberty or civility. Just the stark silence of imprisonment. At least he remained unchained.

Even the ticking of the Earth seemed distant from him now. He would have done better to remain in New Haven and hurl himself on the mercy of Master Bodean's sons or the criminal courts. Even a thief or a debtor might eventually win free. Here, there seemed little chance of Hethor walking away. Still, he spent much time thinking on what he might say in a last, desperate plea.

Around late morning, judging by the angle of the niggardly sunlight from the tiny barred window, there was a screaming of birds outside, followed by eerie silence. Even the street had fallen still. At the same time, what he had taken at first for a cloud shadow deepened to a true darkness.

The silence beyond his window was shattered by the peal of church bells. Dogs howled; firearms were discharged. Had the world's turning stopped of a sudden? He was too late already!

Hethor realized that if the Mainspring had seized in that moment, Boston would be trapped in light, not darkness.

In that strange midday darkness, the door opened. Despite a dozen resolutions to remain firm and spirited in the face of what might take place, Hethor turned with questions on his lips only to be stopped by whom he saw.

William of Ghent had come to him.

The sorcerer was dressed in street clothes now. Neither a gentleman nor a mystic by his attire of nondescript black suit and gray cravat, William could have passed for any tea trader fresh from bidding in some dockside warehouse.

The ice-blue eyes bored into Hethor like the gem-tipped drills of Master Bodean's trade.

"Did you end the world?" Hethor blurted. Not what he had hoped to begin with.

William looked surprised. "What? You credit me with far too much."

"The sun is gone."

"It is a solar eclipse, boy."

"Oh." Hethor was seized with embarrassment. He knew perfectly well what an eclipse was. The peculiarities of the sky were part of clockmaker's lore. Master Bodean had not neglected his training in that regard.

"Still not thinking." William's tone was not unkind. "No more than you were this morning in the audience. That was poorly done, I'm afraid."

Hethor stared at the dirty floor. He realized the dark stains were probably blood. "I had sought a different outcome," he mumbled.

"Mister Phelps tells me you are not a madman, nor a fool. You would never have come back up the stairs in the first place were that so." The sorcerer seemed sympathetic. "What had you hoped for?"

"An honest audience." Hethor looked up. "Some attention to my words. It is plain truth I tell you, sir."

"No one comes to court for plain truth, my boy."

William began to pace the perimeter of the room. "The question of Heaven is tricky. There is no denying Creation, certainly. But some look for God in every shadow and sunrise." A smile quirked. "Even in eclipses, perhaps. Others find His long absence telling. Are you a Rational Humanist?"

"I . . . I don't know." Hethor wanted to have nothing to do with any creed of Pryce Bodean's. And he'd had the evidence of Gabriel in front of him to argue for the close presence of the divine in human affairs. Yet the Spiritualist approach seemed overly comfortable, even facile. "Perhaps I'm too near the question."

"Hah," said William. "Well put." He stopped in front of Hethor. "Look, boy, the world is more than you think. Whatever dream or illusion you had was well told enough for Mister Phelps, but there's far more at stake than you know. Man was never meant to live under the yoke of Heaven. Earth is changing. The wise ones will let it change."

"No." Hethor had no power left but the truth. "I know what I saw. I think you know it, too, sir."

"Maybe I do." William smiled sadly. "And that's the true shame. You could have lived to see the light of day one more time. Ah, well. Regret is for the foolish. Though there's no profit for it now, you might still consider how much better events could have gone for you."

With those words, he stepped out again, leaving Hethor to wonder in the long, silent hours that followed what he might have done differently.

"NO MORE little rooms for you this time, I'm afraid." Ellis half dragged Hethor down a different brick tunnel. This one led deeper underground, far from any windows. The big man carried a small bull's-eye lantern in his free hand to light the way. "Judging by the look on Lord William's face, I do believe that you've gone and forked the duck."

Hethor made no reply. He just stumbled after the sergeant. What was he going to do? He had failed in his mission, failed so thoroughly as to remove himself from any possible hope of redemption. And that bastard William had sealed his fate with nothing more than a word.

"Can you take a message for me, Sergeant?"

"You've got a ma'am somewhere wondering after you?"

"No." Hethor had no memory of his mother at all, and only the one, slim year with Mistress Bodean to fill that hole in his heart. "But there's a man who drinks down at Anthony's on Pier Four. Malthus, Malgus. Something. Tell him I'm here."

Ellis stopped in front of a huge iron-bound door to fish out a key. "And why would he care about you, lad?" the sergeant asked gently.

"He won't care about me at all." Hethor stepped quickly through the door so Ellis didn't have to shove him. "But he might care about my message."

The door slammed shut, the sergeant's final words, if any, muffled by the wood.

Hethor stepped into the darkness, sweeping his foot carefully in front of him. He realized he was in a tiny chamber rather like a mudroom except for being deep underground. He found something solid that thumped at the knock of his boots. A moment's exploration with his hands revealed that another door stood in front of him. In a rush of panic, afraid of being locked in a little closet to starve, Hethor grabbed for the latch of the second door and threw it open.

Beyond there were stars. Tiny glints twinkled high and low.

Hethor stood blinking, trying to figure out what it was he saw, until he realized that a multitude of candles was set before him. Dark, ragged shapes stretched between them.

Some moved.

A bent man approached Hethor, took his hand, rubbed Hethor's clean fingers between grimy calluses. "Welcome, son," the man whispered in a voice so tiny Hethor had to lean forward to hear it. "Welcome to the pit of the candlemen."

The bent man led Hethor to a pallet of rags between four lit candles. Up close, Hethor could see that pounds, perhaps hundredweights, of wax were melted in flowing mounds to serve as bases for those tapers that yet burned. It was a century's worth of candles or more, burning down here forever. He wondered how long the bent man had been here.

He also wondered how long the pallet's previous inhabitant had been here.

He lay back with the top of his head pillowed against flows of wax and listened to his breath and his pulse and his unshed tears, listened to the sputtering pop of the candles and the ragged breathing of the candlemen, listened to the gentle sweating of the bricks and stone beneath the wax.

Under it all, the world turned, the rattle ever louder. Hethor didn't even have to strain to hear it. There was something wrong. Some escapement or fusee was out of time with the gears of the world. God's Creation was like a sick clock not yet gone to ruin but set almost inexorably on that path.

Lost among the candlemen, Hethor knew with a terrible certainty that the world was going wrong. Only he could fix it.

Only he couldn't, not here.

The little lights flickered, spotting the darkness even as Hethor slipped into exhausted sleep, dogged in his flickering dreams by William's voice.

THREE

"**BREAK YOUR** fast, boy?"

Hethor awoke with a start. His body spasmed against cold stone. Darkness around him glittered with tiny flames, each point of light bringing his memories back with it. He had been dreaming of his feather pillow and pallet in Master Bodean's attic, and how only a week before, his greatest worries had been steering clear of Headmaster Brownlee and improving his command of the art of filing the correct gear ratios onto the smallest of the blank wheels.

"I'm sorry," Hethor whispered to the candleman who crouched next to him on hands and knees. "I'm not hungry."

"Never hungry in this heart of stone," the candleman said matter-of-factly. "Not no one. Still, a man's got to eat if he's going to live."

Hethor supposed the candleman had a point. He pulled himself up into a squat, back and joints protesting from time spent on cold stone and chunky wax, then scuttled after the man who had come to fetch him.

A number of the prisoners were seated in a circle. They were surrounded by a veritable rampart of candle wax.

The top of the lumpy, flowing wall was lit by still more candles. Hethor had no sense of the size of the room, other than of a great space, for the flickering flames made the darkness around them all the more impenetrable.

He would have preferred less light and more vision.

His guide brought Hethor into the circle, patted a place on a little seat of wax worn by years of buttocks, then crawled to his own place.

"Welcome," said another candleman. It might have been the same one who had greeted Hethor the night before. He seemed to be the spokesman.

If it had been the night before, Hethor realized with a shiver. His sense of time told him it was morning. The clattering of the Earth was almost loud here, a metronome overriding the confusion of the darkness, but there was no way to check the passage of sidereal midnight, no validation at all.

No master clock save the one he carried within.

"Thank you," Hethor said belatedly, recovering from his train of thought. "I'm—"

"No," the candleman said firmly as he raised a hand. "We have but one rule here in the pit. Slow, go slow. Your least bit of news is a treasure to be gleaned and passed about from man to man. Do not scatter lightly now what you will prize later."

"I see."

"In the pit of the candlemen, no one sees."

They all intoned, "No one sees."

"I hear," said Hethor with a flash of understanding. He *did* hear, after all, the music of the Earth below all the levels of life. That strange gift he had always had, commonplace to him but seemingly peculiar as some rumored power of a sorcerer from the Southern Earth the few times he had tried to explain it.

He understood their darkness in a basic, primitive way. "What of you, then?"

"We are waiting here," said the spokesman.

Hethor considered that answer. He inhaled deeply,

smelling wax and sweating stone and distant slops and unwashed candlemen. He listened to his breathing and theirs, the hiss of hundreds of candle flames and the unaccountably loud sounds of the Earth. He looked around the glimmering darkness.

Panic clawed his throat. It recalled the sensation of drowning in a river. He'd nearly done so one summer when he was nine, tangled in the rotting branches of an old log in the current, willing to mortgage his soul for one more breath of air.

"Please . . ." Hethor choked out the word, fighting his desire to scream and bolt from the prison even if he had to claw through stone to do it. Surely they all felt that in this place. These men were buried, dead as the Brass Christ in his tomb, with no angel to roll back the stone.

Someone pressed a bowl into his hand. It was cool to the touch, and a little rough. He could barely see it even in the candlelight, but with his other hand Hethor found a pile of boiled eggs. He took one and passed the bowl along.

Soon there was a sound of peeling and chomping as the candlemen ate. Still there were no words.

Another bowl came, almost the same as the first, this one filled with a soppy mess of which Hethor took a fingered scoop. Rolled oats with a trace of honey, he decided from the smell. He passed that bowl, then licked his fingers clean.

When the third bowl came, he finally realized what he was holding. They were the tops of skulls, round as his own head and no bigger. Hethor shrieked and nearly dropped it.

The candleman to his right, who had not spoken before, said in a soft voice, "If you don't like sausage, please just pass it on."

"The bowl . . ."

"We share everything here in the pit," said the spokesman. "Even ourselves, once we are gone."

"What *is* this place?" Hethor asked desperately.

"In eighteen hundred and seventy-one, Viceroy Earl Cornwallis caused engineers from London's Metropolitan Railway to come to Boston and create a tube train here. He built a line from the harbor to the viceregal offices at Massachusetts House. From here it ran onward to the west end of Boston Common."

That was not the answer Hethor had expected. "What?"

"The candlemen's pit is the Massachusetts House Station."

"We even have a locomotive here," croaked another voice out of the flickering shadows. Pride still echoed within the reedy weakness of age.

An underground railroad? In a prison? *They are all crazed.* What had William of Ghent done to him? "And you are the engineers?"

"Some of the oldest of us," said the spokesman. "Some of us were laborers or draughtsmen. Others were placed here to wait for . . . whatever."

"As I am—"

"Observe the rule!" the spokesman interrupted sharply. "Our stories are old, and may be freely told. Your story is new, and more precious than gold."

"What happened to the rail line?" Hethor was trying to find a semblance of sanity among these half-mad, half-blind old men.

"Never opened," said the spokesman. He sounded sad. "Viceroy Earl Cornwallis lost a son under the wheels of our test locomotive before the line was ever opened. In his grief, he had us all shut in here with the murdering machine. I believe they eventually shipped him home wrapped in madness."

Surely Viceroy Lord Courtenay did not mean him to rot here for decades? Hethor thought. He would be mad as these candlemen, and no more useful to himself or the world.

If the world indeed kept turning. He thought back to the fault in the noises he had heard as he had fallen asleep. Something was going wrong in the heart of the world. The Key Perilous would be part of whatever was needed to set it to right. Whatever and wherever the Key was.

"I don't want to be here," Hethor whispered.

"None do," a voice responded from around the circle. "We are lost to life. You will no more escape this place than you will fly across the great Wall at the waist of the world. Not till you are born once more into the light."

"Kennard 'as flown over't," cackled another. "Ain't'ch'a, Kenn? Magic and hoody-men walkin' on corpse-legs beyond, na?"

There was a mumbled response. The circle began to rustle as men shifted their weight.

"Please," said Hethor. "There must be appeal. Some escape."

"'Tis not so bad," said his neighbor to the right. A ragged hand touched his arm.

"We all keep nearby," said another.

Around him, the candlemen began to shuffle closer together, closer to Hethor, their bodies one by one blocking the candlelight as their hands reached out for him. Rough-scarred fingers stroked his face, his hair, his body, tugging at his pants, touching him, touching, touching.

With a scream he leapt to his feet, only to crack his head on a stone arch. Hethor collapsed into the heap of candlemen, terrified for his life. They reached once more for him when a bright light stabbed into them all.

The candlemen screeched, shouted, scuttled away from the brilliant beam. A group of men walked through distant doors carrying bull's-eye lanterns and waving staves.

"Line 'em up," someone shouted. "Every able-bodied man fall in, right now!"

Hethor scrambled on hands and knees toward the newcomers, eager to be away from the candlemen, no matter what the cost. He tried to get to his feet, but the throbbing in his head made him sick to his stomach. He missed his footing and slid flat on the floor.

"Come along, you monkeys, or you'll be billy-damned sorry," roared the shouting man.

Choking, Hethor got to his feet. He staggered forward. "Wait for me," he gasped. "Please, wait."

"This place is scuppered," said another voice in a thick Scottish accent. "Dinna see what the fewk we come for. Wastin' our time with them broken old bastards. Dark as yon eclipse in here, 'tis, and them all blind as stones."

"No!" Hethor tried to shout, but his stomach heaved so hard the words came out in a strangled cough.

Hands grabbed at his ankles and his calves, tugging him back into the flickering darkness. A wave of fury and fear drove Hethor forward. They had come for him. He knew it. He fought his tormenters to chase after the lanterns bobbing through the door. "Wait for me!" he shouted.

The last one in the line paused, the light sweeping back once more into the pit of the candlemen. It caught Hethor in the face. He madly waved even as more hands tried to pull him down. Hethor kicked a candleman in the face, then stumbled into the lantern's glare.

"Well and you're nae prize," said the Scottish voice. A great hand grabbed Hethor's shoulder and yanked him out the first door, then the second, into the brick corridor beyond.

"Is he fit?" asked the first man, the one who had shouted for the prisoners to fall in.

"Fit enough, by the white bird," said Phelps quietly. The little man stood in the corridor with Sergeant Ellis, a few feet away from the party with their lanterns and staves.

Hethor tried not to stare at Phelps. His message to the mysterious Malgus at Anthony's must have gotten through. They really *had* come for him. His eyes ached in the lantern's glare. Someone felt the muscles of Hethor's arms and shoulders.

Phelps smiled, nodding slowly, acting for all the world like he'd never before laid eyes on Hethor. "He'll do."

Hethor found himself being dragged down the corridor faster than he could walk. He was surrounded by a chatter of voices talking about weight and lift and drag and everything except the most important thing of all.

What were they going to do with him, now that he had been rescued from the pit?

THE GROUP that took him from the prison turned out to be six men including the leader and the vocal Scot. They bundled Hethor into an enclosed wagon of the sort used by the bobbies to round up drunks and criminals. But they all followed him in. He noted that the door was not locked.

Inside the black Mariah with its tiny, high windows, his eyes had a chance to adjust to the light once more. He realized these men with their striped shirts and canvas jackets were sailors. One even wore a gold hooped earring just like the engravings in the Boy's Own books he'd read as a child. They carried on a multisided conversation that seemed to be all talking and no listening.

"Ain't never seen nothing like that place. Like some demon-hell out of the south."

"Straddle me and me mum both, you've been to the Gambia *and* Formosa. Don't bet that's the worser's ever been seen by the likes of us."

"All right, you stupid arse-licker, but 'tain't nothing like it in a proper English city."

"Who the bloody fewk says Boston's a proper English city?"

They all laughed.

"Excuse me," Hethor said.

"What ho," the Scot replied. "New chum speaks."

"I'm grateful for the rescue, but where are we bound?"

More laughter. The one with the earring punched Hethor in the shoulder so hard Hethor was knocked into the man on the other side of him.

"Silly bugger," shouted one of the sailors.

"No, no buggering his sweetness yet," said another.

Hethor subsided, holding his tongue. He'd gotten in trouble enough already these past few days by talking too much.

After about twenty minutes of travel, the black Mariah rumbled to a stop with much heying and clucking from the driver outside. The sailors tumbled out, sweeping Hethor with them onto a pier. A ship was tied at the far end. A little shingled shack stood right beside them. The sign above the entrance read ANTHONY'S.

"Pier Four?" Hethor asked.

"The same," roared the Scot, slapping Hethor again. "Nae time for drinking this morning. Smallwood wants to cast lines and head south before the midday calm. As His Lordship is our captain and our master, cast lines we shall."

"I'm going on a ship," Hethor squeaked. He'd never even been in a rowboat, though he'd swum enough in rivers and ponds as a small child.

"Oh, that you are, my little beggar."

Someone grabbed his elbow, marched Hethor down the pier, and literally threw him off the dock into a little boat with a single mast and eight oars. He had not seen the small vessel before because it was hidden by the pier's height.

"Sit down and shut your bleeding gob," growled Gold Earring, "if you know what's good for you."

Anything is better than the pit of the candlemen, Hethor told himself. At least if this crew killed him, it would be in good honest daylight, not in that dungeon full of half-starved ghosts bent on terrible violation of his body and soul.

Around him the sailors began to row. They chanted as they pulled.

"Starboard, ya great eejit," bellowed the Scotsman at the small man on the tiller. "Or I'll have your sister for brekkie."

The boat heeled and lurched as salt spray broke over

the bow. Hethor tried to poke his head up only to be slapped down by Gold Earring again.

He lay in the bottom of the boat feeling nauseous once more but glad of the daylight as the sailors rowed their little vessel out across the harbor.

"JEFFRIES POINT," bellowed the Scot. "All ashore what's goin' ashore."

Everyone but Hethor found that very funny. Somewhere in the middle of the harbor his stomach had finally rebelled. He'd kept his guts behind his teeth, barely, but his nose stung and his breath reeked. Hethor knew without being told that spewing would be worse than pained silence.

Much worse.

He climbed up, this time without being slapped down into the bottom of the boat, and was helped out onto a muddy flat populated with wooden towers rising from stone footings. Gold Earring spun Hethor around by the shoulder to point back across the harbor.

"See that?" he growled. "Your precious Boston. Say good-bye, candy-arse."

New Haven was far more precious to Hethor than Boston, but this didn't seem to be the time to mention that.

Two of the sailors set anchors far out into the mud flat from the little boat. They then began hiking along a winding path toward the towers. Away from the water. The group was quieter than they'd been since first snatching Hethor from the viceroy's peculiar dungeon.

"Where's the ship?" Hethor asked after a few minutes of walking.

"Look up," said Gold Earring.

Hethor looked up.

Airships—canvas clouds that dripped hemp rope and wooden decks—floated at three of the towers. Great wings of slats webbed with silk drooped from the bows and sterns of the hulls, which were lean and narrow enough to kiss the water. Huge blades hung crossed over each other, screws protruding from the backs of outrigger pods that had steam hissing along their flanks. Nets hung across the canvas gasbags. The Union Jack was woven into them.

"Oh," said Hethor.

"Seeing as how we've yet to climb the ladder, it's a mite early to be saying so," said the Scotsman from the front of their little hiking party, "but welcome to Her Imperial Majesty's Ship of the Air *Bassett*."

"You've been pressed, man," Gold Earring said with a nasty chuckle, "into the Royal Navy, finest fewkin' fleet on air or water."

Hethor knew he should be dismayed, or even terrified, but he was profoundly glad to be shut of the scent of candle wax. And it didn't matter whether this sweep from the viceroy's prison was meant to help him or betray him. The message Hethor had sent to Malgus through Sergeant Ellis had ultimately summoned the press-gang, saving him.

"Thank you," Hethor mouthed as they reached the bottom of one of the towers.

The climb was ferocious, his arms and legs burning, but still it tasted of a kind of freedom he'd never known before.

THE SHIP cast off almost immediately after the press-gang's return, with a great roaring sluice of seawater ballast being dumped. No one on deck commented on their poor catch of one gangly youth. Gold Earring hustled Hethor to a rope locker near the front of the ship, close under the lowering curve of the gasbag.

"You're to stay here, and no moving about, till someone comes for you. Get a real sailor hurt and I warrant you'll know the meaning of pain under our lash. I'll staple your pecker to the rail with a twelve-penny nail, I find you in the way." He poked Hethor in the chest for emphasis. "And listen, little fish. Wind comes up, you tie yourself down to a safety line and hold on."

Hethor crouched next to the rope locker in a small space between it and a rail until a bored-looking boy with blond hair and a pink face came to find him.

"On your feet," said the child, who had to be four years younger than Hethor—twelve or thirteen at most. In contrast to Hethor's increasingly grimy work clothes, the newcomer wore a nicely cut uniform complete with gold-scabbarded sword.

Hethor stood, steadying himself on the rope locker, and wondered what was supposed to happen.

"You are hereby sworn to Her Imperial Majesty's service, at the pleasure of the queen or her appointed officers, under pain of punishment and death subject to the Articles of War and the captain's will."

"What?"

The child cuffed Hethor across the cheek. "Say 'yes,' lout."

Frustrated and enraged, Hethor hit him back. "Don't touch—"

But the child drew his sword and pressed the point into Hethor's chest. "That will stand you twelve lashes, and twelve more, for striking an officer, lout."

"I—"

"Shall we try for thirty-six?" The child waited for a moment, then lowered the sword's point. "I thought not. I am Midshipman Fine, officer in charge of the deck division. You are the most junior of the deck idlers. This means you do what any man on this ship says unless I tell you otherwise."

"Yes, sir." Hethor's back already itched.

"You'll be lashed at the next discipline call," said Midshipman Fine. "Until then, I suggest you stay out of further trouble. You may begin by finding Deck Chief Lombardo and doing whatever he requires of you."

Deck Chief Lombardo, of course, turned out to be

Gold Earring, the man from the press-gang who'd invested his time in harassing Hethor.

HETHOR'S SENSE of freedom evaporated as he scrubbed the decks with a holystone and a broom and tried not to think about the promised lashing. Though on the water the Royal Navy had gone to steam-powered iron hulls, in the air wood was still very much favored for its relatively light weight, flexibility, and ease of expedient repair.

These things were explained to him, lovingly and with great care, by Lombardo. The deck chief seemed to delight in forcing Hethor to absorb cataracts of *Bassett* trivia, with every expectation that they would be disgorged again on command.

"You're lucky," Lombardo growled the morning of Hethor's third day on board. The gray Atlantic tossed white lines of foam back and forth perhaps a thousand feet below the deck. "Most lads have to do five or ten years on the water before they get to the air. Hard work and plenty of buggering. Ain't never seen a press-gang for an airship before."

Hethor's back itched to distraction in anticipation of Middie Fine's promised lashing. The thought of the punishment held a sick dread for him, to the point where he barely listened to Lombardo.

"What the fewk makes you special?" Lombardo asked. His rough-shaven face pressed close to Hethor's ear. "Who the bloody raging hell *are* you?"

"Someone who needed very badly to leave Boston," Hethor said, despite his efforts to keep his mouth shut and just listen. Someone had made an extraordinary effort to bring him aboard; that was clear. *A combination of Phelps and the mysterious Malgus.* The question was, were they working with or against the connivance of the treacherous William of Ghent?

"This ain't no cush berth, you hear? We work damned hard, and we're bound for territory where Chinee airships troll for trouble. You'd best be able to fight, boy, or you'll really be in for it for some hard scut."

Lombardo gave Hethor a shove, doubling him over his broom, and stalked away.

HETHOR FOUND that even in his distress he loved the air. The airship had met only calm weather since leaving Boston, mostly favorable westerly breezes, so the rocking of the hull had been a gentle minimum. He could work the deck along a railing and stare out across the ocean toward the land to the west—though that slipped beneath the horizon soon enough. They often passed among the clouds, towering white geometries like he imagined mountains to be. The ocean below was a pattern of infinite variety, swells moving at cross-purposes, the colored rivers of currents visible, sometimes the dots of ships.

Occasionally he even saw whales.

It was as much magic as he had ever hoped to find in the world. The sounds were strange here, too, the clattering of the Earth replaced with the creak of ropes, the snapping of the gasbag's canvas envelope, and the distant clang of pumps. At night it was like being in Master Bodean's house during a strong storm, when the beams creaked and the roof groaned. Except these were the noises of calm. And the winds were different at altitude, playing a game both harsh and simple. The world that *Bassett* inhabited high above the Earth smelled pure as Creation.

Mindful of the mirage that he and Le Roy had seen from a Connecticut road, Hethor often found himself staring south. He hoped for a glimpse of the Equatorial Wall and the gleaming brass that defined its upper margin. Somehow, that seemed the best direction for him to be headed in pursuit of Gabriel's mission.

Life on the airship had a well-defined rhythm that was not unpleasing to Hethor. They steamed during the day unless the winds were quite favorable for *Bassett*'s limited sail. They banked the boilers at night unless the winds were quite unfavorable. Much of the ship's hull was taken up with tanking for the boilers, which burned a high grade of oil.

Shrouds and lines ran up and around the gasbag and out to the great steering paddles. Folding in the paddles was a matter of daily drill. For Hethor this mostly consisted of standing around holding onto a line while people ran past him yelling. More experienced sailors scrambled up and down the nets on the gasbag as well. No one suggested that Hethor do such a thing.

Between drills he cleaned the deck and stowed rope and other goods into deck lockers. Even the seat of ease, sky air chill upon his hindquarters, was strangely refreshing. Three meals a day, a ration of rum, a morning shave—though still barely required—and a sleeping hammock strung in the night air were the only other things in his life. At night, if he crept close to the rail, the Earth's tracks gleamed in the sky. They were closer than ever, rising from the eastern and western horizons like brilliant horns.

Except for the promised lashing Hethor could almost be happy. He lived in a bubble of quiet unremarked by the other sailors other than Lombardo's harassment. He steered far clear of officers. It was if he sailed the sky alone. He was no closer to the Key Perilous, but he was out of the candlemen's pit and in the open air.

Somehow, some way, he would find his path back to Gabriel's mission.

One afternoon Hethor was stowing a set of brass-bound blocks and tackles normally used when the ship wanted to show her best colors coming into port. The steering paddle crews had used them for a drill.

His clockmaker's eyes didn't like the way the brass had been polished down—there were streaks of fingerprints along the edges—so Hethor took the tail of his Naval-issue cotton shirt and began working the brass to a smoother perfection. He fogged it with his breath, then polished vigorously, wishing he had some of the right oils.

After a while Deck Chief Lombardo squatted next to Hethor on his heels. "Only damned thing I've yet seen you do on this ship that looked like you cared or understood it, sailor." The man's voice was uncharacteristically gentle.

"I've worked with brass a lot, Chief," Hethor said quietly. He buffed the edge of a pulley head. Then, holding it with his fingertips, he stowed it in the locker.

"What sort of brass?" Lombardo asked. "Weapons, musical instruments, fittings?"

"Precision machines," Hethor said shortly. "Clocks."

Lombardo grunted, then walked away. It was the first time he had done so without hitting Hethor.

Hethor took that to be something of a victory.

A CHANGE in the creaking of the spars and shrouds told Hethor that new developments were at hand. The ship was changing its behavior. Even the smell of the wind was different. He stowed the last of the brasswork and sidled over to the rail.

A scattering of islands lay in the gray sea, the little spots of land shaped like crescents and sickles, all thin and long with many curves and bays. None seemed to have much altitude. *Bassett* beat downward, her great propellers straining—Hethor was given to understand that fuel for the engines was more readily replaced than any venting of the precious hydrogen. Below them he could see dozens, perhaps hundreds, of whitewashed buildings scattered among the trees. Some of the trees appeared to be pines. Others were strange, great stalks with bushy heads.

Four familiar wooden towers rose out of the waters of one of the harbors. Airship masts.

"Bermuda," said a sailor leaning on the rail nearby.

"'Twouldn't do to jump ship here. Whole place is nothing but Royal Navy. Nice enough, mind you."

Bermuda. Hethor had heard of it, traced the tiny dots on maps of the Atlantic in the library at New Haven Latin, just like he'd traced the dots of Hispaniola and Cuba and Jamaica and half a hundred other islands of the Northern Earth.

He'd always thought islands were a sort of magic, life erupting from the hard, salt ocean, a fringe of existence on the watery desert. A challenge to the ruling powers of sea and sky.

That in turn made Hethor glance at the southern horizon. They were still too far north to see the Equatorial Wall, but the very idea of it seemed to hang heavy over the line of the ocean. Even at this latitude, the horns of the Earth's track had shifted, flattening out a bit.

"You'll see it afore we hail Georgetown, boy," the sailor said, following Hethor's gaze. "You can jump there if you've a mind to, but there's nothing that far south but howler monkeys and headhunters and creatures come down off the Wall. Like enough to the far side of the world, I figure." He broke into a toothless cackle. "It'll be a while before we see a good English port with good English food and bad English women."

Bosun's pipes began to whistle a new pattern Hethor hadn't heard in his few days aboard. They were approaching the mooring mast. Most of the deck idlers had jobs. Hethor scuttled back to his post by the fo'c'sle rope locker. He was all alone up there. The engines chuffed, propellers whining, as *Bassett* dropped her steering paddles and set wide stuns'ls to bring her into position on the mast.

The ship yawed in the wind, gasbag booming overhead. Hethor watched a man atop the mooring mast fire a harpoon upward. It cleared the bow and skittered across the foredeck, a large, narrow-armed, blunt-tipped spike that slid backward just as quickly to catch on the reinforced forward railing.

A group of deck idlers rushed up, secured the spike,

and lashed its line to a capstan. They sent a thicker rope down along the first rope, and locked the line into a massive winch. Working in concert with men on the mast, the idlers carefully warped *Bassett* into her mooring. A rope ladder was thrown across from deck to mast. The men on the mast secured it, saluted, then began the long climb down, two hundred feet or so to the water below where they had a little boat tied to the base of the mast.

Hethor stepped over to the rail and looked down. Purple and blue blotches stained the glass-green water. *Coral?* he wondered. Slim shapes slid along the pale bottom. Surely those were sharks.

The bosun piped a new call. A swirling mass of sailors gathered amidships on the upper deck. Two hands set up a little awning as Hethor scrambled to find Lombardo and the deck division and fall in with them.

In moments the crew was silent, ranked in neat arrays. Three men in neat blue officers' uniforms came out to stand beneath the awning. Hethor had never seen them before, though he presumed from all the gold braid that the one in the middle had to be Captain Smallwood.

"Attention, attention," the man with the least amount of braiding called. Hethor thought he might be a senior petty officer, but he had yet to master the nuances of rank other than the fact that everyone on the ship was above him. "General muster of the ship's company is called to order, Her Imperial Majesty's Ship of the Air *Bassett*, Josiah Smallwood commanding. Whereas we are safe in a friendly port, shore leave is granted in watch rotation. Your chiefs and officers will tell you off. She lifts air at four bells of the forenoon watch, day after tomorrow." He paused, looking around. "Discipline parade is now called. Seaman Jacques, step forward."

Oh, thought Hethor. He had almost managed to forget about his lashing.

Lombardo stepped forward with him. The chief took Hethor's wrists in hand from behind and propelled Hethor to a post set beside the awning. A rope was quickly looped and his hands pulled up and forward, over his head, straining Hethor's shoulders.

"Oh, God," whispered Hethor, "spare me from this pain." He was terrified, sweating his fear, legs trembling. He had seen people lashed back in New Haven—thieves, harlots, wayward apprentices. The sheer magnitude of their suffering had been overwhelming, flesh torn to ribbons, blood streaming down bare backs, wretched screams of pain and terror while the crowd threw fruit and stones and sometimes tossed pans of saltwater.

His shoulders tensed more, threatening to pop loose, as someone tore his shirt free.

"For the crime of striking an officer, Seaman Jacques shall stand for twice twelve lashes," said the petty officer in a bored voice. "It is presumed that he will draw moral profit from this lesson. Division Chief Lombardo, you may administer the punishment."

There was a moment of creaking silence. A deceptively cool breeze played across Hethor's bare back. The first slap of the lash came with a snap of leather and a near-blinding surge of pain like a brand searing his flesh. "One," roared the assembled sailors as Hethor fought not to scream.

"Two." He bit his tongue. Blood filled his mouth.

"Three." Hethor's back felt like it was blistering in a fire.

"Four." He screamed and would have collapsed if his wrists were not tied above his head.

"Five."

And onward, until the world was a blinding glare of pain and the blood spotting the deck around his feet became a muddy red kaleidoscope in the blur of his vision. At the count of twenty-four, Hethor had nothing left to him but a sharp smell of coppery blood and the salt sea below. A veil of pain had drawn over his thoughts.

"Here you go, sailor," Lombardo said, tugging Hethor's hands free of the post. Others bound something new to his wrists. Was he to be imprisoned now?

Hethor tried to fight, to push against this new torment, but Lombardo grabbed his head and hissed in his ear, "Hold still, you stupid git; they're helping you."

"And ye'd best hang on t'it," said the Scot who had led Hethor's press-gang.

Hethor blinked his eyes open as a gaggle of grinning sailors picked him up and charged across the deck shouting and singing.

"Oh, oh, oh, *hell*!" Hethor screamed as they pitched him over the rail, two hundred feet above the Bermuda lagoon, which stretched louche and shallow beneath *Bassett*'s mooring.

His hands jerked upward to add a new level of pain to Hethor's abused shoulders, counterpoint to the ruined horror of the skin of his back. Hethor looked up to see a rounded cap of silk billowing above him. It seemed to be slowing his fall.

For a few astonished seconds he hung in the air as if he were some baby spider on its spring migration, grown great and large. Silk or no silk, the water rushed up to meet him with a slap like the flat of God's hand. Hethor's knees drove up to his chin, slamming his head backward and loosing a new round of blood in his mouth as the sea-water of the lagoon washed his lacerated back in yet another wave of agony.

He swallowed his scream in time to avoid gulping down the ocean, and fought the ropes and silk to find the surface.

Then sailors were falling out of the sky to hit the water around him. They whooped and screamed as strong hands held Hethor up and tore his harness away. Someone pressed an oil-soaked cloth against his back even under the water. People called his name in the accents of a dozen different nations. The mob swam him toward shore, perhaps a quarter mile away, chattering of rum and prostitutes and gambling.

On the beach, shivering, half dead from the pain and the fall, Hethor stood wrapped in a dry blanket. A square of silk was stretched beneath it to cover the wounds of his back. The mast crew had met the sailors there with supplies and advice.

"New chum," said one of the Bermuda mast men to Hethor. He was as dark as the West Indian back in Boston had been. "Most bastards don't make the jump with a cat-scratched back. You're a hard case, mon."

"That wasn't punishment?" Hethor gasped.

"Well, the cat were." The mast man smiled. "I seen your back before Shinbone put the silk on it. You took your thrashing bloody fewking good, whatever it was you did to earn it. But the jump, mon, that's what makes you a sky sailor."

Bassett's crew and the mast men swept Hethor off in their midst, still carrying him toward a haze of rum and hemp, and even a prostitute someone else paid for, though all she did for Hethor was dab ointment on his back and sew up the wider wounds. She bathed them in yet more rum, which seemed to be what passed for water in Bermuda.

HETHOR AWOKE facedown in a hammock. His mouth was thick and foul as it had been after drinking corn liquor with those Connecticut turnip farmers. His back had achieved a sort of ethereal state of pain, the skin and muscles seeking to float away from his body on some mission of their own.

The swaying of the hammock convinced Hethor that the ship was under way. He turned his head sideways expecting to see the horizon, but found only wood and an oddly angled view of a small desk. A man sat writing at it.

"I . . . ," Hethor croaked.

"Awake, are you?" the man said without turning around. He had the soft voice of someone from the Virginia countries, far to the south of New England.

"Yes." Hethor could barely get his voice working.

The man turned around. He was dark-haired, balding

at the top, with sharp brown eyes and a rounded face that said nothing of his profession. Met on the street, Hethor might have thought the man a greengrocer or ostler. Even his clothes gave no clue. Instead of a uniform, the dark-haired man wore a blue linen shirt and duck trousers.

"Most of the new chum go through their trials one at a time. You managed to encompass a flogging, an initiation, and a shore leave in one heroic attempt."

Hethor had difficulty remembering the past day or so. On consideration that might be something of a blessing. "Uh," he managed to say.

"Malgus, Simeon Malgus." Malgus rose and pushed his chair back. "Navigator on our HIMS *Bassett,* and lieutenant in Her Imperial Majesty's navy. And you are Hethor Jacques, mysterious seaman recruit late of New England."

"Yes." *Malgus*, thought Hethor. He'd heard the name before. Of course. His message to Anthony's had gotten through. God bless Sergeant Ellis. And, Hethor had to admit, a bit of his own quick thinking.

"Chief Lombardo tells me you know something of clocks."

Hethor tried to sit up. He found he was too weak. "Yes. Apprentice, sir." His voice was returning.

"Clockmaker's apprentice." Malgus stood over Hethor's hammock with a gleam in his eye somewhere between pity and humor. "The holiest of arts, clockmaking. Imitating the Tetragrammaton in His wisdom. Arranging the hours of a man's life as He chose to arrange the universe."

"'S just time, sir." Master Bodean would have said that, though Hethor never quite believed it.

"Just time. You could say that. Everything is just time—the Earth's spinning on her track in the sky, the motions of the moon and planets, even the slow unwinding of our own bodies. Did you sleep through the earthquake?"

Earthquake. A cold stab of fear shivered Hethor's

heart. He had felt flaws in the motion of the world, but those were too easily forgotten sailing the skies. "What earthquake?"

Malgus smiled, almost malicious. "Just as we cast off from Bermuda. One of the mooring masts collapsed, and there were fires in Hamilton port town. Captain Small-wood ordered us to press on instead of returning to render aid. Urgent business west and south."

"Earthquake." Hethor closed his eyes, listening, to see if he could hear the clatter of the world. The ship creaked, and his own breath and Malgus' both masked some of the sounds; but even here high in the air the movements of the world still echoed at the bottom of all the other noises, a fractional step removed from true silence.

And it sounded wrong.

"You hear it," Malgus said, his voice hardly more than a whisper. "You hear the changes."

Frightened, Hethor opened his eyes. The old farmer Le Roy had told him to seek out Malgus with his story. He'd finally found the man out after some missteps, and Malgus had in turn effected his rescue from the pit of the candlemen. But after his experiences in the viceroy's court Hethor was in no wise eager to share his thoughts further. Something about Malgus, his manner or his intensity, moved Hethor to guard his tongue, albino toucan or not. "I don't know, sir," he said. "I don't know what you're talking about."

Malgus' eyes narrowed. "Maybe you do and maybe you don't, sailor. I can't make you something you're not. But I don't want all your training to go to waste. Captain Smallwood has graciously permitted me to take you on in my service in order to properly maintain the instruments of navigation. You do that without embarrassing me, and I'll teach you how to use them."

Lombardo had been right. It *did* matter to Hethor what he did, that he had work he understood and cared for. And navigation was essentially the art of observing God's clockwork in the heavens. This . . . offer . . . from Malgus was another step toward fulfilling Gabriel's mission. "Thank you, sir."

"Now go back to sleep," said Malgus. "You won't be good for anything for a day or two yet. Not with that horrid back. The loblolly boy will be in later to see to your dressings. I daresay whoever sewed you up in Hamilton town knew his business well enough."

Hethor didn't even know her name, but he was grateful to the woman.

TWO DAYS later, Midshipman Evelyn de Troyes showed Hethor to the navigator's cupola. De Troyes was Malgus' assistant—apprentice in point of practice if not by law— though as a middie he had other duties as well.

"On the water," said de Troyes, a small man with sun-dark skin and pale-streaked hair, "all the officers practice navigation. It's a more difficult art in the air. Though the captains and the mates are supposed to do it as well, in practice it's mostly us."

He stopped talking as he and Hethor stood beneath the midmast. The "masts" were misnamed, in that they did not carry the sails, which were borne by flying spars reaching outward from the middle decks. *Bassett's* masts did not even correspond particularly to the masts of a sailing ship on the water. Rather, they were vertical members that were the primary structure anchoring the gasbag to the hull. As such they offered the easiest access to the interior of the great envelope. When he first boarded *Bassett,* Hethor hadn't been allowed anywhere near the midmast or the gasbag.

"Drop all your metal in the bin there," said de Troyes. "No buckles nor blades nor flints nor nothing to strike a spark. Then up the ladder. You first, all the way to the top. Can't get lost on the way."

"Me first?" Hethor unclipped his belt and took his flint and striker from his pocket. He grabbed the rubber-coated iron rungs.

"I want to watch you climb. If you have too much panic in you, we'll have to send you back to the deck division. Brass or no brass."

Hethor climbed like his heart was in it. The stretch-and-reach of the ladder tugged at his wounded back hard enough to bring stinging tears to his eyes. Hethor ignored the pain. *I must please de Troyes enough to keep my post with Malgus,* Hethor told himself.

The midmast rose perhaps eight feet off the main deck before it passed within the canvas skin of the gasbag. There was a flap there, set in place with rope and wooden toggles, that closed off the interior. Hethor flipped the toggles free, let the flap drop, and climbed past.

The inside of the gasbag was dimly lit by a very few electricks strung along the midmast. Hethor hadn't even realized that *Bassett* had electricks. He wasn't sure how they would be powered. The midmast climbed upward at a point where four gas cells met. They were made of silk, stiffened with varnish and rubber, crisscrossed with a fine mesh. Everything reeked of stale air and tar.

It was like being surrounded by billowing sails, though there was no wind in here. In fact the interior was quite hot. The shadows were just as uncomfortable as the pools of light from the electricks. Even cramped by the proximity of the gas cells there was a sense of vastness to the space, though Hethor knew the gasbag wasn't much past a hundred feet in height and somewhat wider in cross-section. The quiet was eerie, too, just the slick noise of his hands and feet on the strangely soft rungs, and a very faint thumping like the slow beating of a giant heart.

"Hydrogen pumps," said de Troyes behind him as they passed a narrow fore-and-aft catwalk at the midpoint of the climb. "Keeping the cells balanced and trimmed."

"Ah."

Soon enough the midmast came to the top of the gas-bag. There was a wooden hatch set in the bottom of a small platform. Hethor paused to study the hatch. It swung down, which was unusual in that most hatches swung outward to a deck. The hatch was smaller than normal as well, about two feet square. It was flanked by small gutta-percha or gum-elastic vents.

"Is there a wind problem up here?" he finally asked de Troyes.

"Good thinking, sailor. Now what can you tell me about those valves?"

"Ah . . ." Hethor stared at them a moment. The vents or valves were designed to allow air to exit without manual intervention. They had no stopcocks or levers. "Gas," he said. "Hydrogen. They let the hydrogen out."

"Indeed. Bad air will kill you. Pay close attention on climbing. If you feel weak or faint, climb down immediately and summon the gas division duty watch."

"Thank you, sir."

After waiting a moment more for further instruction, Hethor undid the ropes securing the hatch—no metal latches up here—and lowered it carefully. Leather hinges squeaked. Wind whistled past the opening, carrying the sharp fresh scent of clear air. As he looked up, squinting into the light, Hethor saw only watery gray clouds.

He scrambled up onto a platform about four feet wide and five long. The hatch was set almost in the middle. Unlike the main deck there was no railing to speak of here, but rather a built-up lip around the edge perhaps a foot tall, with a number of hooks set into it as well as a few stanchion braces. Hethor wasn't willing to stand upright in such an unprotected place, so he squatted on his heels.

The wind plucked at him as Hethor looked around to better understand the layout of the platform. The gasbag sloped away to his left and right, while a narrow plank catwalk, completely unrailed, marked the spine of the ship. The curve of the gasbag seemed to invite a dive, to slide slowly along it, moving faster and faster until one tumbled into the open air to fall to the sea below—how far? A thousand feet? Two?

Except for directly fore and aft Hethor found he had an

unobstructed view of the horizon. The height, with no railing or restraint around him, was unnerving, but not debilitating.

Back in New Haven he'd never imagined such things. Gabriel had indeed set him on a journey. This almost made the agony in his back worthwhile.

"We're gaining altitude," said de Troyes, scrambling up onto the platform and sitting tailor fashion. "Trying to rise high enough to weather the coming storm. Down too low an airship can be driven into the water. Oh, and welcome to the navigator's rest."

Hethor looked at the ragged, overcast sky, the darker clouds piled in the distance. "Is that southeast?" he asked.

"About right. What else can you tell me?"

They had brought no instruments. De Troyes was testing Hethor's education, his common sense, his powers of observation. How would Librarian Childress have looked at this place, at this sky, he wondered? "Hooks for tying us down when there's more wind," he said, thinking through the realities of the position. "Stanchions for the instruments. I assume you have poles."

"Staves, actually. Wouldn't do to pack a metal pole up through the gasbag." De Troyes nudged the edge of the platform with his foot. "These planks open up to our lockers. Ropes, staves, even a few brass chains stowed in there. One of your jobs is to make sure everything needful's present and available at all times. Once in a while we lose a rope or something over the side."

Once in a while we lose a navigator over the side, Hethor thought.

"Anything else?" de Troyes asked.

"Equatorial Wall's that way." Hethor pointed south before looking up. "If the sky were clear and the light just right, we could sight in on Earth's orbital tracks and work out our position. I assume you have books and tables for that."

"You can hear midnight very well up here, too."

Sidereal midnight, when the great brass teeth atop the

Equatorial Wall met and meshed with Earth's orbital track, clattering against the vast ring gear set in place around the sun by God himself. Hethor had used that moment for setting clocks back in New Haven, the precise timing of the world's turning, adjusting for longitude to arrive at the correct local hour. "And of course, you set your clocks by it up here, too."

"Another duty of yours. Lieutenant Malgus has a boxed set of marine chronometers. You can carry it with a strap. Set one face to midnight based on your observations of sidereal time. Later we compare that face to the other face to establish longitude, how far we've traveled east or west."

"Or to establish the error of the timepiece."

"Clockmaker." De Troyes managed to make it almost a curse and almost a blessing in the same breath.

"So I'm to climb up here for midnight?"

"And twice during daylight, to check the supplies and equipment. And whenever we have time to teach you something new."

Hethor decided there could be no finer duty on *Bassett* than to climb the midmast to set the midnight hour.

THE STORM broke on them that afternoon in a swirling fury, wrenching *Bassett* in every direction but forward for some hours. Rain drummed on the gasbag like all the tom-toms of the Iroquois while wind shrieked and howled among the shrouds. Hethor was back with the sailors of the deck division temporarily, securing cargo and equipment and watching for storm damage. It was worth his life to even take a few steps, but at least at altitude they did not have the roiling seas clearing the scuppers with each roll of the ship. Just more rain than he'd imagined possible, and a drop over the rail that no one could survive.

He held tight and did as he was ordered. The tempest died down just after sunset, the clouds skating away to reveal a sullen moon sow-bellied on the barely visible thread of her track, and a few persistent stars.

"Don't worry," Lombardo said as he patted Hethor on the shoulder at chow call. "When we hit a real storm, you'll know why air sailors never marry. Her Imperial Majesty doesn't want to pay all them bloody widows' pensions." With a laugh, Lombardo sent Hethor back to de Troyes and Malgus.

That night after a long session on the main deck working with the boxed chronometers, de Troyes sent Hethor up the midmast on his own. "Fall off if you must," the middie warned, "but don't lose the instruments."

Hethor made the climb at five bells of the evening watch. He met one of the gas division among the cells, a fellow he didn't know who nodded in the electrick dim. Up, through the wooden hatch, and onto the observation platform. His whipped back hurt less and less, either with the passage of time or the joy of meaningful work.

The moon was waxing toward full, dangling on the thread of its tracks. The lamps of the stars were bright as ever. Sitting amid light and beauty, Hethor carefully tied the boxed chronometer to two of the hooks, then flipped the catches to open the lid. There were three dials just as de Troyes had shown him. One was set to Greenwich time. The second was set to the last properly measured reading. The third was his to adjust, though it still matched the second at the moment. Radium dials gleamed against ghostly white faces, while more radium dots marked the little knobs that would reset the time.

He wondered what mechanisms were within, whether this was of the new machine makes from Lancashire and the Germanies, or if an honest horologist had cast and cut the gears with a knowledgeable hand.

A few high clouds scattered pale smears across the heavens, but mostly the lamps of the stars were clear. This close to midnight, Earth's track gleamed above the southern horizon as their face of the world came to kiss the orbital ring. The moon's track crossed half the sky as well, her offset to Earth's plane all the more obvious from this vantage. He closed his eyes and listened, the gentle damp breeze no distraction at all. *Bassett*'s engines thrummed somewhere far below. The hydrogen pumps cycled. He heard his breath, as always, and the creaking of the ropes and the booming of the canvas gasbag.

Beneath it all, the rattle of the turning world. The sound seemed restored now, without that false note he had sensed back in Malgus' cabin.

But midnight was coming. Already the hour brought with it a louder version of the clatter than he'd ever heard before. Higher up in the pure ocean air and much farther south than his New Haven home, Hethor was closer to the sound. Eyes still shut, he found the interrupter on the adjustment face of the boxed chronometer. Hethor was ready to reset to midnight so Malgus could calculate how far the storm had thrown them off course.

The sidereal clatter approached a crescendo, less a chattering racket here, he realized, than the sound of true brass on true brass. He listened, waiting for the peak, knowing when it would come.

Hethor pressed the interrupter to set midnight at the proper moment. At his bidding the boxed chronometer did its job, faithfully recording the hours of their passage.

Only one thing was wrong. In his heart, in his head, wherever it was that he always knew the time, midnight was almost three seconds late.

The sun rising dark as a cinder could be no more horrible. This was not the way of the world. It simply wasn't.

The archangel Gabriel had been right. The world was winding down, slowing. The Mainspring needed to be wound. Hethor had proof now. It was no longer a matter of faith. The problem was, who could he tell? How could he make the truth known?

He didn't trust Malgus, or anyone else for that matter, but he could not find the Key Perilous on his own.

Hethor unlashed the boxed chronometer, stowed the

ropes, and slowly made his way back to the main deck. He would have to develop objective evidence independent of his inner sense before he could convince anyone else.

Simpler, he thought, *had Gabriel come to Queen Victoria herself.* Her Imperial Majesty could have set whole armies and navies in motion to search for the Key Perilous.

Instead of just him.

FOUR

APPROACHING SEVENTEEN degrees latitude, Hethor saw the Equatorial Wall for the first time in his life. He and de Troyes were up in the navigator's rest, reviewing the basics of a sextant, when de Troyes stopped what he was doing, picked up a telescope, and pointed it south.

"Here," he said after a moment, handing the telescope to Hethor. "Tell me what you see."

"A line of clouds on the southern horizon." Hethor swept the scope. "But it's a *huge* storm."

"Biggest storm the world's ever known," said de Troyes with a laugh. "A hundred miles of brass-topped rock, haunted by ghosts from every age. It will never blow over, not while God's universe yet runs onward."

"*That's* it," Hethor breathed. Somehow he'd expected forests of monkeys, exotic crystal cities, wizards' palaces. Not just a smudge where sky met horizon.

"Keep an eye to the south," said de Troyes. "The Wall grows closer day by day."

BASSETT **CALLED** at Georgetown in Guyana to take on more fuel as well as undergo the dangerous process of topping the hydrogen in the gas cells before striking east for the Cape Verde Islands. Everyone but the senior officers and the gas division were given a mandatory shore leave during the hydrogen work. The pumps and fittings grew brittle over time with exposure to the noxious gas, and so close inspection was critical at every operation. Hethor had been given to understand that results of error were spectacularly fatal. Every Connecticut schoolchild certainly knew about the *Hibernia* disaster, which had rained fire in the sky of New London.

He was glad enough of the chance to work on his ideas. Hethor took his notes and observations on the errors of midnight, hoping for a chance to collate them in private in some flophouse room. The Equatorial Wall had gotten quite large so far south, but little more definite, the curvature of the Earth's track even flatter here. Sometimes he thought he saw sunlight sparkling off the brass gear teeth high atop, where the Wall would mesh with the track. No matter how hard he looked, Hethor couldn't be sure.

Not yet.

Now he and a few dozen others were crammed in a small barge being rowed by brown-skinned natives who smiled and rolled their eyes at secret jokes but said nothing. The air was so hot Hethor thought he could have made stew with it. No one complained.

"Hey, boy, be y'goin' to Madam Fossiter's wit' us?" growled the big Scot from his press-gang, whose name Hethor had learned to be the somewhat unlikely Threadgill Angus al-Wazir. Al-Wazir was the chief of the ropes division, the crew that handled the lines and shrouds, deployed the sails and steering paddles, and worked the outside of the gasbag as needed. The rest of *Bassett*'s crew called al-Wazir and his men the "airheads," because they spent so much time with nothing more beneath their feet than a bit of rope, and often not even that.

"No, I believe I'll do a little exploring." Hethor smiled. "I always wanted to see a monkey."

"To be sure, Madam Fossiter has got some fewkmonkeys, too, if that be your taste," shouted one of the other airheads. They all laughed.

Al-Wazir gave Hethor a somber look. "Feller shouldn't work too bloody damned hard on his leave day." He winked.

"Oh, hard ain't in it," said Hethor, which provoked another round of laughter.

There was more chatter about the merits of different girls, as compared by shade of skin, size of jugs, and other, more obscure criteria with which Hethor was unfamiliar. The barge finally thumped against a decrepit dock, pilings silvered with age and salt. The structure looked ready to fall into the ocean and strike out on its own. The dock could scarcely ask for greener shores, however, as the streets of Georgetown seemed to be nothing but whitewashed walls and vegetation denser than anything Hethor had ever seen.

Where Hamilton town had been scattered with palms, a tree previously unfamiliar to Hethor, Georgetown was host to an entire menagerie of plants, flowers, insects, even animals that all might have come from the Southern Earth, for all Hethor could make of them. This was as much a city of his imagination as anything he might hope to encounter up on the Equatorial Wall.

A large spotted cat padded by on a silver chain held by a gleaming black man, himself chained at the neck, though no one held that one in turn. Three white children carried a pole with a shaggy green animal hanging from it that looked like nothing so much as a taxidermist's mistake, except that one doleful orange eye turned in its socket to follow Hethor's progress. Gap-toothed women of some sun-browned race sold fruits from little trays, the brilliant, bilious colors of their skirts competing with the unnatural hues of their produce.

Hethor pushed his way through the crowded, urgent streets, slipping on mud and dodging carts—no electrick taximeter cabriolets here—until he found a quiet park around an equestrian statue. He leaned against the statue's marble plinth, screened from the raucous streets by walls of bushes covered with bright flowers larger than his head, and spread his notes between the horse's iron hooves.

The day wore on in the street beyond the bushes while Hethor reviewed his calculations. Distant thunder rolled, announcing some afternoon storm on the way. People screamed and shouted, but he was lost among the seconds and the time.

Gabriel had come to him the night of May 21st, 1900. Hethor had left New Haven the evening of May 22nd, presented himself to the viceroy on May 28th—the day of the eclipse—and been hauled into service aboard *Bassett* on May 29th. During that sequence of days, something in the turning of the Earth had bothered him, though Hethor didn't know what.

They'd made Bermuda June 3rd, and his services had been taken up by Lieutenant Malgus starting on June 6th. June 7th was the evening that he'd become aware that midnight was late, and he'd had the nights from Bermuda to Guyana to confirm those readings under the bright light of the waxing moon.

The delay was slightly variable, not increasing much past three seconds. Hethor thought the relative stability of the error was probably good—as opposed to, for example, getting worse every night. De Troyes had shown him how to shoot readings with a sextant. Though he actually was able to establish *Bassett*'s location with reasonable accuracy, Hethor hadn't yet been able to figure if that would give him more effective, objective proof of the time slippage. The orbital track was so uniform, flawless as anything crafted by God should be, that even with the help of *Bassett*'s most powerful spyglass he couldn't locate a usable distinctive mark on it and monitor the apparent motion of that mark as Earth approached.

They'd also been heading almost due south, toward the Equatorial Wall and all the mysteries that it entailed.

With that thought, Hethor glanced up at the dark line looming farther along their course, visible even above the swaying, bright-flowered trees. He was still too far away to make out details, but the bulk was as real as Earth's bones now.

Reflecting on *Bassett*'s unspecified mission against Chinese adventurism and empire building along the Wall, Hethor wondered if some Oriental sailor was even now looking north into English lands and pondering the strange thoughts of white people.

"Hethor." It was Malgus. The navigator had stepped through the bushes into the park behind Hethor while he was staring at the southern horizon and thinking of the enemy.

Hethor whirled, startled as if caught in some misdemeanor. "Sir?"

Malgus walked to the base of the statue, pushed Hethor aside with the arched tips of his fingers, and began to flip through the loose sheets of Hethor's calculations. He read for a few moments, glanced up at the sky, then turned his gaze to Hethor. Malgus' sharp brown eyes glinted like knives.

"You've been shooting your own observations up on the navigator's rest."

It wasn't a question.

"Yes, sir," said Hethor. Should he now tell Malgus about Gabriel and the Key Perilous, and the slowing of midnight? The man had been recommended to him, after all. "I was curious about some things."

"Curiosity does not become the common seaman." Malgus picked up the papers and folded them, pinching the edge tight, before slipping them inside his linen blouse. He seemed curiously unemotional, neither angry nor passionate. "I'm reassigning you to the deck division. You can work your curiosity out sanding spars, or whatever task Chief Lombardo sets you to."

"Sir—"

"No." Malgus' eyes narrowed. "Stay away from all of

this." He patted his shirt where the mass of papers bulged. "For your own thick head's sake, if nothing else."

Hethor's back itched, the still-healing wounds in sympathetic anticipation of another lashing. "Yes, sir."

"Go have a quiet drink somewhere, sailor, and meet the barge when it shoves off at dawn."

Hethor couldn't face al-Wazir and other sailors, people who were almost his friends. Instead he eventually found some of the ship's marines busily wrecking a bar that had earned their disfavor. He pitched in to the effort, not even slightly drunk, but just for the pleasure of breaking glass and sheer, howling lawlessness, something Hethor had never before experienced in his life.

Afterward, the marines bought him gin and a monkey. Hethor drank all the gin and gave the monkey to a one-eyed slave who tried to bow down before him.

TWO HOURS out of Georgetown the next day, heading east along the jungled coast, Hethor nursed a headache that hurt more than his healing back. In quiet agony he scraped paint off the fo'c'sle chaser gun mounts when a shouting went up among the ship's company. He looked over the rail to see the trees along the coastline swaying, as if a titanic breeze were passing, while the brown ocean slopped like water in a basin.

"Earthquake, by damn," someone called. Hethor looked up, south past the curve of the gasbag toward the gloomy shadow of the Equatorial Wall. Brass glinted high above it, so many bright diamonds in the sky.

What could he hear? Himself, the men, the ship, a grumbling groan from below—was that the ocean?—and underneath it all, the world stuttering.

The groan turned out to be an enormous wave. The height was hard to judge from above as the ocean swept the jungled coast, biting acre-sized chunks right off the shore while it flooded far inland. Clouds of jewel-colored birds were set to panicked flight, like stars flaring within the green depths, as the faint screams of monkeys echoed from far below.

An explosion rumbled in the west.

Hethor looked back across the mid deck of the ship, past the poop and the helm, to see a burning flame in the western sky. The hydrogen stores at Georgetown must have caught fire, he realized.

He tried to remember if there had been another airship at mast when *Bassett* had cast off to pull away, but his own misery had kept Hethor from paying much attention this morning. He imagined jumping from a burning airship to the water below, clothes and hair aflame, only to have the gasbag settle from the sky like a hot canvas cloud.

Hethor terribly missed Master Bodean in that moment, the cool simplicity of his clocks, the counting of the hours, and his own narrow attic bed.

THEY CROSSED the Atlantic in the face of two more storms, over two weeks' air time to the Cape Verde Islands and the way station at Praia, counting in the lost headway from the adverse weather. Everyone who moved on deck was lashed with a line, which did little to reduce the frightening dangers of the wind. Deep in one of the storms, the number six starboard gas cell sustained a hairline slit, some fault in the reinforced silk wall. Two sailors in the gas division died of the bad air before the problem was discovered and repairs effected.

Hethor was just as glad he was not climbing topside to take his sightings in such foul weather. But in turn, he felt guilty for not doing his part to help de Troyes and Malgus. He would *have* to find a way back to that work. The navigation was what brought Hethor closer to Gabriel and the mission for the Key Perilous and the Mainspring.

Lombardo was almost kind to Hethor during this time, perhaps out of respect for Hethor's unexpected skills at navigation, for all that their application was in abeyance now. The men of the deck division finally took Hethor in as their own, passing him off a few times to the ropes division to test his head for heights. After the navigator's rest, the shrouds and ratlines held no fear for Hethor, though he took little joy in them, either.

He never saw Malgus during the crossing, save once or twice on the poop, the navigator conferring with his brother officers. De Troyes would not speak to Hethor when their paths crossed.

There was a muster for the funeral of the two sailors from the gas division, over which Captain Smallwood presided. Almost the entire ship's company stood in the waist, as they had the day Hethor was lashed. The memory made his spine shiver and the skin of his back prickle with an echo of pain. The captain did not consult Holy Writ during his homily.

"The Tetragrammaton in His infinite wisdom hung the lamp of the sun amid our sky to light Earth's way around her orbital track." Smallwood's measured cadences were as grand as any New England deacon's, his voice booming across the sharp wind that whistled and groaned among the shrouds.

"So He has caused human affairs to be ordered, with Her Imperial Majesty Queen Victoria the lamp amid England's sky, her wisdom lighting all our ways. We of the Royal Navy struggle at the edge of darkness, that England might sleep secure. Always, the Chinese is our enemy. As we defeated first the Spanish, then the French, then the Turk, and even the Iroquois, so shall we best the Middle Kingdom.

"But there are other struggles for England, against capricious Nature and dread disease and vile savages dwelling in the wilderness. Seaman Abehr and Seaman Rountree both gave their lives in that struggle. That they were not bested by Chinese shot robs them of no glory. That they died quietly, as men asleep when the air grew foul, robs them of no valor.

"No, we commend them as heroes to the good English

spirit, light bearers of civilization. For this moment, Abehr and Rountree are the lamps of our life here on Her Imperial Majesty's Ship *Bassett*. Let their shining example guide our lives. And so we pray, as Jesus taught us . . ."

"Our Father, who art in Heaven

"Craftsman be thy name

"Thy Kingdom come

"Thy plan be done

"On Earth as it is in Heaven

"Forgive us this day our errors

"As we forgive those who err against us

"Lead us not into imperfection

"And deliver us from chaos

"For thine is the power, and the precision

"For ever and ever, amen."

The rumble of the sailors' voices died with the last of the prayer. Hethor sketched the sign of the horofix across his chest. A young man with curly hair played a song upon a horn, a tune that Hethor didn't recognize. Wrapped in canvas that must have come from repair stores for the gasbag, the two bodies went overboard. Hethor imagined them tumbling like autumn leaves through the high winds, swirling to the ocean far below.

Smallwood called them to attention once more. "Though it is perhaps premature to speak of this, I shall say a few words about *Bassett*'s purpose on this voyage."

The silence that followed was strained, to the point where Hethor could almost hear ears crinkling as they stretched to capture the captain's next words.

"The Bible tells us that King Solomon built forts and mines along the Equatorial Wall," Smallwood said. "Therefore we know this to be true. History tells us that the Roman emperors set garrisons there, to send back beasts for the games, and to see what might be found. Even the Knights Templar were said to have a chapter house on the Wall during their days of power.

"Her Imperial Majesty's government has decided that

England will assert her rightful place in the powers of the Wall, to the glory of our queen and the confounding of our enemies."

The sailors cheered then, tossing hats and stamping on the deck. Smallwood held up a hand.

"We are dispatched to render aid to an expeditionary force under General Gordon, who requires aerial assistance. *Bassett* will earn a place in history in these coming months. Every man of you will make your name with her."

The cheering erupted again, nearly a riot this time. Smallwood nodded and went belowdecks. While the sailors danced and chanted, Hethor went back to his scraping.

SIXTEEN DAYS out of Georgetown they reached Praia in the Cape Verde Islands. The town was on the southeast shore of an island perhaps twenty miles wide. Tree stumps and mudslides seemed to be the main features of the place, though the water was pretty enough. Praia was a miserable little town, what Hethor could see of it. Shanties spread out from the dilapidated waterfront. There was a small fleet of fishing boats, and one honest warship flying the Union Jack. A few pale stone buildings rose above the wooden shanties, their red tile roofs patched, whitewashed walls blotchy and faded. There was nothing of the festival air of Georgetown, or even the welcoming faces looking up as at Hamilton.

Here the captain gave no shore leave. After exchanging flag signals with the ship at anchor, *Bassett* made a quick stop at the port's lone, rickety airship mast to take on more fuel for the engines. Smallwood promptly cast off again, beating south and east for Conakry and the Guinea Coast.

Ten days further sailing, Conakry was little better. The port itself was at the end of a narrow peninsula warded by a pair of sickle-shaped islands that could have been lifted from the Bahamas. The land beyond alternated between a dustier version of the Guyanan shore and dreary swamp.

No liberty was granted there, either. Even with his ship-fever at being aboard too long, Hethor was almost glad. Where Georgetown had been a vibrant city of colors and life, Conakry looked to have been felled by a recent war, to the point even of fires burning and dust clouds rising along the peninsula. There had been three airship masts, all now toppled into the shallow water, so *Bassett* went through the longer and slower process of dropping drag lines and being warped much closer to the ground than would ordinarily have been deemed prudent while on deployment.

Smallwood went down with certain of his officers, including Malgus, while Hethor idled with some sailors from both the deck and ropes divisions. Threadgill al-Wazir led the detail.

"Have the Chinese been here?" asked Hethor.

Al-Wazir laughed. "And they'd be letting us tie up then, and send the captain ashore for confabulation? No, if the Chinee were here they'd have met us with flaming hell and hot rockets, you can be fewkin' sure. I'd wager another of these quakes yon ground has been stricken with." He beamed at the dozen or so sailors standing at the rail. "There's times I can easily recall that life in the air is the bloody finest life of all."

"Life's not so easy now." Hethor looked down at Conakry and wondered about his native New Haven. Had the earthquakes rung the church bells there? Or were things worse?

"I'm no a-liking bein' this close down," grumbled another sailor, a thin Jerseyman most of them called Dairy. "Herself the ship's an albatross waddling along the shore."

"Aye, and if the Chinee approaches," said al-Wazir, "we'll just brandish you lot and they'll flee in terror of your ugly mugs."

Conakry was able to provide fuel and seawater ballast, though with all the damage to the port, the ship's work parties had to go down and pump by hand to supplement the electrick pumps aboard *Bassett*. Hethor was glad enough not to draw that duty. He found himself afraid of the African coast, and doubly glad when *Bassett* cast off and made air once more.

THE AIRSHIP cut south and east along the Guinea Coast, angling toward the Equatorial Wall. This was dangerous, Hethor knew from deck gossip, straying away from a base with no relief ahead of them. Airships were not like naval vessels, which went where they pleased, and could take on supplies or find repairs in any port. Or in need, any empty harbor. The industry required to supply oil and hydrogen was substantial. Far more than any airship could carry on its own.

Sailors were a superstitious lot, but the awe of being near the Wall seemed to outweigh even the concern at leaving a friendly port too far behind.

Every day the massive bulk became more and more visible, until Hethor could see the cloud banks towering against the Wall, stretching so high he must crane his neck to look. It was like studying a map through a clearing fog—his view grew ever more sharp, revealing features such as great cliffs and ledges, which in turn grew to forests and meadows, and tumbling waterfalls that had to be wider than cities to be visible from this distance.

There was an eerie quiet to the Wall, so unlike the forests and fields of New England or the tropical chaos of Guyana and Guinea. Hethor felt he was staring through a philosopher's glass. Or perhaps overlooking some magnificent daguerreotype tall as the horizon.

Silent or not, he could smell the Wall: soil and trees and the pure scent of life, buoyed by water and sunlight.

Hethor found the same sense of being pulled that he'd encountered atop the gasbag. It seemed as though the Wall were a magnet, and he were made of metal. He felt as if he could simply leap from *Bassett*'s decks and sail over Africa like a frigate bird to meet the rising country God had laid before him.

Sunlight made the air far up on the Wall sparkle even well into the night. Dawn, when it came, was preceded by harbingers in the form of sky-high spears of gold and gray—light, of course, striking the Wall from far to the east where the sun still hid her face from Earth's rotation. Storms moved at night across the great face, lightning playing like sparklers set for Guy Fawkes Day in a blue celebration writ large across the vertical miles.

Every air sailor knew that the higher a ship went, the less strong the air became. The very atmosphere grew weak upon departing farther from Earth's embrace. Eventually it grew thin and bad, so that men sickened or died. Whole ships could be lost.

How then, Hethor wondered, did there come to be air so high up on the Wall, air thick enough to brew storms and build forests? He asked al-Wazir, who continued to show him far more kindness than Lombardo ever bothered to.

"Well, and that's a good question, friend," al-Wazir burred in his Scottish accent. "It must be because the good Lord God made it so. Surely if He can hang the lamp of the sun with nae more than the heavens themselves for a hook, He can make air stick to His Wall. Think on this, that air up there is still close to the ground. 'Tis just different fewkin' ground."

"Different ground ain't in it," said Dairy, who was listening nearby. "There's cities made of jools up there, boyo, and giant iron men that stride the lands like locomotives, their steam hearts shrieking loud as any Mick's banshee bastards."

"Dairy." Al-Wazir's voice was a warning. "They's just tales, and more than twice-told, so less than the voice of rumor."

"Captain Smallwood said the Romans were here," Hethor blurted. "Couldn't there be cities?"

"Of course." Al-Wazir sounded surprised. "Roman cities, and African cities with sorcerers from beyond the Wall. Even cities full of bloody monkeys. It's just there ain't no cities of jewels, if you take my meaning. For how could such a thing be possible? Where would you mine a diamond big enough to make a house from?"

In the face of the Wall, all things seemed possible. "If cities of monkeys, why not diamonds the size of houses?"

"Apes," muttered Dairy. "They's apes. They hates to be called monkeys. One of them served on the old *Firepot,* afore she lived down to her name over Corunna and kilt all them Spaniards in that great huge exploding."

"Ain't never been no fewkin' apes on any ship of Her Imperial Majesty's navy," al-Wazir said with a grin, "excepting you bloody deck apes. Though I daresay I'd rather have half a dozen rain-forest silverbacks than you lot. I expect they'd work harder and give less sass."

"Have you been to the Wall before?" asked Hethor.

"No, but my da went oncet." Al-Wazir sighed. "He was a wet sailor, for the old Guinea and Atlantic Company's slaving fleet. On *Goodness and Mercy* it was, one them scut-lined three-deck haulers with a square bottom and that widowmaker keel they built out of Clyde in the mid-century. Sister ship she was to *Shirley* and *Day Follower*.

"This was their spring run in, I think, the year of sixty-seven. First mate took a fancy to see what they could find on the Wall, something new that would sell well in Kingston, or even London. Da spoke up just for the chance to go. Captain was a damned sorry-eyed drunk, to hear Da tell it, and waved them off with a smile and a belch. They took a little sloop-rigged boat and sailed south across the Bight of Benin until they struck shoreline at the foot of the Wall.

"Now Da could make this story last for three days. I'm a-going to tell it short, since we've all got work and more to do." Al-Wazir raised his eyebrows at Dairy and Hethor and a few other seamen who had drifted up to listen. "I'll just strike for the sum of the thing.

" 'Twas a short beach of hard shingle and no driftwood or wrack to speak of, with a steep cliff above it. There was a foot-worn switchback trail. They climbed and found a sort of ledge, with some farming among the trees. From there they followed a road higher and higher. Up above a rank of clouds, so it seemed they were climbing to Heaven, they found a city of brass and teak, streets paved with marble slabs laid down like them old Roman towns back home.

"Weren't nobody in the city, it seemed, but soon enough ghosts began to follow 'em—pale things that vanished like smoke when Da and the others tried to get a good look. First mate got worried, decided there weren't nae slaves nor gold, but when they turned around, they was met with a terrible battle by white apes, taller than men, carrying fewkin' spears and bows.

"One thing and another, Da escaped, but he could nae find the road down. He and two of his mates spent weeks on that ledge. They was running from those damned apes and stealing food from the little farms in the forest clearings until they could get down to shore. Never did find the bloody sloop-rig. They came to build a raft. On the way back they lost one man to a water snake bigger around than a draft horse, and finally sailed themselves into Conakry port a year older.

"Da's hair went white as them apes, and though he took ship twice again, the Guinea and Atlantic finally gave him a pension on promise he wouldn't tell his tale in ports nae more. Da came home and moved us all to Lanark, thirty miles from the sight of water, and he drank only with shepherds and oat farmers until the day he died."

"That's a lie," shouted Dairy, " 'coz I met your Da in Bristol port five year back, he was on the docks sellin' oysters to the quality trade."

"Ain't no lie!" Al-Wazir threw a blow that sent Dairy reeling. "Ya fewkin' scut-faced poxwhore. If I said it, 'twere true. That's why I'm ropes chief and you're nae but a sloppy hand with a fat bleedin' mouth!"

Hethor slipped off to some more paint scraping, but later he sought Dairy out. "Why'd you say that?" he asked, both of them hunkered down in the orlop, where al-Wazir had set Dairy to hunting rats.

"He ain't never tole the same story twicet," Dairy whined. They were crowded close in stinking shadow. Dairy's rat-killer gleamed by the lantern light. "Cain't call him on it 'coz he's bigger and practically an off'cer besides."

Hethor certainly knew what came of challenging officers. He had the scars to prove it. "So you met his da?"

"White-haired man sellin' oysters and mutterin' that there was apes in the rigging of the ships. Cain't say more than that, 'cept he hugged al-Wazir like a son when we rowed in from the Bristol masts. The Wall, it takes things from a man, and don't never give them back." Dairy glanced up at the low wooden deck just above their heads. "God almighty did us no favor there, when He covered it with magical critters."

AS THEY grew closer, a chill wind blew down from the Equatorial Wall with a frightening consistency. The air pushed out into the Atlantic chop that fringed the base, beating the water to a dangerous froth. It was clear to Hethor that Captain Smallwood was looking for something, because *Bassett* beat back and forth across that wind for days, sometimes straining her engines, sometimes almost drifting.

Great, forested knees of rock, bigger than mountains back home, stood out from the base of the Wall in some places. In others, there were shattered slopes that a sailor who originally hailed from some goat-ridden peak in the Basque Territories called "scree." These scree fields were forty miles wide and thousands of feet high, covered with little rivers of sliding rock. Hethor thought they looked like Hell itself.

On the sixth day, *Bassett* crossed over a port town with cyclopean stone wharves, and tiny houses of wood and leaves built atop great, step-carved blocks. The airship was perhaps a thousand feet above the water then. Hethor watched tiny figures swarm out, surrounded by speckles that he finally realized was a shower of stones being thrown upward.

On the eighth day, the airship rose to the three-thousand-foot level and approached another of the protruding knees of the Wall. This one had a ledge atop it, more like a plain the size of a county back in Hethor's native New England. There was plentiful evidence of prior farming there, fence lines and irrigation ditches, but the fields looked to have been abandoned for quite some time.

Bassett made her way over those fields, tacking back and forth across the ever-present wind. Almost all the officers and division chiefs lined the rails, looking down for something. No one passed the word to the hands, but the sailors peered over, too, when they could find space to stand far enough from a watchful, commanding eye.

After several hours, de Troyes shouted out, "I've got it." There was a general swarm to the starboard, sufficient to disturb *Bassett*'s equilibrium. Hethor joined the mob, stepping up a ratline and clinging to the steering boom even as the officers shouted half the men back to the port side so as not to unbalance the deck.

Below them, on the east bank of a large stream, was a stone arrow pointing west, over the stream and parallel to the line of the Wall. The rocks were whitewashed for greater visibility. Another set was arranged in a crude pattern that Hethor finally deciphered as a lion and a unicorn.

English hands had made that sign.

Bassett beat her way downward as she had in Conakry. Only this time half a dozen men from the ropes division, including both al-Wazir and Dairy, leapt overboard on their silk parachutes. They dragged with them a fine silk line that spooled from a great drum bolted to the starboard rail amidships for that purpose. Another ropes division hand minded the drum, throwing the brake as soon as the party landed in some decent order, so the line would not run out.

They passed down larger lines until the shore party could belay the central anchor to a stout tropical hardwood and help guide *Bassett* to within a hundred feet of the ground. There was no question of actually landing the ship. Her Majesty's airships rarely touched the Earth. Hethor and some of the other deck idlers manned a bosun's chair lashed to the port rail opposite the rope winch, which one by one sent down Captain Smallwood, Lieutenant Malgus, Midshipman de Troyes, and the first mate, Commander Dalworthy, to investigate, along with three marines. Everyone who went ashore was armed—pistols for the officers, carbines for the marines.

Once the officers and marines were safely landed, the men of the ropes division came back aboard. Dairy was sent up first. His ankles were wrapped in a cut length of manila line.

"Near broke me feet off on t'landing," he told Hethor with a lopsided grin, his face flushed, before the loblolly boy and two idlers carried him off to Dr. Firkin.

Standing by at the bosun's chair, Hethor peered over the rail to watch as the officers inspected the arrow and the crude sign of the Empire. Malgus took some readings with an instrument. Smallwood and two others paced away from the arrow to look westward, perhaps searching for some sign visible only from the ground.

Someone shouted faintly, and a bell rang. Hethor had never heard that bell before, but the sailors began to mutter, "Sky watch." Sky watch was the little nest at the bow of the gasbag. Hethor understood it to be like the navigator's rest, save that a hand from the gunnery division always stood watch there.

Then he heard a little popping noise.

Hethor looked around, trying to find the source.

The sailor next to him, a tall Welshman, said, "Swivel gun on the sky watch. We're under attack."

There was a great shouting belowdecks as the ports were knocked open and the guns cranked out on their carriages. Hethor could still see no enemy—was it a Chinese airship, descending from above? No one on the deck seemed to know either, but the officers on the ground beneath were now running about in alarm as the marines aimed their carbines skyward.

The slack rope jerked, signal to raise the bosun's chair. Hethor peered over the side as he and the Welshman began to crank the little winch. Captain Smallwood was rising up to take immediate command of his ship against whatever trouble was a wing.

The attackers came falling past *Bassett*. They were angels armed with swords and bows. Gabriel's sacred band, Hethor thought with a bloom of panic, come looking for him.

But the angels did not spread their great wings and swoop up to *Bassett*'s decks to carry him away. Rather, silent as stones they dropped to the ground amid the crack of carbine fire from the marines down there as more shots came from the ship. Someone in the gunnery division depressed a two-inch gun in one of the belt turrets, trying to get an angle, but succeeded only in rocking the ship and splintering distant trees.

Still madly yanking on the handle of the winch, Hethor released the breath he hadn't known he was holding back. These were not angels, not of Gabriel's order in his pale, glowing glory. These were tall, thin men, leathery as pemmican, with skin the color of fresh-baked bread, and huge, ragged tattoos around their eyes, across their cheeks, encircling their nipples and crotches. The tattoos were red and black in a random pattern like wounds both fresh and pustulant spread across their bodies. Their wings were motley, as if sewn from the plumage of a dozen different drab birds.

They were no angels. They were winged savages.

Only their weapons were fresh, clean, crisp, catching a marine on the ground through the eye here, there smashing Midshipman de Troyes with a great bronze sword. Hethor saw the young officer's head bouncing away from his staggering body like a cricket ball on a pitch.

In a moment of grief-stricken pity, he lagged on the winch, but the Welshman kicked Hethor hard.

Together they helped Captain Smallwood over the rail. Smallwood was a man possessed, shouting as he came, face as red as the savages' tattoos.

"Stand by to repel boarders, break out the polearms. Marines on the rail, every last red jack of you. Where's the second mate, damn me? I want the grenadoes ready *now*! Mister Fine, I need you."

He sprinted away toward the poop deck, trailing commands, as Hethor and the Welshman let the winch trail out again. Hethor chanced to look down once more to see three of the winged savages bent over a marine, rending his corpse by hand. Another chased Dalworthy to his death. Two more lopped the arms off the last surviving marine, forcing the lobsterback to dance in a staggering circle.

Where was Malgus? he wondered, arms once more slowing on the winch.

Next to Hethor, the Welshman let his own pace lag as well. There was no one alive down below but the savages now. The remainder of the ship's marines were firing from the deck with angry abandon. Some of the ropes division tossed grenades over the side, shouting out the names of the dead.

Amid the fall of powder, shot, and curses, Hethor wept as he aided the Welshman in winding back the chair. Below them, the savages spread their wings and flew upward in the afternoon sun. The attackers briefly seemed to be angels again in the golden glare as the ship's two-inch guns barked across the open air.

Bassett had killed none of her assailants, taken no lives in vengeance, though Captain Smallwood stood at the stern rail and lit off his brace of antique chasers, then emptied the chamber of his far more modern Colt revolver.

In the end, they merely disturbed the crystalline air of the Wall. A few bloody feathers remained behind, but the

winged savages had all departed, apparently carrying
Malgus with them. *Bassett* had only her dead.

HE SAT against the lee rail with the Welshman and two
Danish brothers from the ropes division, Swine and Wine.
Surely their mother had called them something else.
When Hethor chanced once in a while to overhear them
chattering together in the singsong tongue of their youth,
they seemed to trade names with similar sound but more
dignity. The four of them shared a butt of watered grog
and a handful of boiled eggs.

"Cap'n'll be angry enough to light a fuse on his temper," said the Welshman in a morose tone. "'Em as carried off our navigator and could'a murthered all of us in
our bunks."

"Too close," said Swine.

"Ya." Wine, speaking. "The Wall is more than we
should work."

Hethor had a different purpose than simply surviving
till *Bassett* made home port. "It was those winged savages. Why there's such things in God's world I don't understand." Was he being disloyal to Gabriel, too? Surely
the creatures that had attacked them were mockeries.

The Welshman shook his head, nodding toward the
cliffs. "Sendings. From beyond the Wall. Them sorcerers
got fire in their eyeballs and the magic of the Devil in
their fingers."

"Walking dead," said Swine.

Wine: "Ya. Like saints but different, ya."

Hethor wanted to protest that it was not so, that the
world worked on a more rational basis—the Creator would
not have built so mechanical a sky, then set uncanny ghosts
to bedevil them all. But the evidence of his own experience
had put the lie to that idea already. "The Southern Earth
cannot be so different from our own, can it?"

"Oh, my boy . . ." The Welshman actually smiled.
"Fleets of golden ships sailing oceans of spice."

"Gold doesn't float," Hethor said.

Swine and Wine chuckled until the Welshman gave them both a dirty look.

"'Tis the magic, you fewking whelp." A boiled egg crushed in his hand. "Beyond the Wall there's great men like graven images waking from their dusty sleeps to cast glamers upon us all. Be glad you're of the north, where Her Imperial Majesty watches over good honest sailors everywhere."

SMALLWOOD STOOD beneath his awning once more. Marines lined the rails with carbines in their hands. Hethor had not seen such a show of force since joining *Bassett*'s crew. The captain was angry, though this was cold anger like the edge of a sword, in contrast to his hot rage in the moment of the attack.

No man among the ship's company had whispered against Captain Smallwood for coming aboard during the fighting. It was understood that his first duty was to HIMS *Bassett,* to the ship and her company and her mission. The Articles of War, naval tradition, English law, and the custom of sailors all required him to do so. That the captain had fled the field of honor, leaving five dead and one missing in his wake, was a tragedy worthy of a Greek hero. In staying where he was, he would have betrayed his command. In leaving the fight upon the ground, he betrayed his brother officers.

Anger mixed with pity throughout the ship's people.

Now there were five corpses sewn into stained canvas, doubled thick because so many of their parts and pieces were loose. Captain Smallwood stared down at them as he slapped his thigh with the ship's Bible.

"Our Brass Christ," he said suddenly, in a sharp, low voice much unlike his usual firm tones. "Our Lord, He suffered on the Roman horofix. The gears ground closer to His hands and feet. The spike sprang forward by moments toward His heart.

"Yet even in His hurt, our Lord prevailed, taking the sin of the world into him. In time, his tormentors were struck down. Rome . . ." Smallwood seemed to lose his thought for a moment, then collected himself. "Rome *burned*."

The captain stared around at the ship's company, the continued slapping of the Bible slowing in tempo to a dirge. The air had turned foetid, the ever-present wind suddenly silent as any distant family members at a funeral. The thick scent of blood and rank death curdled the air of the deck. Hethor's neck tingled as Smallwood's gaze swept past him, lit on Lombardo—they were arranged by divisions—then back a moment to Hethor. The captain's eyes burned hotter than the day, a bright fever in their brown depths.

Vengeance, Hethor hoped, rather than the fires of madness.

Smallwood continued to slap the Bible. Then, as if noticing for the first time that he held it, he looked down at the book before opening his hand and letting the leather-bound volume tumble to the deck. It fell open, pages fluttering for a moment before it settled as limp as the wind.

"Rome burned, men," Smallwood continued, "for her sins. Lieutenant Malgus awaits rescue, having been carried off by these vicious savages. Five of our ship's company lie dead on an altar of pagan treachery. As we have been ordered to do, we will find General Gordon. With his men and our own stout crew, these savages will pay for their insult to our lives, our honor, and our gracious queen."

A horn began to play, off-key, and the company sang "God Save the Queen." Hethor thought it an odd choice for a funeral hymn. As the last flat notes trailed off, Smallwood said in his usual command voice, "We will bury our dead over honest water when next we find it, that those winged savages shall not pick among the bones of honest Englishmen. Ship's muster is dismissed."

The crew scuttled to their stations, those off-watch back to their hammocks and hidey-holes. Hethor stood before the canvas lumps that had so recently been men.

Though none were his particular friends, de Troyes had been kind and thoughtful to Hethor when no such consideration had been warranted.

The ship's Bible still lay there, one page folded over, the other with a penciled highlight glittering in the late-afternoon sun.

Curious, Hethor picked it up.

It was open to the Book of Job, Chapter 41. He read the underlined verses aloud softly. It was as close as he could come to saying a benediction to the dead and a prayer for the missing.

" 'Canst thou draw out leviathan with an hook? or his tongue with a cord which thou lettest down? Canst thou put an hook into his nose? or bore his jaw through with a thorn? Will he make many supplications unto thee? will he speak soft words unto thee? Will he make a covenant with thee? wilt thou take him for a servant for ever? Wilt thou play with him as with a bird? or wilt thou bind him for thy maidens?' "

"Seaman Hethor." It was the second mate, Lieutenant Wollers. "Captain Smallwood will see you at the second bell of the evening watch." He looked Hethor up and down. "Come clean and fresh as you can make yourself, boy."

Hethor nodded. He handed the Bible to Wollers with an abortive pass at the sign of the horofix. "Aye-aye, sir."

"Thank you."

If Captain Smallwood had been angry in defeat, Wollers was simply defeated. The officer walked away slope-shouldered and tired.

Hethor moved among the watchful marines to the water butt, the better to clean his hair and ears.

EXCEPT FOR his trips to and from Lieutenant Malgus' cabin during his stint as the navigator's assistant, Hethor had spent no time among the ship's officers. In the quiet of the evening, he made his way aft, down the narrow companionway, past Malgus' cabin and several others before presenting himself to a marine who stood guard outside Smallwood's hatch. The entrance to the captain's cabin was an ornate thing, carved with classical motifs of nereids and sirens. So far as Hethor knew, it was the only such hatch on the ship.

"Seaman Jacques reporting to Captain Smallwood as ordered."

The marine was an older man with a ruddy face lined as a plowed field. He frowned, then reached over to knock without taking his eyes off Hethor.

The hatch cracked immediately. Wollers peered out. "Seaman Hethor. You are timely." He tugged it all the way open, ushering Hethor into the cabin beyond.

It was the stern cabin. Three narrow windows glinted in the flickering light of electrick lanterns. The ports showed muted colors of stained glass, which would likely be glorious when the ship sailed away from the sun. Other than the carven door and the colored windows, the captain's accommodations were austere—two sea chests, a bed folded up to become a writing desk, two chairs and a bench and a chart table.

The only luxury was the sheer size of the cabin. In no other respect did the place resemble the carpeted expanse of silver ornaments that deck rumor attributed to Smallwood. Hethor had never thought the captain a man of excess. He was glad to see himself proven correct.

"Thank you for coming." Smallwood was seated, Dr. Firkin standing behind him. The captain waved Hethor to the bench. A signal breach of naval etiquette. "We must speak with you on matters of grave concern to the ship."

Had the viceroy somehow sent a message? Hethor thought in panic. Was he to be turned out, or clapped in irons? Surely not, if they had asked him to come astern, cleaned and dressed. Would Smallwood take him farther from Gabriel's charge?

"I am ready to serve, sir." Hethor tried to press the nerves out of his voice.

"The loss of both Lieutenant Malgus and Midshipman de Troyes is a terrible blow to *Bassett*," Smallwood said. "Especially with Dalworthy dead as well. We are short-handed now for watch-standing, with no one to fill in for our navigators. It is my understanding that Lieutenant Malgus trained you in the instruments of his craft before dismissing you back to Chief Lombardo's service."

"Yes, sir." Hethor paused, uncertain. "I have some talent and experience with fine mechanisms."

"So you can take readings, and establish position?"

"He had not time to teach me to plot charts, sir, but I can set the clocks and take our latitude, calculate present speed, and such tasks."

Wollers, in the other chair, exchanged glances with Smallwood, who nodded and cleared his throat before continuing. "But you could take the measurements, and consult with Lieutenant Wollers with regard to the charts?"

This was not how he had wished to be restored to his work. Though Hethor felt a rush of excitement, it was nearly balanced by a parallel rush of shame. Excitement won through though—he would be free of the petty tyrannies of the deck, working again with the instruments and the mathematical precision that he had loved under Master Bodean and again under Lieutenant Malgus.

"Sir . . . I would be pleased to aid the ship as you command." The captain had to be desperate, to be asking him with such politeness.

"It is for England, son," said Smallwood, forcing a smile. "We have a crude map with rough directions, left by General Gordon's expedition. It was recovered from the site of the massacre. *Bassett* is to bear east another ninety or so knots, and look for a certain bay in a cliff, about six thousand feet above the level of the sea. That is rather above our normal cruising altitude. It is my understanding that this bay may be hard to locate by eye, due to a tricky lay of the land. Sadly, our charts of the Wall are necessarily incomplete.

"You, Seaman Jacques, must guide us there, with Lieutenant Wollers' leadership. The entire ship's company, and the noble memory of our dead, shall depend upon your skill."

"Yes, sir," said Hethor, his elation melting to misery. He wanted freedom, not responsibility. Captain Smallwood might as well have kept him in chains as set him to this task.

But it wasn't just Smallwood, it was al-Wazir and Dairy and Lombardo and the Welshman and all the men of the decks and ropes and gasbag who needed him. Perhaps most of all, Lieutenant Malgus, in spite of his strange behaviors and secretive ways, needed Hethor's help.

Wollers showed him out and walked him to Malgus' cabin. "It would not be seemly for a common seaman to bunk here," the second mate said, "but as this is also the chart room, you may use this as your workplace. Keep your hammock on the deck and mess with your division and watch. You will need to take the midnight hour each evening. Do not fall prey to sleep when you return here with the box clock."

"Aye-aye, sir."

The officer departed, and Hethor dropped to a seat on the low stool at Malgus' chart table that he had originally mistaken for a desk. He looked about the tiny cabin. No windows, just two cupboards for the instruments, a sea chest, and a narrow bunk that looked far less desirable than his own hammock. And the chart table. There were sheets upon sheets of charts stored in the drawers that made up its pedestal.

Nothing here spoke of the life of Simeon Malgus, lieutenant, RN. Hethor studied the chest. There was a fresh wax blob over the latch. It was marked with the captain's signet, or possibly the purser's seal. Despite Smallwood's words of rescue, the officers had written Malgus off for dead, then.

Hethor tugged open the chart drawers. The maps lay

within. They were densely packed, printed on a fine paper almost as thin as onionskin, the better to stuff them in so that there would be a sufficiency for *Bassett*'s long voyage.

"I seek the Wall," Hethor told the empty room and, perhaps, Malgus' ghost looking on.

He flipped through charts of England's water and sky lanes, penciled notes of trans-Atlantic navigation, down the drawers to New England and the Virginia Country and Georgia, down again to the Caribbean.

Malgus had been particular in his organization.

Hethor looked through another pair of drawers. These charts were more like sketches, not the printed and tinted sheets from the higher tiers. The papers were covered with rough coastlines and altitudinal cross-sections, notes on bays and harbors and plateaus along the Wall's Atlantic coast, right to where it met Guinea.

Carefully turning those fine sheets, he found a different chart, of Earth's track around the sun. It was edged with notes on the cycles and epicycles of the balancing system. Someone—Malgus?—had sketched in the hand of God, a key held within His fingers.

Hethor's heart fluttered.

The Key Perilous.

On the back was an elevation of a temple, in the Eastern style like something the Middle Kingdom would have built—he had been told that Jerusalem and Constantinople were full of them, from the days of the Horde before Spanish steel and English leadership had driven the Chinese and their pony warriors back almost all the way to the Indus. The temple seemed to stand against a cliff face, if Hethor could trust the artist. In lettering that was definitely Malgus' hand, the caption on the sketch read, "Return, reconsider, rebuild. No heart."

He put the papers away as seven bells of the evening rang. Time for the box clock, and the long climb to the navigator's rest.

For a moment, Hethor's heart skipped again at the

thought of the winged savages coming by night, swooping silent over the spine of the airship like sharp-shinned hawks over a stubbled field, to carry him off as handy as any squeaking mouse. He shook the image away. There was a job at hand, and a need, as well as a chance to make more of himself than any he had had since being expelled from New Haven.

THE NEXT morning he sat with Wollers and reviewed the charts that Malgus had left behind, as well as the crude sketch recovered from the ground.

"The bay is here on the drawing," Wollers said, "with a warning, 'Not easily spied.' I do not see anything like it on Malgus' chart."

"We are somewhere in this area." Hethor stabbed his finger east of the great knee where the battle had taken place, marked on the chart as Sepulchrum Caii. *Grave of Caius.* "If the distances are correct, unless we meet a storm we shall be within a few knots of the bay tomorrow shortly after dawn. I do fear we shall have to climb quite a bit higher to reach it. I recommend we slow during this coming night so as not to overshoot our mark."

"Agreed." Wollers turned the chart as if he could find wisdom in another lay of the land. "I will pass that order. During this day, see if you can establish the possible location of this high bay. There may be some pattern in the knees and columns of the Wall here that lend themselves to such concealment."

They all *lend themselves to such concealment*, thought Hethor as Wollers left the cabin. Nonetheless, except for his noontime measurements, he sat and sketched possible configurations of the land, trying to imagine the complex topography of the Wall in terms of the ways that clockwork fit together. There were always many solutions to a problem of horological design, but usually only one that truly made sense, made art of the mechanical soul of the thing.

He thought the Wall might yield to the same logic.

Working as he did, Hethor also had time to listen: to his breathing, feet pounding the deck overhead, and more distantly within the hull, occasional groans and shudders from the gasbag, the wind playing in the rigging.

And, as always, the rattle of the Earth's turning, the springs deep within the planet's shell powering the days and seasons of the life of man. Here in the air, so close to the Equatorial Wall, whatever the reason, Hethor could not hear the dissonance he had detected previously. The world's windings sounded normal once more.

WOLLERS AWOKE Hethor just after dawn. "Come, now, to the poop."

Hethor rolled out of his hammock, dragged his fingers through his hair, and trotted after Wollers across the main deck and up the ladder to the poop deck. He'd never been there before.

Midshipman Fine seemed to have the deck watch. He glared at Hethor with undifferentiated malice. Captain Smallwood stood near the tillermen, staring off the starboard side at the face of the Wall. It was forested here, insofar as Hethor could tell in the orange glare of the morning sun—narrow, tall trees of a light green and passing strange canopy. Nothing like the stout forests of New England, nor even the tropical hardwood riot of Georgetown. This forest swayed in the wind, as though the trees were no more than giant reeds.

"What do you see, sailor?" Smallwood handed Hethor the spyglass.

Almost shaking with pride, Hethor put the glass to his eye. He knew something of optics from his work with Master Bodean, and had made use of a glass in his duties as navigator, but this was the first time he had been called upon to render intelligence from the view. And by the captain at that. Hethor hoped not to disgrace himself. After a few moments of confusion, he found the shaking forest and scanned it.

"What is our altitude, please, sir?"

"Just over six thousand feet," said Smallwood.

The correct part of the Wall then, for all that it loomed ever higher over their heads like the edge of God's Creation. Hethor wondered why his breathing did not labor, as he had been told it would at higher altitudes.

He studied the shadows creeping away from the dawn. "According to what I understand of our charts," he said, "there is a knee in this rock face. It would seem that this forest hides that cliff, folding it away in a blanket of green. If we make ten degrees east of south, dead slow, and watch our marks, I believe a narrow valley will open up. Cool, dark, and hidden."

"Good." Smallwood took the spyglass from Hethor and snapped it shut. "Remain here with Lieutenant Wollers, and send a runner soonest you are certain. I must go forward and prepare for a shore party."

Hethor stood as the airship slowly eased toward the blanket of forest, marveling at how the green seemed to part as they approached the edge of the knee. Once he knew to look for it, he could see in perspective that the more distant forest past the gap boasted a smaller appearance. The narrow, shake-shouldered trees made that hard to find and focus his attention on.

"Bamboo," said Wollers suddenly. "A Chinese tree, like elms for the devils."

They entered a valley not as narrow as it had seemed, sort of a tall fjord cut from the stone-bordered sky. The tillermen slowly eased *Bassett* around a great bend to reveal a giant harbor of the air. Its contours were approximately the shape sketched in General Gordon's map. A city stood there, rising high into the morning sun and plunging to the shadowed depths of the harbor. It was all of wood and wicker, vertical towers and ladders and bridges and cunning battlements balanced on ropes and poles. There was a scent of morning mist, and damp wood, but he smelled no cookfires, no brawny reek of bodies, no oiled scent of commerce.

The city was quiet as a churchyard.

"It rises for miles." Hethor stared upward, wondering where the folk who had built the place had gone.

"A vertical, wooden London," agreed Wollers.

"I wonder if we are at the proper altitude," Hethor said. "Gordon's column could have passed through this great maze anywhere. It would be like looking for a single man in downtown New Haven."

Together, he and Wollers scanned the vertical face, looking for some sign or clue indicating the passing of a British force.

"There." Hethor pointed at a spot a few hundred feet above their present altitude. "Those dark streaks against that pale palisade. Someone has lit cooking fires here, and recently. We should send a runner to the captain." *Librarian Childress could have done no better a job of observation,* he thought with a swell of quiet pride.

Wollers moved to pass the word, while Hethor watched his mark. The ship rose carefully, as pained and cautious in her movements as any arthritic matron.

The architecture was impressive. Entire forests had died to make this city. Hethor realized this was a place where a race such as the winged savages could dwell in comfort. His awe quickly collapsed to fear. A thousand savages could tumble upon *Bassett* and worry them all to their deaths in the shadows far below.

A signal gun went off, the sharp report startling flocks of birds and bats. They rose in thick clouds from the forest that grew throughout the city.

Hethor bit his tongue to hold in his shout of fear as fluttering wings in their millions met the sky all around *Bassett,* like dogs that would run before hunters of the air.

FIVE

THE MARINES already assembled in the waist of the ship ran to the rail. Their carbines crackled as they shot wildly into the mass of birds and bats that darkened the air around *Bassett* like smoke from a burning city.

"Belay that firing immediately," shouted Captain Smallwood as he returned to the poop deck.

Officers and petty officers about the ship took up the order. The marines quickly stood down. Their lieutenant ran up and down the ranks berating his men. The clouds of winged creatures surrounding *Bassett* dissipated, seeking higher ground and more peaceful roosts.

Wollers barked a series of steering orders to the tillermen and the ropes division, lest the airship drift into the walls of the city that now surrounded them. Hethor glanced backward, over the stern rail, to see blue sky beyond, ocean sparkling below. The Guinea Coast was a dark and distant line looming on the horizon.

Honest terrestrial soil, so comfortingly horizontal, had traded places with the ever-vertical Wall, which itself had once been the foreboding shadow in the distance.

He turned back to the city. Seen from such a short range the place was more ornate than he had originally thought. Ladders and stairs led up, galleries and bridges leapt across, while a whole nation of men could be hidden behind wooden walls and reed-mat screens, living like chimney swifts in this upsweep of wood.

"Bamboo." Captain Smallwood stared at the immensity of the city, lost in thought. "The Chinaman's steel."

Hethor bit back a question. The captain had not been talking to him. But then Smallwood turned and stared at Hethor as if he were some ape hauled aboard by a foraging party. "You're no Malgus," Smallwood said, "nor even de Troyes, God rest his soul, but you're who we have. Are you able to come ashore with the party?"

A captain asking a crewman for his preferences. Hethor would have been no more surprised had Smallwood grown wings and leapt from the deck to join the flying savages. "I . . . sir . . . ," he began, then stopped. Did he want to leave *Bassett*? He was afraid of those bronze weapons and the long, sinewy arms of the winged savages, but something in this place stirred both his inner artistry and his sense of the mission entrusted to him by the archangel Gabriel.

"It is a matter of the safety of the ship," Smallwood said. "If you are lost, then one of my officers will need to perform your duties. I am already rather understrength there. But I expect to find maps, logs from Gordon's expedition, somewhere in that city. There may possibly be specialized instruments for navigating the Wall as well. Your aid may prove invaluable."

"Permission, sir," Hethor said, then gulped. "Permission to accompany the shore party, please?"

"Granted." Smallwood turned away to the logistics of safely tethering his ship in this environment and subsequently landing the party.

Apparently forgotten, Hethor stood at the stern rail and craned his neck, trying to stare up past the gasbag. This close in to the aerial harbor it blocked most of his view, but he saw great legs of dark wood—teak, perhaps?—supporting some of the buildings above them. The legs looked to be milled from single logs. If so, the trees from which they had been cut would have been giants almost beyond Hethor's imaginings.

He looked onward, at the balconies and battlements and buildings. They were as ornately layered as any German clock, hinting at architectures within architectures like Christmas crackers. He wondered if each building could be shredded to reveal a smaller one within. After a while, two facts came to his attention.

There was no glass, anywhere.

And there were no clock towers.

A people with clement weather and no commitment to time, perhaps. Or primitives, savants of bamboo and wood, with no metallurgy. Though the winged savages had wielded bronze weapons to deadly effectiveness.

ONCE THEY reached the altitude of the fire scars Hethor had spotted, al-Wazir got *Bassett* warped to a reasonable anchorage by an expedient Hethor had never before witnessed. The ropes chief harnessed two volunteers to what looked like oversized parachutes coated with gum-elastic. These he stretched over the rail. He then had the gas division inflate them with hydrogen via a hose dropped down from the gasbag.

The faux-parachutes quickly rose to become medium-sized copies of the great cells that crowded the bag overhead. Each was close to twenty feet across its fat belly, already crowding hard against the ropes restraining them. The sailors were put overboard, secured by narrow ropes wound on winches. With much shouting and encouragement, they bobbed out into the open air to fly upward as though driven by springs.

Al-Wazir winched them back down close to the ship. The ropes chief then had deckhands toss out a secondary line that was used to pass weights to the flying sailors until, while they still strained at their tethers, they no longer sought to rocket heavenward. The flyers then each deployed two canvas sweeps, handheld sails—oars of the air—with which they each slowly made way, beating across the wind toward the structures of the city.

Hethor could not decide whether to be fascinated or appalled. Both sensations warred within him. He longed to soar as those sailors did, yet their lives were bound so close in hand by the strength of their harnesses and the integrity of their little gas cells.

The two made it to shore, perhaps a hundred yards apart. Each secured himself to a pillar. Heavier lines were passed across to be secured in turn. Finally *Bassett* was warped in toward the cliff. She turned her stern to the land as she went so her steam-driven propellers could push her toward the bay's mouth at need.

The whole operation took perhaps three hours. Hethor stayed on the poop, hanging back by the stern rail in order to remain unnoticed. Or perhaps Captain Smallwood was merely keeping a convenient eye on him there.

Once the ship was brought to rest, al-Wazir had his division run additional ropes across from the aft anchor point until a three-rope bridge was made. He then piled a number of parachutes on deck next to the stepping-off point, saluted the poop, and shouted, "All's ready for shore detail, Captain sir!"

Smallwood returned al-Wazir's salute, then ordered the marines across. Their lieutenant split his force in half. One squad remained stationed on the ship's rails, carbines locked and loaded, while the other squad shouldered the parachute harnesses and crossed to secure the landward side.

Or cliffward side, Hethor thought, depending on how one chose to view the deployment.

The marines took up positions in the galleries and walkways opposite *Bassett* with much kicking of wicker doors and poking of carbines through windows. Eventually the all-clear was shouted.

"Seaman Jacques," Smallwood said. "Stay close to Lieutenant Wollers. If I need you, you will be called upon.

You are specifically not permitted within areas the marines or I myself have not yet checked."

"Aye, sir." Hethor glanced at Wollers, who favored him with a sympathetic grin.

He followed the second mate down to the waist to gather a leather water bottle from Cook and strap on a parachute—which despite Hethor's experience in Bermuda he had never done since of his own sober will. Once prepared, they stood on line for the rope bridge.

It was then, waiting on deck behind Wollers and in front of the loblolly boy, that Hethor became afraid.

THE ROPE bridge was about a hundred feet from the braces at the ship's rail to its endpoint against a teak-pillared galleria that could have come straight out of Venice or Constantinople. The two lines Hethor grasped were no thicker than his thumb, each bristly with hand-scarring hemp.

He wished he'd brought gloves.

Hethor glanced down at his feet. That line was the same insufficient diameter as the other two, curled under his leather shoes just before the heel, bending and swaying with his weight. All of that was alarming enough. Worse, he was nearly paralyzed by a gut-wrenching view of thousands of feet of wooden city and stone cliffs below, vanishing into a very distant perspective of mists and shadows.

It was as if he stood atop a shaft leading straight downward to a cold, dark hell.

"You knew this," Hethor said to the air around him. "You worked the charts; you knew the altitude." His hands wanted to let go, his arms to spread so that he could fly like a bird, soar into the misty depths with all the freedom of a falling leaf. He could feel the pull of the distance. The depths almost had a voice of their own.

"Hey," said the loblolly boy, coming up behind Hethor. "Move it along, Clocks."

After the marines had crossed individually, al-Wazir had ordered tighter spacing in the interests of time. Hethor glanced back at the ship's doctor's assistant—what was his name? The loblolly boy was literally a boy, perhaps eleven years of age, sent on this mission because Dr. Firkin would not cross. Up in the fo'c'sle the common sailors said Firkin had no head for heights. That seemed to Hethor an odd thing in an airship officer, even the ship's surgeon, who might be excused some failings due to the nature of his appointment.

"I'm moving," Hethor grumbled. He was glad for the interruption from his contemplation of the awful depths below. He narrowed his eyes, looking only at the ropes in his hand, and continued crab walking toward the anchoring galleria. Behind him, the loblolly boy cursed and grumbled out his own fear, using Hethor as a target.

For once Hethor didn't mind such treatment.

Then he was being helped onto the galleria. The wooden affair seemed much less solid as he set his weight upon it, creaking beneath the bulk of so many beefy Royal Navy tars. Wollers, who had stepped off the rope bridge well before Hethor, grasped his shoulder with a firm hand as they stood at the arches that opened out toward *Bassett* floating at anchor in the empty air.

Hethor had never before experienced a level view of the airship. From below, approaching a mooring mast for example, she was just a large, dark shape in the sky, resembling the outline of a snail or slug. From the top of a mast, she was too close to be anything but an immensity of gasbag and wooden hull.

From the galleria of the vertical city, though, she was beautiful. The hull was narrow and graceful in proportion. The lines seemed too sharp for an oceangoing vessel, though Hethor supposed she could land on water at need—at least until the pitch-sealed traps and hatches along her keel line flooded.

From the side, the gasbag took on a more imposing appearance as well. The catwalk he had seen from the navigator's cupola ranged almost level from fore to aft with just the gentlest of curves until the nose dropped sharply like a beak. Aft, the gasbag ended in a more rounded arc, with a sort of fold at the top.

Bassett was beautiful indeed, a veritable raptor hunting the airways of the Empire for Chinese intruders. And now, chasing down the ghosts of history.

Wollers said, "Come on, we've got to start looking in these rooms. The marines found trash in there. It's up to us to determine if that's good English trash or something left behind by wogs or those damned flying horrors."

Hethor would have wagered on good English trash. The vertical city gave an impression of absolute desertion. Who would be here to make such a mess, now that the original inhabitants had fled, or died, or whatever had become of them?

So they stepped into wooden-floored rooms with wicker walls. Clever shafts let the sun in from above, though the light wells seemed to be baffled against glare and rain. As a result the illumination was indistinct, filling the rooms with a gentle, shadowless glow. The floors popped and creaked as Hethor and Wollers walked, but not with the noises of decay and collapse. It was almost like music.

Hethor had a vision of dancing in a room like this, the rhythms rising from the very feet of the partners. The buildings seemed tuned to the movements of those who dwelled within. Perhaps this is what the builders had intended as well.

But the true glory of the inner rooms was the weaving of the wicker walls. Many shades and textures of the narrow laths had been used, so that the walls were each a work of art, depicting landscapes, people at their work, great festivals, the brassy gearing of the heavens, and so forth. Hethor could have simply stared at the woven panels for some time, but Wollers tugged him on.

"The rooms are darker and cooler along the cliff face," the second mate said, stepping through a door with a knee-high threshold beam that rose from the floor. "One of General Gordon's scouting parties would be more likely to bivouac back here. They would feel they had a more defensible position."

Sure enough, Hethor noticed crumpled in one corner a waxed sheet of paper, the sort that the marines unwrapped to get at their carbine bullets. Another high threshold beam, and they were in a much darker room. This one showed evidence of a fire on the floor. The ornate walls had been defaced, which made Hethor wince. More rubbish, as well—bones from some dinner piled in a corner, scraps of paper, a loose button.

He picked the button up. It was brass, with the lion insignia of the British Army embossed on it. "This isn't from *Bassett*, sir," he said to Wollers.

Wollers took the button. "Good. So they *were* here. Well, if they left us a message back at the Sepulchrum Caii, they probably left one here as well. Let's work our way along the cliff face."

The wall leading east had been torn open, the beautiful wickerwork bayoneted to provide easy access to the next room. These buildings had stood here for a length of time Hethor couldn't even imagine. Now brief occupation by English troops had savaged their beauty. *Oh well*, he thought. *At least they didn't set fire to the city with their cooking.*

Hethor followed Wollers through a line of rooms. Wollers kept looking left and occasionally called to make sure they weren't passing beyond the line of *Bassett*'s marines outside along the railing. Though they disturbed very little dust, Hethor got a clear impression that no one but Gordon's soldiers had been inside here for quite some time. Perhaps decades, or more.

It was like going into one of the old storerooms at New Haven Latin, where not even the janitor had been in years—that same sense of desertion, yet with watchful emptiness.

They stepped into a larger room. This space took advantage of an apparently natural depression in the cliff wall to extend farther back. This had obviously been a sort of headquarters, for there were still a few sheets of paper tacked to the walls. A pair of campstools leaned forgotten at the back of the depression.

No good foot soldier would use a campstool. Even Hethor knew that.

Wollers cried out, a shout of discovery, and moved the folded stools aside. "A dispatch case," he shouted, and pulled open the leather flaps. It still held papers within. Wollers glanced at Hethor. "Letters, not maps. I think we've found what we came for. I'll be taking these across." He thought for a moment. "You should wait at the rope bridge, attending the captain's pleasure."

"I want to go back through these rooms," Hethor said, "retracing our steps. The panels interested me."

Wollers stepped to the torn-open doorway where Hethor stood, peered over his shoulder for a moment to sight along their recent line of travel. "No harm, I suppose, since we've been there already. Don't go anywhere we haven't already passed through."

Humming to himself, the second mate headed out the door, toward the gallery and a quick trot back to the railing and faster access to the rope bridge.

Hethor stepped away from the room and returned to the little chamber they'd last come through. All the trash and casual vandalism depressed him. It was akin to disturbing a church, or a grave. Had Gordon's soldiers no sense of the sacred nature of this place?

Or did that feeling only come from within him?

He closed his eyes and listened carefully, separating the sounds.

His own breathing, as always. Distant grumbling conversation from *Bassett*'s marines. Footfalls echoing from the wooden floors of the vertical city. The gentle creaking of its timbers. One of *Bassett*'s engines thumping in a slow mechanical heartbeat. Wind whistling through the arches of the galleries and pillars outside. The clicking and clattering of the world's turning, though it seemed different up here on the Wall, both more distant and more immediate, the way a gunshot at the edge of hearing can grasp the attention.

There was a sudden, close flutter of wings, along with a gust of rank scent. Hethor threw himself to the floor. He cried out as he opened his eyes to see whatever was flying at him with murder in its heart.

Nothing.

Nothing but feathers spinning in the air, three long pinions as great as Gabriel's.

Or those of the winged savages.

And in the middle of the floor, something new. A little brass plate, like the nameplate that had been screwed to the lintel of Master Bodean's shop door.

It had not been there before, when Hethor and Wollers had walked through the room. It had not been there just now, when he had stepped back to close his eyes and listen.

Whatever had flown through like an owl unseen beneath a new moon had left that plate behind, though he'd heard no noise but the wings.

Hethor cautiously edged into the room to approach the plate. It was rectangular, perhaps ten inches by fourteen. No screw holes in the corner. And instead of raised letters, or the usual Roman style of engraving, it looked to have been scribbled upon by someone in a hurry with a pen or stylus capable of cutting brass.

Not brass, he realized as his fingers touched it.

Gold.

He picked up the plate. A tablet, really. It *was* gold, more wealth than he'd ever held, or even seen, in his life. Not beaten thin, either, but of some thickness. Perhaps a quarter inch. Even if it were leaf, over silver perhaps, it was still quite valuable. Immensely valuable, if it were solid gold. Though it didn't weigh nearly enough for that mass of pure metal.

Gold leaf, then. Or plating. Over something light, such as aluminium, perhaps.

No matter, he thought. Hethor instead stared at the scribbling. He thought he might recognize some of the characters, but he would have to copy them out, decompose the original maker's scribblings into rational letters. He refused to think on it further. Hethor knew he should run for Wollers or Smallwood right now—to do anything else was a form of betrayal, almost a mutiny.

But this was what Gabriel had sent him for. His allegiance to the archangel trumped even the claims Her Imperial Majesty's navy had upon him. He needed to understand, before they took it away from him. As they surely would.

Feeling distinctly unworthy, Hethor slipped the tablet under his shirt, let it slide down behind his rope belt. The thing was cold, but not too big to carry in that manner albeit heavy enough to press uncomfortably against him.

It was not stealing, Hethor reasoned. He would take the tablet to Malgus' cabin. There he would stow it in the map chest, and work to translate the text. Once he knew what it said, what it *meant,* found here surrounded by feathers in an inner room, he would tell Wollers and Captain Smallwood.

Then he would tell them immediately, he promised himself.

Hethor found his way back to the rope bridge. He was nervous, though those around him seemed to think he was merely struggling to find his own head for heights. He was grateful for their gentle contempt. It kept them from looking too closely at the way he crouched slightly, hands folded across his waist, protecting the golden tablet.

STRUGGLING ACROSS the rope bridge on his way back to *Bassett* with his parachute pack weighing on his back, Hethor found himself torn between fear of the abyss yawning for thousands of feet below him and concern for the tablet cutting into his groin. Somehow, he was again crossing with the loblolly boy. This time the lad was in front of him instead of following with complaints about his slow progress.

One foot, other foot, Hethor thought. *Don't stop, don't think, don't look. One foot, other foot.*

The ropes jumped. The line in his left hand dropped away slack. Hethor shrieked, grabbing the right-side line with both hands, which threw him off balance. He realized that not all of the shrieking was coming from him.

He looked down. The loblolly boy fell into the towering pit of wooden city and cold stone, hands slapping at his chest. Was he trying to fly?

Then the parachute blossomed, a square of silk tied at the corners and sewn to a harness of lightweight lines. That upward tug was a feeling Hethor well remembered from his jump at Bermuda. The loblolly boy disappeared beneath that puffed blanket of silk, though he did not stop screaming.

Hethor stood with both fists wrapped around the remaining hand rope, shivering in the wind, during the minute it took the loblolly boy's voice to fade and the longer minutes that it took for his parachute to vanish from sight in the distant, misty shadows far below.

He finally realized people were shouting at him, both from the ship and from the shore. Hethor tore his gaze from the abyss beneath his feet to see Wollers at the rail. The second mate waved his hands as if he could reel Hethor in by main force.

I cannot do it, Hethor thought. *No more steps. Unless I grow wings, I'm never moving again.*

"Bring it in, sailor," Wollers called. His face showed profound relief that he'd managed to catch Hethor's attention.

Both hands still clutched tight on the remaining rope. Hethor shook his head. The motion caused his body to twitch. The golden tablet dug into his groin.

Wings rushed in Hethor's memory, the smell of savages

overlaying the image of angels. He had to get the tablet to Malgus' cabin.

"Left foot," Hethor whispered, sliding that foot along.

"Right." It moved a few inches.

"Left hand." If he didn't open his fist, he could keep his grip.

Wollers shouted more encouragement.

When they finally pried Hethor off the rope to get him onto the ship, al-Wazir handed him a flask of brandy while Lombardo pounded him on the back. "Good work, son," the decks chief whispered.

"What about the boy?" Hethor asked, imagining himself plunging into cold shadow, twisting beneath the silk of the parachute.

Al-Wazir shook his head sadly. "Naught Cap'n'll do for 'im. We're serving 'neath the Articles of War out here. Cain't spare the time to drive her down and look."

"Besides," Lombardo added, "he's most likely dead already."

Hethor felt sick. Falling, only to be abandoned. He sat down and shivered.

A few minutes later the second mate sought him out. "I need to go to Malgus' cabin," Hethor told Wollers. "I want to look at the maps. I . . . I need to concentrate."

Which certainly wasn't a lie.

"Very well," said Wollers after a long, careful look. "Proceed."

Hethor limped off, cramped from panic, muscle strain, and the attentions of the golden tablet. He still couldn't remember the loblolly boy's name. He figured he would hear it at services.

STILL SHIVERING, Hethor studied the lettering on the tablet. He would have taken a rubbing but did not possess any charcoal. He would have to beg some from Cook later. So he was reduced to handling the gold itself. The metal was velvety, almost warm.

The lettering resembled handscript, but not of the Roman or Greek alphabets. It was more like someone hastily had written Chinese or some other language where the words were little houses folded over their ideas instead of built from honest letters and sounds.

Or not.

This tablet was a gift, to him. God had spared Hethor's life in crossing the abyss, taking the loblolly boy in his place. An angel had come to him in that little room in the vertical city. It must have been Gabriel or one of his angelic servants, Hethor reasoned, because any of the winged savages would have killed him where he stood. Those great feathers were too large to have found their way into that chamber by any other agency.

Hethor traced his fingers over the script on the tablet. There were six lines, with some repetition of the symbols between them. Like a bit of verse.

But this was a *gift*.

A message from God.

Could it be God's name on the tablet? The Tetragrammaton was both the name of God and the name of God's name. The word simply meant "four letters," after all. "YHWH," the four letters of the Hebrew word for He whom the Jews would not name.

Hebrew. What if it were not Chinese, but Hebrew? Hethor knew a little bit about Chinese script, but he had also seen written Hebrew at New Haven Latin, in biblical studies and discussions of the Roman occupation of Judea.

The Hebrew word for the Tetragrammaton began with a letter that looked like an apostrophe followed by one that looked a little like the Greek letter "π." Or maybe a lowercase English "n." Hethor scanned the tablet's strange, looping, sloppily crafted script. It did not follow the forms of the Hebrew alphabet, not as he understood them.

Lines one, four, and five had similar symbols that might have been the name of God. As that thought occurred to

him, Hethor for a moment heard the clattering of the
world, as if midnight had come upon him in the navigator's rest.

He slipped the tablet into a drawer in Malgus' tiny map
table, covering it with charts of the Orleans and Texian
coastlines. Then despite his orders he lay down on Malgus' bunk and thought about Gabriel, God, and the Key
Perilous. Eventually Dr. Firkin startled him awake by
banging open the door and saying, "Best get on deck,
son."

IT WAS near sundown, judging from the view to the north
off the port rail. The bay of the vertical city was already
deep in shadow. Between the obscuring gasbag and the rising walls of the cliff city, Hethor could not see the heavenly brass in the eastern and western skies. Still, he could
almost feel it.

Absent a body, there was no funeral for the loblolly
boy. Captain Smallwood had elected to have a crew
muster nevertheless. Hethor scuttled out of the hatch
from officers' country and slunk to the back of the assembled divisions, praying Smallwood did not take note of
his tardiness.

". . . and so we hope that young Mister Davies found a
safe landing and path to the Atlantic shore, that he might
someday make his way home," Smallwood said. "May
God grant us all that grace." The captain stared around at
his ship's company. "Dismissed."

Hethor started to turn away with the rush of sailors
eager for the mess, or perhaps their bunks, only to have
Dr. Firkin grab his arm. "Wait."

A few moments later Smallwood was surrounded by
his remaining officers: Wollers; Lieutenant Prine, the third
mate; Lieutenant Commander Cocini, the aeronautical
engineer who commanded the gasbag division and over-
saw the engines; Ensign Mayhew, the pilot and master of
the tillermen; and Marine Lieutenant San Lorenzo. Only

the middies were missing, standing watch on the poop or elsewhere, and Dr. Firkin himself, still to one side of the group with his hand on Hethor's elbow.

"Let's go," Firkin said in a low voice. "Officer or no, you're the navigator. You need to hear this." He steered Hethor into the officers' conference.

"There you are," said Smallwood, noticing Hethor. The captain stared him up and down. "Are you fully recovered, Seaman Jacques?"

Hethor almost blurted, "From what?" Instead he simply nodded. "Yes, sir."

"Very well." Smallwood marched to the midmast, removed his buckled shoes and belt, dropped his dagger, and climbed to the trapdoor set in the gasbag. The other officers likewise began divesting themselves of their accumulated metal.

Hethor was astonished. It had never occurred to him that the captain might be willing or able to climb where the tars went.

Then Smallwood was through, crawling up into the gasbag. Wollers followed the captain with a backward glance at Hethor. The rest of his officers climbed after.

Hethor went last, waved on by Dr. Firkin. "With all respect to Captain Smallwood," Firkin said, "I'm not cut of the right stuff to stride the catwalk." Hethor nodded, not sure what to say. He climbed into the hot, billowing darkness of the gas cells. The worn heels of Lieutenant San Lorenzo's stockings bobbed above him.

When Hethor arrived at the navigator's rest, Smallwood had walked perhaps twenty paces forward along the catwalk. There the captain stood with his hands folded behind him to stare up at the Wall, as unconcerned for the exposed height as though he were in his own cabin. The canvas surface of the gasbag sloped gently away to both sides to form the predatory curves that Hethor had admired from a distance. Up here, he felt far too close to the edge and the fate of the loblolly boy.

They had not even parachutes to break their fall.

Though that might actually be a blessing, Hethor supposed.

The other officers were strung out behind the captain. Cocini was as unconcerned as Smallwood. The rest displayed varying degrees of nervousness. Hethor was just as happy to stay in the navigator's rest with its useless railings. They at least kept his mind calm and defined the space on which he stood.

Smallwood pointed up at the Wall. Hethor followed the line of his hand. It was like looking across at a horizon, except this horizon was straight up. Through some trick of the light, the distance glowed, a sort of sunrise from the south. This made Hethor think of the brass gear teeth sparkling atop the Equatorial Wall. The gleaming horns of Earth's orbital track were clearly visible directly overhead, extending to the east and west. Though they stood in deep shadow, there was still sufficient sunlight to make out features on the Wall in the many miles it towered above them.

Between here and the upward horizon, Hethor saw more forests, meadows, scree fields, the pale glow of ice or snow, what might be cities sparkling in the distance, drifting banks of cloud or mist—a world's worth of land hung over his head, all clinging to the near-vertical.

"Gordon's notes indicate that he was trying for the Diamond Palace," said Smallwood. "At one time Emperor Hadrianus caused a fort to be built there for the Fourth Massalia Legion. Gordon hopes to establish his command therein for a long-term occupation of this portion of the Wall."

You could no more occupy the Wall, Hethor thought, *than you could occupy the Atlantic Ocean.*

"General Gordon's notes further indicate he hopes to find some sign of the Roman presence yet lingering in the fort."

After all the many centuries since the Empire's collapse? Hethor could hear the smile in Smallwood's voice.

"Our best interpretation of what we have discovered

thus far is that Gordon's forces decamped about two weeks past. With great reluctance, I am detaching Lieutenant San Lorenzo and half his force to follow the general's line of march to search for more direction from him, and perhaps catch his rearguard. San Lorenzo will also take a party of seamen to be chosen by Lieutenant Wollers subject to my approval. *Bassett* will rise to the Diamond Palace with the expectation of arriving prior to Gordon's force. There we will perform an aerial reconnaissance, then rendezvous with the good general if that is at all possible. Do I hear any discussion?"

By no means was Hethor going to say anything here, where he really had no business being. Still, he was certain that Smallwood's plan was foolhardy. The entire company of *Bassett*'s marines had barely sufficed to drive off the winged savages in their last attack. He dreaded a reprise.

Ensign Mayhew spoke up. "My pardon, sir. I know we are short of officers to stand watch, so it might be difficult for one of us to volunteer and still keep the ship in good order. Perhaps you could send a division chief, al-Wazir or Lombardo, to keep the tars in line." He added hastily, "Sir!"

Smallwood nodded. "I will take that under advisement. Now, before it falls fully dark, look at that great col there." He pointed upward toward a bare cliff of rock amid the endless wooden buildings. "See how it rises out of a split in this vertical city? According to Gordon, a trail rises there that cuts east beneath the galleries of the city before heading upward. Lieutenant San Lorenzo, does that seem to you a reasonable path? Should *Bassett* rise to discharge you there? Or would you prefer to set out from our current moorage?"

The discussion spun off into a lengthy argument about routes, supplies, and support. All of what was said had only the basis of pure opinion, since as far as Hethor could see, none of the officers knew any more than he did about the rigors of marching up the Wall. He remained silent, watching the stars come out. He spotted the thin tracery of the orbital track of Venus. It was the faintest counterpoint to the moon's circumterran thread, a sight rarely seen from New Haven, which filled its sky with constant smokes and fogs of industry as well as electrick glares overwhelming the lamps of night. He also saw faint ghostly colors that seemed to pass back and forth high above him on the Wall. Like faerie fires in a swamp, save that they might be miles wide for all he could determine.

Then it was time to go down. As last man up Hethor led the way back to the deck.

SOMEHOW SAN Lorenzo's party was organized and ready to cross the rope bridge at dawn. Hethor had slept in Malgus' cabin, improper as that was, because he was afraid to be too far away from the gold tablet. The fact that he'd held in his hand something that might carry God's very words made his skin crawl and prickled the hairs on his head. Though the tablet had seemed almost ordinary the day before, separated by a night's memory and the wearing of time, the event seemed a miracle. Much as with his original encounter with Gabriel.

He was on deck, standing uneasily with his division to watch the proceedings. The Welshman stood to one side of Hethor while Dairy sat on the other, resting his wounded ankles. The two dug their elbows into him and ribbed him about his "promotion" to officer country.

The marines went across one by one. As they landed, they secured the gallery once more. After them a mixed group of sailors from ropes and deck, along with a few from gunnery, followed. Hethor wondered if they were volunteers. Lombardo followed, favoring Hethor with a final glare as he wiggled out onto the rope bridge.

After the men were landed, the rigging of the rope bridge was changed and supplies were sent over—mostly ammunition and tools, along with some canvas.

Apparently the party would be expected to forage on its way up. As there was little to eat in the vertical city except the bamboo and wicker of its walls, Hethor hoped their march would be quick and successful.

The bosun piped them away, followed by a salute from Smallwood. With a casting off of the mooring and bridge ropes, the shore party was gone, so many flickering shadows among the galleries and balconies. Under al-Wazir, sailors from both the ropes division and the deck division reeled in the bridge lines and broke down the winches. At the same time *Bassett*'s engines beat her away from the wood-encased cliff face and back to the comparative safety of the open air at the center of the bay.

Hethor set to working with his division at the stowage of the ropes and reshifting the deck cargo and equipment that had been disrupted by the staging of the shore party's departure. A shake of the head from al-Wazir quickly warned him off. He returned to Malgus' cabin instead, deep in contemplation of the gold tablet.

Though the writing was not Hebrew, Hethor was increasingly convinced that the four letters he saw were in fact the Tetragrammaton, God's name, inserted in the text just as a scholar at Yale might insert a word or passage of Greek in an English text.

Which left the rest of the language to be deciphered. He had some Latin from his studies at school, but this was a different order of problem entirely. One he was clearly not competent to solve. Simply staring at the tablet did nothing. He only cramped his hand attempting a precise copy of the shaky loops and swirls of the writing.

Chinese didn't loop, did it?

Somehow Hethor had trouble believing that God would speak Chinese, at least to him. Or maybe at all. So surely if this was a message from God, Hethor was meant to be able to read it.

There were other repeated symbols. One appeared in both the first and second lines. Another one in the third, fourth, fifth, and sixth lines. A devotional term? But God wouldn't pray to Himself.

He thought about the Eastern alphabet that the Constantine heretics used. That didn't make sense as an explanation—as he understood it, the Eastern lettering resembled both the Latin and Greek. This decidedly did not.

Hethor returned to considering Hebrew. *Bassett* carried no chaplain, and as far as he knew, none of the officers or crew were secret Jews. Would anyone else on the ship have a Hebrew dictionary or grammar? Dr. Firkin, perhaps.

Concealing the golden tablet in the map chest once more, Hethor went up on deck. Firkin was unlikely to be in his cabin now. Since the loss of the loblolly boy the doctor spent most of his time in his surgery under the fo'c'sle or out on the deck, though he assiduously avoided the rail. As Hethor stepped out the hatch, he noted *Bassett* was rising, still within the vertical city.

Walking across the deck, Hethor wondered how he would explain his request for a Hebrew text. Then he heard the faint bell of the sky watch and looked around in panic as the swivel gun popped again. The noise echoed faintly from the front of the gasbag.

This time, *Bassett* was better prepared. Marines poured onto the deck. Each soldier carried two carbines, which they shared out to eager sailors. Within moments the rails were lined with excited marksmen of varying skill.

Winged savages fell past the ship, flying through a storm of fire that sent the smoke and reek of powder across the deck like a fog bank. Hethor didn't see any of them tumble from the sky. They would be back in moments, all of the fliers, to stalk the decks in their hideous glory.

These were a true mockery of God's angels.

Then the mockery was over the rails in a wave of a dozen or more. They whirled like fire dancers, brass swords gleaming in the morning light, and passed among

the lines and shrouds like so many great moths drawn to
slam into the ship's company. They swung their blades,
and some drew bows to send arrows into the row of
sailors and marines still firing upon them.

None of the winged savages so much as shouted, let
alone said a word. All fought in eerie silence save for the
clash of arms.

Lacking a weapon, Hethor scrambled to the forward
rope locker. There he pulled out a pry bar intended for
levering the winches as they were mounted and dis-
mounted. He was no fighter, but it might serve to keep
one of those brilliant, flashing swords at bay. And woe
betide the winged savage he could swing at from behind.

Despite his prudent thoughts, Hethor waded screaming
into the fight, slipping on blood and gore, almost tripping
as his right foot rolled away from someone's severed
hand. The pry bar made a whooshing noise as he swung it
to connect with a winged savage's arm with a crackling
like a snapped branch. He pulled it over his head and
whacked another one on the muscled mass that enclosed
its wing joints, between and just below the shoulder
blades.

Al-Wazir was next to him. The ropes chief bayoneted a
savage as he grinned through a blood-splashed face. He
shouted something to Hethor, who only heard the word
"right," then swung about to help Dairy, who had been
fighting the whole time from a seat on the deck and now
seemed to be missing at least one arm.

Hethor laid in again with his pry bar, feeling something slick slide off his arm just before a spray of blood
erupted. He glanced that way to see the Jerseyman dying,
the man's half-toothed grin collapsing in pained surprise
as his body separated from shoulder to waist in a fountain
of blood and offal.

So Hethor turned again, still swinging, though his
palms stung terribly. He felt beaten, bruised, but not
sliced. Somewhere nearby Smallwood shouted as pistols
crackled. More carbine fire popped. At that point Hethor

realized that he was completely surrounded by the winged savages. He was alone in a circle of them.

Swords poked out at him, not killing blows. They were trying to force him to drop the pry bar.

Hethor held it out in front of him, two-handed like he might have pulled on a line. "Oh, no," he shouted. "Not like Malgus!"

He saw Dr. Firkin, covered in a bloody apron, shouting at him. The surgeon seemed to be waving Hethor on. Then, grinning their rotten-toothed grins, the winged savages moved closer in, until one of them managed to grab his pry bar on the left extension of its swing. After that their hands were all over Hethor. They grabbed, pinched, the horrible ragged nails cutting into him. It was like his nightmares of the candlemen.

And worst of all, they still made no sound other than their breathing. No shouts, no curses, no taunts.

"By the white bird . . . ," Firkin yelled, still waving Hethor onward, but the winged savages rushed Hethor toward the rail and threw him over. They dove after him, taking two marines and Midshipman Fine with them in their wave of flesh. Hethor screamed as loud and shrill as the loblolly boy had, terrified of the fall and more terrified of the savages. Two of them folded their wings and dove after him, grabbing Hethor by arms and legs. They swung him between them as their wings beat for altitude.

He watched the other three from *Bassett* fall screaming down the bay of the vertical city as a last few rounds of gunfire pursued Hethor and his captors. Moments later they were winging through open air, almost peaceful save for the cruel hands nearly breaking his ankles and wrists. In addition, the weight of his own body conspired to disjoint his knees and elbows.

Somewhere in the first stages of shuddering flight, Hethor forgot his fear long enough to feel a great pang of regret for the golden tablet. God's word had been sent to him and him alone. It now lay abandoned in a chart drawer that would not be opened for months to come.

Nor indeed, ever opened at all, if *Bassett* did not manage a return to a friendly port.

He twisted his head to look over his shoulder, down into the vast, endless pit. The winged savages were moving so fast that even the massive gasbag that made up the bulk of *Bassett* looked like nothing more than a leaf floating on a dark pond from the increasingly higher vantage toward which he was being lifted.

SIX

HE SWUNG free in the chill air of the evening. The pain in his arms and legs stretched in his mind like ropes fraying to the point of separation. Hethor was lost in his suffering—frightened, lonely, keenly aware that he would most likely never see *Bassett* again. The savages who had taken him had been flying for hours, well into twilight's gleam. The airship was long lost to sight, as was the vertical city.

He'd never meant to be a sailor, but Hethor would miss them—the dead and living. And so much had been left behind. The golden tablet, most of all, but other answers, too. What had Dr. Firkin been trying to tell him? His life seemed already forfeit. How much else had he lost?

Hethor spent time in fruitless contemplation of that question as they rose further into the evening. His captors flew very fast, though the beats of their wings were lazy enough. It was as though they were borne on the invisible hands of God. In the gathering twilight, Hethor could see lights on the face of the Wall—campfires, perhaps, or settlements, though he was hard-pressed to tell what exactly they might be. Some flickered—his captors perhaps flying over a sheltering forest. Others gleamed as hard and bright as good English electrics.

As night finally settled full on, the winged savages chose a ledge on which to alight. It was relatively narrow, perhaps twice the width of a cart track. The flat stone vanished into darkness before Hethor could spy either end. He had no doubt the only way off was into the open air. His captors were far too cunning to choose a site that would leave them vulnerable to attack by enemies or animals.

He had no doubt these man-beasts had enemies.

An even dozen of the savages settled onto their ledge. They wrapped themselves in their great, ragged wings and went to sleep. Not a word was exchanged, no meal was shared—nothing that would substantiate the kinship with man so broadly hinted by their bodies and faces.

Remaining firmly seated on stone, Hethor scooted over to the edge of his little territory. It was sharply defined, sheared clean off by some slide or breakage. The image of an undercut beneath the ledge kept him from the very precipice. Still, he sat close, trailing his fingers through pebbles and looking north across a sea of clouds that roofed the Bight of Benin and the African coast.

He reckoned on being at least three miles above the sea, maybe five, but there was no noticeable thinness in the air like the sailors had spoken of in their tales of high-flying airship battles with the Chinese. It was the Wall, of course. Whatever energy of Creation God had put into raising this support for His gears had encompassed the thickness of the air.

Why?

Surely a vacuum would have sufficed.

The answer came to Hethor: so that men could live upon the Wall, or even at the top. Why, he was not so sure. Perhaps to be closer to God.

The thought of men caused Hethor to look over his shoulder and make a small study of his captors.

They were so much like Gabriel in their form, though

the horrid tattoos and stringy bodies were a crude echo of the angel's perfection. These savages also seemed mute as fish, in contrast to Gabriel, or Hethor himself. Hethor wondered how they communicated. What passed between them to exchange the skills of combat, or sword smithery? Were there winged mothers somewhere mouthing silent lullabies to rude little cherubs in their stone cradles?

A thought struck him. Man was made in the image of God. The winged savages seemed to be fashioned in the image of the angels—a lesser Creation in an imitation of a lesser model.

He stared across the starlit sea of clouds for a long time, ignoring the rumbling hunger in his gut, and wondered what the golden tablet had signified.

DAWN AND a thicket of rustling noises brought wakefulness to Hethor. He'd slept through the midnight rattle high above, as well as ignoring his hunger and the persistent ache in his arms, legs, and bladder. He looked around.

He was still perched upon the ledge. So were the dozen winged savages. They were spreading their pinions wide to warm them in the morning sun. That explained the rustling noise. For the moment his captors were ignoring him.

Hethor crawled to the rim of the ledge, keeping his weight as far back as possible in case the imagined overhang was real. Peering over, he saw no cliff or rock angling forward just below him. Some distance down was an apron of meadow, dotted with pale spots that might be sheep, or mountain goats. The Wall spread gradually outward from the field, acquiring a bit of slope until it eventually met the sea in a gleaming line far below.

Four of his captors sprinted over the edge. They snapped their wings wide to circle for a few moments before folding them again to drop into a dive. Hethor watched them plunge the thousand feet or more to the meadow. The lead savage snatched one of the grazing animals right off the ground. The others flew guard as the hunter's wings beat hard, straining to bear the prey upward the same way that two of them had carried him the night before.

The sheep was deposited onto the ledge still bleating its terror. One of the other winged savages dispatched it with a sword blow to the neck. They fell upon the poor beast, tearing with fingers and mouths in a whirling mass of wool and blood and sloppy purple-red fragments.

Hethor turned away, his stomach churning. He could do nothing to shut out the slurping and crunching noises that continued for some time behind him. *We eat them too,* he thought.

Then two of the winged savages grabbed his arms, leaving bloody prints on his canvas shirt, and hauled Hethor to his feet. One of them handed him a bundle of bloody rope—no, tendons from the unlucky sheep—before making circling motions around its own waist.

He stared at the slimy, warm things flopping within his fist. What was it they wanted?

The winged savage slapped his hand—lightly, not to hurt—and made the same motions, followed by a mime of lifting.

Harness. They wanted a harness with which to carry him. It would be a less tiring method for them to fly him away. Hethor doubted it was out of any particular concern for his comfort. These creatures had been charged to deliver him somewhere, reasonably intact.

At least they weren't going to eat him like that poor sheep.

He had no idea if the tendons would hold raw and uncured, but given the way the winged savages had chased and caught him after tossing him overboard from *Bassett,* perhaps that didn't matter. He was far past the point of being horrified about falling—everything that was happening now was no less frightening than the prospect of another fall.

The tendons knotted together to about five feet in length. He would need three or four times that to form even a simple bosun's chair. Hethor gestured with his arms spread wide, showed them the bloody rope, then held up three fingers. Three more spreads of his arms.

The one who had handed him the tendons simply stepped sideways several paces and fell off the ledge, followed by several more.

They were back shortly with more clusters of sheep tendons. At least Hethor assumed they were sheep tendons. He tried not to imagine the scene in the meadow below. Taking the wretched, bloody things in hand, he set to making his ropes and from them his chair.

THEY WERE airborne, sweeping past a land of rubble and stunted trees. Hethor felt ill, having slaked his thirst on sheep's blood. That was not a good substitute for water. He hung between four of the savages, roped about his legs and chest with the stretching, bloody mess.

Looking at the ravaged country, it seemed to Hethor as though a great battle had been fought. Several times he saw creatures lumbering through the rubble. They were enormous things that gleamed of brass and crystal, but they never turned their barrel-shaped heads toward him.

The monsters were hunting each other, he presumed, until he saw the column of men.

From his vantage among his captors, Hethor could not make out many details. He tried anyway. There looked to be hundreds and hundreds of them. They were spread out along a trail through the rubble. A team of mules dragged some light artillery at the tail of the column. Squinting hard, Hethor could see men hastily digging farther up.

A firing point, he thought, in their defense against the brass-and-crystal machines.

"Ahoy!" he screamed, releasing his grip on the slick ropes of his harness to cup his hands, though that threatened to pitch him forward over the abyss. "Ahoy there!"

Two of the winged savages jerked the ropes they carried. Hethor looked up into their angry black eyes. They might not talk, but they certainly had ideas, he realized.

He considered screaming again but decided not to. Dangling over so many miles of open air, his options were limited.

The winged savages swept upward past the column. At the head, Hethor saw a Union Jack on a staff—an enormous battle flag being carried in the van. Just ahead of the flag were more soldiers firing their weapons up the hill as another of the brass-and-crystal monsters shambled down their trail. It seemed unaffected by the efforts at defense.

The world lurched with a grinding noise that rang inside Hethor's head as loudly as if a gear had stripped itself while still in his hands. Everything below stopped for a moment, men and monsters alike. Clouds of dust billowed up from the surrounding rubble. The Wall emitted a groan deep as a wounded beast the size of an entire world.

Hethor watched, his mouth frozen open, as the entire landscape of rubble and trees began to slip. A full section of the Wall was giving way, he realized. The hunting machines felt it first, swaying with their height; then a ripple of panic spread through the men in Gordon's column, their reaction visible even from Hethor's vantage.

The winged savages had beaten their way above this battlefield, but Hethor continued to stare as the land slipped away beneath him. The moving surface was but a flake off the Wall, though it looked to be forty or fifty miles wide and several miles high. It was like watching Long Island vanish.

The slide began to fold in on itself. Rocks and dust washed over the scrambling men and the machines that persecuted them, until everything was lost in a great cloud of gray. He glanced up to see towers toppling from a higher ledge, more brass and crystal like the hunting machines, shattering as they fell. Their destruction sent brass collars and domes spinning in the air, giant missiles that weighed tons.

Was the entire Wall slipping away?

Was the entire world slipping away?

He closed his eyes, grabbing tighter to the bloody ropes that bound him, unable to look. He let the roar of millions of tons of stone engulf him as surely as it had the men of Gordon's column.

Except that he could fly away. All they could do was be crushed or fall.

Still the savages flew upward and upward, while Hethor listened to the clattering of the Earth stutter, then right itself, only to stutter again. The Mainspring was indeed troubled, he thought. How far was he from the Key Perilous, and Gabriel's mission?

Climbing ever higher into the sky, Hethor wept for longer than he cared to keep count of.

THEY FLEW past wonders, Hethor and his captors, so many that the sights became commonplace.

A city carved out of a looming cliff face in the form of dozens of standing men. Each had a sloped forehead and enormous nostrils, tiny windows and balconies all about their bodies.

Fresh scars on the Wall from the earthquakes, long tails of destruction below them. Tongues of smoke and steam hissing from cracks in the erased landscape. Even once, what Hethor thought were enormous snakes or giant, sinuous lizards that must have hatched beneath the stone.

A forest of trees, each taller than any he had ever imagined, like masts for a ship of giants. Their tops burned in apparent perpetuity, while flaming birds circling the roiling orange mass.

Glaciers hanging in dark clefts, overrun with furry beasts that seemed to glow within their shadows. Larger, dimmer glows were embedded in the darkest regions of the cleft behind them.

He tired first of cataloging them. Eventually, he even

tired of witnessing them. He dropped to sleep, until he was eventually awoken by being thumped onto stone.

This was another ledge, narrower than the first. The air did feel somehow thinner and colder here, though Hethor still seemed to be in no danger of freezing. It was close to dusk once more. He glanced up to see a brassy gleam in the vertical horizon above him. Their angle continued to grow narrower, the horns of the orbital track widening to a line.

They were approaching the gears, then.

He turned to look out and down. The view made him gasp for breath. Hethor collapsed onto the ground and scooted to place his back against the stone of the Wall.

The Earth curved away below him, as if to replace the lost curve of the horns of brass in the sky. Clouds dotted the ocean like the sheep had dotted the meadow that morning. He could see the shimmery blue of daylight down there. Yet when he raised his eyes, he saw stars surrounding the moon's track, which in turn gleamed bright as he'd ever known it. Hethor thought he might reach out and touch it.

This was what the eyes of God saw. Or at least the view granted to His angels.

Hethor's gut, empty for a day, rebelled, seeking level ground and a safely familiar horizon. He leaned over to choke out the bile, the heaves in his stomach and chest preoccupying him even as his throat and nose stung. Finally, Hethor found himself studying the tiny insects that crawled among the stones of the ledge.

Anything but looking out at that terrible view again.

He leaned away from the puddle of his spew, curled tight against the rock wall, and shivered into night's darkness. Hethor wept for the men and lands that had died and wondered when his turn would come.

THE WINGED savages kicked Hethor awake the next morning. He felt shrunken, dried out. His tongue was a strip of leather. One of them handed him a broken gourd that proved to contain a small amount of water.

Where had they gotten *that*?

Hethor drank, eager but slow. He was terrified of spilling the liquid. He broke off a few fragments of the gourd for something to have in his mouth.

He was almost feeling well again until they seized his sheep-ropes and dove over the edge of the ledge. Wings snapped wide to take to the air as the gleaming dawn of the world was spread below him.

This was certainly the place where Satan had taken the Brass Christ to tempt Him with the kingdoms of the Northern Earth. Seeing the kingdoms of the Northern Earth mostly made Hethor ill and frightened, summoning a scream from his depths that he had to work to swallow without releasing.

They continued to climb, but today his previously tireless captors seemed slower. Hethor worked on his nerve, peeking through squinted eyes at the world below him now and again, trying to reverse the fear. Wherever they were taking him, "up" figured prominently. Hethor would have little use for his terror. It would not serve him on his mission from Gabriel, to find the Key Perilous and wind the Mainspring.

So he concentrated instead on his hunger and his thirst, ordinary and reasonable demands of the body however extreme they had become. He let that distraction occupy his fears while he looked across the kingdoms of the Northern Earth. Once the veil of fear was drawn aside, he saw that the world was beautiful.

THE AIR grew thinner and colder through the day, the Wall increasingly desolate. The winged savages were definitely moving even more slowly now. Either they were tiring or up here they were less buoyed by whatever supernatural power lent them the immense speed and ferocity they had displayed at the lower altitudes. Hethor began to stare upward, at the stars that shared the sunlit sky, hoping for a clear look at the brass gearing that topped the Wall.

With a rush they were over the lip of a cliff. The ground was flat instead of rising. Though the air was cold and thin, there were orchards and fields and copses of wilder woods. Behind it all, set back several miles from the cliff edge, rose a towering cliff face of brass.

Hethor looked up to see the angle of the gear teeth making a valley within the brass almost directly in front of him. He estimated at least a mile from the ground to the base of the tooth, with the angles rising past any sense of distance he could find—there was nothing by which to judge. The brass gearing was pure and unsullied, in contrast to the Wall's teeming lands of people and creatures and wondrous cities.

Here was the very touch of God's hand.

Hethor closed his eyes in silent prayer for a moment as the winged savages skimmed over the orchards. He traced the horofix in the air before him with a trembling, fearful hand. When he looked again, his captors were depositing him in front of an imposing building, releasing the sheep's tendon ropes before spiraling away on the thin air. They ignored him as though he'd never been there in the first place.

Just like that, he was alone.

The building rose in front of him in the style of one of the fabled temples of the Middle Kingdom. Somehow even the thought that the Chinese might already have conquered the Wall couldn't stir Hethor's concern. The structure was tall, perhaps four floors in height above the substantial marble foundation, with red lacquered pillars and a green tiled roof that swept to an upward curve at each end. Narrow windows almost the full height of the faded yellow walls punctuated the face of the temple—Hethor knew this had to be a temple—their frames filled with a carved wooden filigree that reminded him of the scenes woven into the wicker panels of the vertical city far, far below.

But most importantly, an ornamental pond shimmered in the walkway just in front of Hethor. Golden carp flickered among the water lilies. He staggered forward to collapse into the pool, letting the cold water enclose his sore, chapped skin, his bloody lips, sucking it into his thirsty mouth, then spitting it out almost as fast when he choked, only to drink it in again.

At that moment Hethor would have traded his soul to be a fish.

He eventually sat up, his throat and gut aching, needing desperately to urinate, and wishing that there was food to hand. Hethor solved the urgent problem first. He then briefly considered the carp before stripping a water lily loose to chew on its pale underwater root. The orchards behind him, perhaps.

It was a place to make him believe the wildest tales of the magics and sorcery of Southern Earth, as real and miraculous as the saints of the Brass Christ.

Dripping, he climbed out of the pond to stand shaky on the tiled walk. The sheep's tendons still clung to him. They were wound tight. Hethor spent some minutes working the dreadful things free. As the wind and the cold air were chilling him, he reluctantly abandoned his ideas about the orchard in favor of the shelter of the temple's pillared portico.

He glanced back as he stumbled along the walk. There were stout, hairy men among the trees now, wrapped in orange robes. None returned his looks that he could see, but Hethor thought he recognized them from the city of the stone man-towers. Or not-men, perhaps. These folk had something of apes about them in both their hairiness and in the flatness of their faces with enormous nostrils and sloped foreheads.

There were three marble stairways ascending in parallel to the temple portico. Carvings covered marble ramps between them, depicting dragons chasing clouds up their slope. Hethor chose the right-hand way. With a grip on the marble banister, he limped upward. He wanted to be out of the wind very badly. Climbing the stairs was making his legs shiver and threaten to fold flat. Even after slaking himself in the fish pond, his thirst was still great to the point of madness.

The portico at the top faced three wooden doors, each lacquered red in the Chinese fashion. These doors were as tall and almost as narrow as the windows farther along the face of the building. There were gold filigree panels inset upon them, no broader than Hethor's hand, but running high up the door. Above the doors was a large blue panel with Chinese writing on it in gold, incomprehensible as Hethor's lost tablet.

He stepped to the closest doorway and saw that the threshold was a high beam, just like in the vertical city miles below. Hethor touched the door panel with his fingertips. It swung noiselessly open. Dust-specked light beckoned from inside, golden beams falling from some high clerestory. Furniture loomed in the shadows like monsters in a well.

Hethor stepped over the high threshold. Immediately he was out of the cold wind and into a silence so profound it seemed to echo. The peace was broken only by the faintest susurration, as if someone whispered in the distance, or walked carefully in shoes of silk. The sun-dappled hall was easier to see once his eyes adjusted to the interior. Enormous tapestries hanging on the walls featured bulk-muscled devils or gods with skin of unlikely hues and far too many eyes. Low lacquered tables stood beneath the hangings, their legs slightly bowed out, each holding a vase or bowl or jade statuette. The center of the room was dominated by a great metal statue. Or perhaps it was a suit of armor. Though with a height of almost ten feet, Hethor was unsure who would wear such a thing.

The vases and bowls placed artfully about did not seem to be the sort that might contain water or food, so Hethor resolved to strike farther in. As he walked past the metal statue, one great arm shot out, a gloved fist the size of his head nearly touching Hethor's chest. It made no noise at all.

He shrieked and jumped backward. The distant sounds fell to utter silence as the armored head swiveled to face him. Was there a gleam within the dark eyeslit of the helmet?

"I need water," Hethor gasped.

The armor turned in place, still eerily quiet, then walked away from him, into the interior of the temple. Stumbling in his chill and his fright, Hethor followed it.

The journey was short, but astonishing. They passed through a series of similar rooms—high-beamed thresholds, tapestries on the wall, dusty sunlight from above— each holding different works of art or science. In his urgency to keep up with the walking armor, Hethor did not stop to look. Nonetheless some things caught his eye.

There was a boulder of jade, taller than he was, worked cunningly into the semblance of a mountain, or perhaps the face of the Equatorial Wall itself. Tiny roads were carved into it, little farms, villages, even castles and stout walls around which jade battles raged. He could have stared at that alone for hours.

Another room held a man whose waist was embedded in a tabletop. A chessboard was set in front of him. The man was turbaned and bearded like a Turk, grinning and glaring from his dark-skinned visage. Hethor, briefly startled, realized that this was an automaton—a gaming machine of some sort. Others of the same ilk lined that room, but he was still staring at the Turk as he passed through. The Turk's head swiveled to stare back.

On they went, through rooms filled with armaments and maps, animals stuffed and mounted, a demiglobe of the Northern Earth rendered in stained glass and silver. Finally the armor stopped before a set of doors that seemed no different from the rest. There it resumed its ordinary, settled state.

Hethor edged past the enormous metal thing—for all its mobility surely another automaton like the Turk, as it had never spoken or even breathed to the best of his hearing—and pushed at the middle one of this last set of doors.

The interior of the next room was white, much brighter than the dark reds and golds through which he had passed. There were wider windows and floor mats woven of welcoming straw. A man in a blue jacket sat with his back to Hethor, cross-legged on the floor, facing a low red bed or couch on which a sallow man in saffron robes sat, also cross-legged.

"Welcome," said the sallow man. Hethor realized his host was Chinese, though the man spoke ordinary English. "Your journey has been long and perilous."

The other stood and turned—it was Simeon Malgus!

"You . . . ," Hethor began, then stopped. He was shocked at seeing this man who had been lost to the winged savages.

As he himself had been lost, Hethor realized—at least from the point of view of *Bassett*'s captain and crew. Was Malgus on a mission from God as well? The navigator had hinted at such in Georgetown, when he seized Hethor's notes and warned him away from further inquiries. As for Firkin's last words to him . . . the doctor must have known Malgus' true nature.

"And you," Malgus said. "Welcome, Seaman Jacques. Though I don't suppose you're here on a sortie from Captain Smallwood."

"I was taken by those winged savages. Just as you were." *Or by you,* Hethor thought with a chill shiver of betrayal.

"They are not savages," said the Chinese gently. "All of Creation serves God, though some of His creatures pursue purposes opaque to such as you and I."

"They tore apart five of our men to capture *him*," Hethor protested. He pointed an accusing finger at Malgus.

The Chinese bowed slightly from the waist, hands

palm-to-palm in front of him. "How many died for you to be brought here?"

"At least three," Hethor said grudgingly. "Probably more."

"Are you to blame?"

"No, I—"

"When people fight them," Malgus interrupted, "they fight back."

"But—" Hethor stopped himself. Then: "You sent them, didn't you?"

Malgus' face flickered with the ghost of a smile. "I no more call the winged savages than I can call the storm."

Hethor gave the Chinese a long, slow look. "You, then? They did not come to me on their own."

"Who am I to say?" He tipped his head forward. "Enough," he said. "I neglect my hospitality to you." He pressed his palms together again. "I am the abbot of the Jade Temple. The esteemed Mister Malgus you already know." He paused. The silence invited Hethor to speak.

Hethor stopped, took a deep breath. "I am Hethor Jacques, a seaman on Her Imperial Majesty's ship *Bassett,* of late stolen away by those creatures. I began as a clockmaker's apprentice of New Haven, Connecticut. In New England. In America. And I am very thirsty and hungry."

"I know where Connecticut is," said the Jade Abbot gently. "And I know what it means to suffer terrible thirst and hunger." He clapped his hands once, very gently. Hairy men of the same race as those in the orchards outside promptly streamed into the room. Their robes were orange as well, and their hairy feet were bare.

This group brought trays to set before the Jade Abbot, Simeon Malgus, and Hethor, along with great ewers of water, lengths of linen, and a small stool for Hethor to sit upon. They came and went in one lengthy, sinuous movement, as the waves wrapped around the rocks upon the Connecticut beaches. They left only their offerings behind.

Hethor studied his tray for a moment, even as he reached a trembling hand for a ceramic cup of crystal water. There were dates, olives, apricots, along with a seed-covered dark purple fruit he could not name. Little balls of rice with bits of vegetable in them. Flat leaves rolled up around yellow paste. A small bowl of steaming soup that smelled both alien and delicious.

Chinese cooking? Hethor had heard of monkey brains and dog stew and warm plates of slugs. This food was appetizing, almost ordinary even in its unfamiliarity.

Malgus had a similar tray, but the Jade Abbot's held only two dates and a pomegranate. Hethor sipped his water as the Jade Abbot folded his hands again.

"Homage to the Divine, homage to the Spirit, homage to the Community," said the Abbot. "Blessing on this food and those who made it."

"Thanks be to God," Hethor said. He knew a prayer when he heard one, even if it was to some heathen Chinese deity.

For a while he became lost in the flavors on the tray. The fruits were wonderfully fresh, the seed-covered one filled with a tart, fibrous flesh pale as ice. The rice balls were tangy, the soup vinegary and sour and peppery all at once, while the paste within the leaves proved to be an unexpected admixture of bananas and corn. The smells wove with the tastes to settle Hethor's stomach and smooth his sense of self back to something resembling the ordinary.

Hethor finally emerged from the spell of the food to find both the Jade Abbot and Simeon Malgus studying him. The Abbot had not touched his sparse meal. Malgus snacked slowly.

"I'm sorry," Hethor said, unsure what he was apologizing for.

The Jade Abbot smiled. "Sometimes there is immense pleasure in observing the satisfaction of others."

"Feel better?" Malgus asked.

Hethor poured out some more water and took a long

drink before answering. "Yes," he said, "though I expect I should clean my clothes soon."

Malgus nodded, with the ghost of a wink.

The Jade Abbot smiled. "Now that you are rested and returned to sound mind, how may I help you?"

Hethor studied Malgus for a moment. "What is he doing here? For that matter, what am I doing here?"

The Jade Abbot also stared at Malgus, who cleared his throat and stared briefly at his hands before meeting Hethor's eye.

"As should be clear to you, I am not merely an officer in Her Imperial Majesty's navy." Malgus sighed. "I took an oath at my commission, which I continue to regard seriously. But I also serve other, higher callings."

Nothing is higher than this place, Hethor thought, *save the gears themselves*.

Malgus continued. "On the other side of the Equatorial Wall lies the Southern Earth. It is vastly different from our contentious, industrialized Northern Earth. Where we have smoky mills and laboring children and great cities of brick and wood, the Southern Earth has cathedral forests whose dwellers live free of misery, without even the need of labor for their daily fare. Where we have competing empires shaking the very air with the thunder of their cannon, the Southern Earth shakes to the thunder of hooves as great beasts migrate across endless plains. Where England and China each struggle to bend Creation to their will, the Southern Earth abides comfortably in the lap of God's world. As man was meant to do."

"So you are an agent of the South?"

"No, no." Malgus shook his head, irritated. "It is not so simple. There is no 'South,' in the sense that there is a China or an England. There are just races, the hairy men and the fliers among them, who live side by side with men very similar to ourselves. There are animals and forests and oceans untrammeled by steel and flags. If I am an agent, I suppose I am an agent of Creation." His voice trailed off a moment; then Malgus gave Hethor a look that was almost haunted. "But yes, it could be said that in part I serve the interests of those who abide in the Southern Earth."

Hethor was skeptical, but could not find it in himself to be scandalized. "As well as your oath to the queen?"

"In a practical sense," said the Jade Abbot in a pleasant voice. "Do not be swift to judgment. Malgus takes counsel with me from time to time. I have certain . . . counterparts on both sides of the Wall. Every soul has its place in Creation. Some of us are blessed with an occasional glimpse of how those places are fitted together."

He would find no higher, holier destination than this, Hethor realized. As best he could tell, Malgus had never betrayed his trusts, not directly. Though he supposed Captain Smallwood might see that question quite differently. Nevertheless, the Jade Abbot was a man closer to God than Hethor ever would be.

"So you are holy, and Malgus is worthy. What about me? At least three men died to bring me here. Why?"

"Were you not bound upward already?" the Jade Abbot asked gently.

"I am searching for . . ." He had been so cautious of his tale, since the disaster at the viceroy's court in Boston. Perhaps it was time to entrust his story to words again. "I met the archangel Gabriel," Hethor blurted. "He came to me in New Haven with a message. Was he one of those winged sav—flyers?"

"Are you a savage?" The Jade Abbot's eyes sparkled with amusement.

"No. Neither do I resemble an angel."

"There are many races here upon the Wall and in the Southern Earth," Malgus said. "Different images of God's will, perhaps. But if your angel spoke to you, he was not of the winged folk. Manlike though they are, and of some little intelligence, the fliers do not have the gift of speech. Their blessings lie elsewhere. As do their services."

"Angels are what you make of them," the Abbot said.

"Up here in the sky, so close to the gears, we hear the voice of God every day when the track of the world thunders overhead. I have never seen a messenger of Heaven in the flesh, though there are signs aplenty of God's will in the world."

He leaned forward slightly, communicating a certain eagerness. "If you have truly seen an angel, you are blessed. You would be welcome and more than welcome to remain here in the Jade Temple. You would be a member of our community of spirit, and take part in the nightly Sacrament of Listening."

"No," said Hethor, blushing. He had no desire to live here in the thin, cold air among hairy men and walking statues. Even so, the invitation was a balm to him. *Bassett* had been home, however briefly. Before that, Master Bodean's house. Here was another home, freely offered. It was tempting. "I must be free to move on. Gabriel's message was a warning. The Mainspring of the world is running down. I must find the Key Perilous and wind it again."

Hethor crossed his arms and set his lips, awaiting scorn and worse.

Malgus did not disappoint. The Englishman burst into laughter. "The Key Perilous? You've been reading too many penny dreadfuls, boy. Or drinking belowdecks with entirely the wrong sort of Spiritualists."

Hethor cringed at the navigator's words.

"Simeon." The Jade Abbot's voice was a warning.

"I'm sorry, boy," Malgus said, his tone gentler now. "You were taken in by a mummer or a magic lantern show."

"Perhaps," the Jade Abbot said. "But there truly is a Key Perilous."

Hethor stared at the Abbot, his humiliation forgotten as quickly as it had arrived. Malgus wheezed, as if he struggled to raise objections.

"It is real enough," the Jade Abbot continued. "Though certainly legendary as well. When your Christ was broken on the wheel-and-gear of Roman punishment, He left you seven Great Relics. The Key Perilous is one of those."

"Where is it?" asked Hethor.

"I do not know." The Jade Abbot smiled. "But there are those who might. Christ's word has never found favor in the Southern Earth. The Equatorial Wall blocks much besides the guns of Englishmen from crossing over. But the Relics did cross, centuries ago and more. There are wise men in the South who may well know where to find the Key Perilous.

"Whether your vision of Gabriel was false or true I have no way to say. But there is something wrong with our days of late. The gear has slipped, and the Wall shakes like a dog awakening from sleep. You are the first person to bring a theory to my ears that is neither sheer foolishness nor self-serving."

The Jade Abbot gave Malgus a long look, then turned his small smile back to Hethor. "I feel free to say that Simeon would be pleased to escort you over the Wall and down the other side. There he can help you find and meet with these sages of the Southern Earth who might guide you further in your quest."

Malgus choked on his water, setting his ceramic mug down as he sprayed the woven mat at his feet. "I have important work afoot in London and Damascus," he cried. "My contacts in Boston bear fruit, and I—"

"Simeon," the Jade Abbot said again in that quiet voice. "Other men and women will carry your standard a while. This is a chance unplanned for by any of us. We should bow to God's will, even when His hand touches us unlooked for. Especially when you are fit to lead him across and down the other side, and you are here now. There is no coincidence in this world."

"I will of course bow to your wishes," Malgus said stiffly, "as you have heard my protests and judged them according to your wisdom. If we are to go this midnight, I must make preparations." He stood. With a nod to Hethor, he stalked from the room.

"I have to believe this is the right thing," Hethor said. "But it is so easy for me to doubt." Was he ready for the Southern Earth? Going beyond the Wall was an irrevocable step.

"When the angel came to you in New Haven," the Jade Abbot said, "did it give you a map, a compass, instructions to follow?"

"No. Just a warning."

"So without knowing what the right thing was to do, you found your way here."

"Yes. Through peril and happenstance." *And perfidy*, he thought, but this did not seem the time to complain of his ill treatment at the hands of William of Ghent. For one, Hethor had never been certain what if any connection pertained between the sorcerer and Simeon Malgus.

"It seems to be a great happenstance indeed that you are here. Many hands must have touched your journey. A prayer shared across miles and days. Is this not true?"

Hethor nodded, thinking of Librarian Childress and the viceroy's man Phelps and all the other people who'd helped him. Even Pryce Bodean had advanced his cause, in a peculiar way. It seemed odd that the petty, vengeful divinity student might have been working God's will. Or perhaps they all followed some strange magic from beyond the Wall. Drawn forward by the Key Perilous, as it were. *Even William?* He wondered.

"Trust the divine," the Jade Abbot said, "and you will be rewarded. You have not been wrong so far."

"Many have died," Hethor whispered, thinking of the earthquakes and the attacks. "Lost their lives so that I might reach this place."

"The world winds down. This is the reason for your journey. So their lives would have been lost regardless of your passage, yes?"

"Perhaps." Hethor felt miserable. "Probably."

"The account does not lie with you. It was time for their souls to pass onward and follow the wheel once more."

"Maybe. But I would not like to be the reason for their deaths." Hethor paused to frame his thoughts. "Still . . . sir . . ."

"Yes?"

"The way Malgus laughed. It was not he who sent the savages to tear me from *Bassett* and carry me up here. He would not have troubled to do so."

"No, I think not."

"So it must have been you, right?"

There was a long, thoughtful silence. The Jade Abbot's smile deepened. Finally he said, "You do the work of Heaven. Are not all the ranks of the celestial realm arrayed in support of your mission?"

"But the winged savages are not angels," Hethor said.

"Indeed." The Jade Abbot clapped his hands. "You need a bath, some sound sleep, and at your age, I would imagine another meal soon as well."

The subject was clearly closed. Following his host's lead, Hethor glanced at the Jade Abbot's sparse tray. "You are not so old, sir, to live each day on three fruits and the thin air of this high place."

The Jade Abbot laughed. "You may guess at my age, young man, but you will never arrive at the truth. Now go."

In response to the summons, two of the saffron-robed hairy men took Hethor by hallways different from those he had entered through. These were more ordinary, with shelves to hold linens and little cabinets that smelled of fruit and wine. They left him soaking in a great wooden tub with long-handled brushes and three differently scented cakes of soap. Sleep took him there, lying in water stained with sheep's blood and the dirt of the Wall, but Hethor was beyond caring.

MALGUS ROUSTED him out of the tub some hours later. Hethor was glad enough of that—the waters had cooled to a chill bath indeed. His muscles were cramping.

"Come on, then," Malgus growled. "We'll attend the Sacrament of Listening. We're to set out immediately afterward. It's a toilsome journey, with no time to be made up in case of error. Trust me, you don't want to be caught out there."

"Out where?"

"Among the gear teeth. From here, the only sensible crossing is up the brass and right over. Believe you me, that's dangerous business."

The gears themselves. Hethor marveled at the thought, to see up close how God in His wisdom cut gears. He wondered what files one would use to shape the movements of an entire world.

"Quit smiling like a fool and get dressed." Malgus shoved an odd, quilted suit at Hethor. "Wear this, and the boots I've brought you. It's damned cold up there. The weather won't be much better coming down the other side. Not till we've gotten to honest, horizontal African soil."

Hethor took the garment. He rubbed the quilting between a thumb and forefinger. It was much lighter in weight than he might have expected from the look of it, and promised to be quite warm.

"Lieutenant . . . why did the Abbot send the winged savages for me?"

"Both of us," said Malgus roughly. "And I couldn't say. For the sake of the white bird, perhaps. He listens to different voices than you or I can hear."

That wasn't any better answer than Hethor could have given himself, but it was probably the only answer he would receive. *On to more practical subjects,* he thought. "When's the Sacrament of Listening?"

"Less than an hour. I've arranged for the rest of the equipment we shall need to be set aside by Heaven's Ladder. Clean up your hair, boy, get dressed, and meet me in the Orchid Garden."

"And where is the Orchid Garden?" There was no answer, as Malgus was already pushing his way out of the lavatorium door.

Hethor smiled. There was no reason for him to be happy, running from danger to danger, but for the first time he felt a sense of purpose. He was finally in control of his own destiny and the charter given him by the archangel Gabriel.

He pressed the clean, fresh-scented cloth of the quilted suit against his cheek. He'd never worn clothes so fine, for all that their quality and warmth bespoke a cold the like of which he'd never known before. The Key Perilous seemed once more within his reach. For good or ill, he had the guide who had been recommended to him so long ago back in New England.

"God meant you to help me, Simeon Malgus," Hethor whispered. He began to dress himself.

MONKS KNELT on mats, a mix of hairy men and humans as Hethor understood his kind to be, though like the Jade Abbot some were of races strange to him. A few were of a much smaller kind, furtive and wispy, almost like he might have imagined the children of the hairy men to be. But their bodies were of the wrong shape for youths of that species, too slight of chest and face, and legs over-long. And they kept to themselves.

He saw no winged folk among the worshipers. Savage or otherwise.

The Jade Abbot knelt on a mat in the front row, though he was set no higher up or farther forward than his fellow monks. To one side, a serious young fellow with the red hair and ruddy skin of a Vinlander or Norseman rang a bell. Incense drifted across the Orchid Garden. The flowers gleamed dimly in the pale glow of the rising moon. Hethor could see the pale, fleshy blossoms hanging among dark trees themselves twisted by wind and careful pruning. A drifting mist lent a jeweled cast to each flower so that the whole garden became a work of beauty.

At the head of the garden, where the land sloped upward, the brass cliff of the gears erupted from the soil to rise skyward. It was smooth as any fresh-hammered sheet for all that the Wall went on to the east and west as far as Hethor could see. The metal shot straight up from him as if it were the edge of the world.

Which, in a sense, it was.

A wooden scaffold clung to the brass cliff. A steep stairway wound back and forth across the frames. *That would be Heaven's Ladder,* Hethor thought. He wondered how his legs would handle the climb, especially with the rapid hike across the breadth of the gear teeth that must follow.

The bell rang again even as a low rumble echoed from the east. The monks chanted in a vibrating language more an answer to the rumbling of God's gears than like any words Hethor had ever heard. The rumbling grew, the noise broadening and deepening into a echoing version of the clatter of the world that Hethor had sometimes heard far down below on the surface of the Earth.

The noise bloomed louder and louder. He began to feel it in the bones of his face, in his wrists and ankles, within his chest. The rumble became so much the dominant force in Hethor's senses that it passed out of the realm of sound, the way the pain of his lashing had surpassed his sense of self, or the way the great storms buffeting *Bassett* had become forces of their own, exempt from the rules of rain and wind.

Even though those around him knelt in prayer, Hethor stared upward. He saw far-distant teeth flash in sunlight, the Earth's orbital track approaching like a falling tower of brass. He screamed to balance the pressure in his ears, his head squeezed to nothing by the divine force of the passing of midnight, ready to throw himself from the distant cliff in a final, plunging sacrament of his own. How could any man face such absolute proof of God's hand in His universe and remain sane and whole?

Then it was gone, the noise and pressure and pain. Blood trickled from his ears and nose. The Norseman still rang the bell, the monks still chanted, but Hethor felt like his body had been riven apart by the sounds of passage and reformed anew.

Malgus touched his arm. "Are you well, boy? Not everyone can appreciate this particular rite."

"I have survived." Hethor realized he was shouting over the echoes inside his head.

"They're at prayer a while longer here," Malgus told him, "but we must be swiftly on our way."

Hethor stumbled behind Malgus to the base of Heaven's Ladder. There, two small packs lay, along with some leather water bags. "I think I expected more equipment."

"Light and fast," Malgus said. "None of this will be needful on the other side." He tugged something out of one pack—it was a pair of small wedges, with buckles and straps. "When we get up top, you'll need to put these on your boots. There's buckles and straps for them."

"Why?"

"You'll see. I'll go first. That way if you fall, you won't hurt me."

THE CLIMB was hellish, if only for its height. Hethor guessed they ascended almost two miles of stairs. The scaffolding grew lighter, thinner, more delicate, until the last part of the upward journey was made on springy bamboo ladders of a single pole, with small points of wood pounded into them for hand- and footholds. These were lashed end-to-end. Hethor could not see how the ladders kept their balance under his weight and Malgus'.

His quilted suit grew hot under the strain, sweat pooling across his back and down his limbs. Even the light pack became a leaden weight. His arms were wooden blocks that banged against his side as he climbed, bruising his chest with his own elbows.

There was no more ladder, but rather a narrow vee cut into the brass. Malgus, climbing ahead of Hethor, slipped perhaps two yards inward. He now braced his back against the vee to strap the wedges from his pack to his boots.

"Ah," said Hethor. The wedges were what would allow them to walk at a reasonable pace across the bottom of the vee. He pulled himself after Simeon, dreadfully glad to be off the ladder, and studied the bottom of the cut as his nerve-dead arms fought his efforts to open his pack and extract his own wedges.

"This gear is wrought as fine as any handwork," Hethor told Malgus. "If I had a glass and a micrometer, I'd wager it narrows down to the limit of my vision."

"This is God's work, boy," Malgus said. "What do you expect? Sloppy shortcuts?"

Given some of the rest of Creation, such as Pryce Bodean, Hethor wasn't sure how to answer that. He settled for strapping on the wedges. They resembled the heels of a woman's fancy dress shoe, except that the angle ran from left to right, or vice versa, rather than front to back, so the soles were on a severe bias.

Wedges strapped on, Hethor tried to stand. He immediately slipped. His left leg plunged down into the vee until the wedge on his boot jammed into place.

"People have broken legs doing that," Malgus said dryly. "I wouldn't fancy a climb back down the other side with such an injury. Watch me." Facing away from Hethor, Malgus used his hands and the main strength of his arms to balance himself in the vee, settled his feet carefully, then walked a few steps away in a gliding motion more similar to ice skating than any normal land-bound gait.

Hethor imitated Malgus' movements. That got him settled on the wedges, whereupon he stumbled forward. He thought of skating on the Quinnipiac River in winter, and tried to smooth out his footwork accordingly.

"Not bad," Malgus said grudgingly. "Before we set out, a quick stop for food and water."

"How long?" Hethor asked. "How far?"

"Twenty miles edge to edge. A hard hike at the pace forced by these shoes, before midnight next, but we'll make it." Malgus took a long drink from his water skin, then slung it over his shoulder. "Unless you'd like to turn back?"

"I didn't come here just to go home again," Hethor said with a twinge. There was no home to go to. He was a failed apprentice in Connecticut, under order of imprisonment in Massachusetts, and absent without leave from the Royal Navy. Southern Earth could only be an improvement. "Onward, sir. Onward."

WALKING WAS miserable work. Hethor's ankles kept wanting to roll inward from the slope of the vee, threatening at any moment to sprain or strain. Which would be deadly if they could not make their way back before the next meshing of the Earth's gear with its orbital track.

Even keeping his hands on the walls of the vee for balance was troublesome. The brass was cold, like a great metal glacier. The chill seeped through the quilted suit. Hands palm down on the metal, even through gloves, seemed to multiply the cooling effect. Hands away from the metal resulted in him slipping all the more, losing his balance or the position of his feet.

Malgus slowly pulled ahead. "I'm not waiting for you, boy," he called back. "If you fall too far behind, we'll meet on the other side. If you make it."

Hethor struggled on, ignoring Malgus' words. It only made sense. If he, Hethor, failed in his crossing, there was no need for them both to be ground between the gears as a result. Arriving ahead of Hethor, Malgus could clear the way on the far side of the gear. Nonetheless, Hethor felt obscurely betrayed by the sense of abandonment, disappointed in some way that seemed illogical even to him.

Even stopping for natural necessity seemed both wasteful of precious time, and somehow blasphemous. Urinating on the gears of God was wrong. Not that he had much choice.

Three hours to climb Heaven's Ladder, he thought, moving on from his third such pause. The process of opening his crotch had let too much cold air inside his quilted suit, and his mind wandered in search of a distraction. Three hours down the other side. That left eighteen hours to cross twenty miles of brass. He'd been struggling for four hours and some, but he had no sense of how far he'd gotten. Daylight had arrived and Malgus was still visible in the distance ahead, so Hethor couldn't be in that much trouble.

Until he realized the sound he heard over his rough breathing was Malgus cursing.

Hethor caught up with his guide soon enough. Malgus was still working his way through a lengthy run of naval imprecations mixed with several other languages, along with a number of terms Hethor had never heard before.

"What is it?" he called from just behind.

Malgus looked over his shoulder. "There's something here."

Hethor's heart suddenly felt as cold as his face and hands. This could be their death warrant. "Is it big? Are we trapped?"

"No. That's not the problem. You don't understand. Nothing's *ever* here. How could it be? The wheels of the universe grind everything to dust once a day." Malgus sighed. "I'm trying to figure what this means, if we should turn back. There's still time."

"What is it?"

Malgus bent, grunting, picked something up, then turned to pass it back to Hethor.

It was a golden tablet, with the same strangely scratched writing as the one he'd found in the vertical city. Exactly the same writing.

"It's a message." Hethor's heart was exultant as any flight of birds. "For me."

Malgus shook his head. "Anything might be true, but I'll be damned if I know why you think that. But if it's yours, sobeit. You must carry it. As for me, I plan to live to see the other side." He shuffled ahead, walking at a pace that even Hethor realized was too fast.

Hethor hugged the tablet to his chest, then opened his quilted suit to slip it inside. His torso nearly froze with the influx of frigid air, and the tablet poked into his belly most unpleasantly. Hethor didn't care.

Gabriel was still watching over him.

This was where he needed to be.

A faint vibration in the brass around him stirred Hethor to motion once more. He might need to be here, but only to pass through. Shuffling in his ice-skater walk, Hethor scuttled after Simeon Malgus as quickly as his wedge-soled boots would allow.

THE TRIP across the brass vee devolved into a painful nightmare of strained leg muscles, freezing hands, and sheer exhaustion. Hethor's lips froze together at one point. The gold tablet within his suit refused to warm—rather it continued to impart a chill to his chest and gut that made his lungs shudder and his heart race. With the coming of dusk, he lost sight of Malgus toiling ahead of him. The sense of isolation brought Hethor nearly to the point of despair.

"Oh, God," he said, stumbling along the vee, "You did not bring me this far to abandon me. Grant me strength, please, to carry on Your work."

By way of answer, Hethor heard a faint clatter. He was heartened by this echo of the music of the world until he realized the clatter was slowly getting louder, accompanied by a rumble.

The gear! The track was approaching!

Hethor began to run, fast as he could on the wedge-shaped clogs, glancing up. Earth's orbital track glimmered close above, a brass roof blocking out what should be his view of the stars.

"Malgus!" Hethor shrieked. "Don't let me die here."

He ran harder, fighting the weakness in his ankles and

calves. The tablet dug in at his waist so hard as to draw blood. Under his steadying hands, the brass walls of the vee felt warmed, as if the approaching contact with the orbital ring were transmitting heat.

The clatter built toward the mind-blanking roar he'd heard at the Sacrament of Listening. Then louder. In the Orchid Grove, he'd been two miles below the gearing, without metal walls around him to amplify the sound.

The same metal walls that would amplify *him* to so much grease. Where was the end!?

"Simeon, help!"

Soon, Hethor could no longer hear his own breathing. His right foot slipped. The wedge-shaped clog tore free from the boot. Hethor found himself prone at the bottom of the vee, sobbing his fear. Not knowing what else to do, he pulled himself onward, scuttling like a silverfish trapped within the pages of a book as the roar washed over him, blanking out all thoughts except the sheer terror of survival.

The brass teeth of the orbital track came for Hethor.

SEVEN

A CHILL breeze worried at Hethor's face. His legs felt peculiar, or more to the point, they didn't feel at all. He could sense his heart beating, but there was no sound.

He opened his eyes, or tried to. The lids seemed stuck together.

His right arm wiggled, but it did not move. Something was wrong with his head, too, Hethor realized. It was hot, and felt heavy as one of *Bassett*'s cannonballs.

Was he back on the airship somehow?

His left arm was free from entanglement. Hethor reached to rub his eyes, fought an unaccustomed heaviness in his hand, and discovered his lids coated with a sticky grit.

Scabbed blood.

Hethor tried to shout his fear, but though his chest heaved, nothing happened.

I am struck dumb, he thought. So this is death . . . silence, and near-immobility.

Somehow, that didn't make sense.

He swiped again at the blood sealing his eyes. The left lid fluttered open, revealing something huge far above him.

Then Hethor understood the world. He was hanging up-side down, nothing but empty air between him and the ledge at the top of the southern side of the Wall. He did not want to think how far down that would be. The inverted po-sition certainly explained the heaviness in his head.

He spent the next few minutes heaving his guts while trying to hold perfectly still against a spinning rush of panic that threatened to rob him of all his faculties. The world remained silent, too silent, but in his fear, he did not have time to consider this. Hethor kept his eyes firmly shut and tried to calm himself.

Concentrate on one thing at a time, he thought. Just like trigonometry. Break the problem down; solve it in steps.

Step one. He was alive.

Step two. His left arm worked.

What about the other arm?

Careful to look only in that direction, Hethor saw that his right arm was still enclosed in the quilted suit, which had snagged on a bamboo stub protruding from a pole.

He could have shouted for joy. He was on the other part of Heaven's Ladder, on the southern side of the Equatorial Wall. Upside down was . . . not good . . . but much, much better than dead. Encouraged, he checked on his feet.

One boot was missing; the other seemed to be in tat-ters. His legs, loyal to the last, were wrapped around the very top of the pole. Leather strips from the tattered boot and bits of the quilted suit formed a knot that kept Hethor hanging.

The gears. He had survived the gears, somehow squeezed out of the end of the vee at the last possible mo-ment, though his boots seemed to have been caught. This time, he did shout for joy.

Nothing came out.

He shouted again, paying careful attention as he did so.

The air puffed in his mouth. His throat buzzed. His lips moved.

I am deaf, but alive. It was still a small price, Hethor told himself.

Back to the trigonometry of survival. Should he unhook his right arm, or his legs next? Which was less likely to send him tumbling thousands of yards down the brass cliff face?

In fact, with both hands free and cautiously working on the accidental bindings of his foot, Hethor tore something loose despite his best efforts and went sliding upside down along the bamboo pole ladder. The ladder on this side had been unfortunately damaged as well, either by Malgus or by his precipitous arrival. Each of the stubbed handholds jerked him back, but his weight pulled him past. He could see the cloth at his ankles unwinding to set him all too free.

Desperate, Hethor grabbed the pole with his hands, accepting a bone-numbing bruise, just as his ankles tore loose. He flipped in place and continued to slide feetfirst. This time he hung on with nearly frozen hands and knees, praying for a stop before a crosspiece tore out his thighs and crotch, or simply smashed his face.

Hethor finally came to a halt resting on his shoulders, legs up in the air on the highest of the scaffold platforms. He rolled aside just in time to dodge two of the pole ladders falling free from the brass face of the gear. He watched them spin away into the two-mile-deep darkness below, took a deep breath, and followed the poles at a slightly less hurried pace down the scaffold stairs.

He had to catch Malgus before his reluctant guide left the ledge on errands of his own.

HETHOR REACHED level ground as light flashed over the curve of the eastern horizon. The world here spread as it had on the other side, a tempting array of lands and kingdoms bordered by broad ocean, in a view that pulled at his eyes and gut much as it had before. Hethor did not have time for such distraction. He had to find Malgus.

A broken trail led away through a riotous mass of bushes that might once have been a garden. There were signs of recent passage. Malgus, of course. Hethor followed, moving as fast as his nearly crippled feet would allow him to.

After a long, hilly descent, he came out just above an enormous building—a twin, Hethor realized, of the Jade Temple. This one was in obvious disrepair. Holes gaped in the roof, and there were mottled patches where exterior plastering or stonework had fallen away.

Reasoning that Malgus might be somewhere within, Hethor hobbled around the near end of the building. Gardens and orchards stretched away toward the rim of the Wall, as neglected as the building. Small figures in white rags ghosted among the trees, perhaps the Southern exemplars of the same race as the littlest monks of the Jade Temple on the Northern side.

Hethor found the main entrance and looked up at the doors, which gaped open like missing teeth. He turned to look along the walkway toward the edge. A man-sized figure was visible in the gloom.

Hethor tried to shout, "Malgus," but there was no sound. He ran, the pain lancing up his legs and right into his head, still screaming silently.

The figure turned. In the rising twilight of morning it resolved itself to be *Bassett*'s navigator.

His guide began talking, jabbing a finger at Hethor, who slowed to a limping stumble and pointed at his ears.

"Can't hear," his lips tried to say. "Deaf."

Malgus looked puzzled for a moment, then nodded. Hethor could see that the navigator was laughing at him. Malgus mimed something long and thin falling, bouncing, then pointed up, and at Hethor.

He must have seen the poles fall, Hethor thought, *and therefore knew I was alive.*

Malgus picked up one of two heavy packs at his feet and shouldered it, nudging the other one toward Hethor.

Hethor pointed to his own distressed feet. "Need help."

The navigator shook his head and settled his new pack onto his back. It also strapped around his waist and groin, seeming to wrap him in a leather web.

Hethor picked his own up and positioned all the straps in the same fashion, though he did not understand their purpose. Somewhere coming off the brass gear, he'd lost the smaller pack Malgus had given him back at the Jade Temple.

Malgus pointed downward, jerking his hand, before turning to sprint along the grass-crazed marble walkway toward the cliff edge. Hethor stumbled after him, wondering if the man had gone completely crackers. Malgus spread his arms as he ran, as if expecting to leap into the air and fly, before doing just that—leaping off the little balcony at the end of the walkway and into empty space.

Hethor pulled himself short at the marble railing to see Malgus falling through the air. The navigator's arms and legs were spread in the "X" shape of the clockwork Christ.

Parachutes, Hethor thought. These were parachutes, just like the sailors used on *Bassett.* Which conjured immediate and unpleasant memories of his jump at Hamilton, and of the loblolly boy falling into darkness below the vertical city.

"I can't do it," he tried to say. But what else could he do? Even if he hadn't destroyed the top of Heaven's Ladder, Hethor was in no shape to recross the brass desert of the gears by himself. It might literally be the work of a lifetime to climb the miles upon miles down from here to the surface of the Southern Earth on foot. Even assuming he healed well enough and he could somehow find new boots in the ruined temple. Not even considering earthquakes, monsters, and suchlike.

But the jump frightened him so very, very much.

He realized that the little hairy men in their rags were approaching. They tossed stones and dung ahead of them. Some carried large sticks, wielding them as spears or prods.

This was why Malgus had been so rushed. He'd been concerned about opposition. Alone and wounded, Hethor could not fight these creatures off. Deaf, he could not negotiate.

Hethor turned, stepped with a wince up onto the marble railing, and let himself pitch forward, screaming so loudly that even in his deafness his skull hurt from it.

AIR BATTERED him, slapped him, pinched him, violent as a storm wind. Hethor imitated Malgus' "X" shape, and found he could follow the navigator downward, steering his body by twisting his arms and legs. The blue-black of the aether, the approaching fire of the sun, the lazy curves of Earth below—all symbols of his failure. He was wounded, deaf, on the wrong side of the Wall, sure to lose track of Simeon Malgus somewhere between here and honest soil.

He had failed the archangel Gabriel, and in failing Gabriel, had betrayed the Tetragrammaton. Now he plunged through the thin blanket of air that surrounded the Equatorial Wall, to arrive a victim in some land he would likely never know the name of.

What if he didn't open his parachute? What if he fell all the way to the ocean, let the warm waters of the Southern Earth swallow him whole? His bad luck would be erased. Gabriel could find another champion.

Then Hethor remembered the tablet still digging into his waist and chest. Words brought by an angel, a message from God, that he had yet to read.

Whipped by the wind, Hethor was still moved to unbutton the top of his quilted suit. He tugged the tablet to the resulting opening and tucked his chin down to his chest to stare at it, as though he could will the words to meaning. They were close, somehow, very close, but simply not present for him. Like when he had first tried to learn Latin.

Looking ahead into the far-distant lands of his descent, Hethor watched Malgus, watched the shape of lands he'd never before seen, watched the clouds grow closer, and the ocean beneath them. Malgus seemed to be steering toward the coast. Presumably he had some port city in mind for his destination.

Assuming the people of Southern Earth bothered with shipping. Malgus had made it sound like a Heaven, all paradise and lions-and-lambs.

Hethor steered after his guide, growing bored even with this glorious view. His earlier despair had given way in the face of first magnificence, then silence, so that in time he reached the same neutral mental state that the Sacrament of Listening had induced.

A bit less than an hour later when Simeon Malgus finally opened his parachute, Hethor discovered that he did not know how to do the same.

Morning light flooded the sky now. The sun shone brilliant on his frost-damaged, bloody hands as Hethor fumbled for snaps or straps or handles or anything that would allow him to release the parachute, to do something other than hit the water like Milton's Lucifer on his final descent into the ice.

Nothing. There was *nothing*.

Hethor screamed his frustration again, though Malgus was much too far away to hear it, and drifting east as Hethor plunged past the navigator's altitude.

What could he do? How could he cheat death yet one more time?

Hethor twisted onto his back, losing sight of Malgus to look up the expanse of the Wall rising above him like the world turned on edge. *Trust in Heaven,* he thought, *and the riches of the world will be yours.* He worked the golden tablet all of the way out from under his quilted suit and took a long look at the crazy-handed writing. He then held it to his chest, trying to catch the morning sunlight to make it flash upward.

God's words make a glorious heliograph.

Refusing to look at the uprushing ocean, Hethor stayed on his back, signaling toward the top of the Equatorial Wall as he counted out the remaining seconds of his life. Help would come, or death would.

They had come for him before, after all, help flying on death's wings.

His ankles, already damaged, nearly separated from his shins as two of the winged savages caught him from below and behind. Their pinions beat upward to pull Hethor out of his fall. He flipped over, head down, and lost his grip on the golden tablet. It tumbled away like a tiny, square shooting star to meet the sea perhaps a hundred feet below.

Hethor's rescuers shifted their grip to his calves, then thighs, trying to hold him in a way that didn't threaten to dismember him. He was beyond caring. He closed his eyes and prayed, really prayed, thanking God for his life in a deep and heartfelt way that he had not experienced since he was a little boy.

Losing the words of God a second time seemed almost as great a disaster as losing his life and failing in his mission.

Eventually the winged savages shifted their stance to take Hethor by his arms and chest. They flew him for a while over a mud-banked coastline, then across an endless topography of jungle treetops not so different from those of Guyana. Which led Hethor to wonder if the Southern Earth was a sort of mirror to the Northern, until he fell asleep in their arms.

HETHOR AWOKE, still in the air, now over beautiful meadows crossed with vast herds of animals he couldn't identify. Trees stood alone or in copses. There were small villages of wood and mud huts by watercourses. *This* was the bucolic paradise described by Simeon Malgus.

He had grown closer to his rescuers as well, matching their muteness with his deafness. This time they had come to him without drawn swords or blood in their eyes.

Or perhaps they were his captors now.

Strong wings bore him over more jungle, and a green-gray river in which toothy logs swam against the current, over a rising set of hills, before circling a valley filled with more jungle. Either the land had risen or they had descended, because Hethor could see enormous butterflies of every color, birds in their flocks, animals leaping among the trees. It smelled verdant and fecund, with that same sharp, startling reek as the jungles surrounding Georgetown. Though the trees and their teemings had a distinctly different flavor here.

Only the shrieks and screams and cackles of the jungle were missing. His ears were lost in fog. The gears had spared Hethor his life, but taken his hearing. Even in his thankfulness, Hethor regretted the loss. How would he carry out his mission?

Trigonometry again. One step at a time.

The winged savages' slowly turning descent brought them to the center of the valley. There a great earthwork fortress stood, all red and brown. It was enormous—an entire city of ramparts, with square towers and slightly sloping walls. The architecture was oversized, as if built for giants with little sense of fancy. Hethor's rescuers dropped him atop one of the fortress' gatehouses. From there he could see that the place, while in good repair, was deserted as the vertical city had been.

Wordless as ever, the winged savages spiraled away into the upper air. Their shapes were soon reduced to dark ciphers by the brassy tropical sun.

Hethor waved them farewell, then set about climbing down off the gatehouse. His legs ached abominably, especially at the joints, but he was more afraid of staying up high with no food or water than he was of losing his balance on the descent.

There was no interior stairway from the gatehouse roof, but a rough wooden ladder leaned against the northern wall where the structure met the main battlements. Hethor carefully worked his way over the brick-and-mud parapet, found his footing on an upper rung, and descended with as much care as any doddering grandparent.

At the bottom, he stepped away from the ladder and turned to see a man slowly clapping his hands. Tall as a winged savage, curly reddish hair and ice blue eyes, wearing a black cassock.

William of Ghent.

Hethor did not have it in him to be startled yet again. He was too tired even to concede defeat or allow the rush of fearful anger he knew he should have felt in that moment. Either this man would succor him or destroy him; Hethor no longer cared which.

William's lips moved, words forming soundlessly. Hethor took two steps toward him, then toppled forward, saved from smashing his face on the battlement by a quick, knee-bending catch on William's part.

They stumbled together toward a set of stairs, Hethor's new host content to speak no more.

IN A great hall at ground level, deserted as the rest of the fortress, William laid a table for Hethor. Tall wooden statues lined the room. They were portraits perhaps of great kings and chiefs of the past, though executed in a style unfamiliar to Hethor—their faces were flattened and elongated, certain features emphasized while others were absent. Shells and beads were inset in swirls and lines across the planes of their carved faces. The patterns of tattoos perhaps, like those he had seen on the visages of Guineans and West Indians in Georgetown.

On a polished wooden table that looked to have been cut lengthwise from a tropical hardwood, William laid out a dish of beans; pitchers of water, wine, and milk; some flatbread of a truly lovely scent Hethor had never before encountered; and a rich, dark stew with peanuts and shredded meat mixed into it. He gave Hethor a bowl and plate. Both were rough-made ceramic painted with patterns of a snake chasing its tail. With them came three cups, one for each drink. William then sat down opposite Hethor with dishes of his own and beckoned Hethor to eat.

Given their past encounter Hethor was still quite worried about William's intentions. He could see nothing for it, however. Not at the moment. Besides which, his guts were rumbling at the smell of the food. Hethor ate, finding himself beyond famished, and the food almost heavenly.

As he finally slowed down, reduced to mopping up stew with shreds of the flatbread, Hethor glanced up to see William studying him. William touched his ear, then shrugged.

A question. *Have you gone deaf?*

Hethor considered ignoring him. This man had, after all, sent him to a living death among the candlemen. But they were in another world now, and time had certainly wrought its changes upon Hethor. Perhaps William had changed as well. Hethor touched his own ear and nodded in response.

Hands close together, then far apart.

Hethor shrugged.

William pursed his lips. He rose and beckoned Hethor to follow. Two rooms away was a large sand table, some miniature animals and men scattered among its hills. William swept up the miniatures, quickly smoothed the table with a small rake, then took a stick and wrote, *For how long?*

Hethor shrugged again. He had no idea if the deafness was permanent. "I don't know," he tried to say. It *felt* right, but he couldn't tell how the words sounded.

A pity, William wrote. Then, *I can save the world. Desire yr help.*

He'd been here before, with William. No. Hethor tried speaking again. "Not a savior."

William smiled, as though he was chuckling. *Earth is in thrall,* he scribbled in the sand.

Hethor nodded, waiting. William was a leader among the Rational Humanists, and had showed his true colors back in Boston. This was their cant, that the Clockmakers had set the world in motion, and would someday return to adjust the windings. Memories began to roil in Hethor's mind. He had been sent down into the dungeons to die by this man. What trust could he have?

Gd's plan is too mchanical. William scratched out everything he'd drawn thus far, then wrote more slowly

and carefully, *You make arguing philosophy a challenge.*
He grinned, a twinkle in his icy eyes.

Hethor refused to laugh. The man truly seemed to possess a likeable core. Strangely so given that he was an
enemy of God's design and Hethor's chief persecutor.
Finding the Key Perilous or not, Hethor knew he must
oppose the works of William of Ghent. The man moved
freely between Northern and Southern Earth, argued
against the indisputable nature of the world, and was
charming to deaf boys in the bargain—when he wasn't
trying to shut them away forever in dark, deep holes.

William was as much or more the enemy as the stuttering clockwork of Creation.

And he was writing again. *We must throw off the
tyranny of God's clockwork.* Another set of scratches. *Let
the Mainspring of the world wind dn, & see what new sun
rises in our skies. We will be savd by an ordrly univers.*

William touched Hethor lightly on the elbow, leading
him along more hallways lined with statues and weapons
and tapestries to a sumptuous room with an enormous
European-style bed. There the sorcerer left him to find
rest. Despite being in the house of his enemy, Hethor
found a deep comfortable sleep for the first time in a very
long while.

HETHOR WOKE to light low in the eastern sky. A new day.
He was still deaf as his bedposts, which was beginning to
make him angry. He rose to find his ragged quilted suit
gone. In its place a fair set of gentlemen's clothes in ordinary New England style awaited him. The pants and coat
were of a rougher cut than Pryce Bodean or his friends
might have worn, but suitable for venturing out of doors
here in the wilds of the Southern Earth. The linen shirt
was smooth and clean, apparently fresh from the tailor.
The tie and kerchief matched one another as well as the
stockings.

He bathed, and shaved with a bright steel razor. His

face had begun to itch since leaving *Bassett*—his beard was finally coming in as more than irritating fuzz. Then he tried on the clothes. Everything fit perfectly, even the new-made boots.

Where *were* William's servants?

Venturing back to the great hall, Hethor found shirred eggs, a baked whitefish, several kinds of squash or gourd he did not recognize, and a pitcher of some sweet, cloudy fruit juice that made his tongue curl. He set to, demolishing the fare as effectively as he had the previous dinner. His body was beginning to feel normal, the aches and pains almost ordinary rather than marks of near death and narrow escape.

As Hethor ate, William of Ghent appeared, seeming no different in dress or manner than on the previous day. Now he had an onionskin pad with him, and some pencils. He flipped open the pad and jotted out a few lines before handing it to Hethor.

I truly am working to free the world, he had written in a glorious copperplate hand, *though I know you do not believe in me or my cause. Grant me a truce, your distrust held in abeyance, that I may show you some things to help you in your thinking.*

Truce, thought Hethor. No. William was too dangerous. A killer, albeit at arm's length and through the lens of law, or at least power. But he smiled, and nodded. "Yes," he said, though his faithless ears recorded nothing.

Another scribble. *There are ways and ways within the world. I will show you some.*

Hethor bowed from the waist, the false smile still on his face.

Once the breakfast was finished, William took up his pad and pencil and led Hethor on a long walk. They passed through high-walled galleries with great beams at the ceiling, up and down narrow stairs, through dark corridors that smelled of mold and rot. It was as though the fortress had grown bigger inside than out, as if William found paths that led to other places in the world.

But the same thin, flat-faced statues were in many of the rooms and corridors they passed. Hethor decided that William was only out to confuse him, in case they came to blows.

Eventually their path led so consistently downward that William stopped and procured lanterns from an alcove, one for himself and one for Hethor. They soon left all daylight behind as passages twisted into the earth, or simply sloped farther downward. The walls smelled of soil and damp, then of flinty stone. There were occasional doors to the left or right, or side passages, some with flickering light, others silent as a midocean night. Hethor was tempted by none of them. The pit of the candlemen was too close in his memory now.

He knew they had walked for over an hour, much of it downward trending, when William stopped before a shadowed grotto. He raised his lantern high to reveal a great door. It was wrought in brass and steel and covered with wheels and bolts. This was a door such as an Eastern sultan of old might have had for his strong room or his harem.

Hethor ran his hands over the wheels and levers, marveling at the construction, then looked at William. "Here?" he asked, or tried to.

William nodded, then began throwing bolts and twisting wheels in a certain order. He sometimes paused to think a moment. After several minutes of unlatching and unlocking, he pulled back on the largest lever, forcing the door open.

Hethor felt a rumbling strain even in his feet. That must have been a great groaning noise to William or anyone else with functioning ears. It did not seem that William came here often.

They passed through the door and onto a high balcony overlooking a great cave. William lifted his oil lamp to cast illumination far and wide. Hethor looked where the light led.

Not far below their feet was a great, spinning field of brass, moving so fast it was a blur. The first and outermost of Earth's inner spheres, their rotation driven by the Mainspring of the world. And here William of Ghent had a private entrance.

William set down his lantern and wrote: *There are nine such shells within the Earth, each powered by the Mainspring. They are what keeps Earth turning, and captive to the mechanical heart of an absent God.*

But God is not absent; He is in the world, Hethor thought. Gabriel had come to him in New Haven, and twice golden tablets had been set before him in ways and places only an angel or divine intervention could have managed. Hethor saw something different than William—Hethor saw power, access to the workings of the world, an entry point through which William could sabotage the Earth's turning, only to cast blame Heavenward.

"You do not believe," he shouted, or tried to.

William smiled again, then scratched out more letters with his pen in his gorgeous calligraphy. *Rational Humanists believe in the evidence of their senses.* He glanced up at Hethor a moment, then resumed writing. *We have had this argument before. God may have made the universe, but the Clockmakers made the world. You of all people should understand.*

Hethor clenched his fists, frustrated. That remained a seductive heresy. William was indeed right, that he of all people should understand. Master Bodean had held little truck with God or the modern heresy of the Clockmakers, sticking instead to his tools and his trade.

What Hethor, too, would have done if Gabriel had not called him forth. He faced away from William to stare across the racing plain of brass gleaming in the light of William's lantern.

Lies. It was all lies. This man had never meant Hethor any good, whatever hopes Librarian Childress might have once nurtured.

He could believe nothing.

The movement below them stuttered. Walls shook, dust

and rocks dropping from the ceiling. The floor slid as though it were river ice in a spring thaw.

William smiled through the chaos, mouthing words Hethor could not make sense of.

Earthquake, Hethor thought. *More of this bastard's doing.* He had seen William work no charms, but here was the evidence. Not a word the sorcerer had told him was true—this man himself was the architect of so much of the world's undoing as well as Hethor's own miseries. He had understood that in his gut since William's cold stare back in the audience chamber at Massachusetts House had first condemned him to the pit of the candlemen.

With the thought of the candlemen and what had nearly befallen Hethor there, his fear for the fate of the world was compounded by an immediate release of pained rage.

Hethor turned and rugby-tackled William in best New Haven Latin fashion. He pushed the great sorcerer to the balcony rail and onto the plain of brass below. Slowed almost to a halt by the earthquake, Hethor could see the complex surface of spikes and cracks and patterns, wrought in seemingly infinite detail—stark contrast to the massive featurelessness of the gears atop the Equatorial Wall.

William tumbled, mouth open as if to scream. The sorcerer landed in a crevice between two serrated formations just as the plain began to move again. The balcony shuddered beneath Hethor's feet. William was carried away, arms waving and mouth twisted into words Hethor could not hear, passing into the distant darkness beneath the Earth.

William of Ghent was gone. Hethor remained trapped within his citadel.

He ran, trying to retrace their steps up to daylight. It was this subterranean labyrinth Hethor feared most— once on the main level of the fortress, he could always escape via a window or over a wall if need be.

The dark hallways did not always lead up, and seemed

to twist more than he remembered, but Hethor kept moving through showers of dust and rock. Doors splintered open from within as he passed them. Light flared down the side hallways. He ignored the chaos that seemed to spawn in his wake and fled upward, ever upward.

Finally reaching the alcove of the oil lamps, Hethor found his way barred by some of William's servants. The tall, flat-faced statues had come to life, taking spears and swords from the walls to oppose him.

Hethor threw his lamp at the servants. He then grabbed clay oil pots from the alcove and followed his lamp with more fuel. The servants caught fire. Their narrow, thick-lipped mouths writhed in what must be terrible shrieks, while their wooden bodies burned with an ugly pork smell that had to be flesh.

For the first time, Hethor was glad of his deafness.

He ripped a tapestry from the wall, rolled it around him, and charged the flaming, milling mass, pushing his way onward by main force. The tapestry heated up within, and smelled abominably as it smoked, but Hethor fought through.

Soon he was in the main level, with its larger galleries and multiple entrances to every room. More of the wooden servants pursued him, while others fought amongst themselves. Hethor continued to run, seeking a door or window, when with a sudden turning he found himself in the courtyard before a gatehouse.

Animal skeletons danced in the yard. Palm trees swayed, and stranger plants twisted and turned, sending out green shoots that writhed like blind snakes. Howling, Hethor bolted for the gate. He found it unbarred, and dragged open one panel of the great doors. He darted through the opening to run across a short stonework bridge that spanned a shallow moat just outside the walls.

He turned back to see smoke billowing into the sky. It was not black but rather many colors—red, brown, green, as well as more subtle hues. Faces swirled and dove within

the roiling clouds; shapes fought to assert themselves before being swallowed again. All the penned chaos of
William's fortress was escaping in the absence of his
magical influence. Hethor stumbled backward, eager to
be away from the accursed place, when he tripped over
something.

A third golden tablet.

"Thank you, God," he said, his prayer silent in his own
ears. Clutching the tablet, Hethor fled west into the jungle,
hoping to strike for the sea and whatever destination
Simeon Malgus had originally intended for them both.

"I WILL not . . . lose these words. . . . I will not . . . lose
these words. . . . I will not . . . lose these words. . . ." Hethor had been breathing the phrase for the three days since
he left William's citadel. The sorcerer's magic-wrought
boots and clothes had held up, much to his relief, but he'd
found little to eat in the jungle. Hethor was certain that
half the things growing, crawling, and flying around him
were delicious, while the other half were deadly poison.
Unfortunately, he could not tell the difference.

He was reduced to sucking on roots and shoots of
small, inoffensive-seeming water plants.

"I will not . . . lose these words. . . . I will not . . . lose
these words. . . . I will not . . . lose these words. . . ."

Each evening Hethor stopped before sundown. He
would find a tree to sleep in away from whatever crashed
heavily through the jungle at night and check it for snakes.
Once settled he chewed on whatever shoots he'd found
that day, then stared at the scratched writing on the
golden tablet until the light stole his sight away from him.

Malgus would be at the coast, somewhere with or near
the Southern wise men the Jade Abbot had spoken of. The
hierophants of this part of the world would dwell in cities,
which meant ports. It made little sense to come inland.
Here was trackless jungle, and no settlement at all save

William's fortress. Hethor wished that he had asked more questions when the Jade Abbot mentioned the Relics of Christ coming over the Equatorial Wall.

Why?

Who brought them?

He did not care for Malgus in the first place, really, for all that the man had rescued him in Boston. Malgus had betrayed Hethor as well, in a sense, with the misleading trick of parachutes coming down from the Wall. Still Hethor did not think Malgus evil, as William of Ghent was. William had condemned Hethor to death, and sought to overturn the order of the world. Malgus simply worked at cross-purposes to Hethor's mission from Gabriel.

Where *had* the man landed in his great fall from the Wall?

"I will not . . . lose these words. . . . I will not . . . lose these words. . . . I will not . . . lose these words. . . ."

On the fifth day out from the fortress Hethor came to a wide river that blocked his way west. He could not begin to judge its depth, for it was muddy and apparently in flood. It seemed narrower upstream, to the south. Hethor picked his away along the bank in that direction, looking for a log or some other way to cross the flow. The flood had a ticking chuckle to it, different from any water he had ever heard.

Heard.

Hethor shouted, dropped his golden tablet into a stand of ferns, and reached up to gently stroke his ears. Insects flew from the left, and he dislodged a leaf from his right.

"Is it me? Can I hear?"

His words were still lost to him, but Hethor could definitely hear the river, though as a ticking, the way he'd always heard the turning of the Earth.

He fell to his knees, kissed his tablet, then looked up at another small noise to see a great, tawny cat staring at him from perhaps thirty feet distant.

Hethor walked away slowly, backing from the cat's gaze, but it sauntered after him. He turned to run. Over his shoulder he caught a flash of movement as the cat sped up. Hethor spun back around, brandished his tablet, and shouted, "In the name of God, leave me!"

The cat pulled up sharply, eyes blazing in a bright reflection of the sheet of gold. It opened its mouth to another sound of clicking before walking back into the blue-green shadows of the jungle.

"I will not . . . lose these words . . . ," Hethor said, his voice at the verge of audibility now. They had saved his life, over and over again.

"I WILL NOT . . . lose these words. . . . I will not . . . lose these words. . . . I will not . . . lose these words. . . ."

Ten days into the jungle, Hethor still followed the river south. He was too weak now to attempt a crossing, so weak he crawled most of the day, dragging his tablet with him. He'd tried to eat other things, eggs and insects, but that just made him sick. There had been more earthquakes, more animals, and once something dark and large that howled its way across the sky, but his memory grew fainter and more chaotic. He had seen a white bird, a parrot perhaps, several times, but could no longer recall why that might be important to him.

He longed for cold chicken and corn liquor, a simple ride in a hearse over country roads, Royal Navy hardtack and rum. He longed for anything but this hot, moldering jungle with its smells of water and rotten flowers and the little clicking noises that always hovered just inside his hearing.

One hand, then another, Hethor thought. One foot, then another. It was good that his boots were so stout, as the ground was tearing into his palms and knees as he crawled, making of them a painful mess.

With a loud clattering, a small hairy foot planted itself between his hands. The shin was almost pressed into Hethor's nose. He looked up, squinting, to green-tinged shadows of a familiar shape.

"I will not . . . lose these words . . . ," Hethor said. His voice sounded almost normal.

The owner of the hairy foot bent down, a spear preceding him, and jabbered in a clicking, whistling sort of language. This was one of the small hairy men, Hethor realized, that had forced him off of the southern ledge of the Equatorial Wall to fall after Simeon Malgus.

Straining, his every movement a palsy, Hethor fished within his coat for the golden tablet. Where was it?

"Have I lost . . . these words . . . ?" he asked, but then it poked him, hurting his hand.

Hethor drew the tablet out and brandished it unconvincingly at the hairy-footed spear carrier.

More clicks and whistles, quite a few of them, accompanied by considerable running back and forth. A conference, then, of the little apes, as they circled around Hethor. Under their clicking and whistling, the clattering of gears, as if the entire world were nothing but automata within automata, every creature in God's Creation a thing of brass gears and rings.

Five or six of the little hairy men picked Hethor up and laid him on their spears stretched crosswise beneath him. Once he was balanced they began to run through the jungle, chanting to the rhythm of their steps. Hethor floated above them in the green-lit shadows like a small, almost-fallen angel making that final trip to ground.

THE NEXT few days were a fevered blur of color and pain, always tinted green, though flashes of every hue in God's palette seemed to pass before Hethor's eyes. Once he awoke to find himself covered in long black tongues, as though his body were vomiting forth what lay within, only to realize they were leeches sucking him dry. He screamed himself back to sleep.

Later, there was a moment of concern from a hairy face, brilliant yellow eyes so close to his their lashes might have touched, a furtive hand upon his forehead. He smelled flowers then, and heard more of the whistling click-speech. Beneath that speech and woven through it there was the clattering of gears and spheres that had dogged his hearing ever since it had first begun to return to him in the jungle.

He awoke one morning in a terrible thirst. His head was clear, but he felt very weak. Hethor was barely able to move his arms. The leeches were gone, but his hands were bound in large leaves, greasy and stretched beneath their coverings. He was inside a simple hut, barely more than a lean-to, walled by vines and fronds woven together in a semblance of privacy. Or perhaps just for shade. It was daytime outside, but the light in his shelter was a uniform aquarian green.

"Water." Hethor rejoiced to hear his own voice, though it was cracked and dry as an old cobblestone. "Please, someone. Water."

One of the little hairy men stepped inside. *No,* thought Hethor, a hairy woman. He wasn't sure how he could tell, for she was thin as any stripling lad, with no bosom to speak of, only a cloth waistband to hide her sex.

Not that he would have looked.

She had those brilliant yellow eyes, like liquid shards of sunlight, set in a small face almost indistinguishable from that of a monkey. She carried with her an enormous gourd. Its skin had been carved in complex geometries that could have been animals, or a junglescape, or just an abstraction of the mysteries of life. The smell of flowers followed her into Hethor's little hut. A familiar scent, one from his fevered dreams.

The hairy woman sat on the edge of the cot where Hethor lay. He tried to prop himself up to greet her, but the effort racked him with coughing, creating lingering pain in his ribs and the muscles of his stomach.

She touched his forehead, patting him with her fingers in such a long and rhythmic way that he wondered if this were speech among her race. She dipped her hand in the gourd to wipe water over his forehead and cheeks before lifting the gourd to his lips and steadying it at the exactly correct angle to avoid pouring water onto his face.

Hethor drank deeply. This water was warm and sweet, almost nectar, though his thirst was so great he would have prized damp mud. The hairy woman watched him carefully, keeping the gourd tilted sufficiently to allow him to drink his fill.

"Thank you," Hethor finally said, pulling his face away from the gourd. He tried to wipe his lips but encountered the waxy slickness of the leaves wrapping his hands.

She smiled, a flash of sharp teeth around long, biting canines, then wiped his mouth for him with the back of her free hand. Small as she was, Hethor realized the hairy woman was strong. She must be, in order to manage the gourd one-handed.

"Thank you," he said again.

She clicked-whistled at him, the sound still underlain by that faint clattering of gears. Was she an automaton? Was he hallucinating? Or was his hearing so damaged that every sound carried that undertone?

"Right." Clumsy, he took her free wrist between his leaf-wrapped hands. "I am Hethor. *Heth-or*."

She chattered, something very much like laughter, then rose from his side and set the gourd on the floor. With a last flashing glance of those sun-yellow eyes, the hairy woman left his hut.

Exhausted, Hethor let sleep reclaim him.

THE NEXT time he awoke, it was to the smell of a stew or soup not unlike what William of Ghent had served him. Had that really been the last time he had eaten? No wonder he was so weak. His face itched, too. Hethor crossed his eyes, trying to see if he'd grown a real beard.

"Hello," he tried to call, though his voice again betrayed him. Daylight still reigned, flooding his hut with that lambent green.

There was a racket just outside, followed by more

chattering laughter. The hairy woman returned bearing a shallow wooden bowl of the stew and a rough-carved spoon. She squatted beside his cot, back on her haunches, and slowly fed him, one little spoonful at a time. Though he could smell meat in the stock, and it made his mouth water, the hairy woman gave Hethor only vegetables and broth. She kept smiling. Her eyes were bright.

He could not recall ever having such attention paid to him. Sick in Master Bodean's shop, Hethor had simply been packed off to his attic room with bread and water to sweat it out, the better not to pass his illnesses to Bodean and his sons. He did not remember much of life with his mother. Hethor presumed she must have fed him as an infant.

Now there was a hand casually laid upon his arm, or tilting his chin, eyes close to his, a ready smile. Somehow it didn't matter to Hethor that she was small and hairy as any jungle ape, another race of man entire—no woman had ever focused her full attention on him, except Librarian Childress for a few brief hours.

This woman, he thought, *is someone of whom the librarian would approve.*

Hethor realized he must still be feverish, to react so to the presence and touch of someone who was little more than an ape. His logical mind, back at New Haven Latin, warred with his emotional mind for a while, as stew kept spooning into his mouth, until his body, warmed and comforted, forced him to stop eating through sheer satiety.

After the meal, as she was wiping his mouth, Hethor asked a question that had been lurking at the edges of his thoughts for a while.

"Where is my golden tablet?" he croaked.

She whistled and stared intently at him.

Hethor mimed a rectangle with his leaf-wrapped hands. "My *tablet*," he said, as though reinforcing the words would somehow help her understand.

The hairy woman chirped. She then reached beneath

him, hands burrowing in the rustling bedding of the cot, before producing the tablet. She stared at it for a moment, turning it in her hands, with an expression somewhere between lust and awe inasmuch as Hethor could read her nonhuman features, then handed it to him.

"Thank you," he said. Then: "I can't call you 'hairy woman.' I am Hethor." Tablet clutched in his elbow, he tapped his chest. *"Heth-or."*

She chittered her laugh again, then said in a passable imitation of his voice, "Heh-for."

"And you?" he asked, pointing toward her.

She clicked and whistled, then again in more or less his voice, said, "Arellya."

Hethor felt a smile stretch his cheeks. "Arellya. A beautiful name."

Taking the bowl, she left.

He studied the golden tablet for a while. It seemed to be more sensible, somehow. Somewhere in the depths of his deafness perhaps he had overheard the language of God, and now the words of the tablet echoed just outside his hearing.

Which, Hethor realized, given the way everything around him now clicked and whirred, might even have a grain of truth to it.

He tried to form his mouth around the strange words, the clusters of letters that might or might not be the Tetragrammaton. What did it mean? Why did God, or Gabriel, or some agent of Heaven, keep sending him this message, over and over? The tablet had been a lifesaver for him. But its purpose had to be more than that. It had to hold a greater meaning.

Though no answers came to him, Hethor felt at peace with the mystery of the words for the first time since they had come to him. He let the tablet rest on his chest, staring out at the leaves and vines surrounding him, wondering where he was, where he should go, what would be next in his quest.

"I must take control," Hethor said aloud, "not be subject

to the whims of the viceroy or Malgus or William of Ghent." Gabriel had charged *him* with finding the Key Perilous, not one of his enemies. Nor even his allies.

Hethor flexed the palm of his hand, thinking of the key-shaped scar the silver feather had left behind, but the leafy wrappings hid any view he might have. He suspected all the abuse he had recently taken had obviated the scar with new damage.

Arellya looked through the curtain, smiled at him, and pulled down the line of leaves and vines.

He sat a bit above a clearing in the jungle. The mighty river muttered nearby but out of sight. His bed, his little hut, were surrounded by the diminutive hairy men. They stood in circling ranks, male and female, young and old, parent and child, each with a little bundle of goods and weapons at their feet.

As Hethor watched in growing horror, with a chorus of clicks and whistles, they all bowed to him. Every last one, even Arellya.

"No," he said. "Not this. Get up, by God. You will not bow to me!"

"Heth-or," they all intoned, like monks chanting. "Heth-or."

He struggled to his feet, swaying. He threw his hands out in an unsteady attempt at balance. "Get up! This is wrong. I'm not here to be your leader. I'm not . . . I'm . . ."

Words failed him. The hairy men continued to chant his name, their heads pressed to the leaf-strewn floor of the clearing, as the brilliant tropical sun blazed down upon them all.

EIGHT

HETHOR TRIED for the rest of that day to get the hairy men to stop bowing and treating him like a god-king. He yelled until they chanted his name in time to his rants. He grabbed one or another by the shoulders and pulled them to their feet, where they would gaze in ecstasy upon his face, boneless as eels, until he dropped them again.

That night, even with the leaf-and-vine curtains of his hut pulled to, Hethor was forced to listen to his name being chanted like a prayer.

The next day, more of the same frustrations.

"Hey," Hethor shouted, "I'm just a man."

"Heth-or, Heth-or."

With "ma-an, ma-an" as counterpoint.

He ran around the clearing, or at least hobbled at a brisk pace. They followed him. That was when Hethor realized his hairy man contingent was growing. More of the tiny folk continued emerging from the jungle.

He tried to pick a fight, shoving and shouting.

They just grinned, chanting his name.

Hethor finally threw a tantrum. He yelled and screamed and leapt about on his still-sore feet until his ankles felt ready to snap. He fetched the golden tablet from his cot and hurled it to the ground.

"Stop!" Hethor shouted. "Someone please just please talk to me!"

He sat at the foot of his cot, back to the crowded clearing, and stifled the hot, tired tears that threatened to burst forth. Somehow this was even worse than the fighting, the cold, the fear. Being bowed to made him feel dirty. He was no slaveholder or raider or workhouse tyrant.

Arellya came and squatted next to him. Her fine-boned hand rested gently on his shoulder. "Hethor," she said, in a quiet, normal voice.

His breath shuddered. "What?"

She clicked and whistled, then tugged at him, trying to make him turn around.

Hethor grudgingly looked.

The clearing was still full of Arellya's folk. Many watched him, but they were no longer in their worshipful array. Some built fires, while others wove shelters of jungle leaves. A group of young males, spears at the ready, stood guard over the golden tablet where Hethor had thrown it in his temper.

He looked at Arellya again. "Thank you."

She smiled her too-toothy smile, took Hethor by the hand, and led him out of the hut to a fire circle. There he ate a pale yellow stew of grubs and fruit. Sitting shoulder to shoulder with Arellya and her folk, Hethor's sense of disgust at being worshipped transmuted to a sort of golden-hearted kinship.

"We are all men, in God's image, are we not?" he asked the circle.

Clicks and whistles all around answered him, so Hethor had some more of the pale stew.

WALKING BACK to his hut in the miserable, stinking heat of the late afternoon, Hethor stopped before the young men guarding the tablet. They immediately opened their circle of spears to let him step forward. When Hethor bent to pick up the tablet, he heard his name whispered. When he stood again and looked around, a number of the hairy men were forming their worshipful ranks again.

Ah, thought Hethor. *The tablet. It is not me they worship; it is God's word.*

He marveled that even jungle savages of such primitive ancestry could recognize the hand of God in their lives, when a sophisticated divinity student like Pryce Bodean had denied the same.

"Who's the ape now?" Hethor whispered with a chuckle. Then he set the tablet back down and motioned for the larger group of hairy men to rise and disperse. He left the spearmen to their guard.

Loath as he was to leave the tablet behind again, it was easier than withstanding the awed regard of the massed hairy men. Besides, they clearly intended to guard it from all comers. They would protect the precious artifact for his future use. Probably better than he could himself.

Inside his hut, Hethor was at least shaded. Otherwise he was more uncomfortable than he had been at any time since being brought to the village. If insects, heat, and smells were what bothered him most now, that probably indicated that he was recovered for the most part from his fatigue and injuries.

Arellya approached, whistling for him from just outside. Behind her, life in the camp went on as usual. She had an old male with her, doddering and pale-furred, with a loose mouth that suggested a complete lack of teeth.

"Hello, Arellya." Hethor was glad to see her.

Arellya flashed her toothy grin. "Hethor." She took the old hairy man by the hand, held their joined fingers up toward Hethor in greeting, and inclined her head. "Kalker."

"Hello, Kalker."

Kalker said something so unlike the usual whistles and clicks of hairy man speech that Hethor didn't catch it all.

"Excuse me?" Hethor said, cupping his ear to mime.

Kalker repeated himself. "Salve."

Salve? *That's Latin,* Hethor thought, though the hairy man's terrible accent would earn him a caning under Headmaster Brownlee. "Ah . . . ," Hethor said. "Quod velles?" *What do you want?*

It was rude, abrupt, and in the infinitive besides, but Hethor was too surprised to work out conversational sentences in a language he had only been taught to read.

Kalker grinned, his lack of teeth becoming painfully obvious. "Loquamur," the old hairy man said. *Let us talk.*

They continued in broken Latin, missing one another's intentions almost as often as they understood. But at least it was common ground, rather than the frustrating impenetrability of trying to speak with Arellya.

"You are Hethor," Kalker said.

"Yes. Me Hethor."

"You are angel?"

"No! Man! Me man."

"God's messenger."

"Not an angel."

"Messenger. One who talks. Bring divine word."

Hethor had to admit this old hairy man living deep in the jungle on the far side of the Equatorial Wall from Rome or New Haven Latin spoke the language better than he did.

"No," Hethor said. *"No divine word."*

Kalker said something he didn't understand.

"What?"

The old hairy man tried again. *". . . gold . . ."*

"The table," Hethor said, incorrectly. What *was* the world for 'tablet'?

Kalker nodded. *"God's word on gold; you bring gold here. You bring God's word!"*

And how did they know it was God's word? *"Are you a Christian?"* asked Hethor.

Kalker let out a long, chittering laugh, then turned to explain something, at length, to Arellya. Eventually she

laughed, too. They both stared at Hethor, bright yellow
eyes gleaming like a brace of twinned suns.

"Christ not for us," Kalker finally said. *"Christ for . . .
men. Only for . . . men."*

"Christ died for all men," Hethor insisted.

"We are not men," said Kalker. *"We are . . ."*

"What?"

Kalker chattered to himself for a moment. Then: *"We
are the correct people, not men."*

"I am a man," Hethor said. *"Tell them to stop bowing
down before me."*

"They do not bow before a man," Kalker answered.
"They bow before the messenger of the words of God."

IN THE evening, Hethor's sense that he heard clattering
gears inside even the smallest things was stronger than
ever. Tiny and hairy, resembling children costumed as so
many apes, the correct people danced before a great fire.
They threw fruits and meat and even their spears and
breechclouts into it. Some fell to the ground, coupling, so
that he was forced to avert his eyes. Drums pounded a
wandering rhythm that filled the night like a heartbeat.
The stars above seemed to waver with the tempo. Even
the bright thread of the moon's track swayed, the sky itself seeming to quake. Clicking and whistling they sang,
the music counterpoint to the rhythms of the dance.

The food on the fire crackled and hissed and raised a
smell not unlike a feast fit for angels. The correct people
raised a sweat of their own, the scent almost sweet and
more than a little challenging to Hethor's nose. Beetles
the size of Hethor's hand and larger flew out of the jungle
into the flames, exploding like little fireworks as they
burned, while enormous moths with crying faces upon
their wings circled above. Ghost-pale birds rustled and
croaked in the surrounding trees.

He sat in front of his hut where Arellya had so often
lately squatted to watch him. There he listened to the

clattering. Even the wind seemed a thing of metal artifice, the crackling flames mechanical in their hunger for the fuel on the fire. Every one of the correct people moved with the clicking of an automaton, yet another counterpoint to their click-whistle language and their shuffling steps. Hethor felt as though he was witness to a great conference of metal men, a sort of coven of fleshly machines met to worship in a jungle lair.

Just as he had lain in his narrow bed in Master Bodean's attic to listen to the clattering turn of the world, so Hethor now turned his ears to the sounds that tugged at them. He was close enough still to his recent deafness to feel a warm and profound gratitude for the return of his hearing, even if it was strained through this metal sieve.

All Creation was artifice, was it not? Anyone with eyes could see that, bearing witness to Earth's orbital track, the gears atop the Equatorial Wall, the mechanical motions of the moon and the stars, even the lamp of the sun. Why wouldn't men, and correct people, as well as animals, beetles, trees, fire, and wind be artifice?

Hethor could not decide if this was heady philosophy or maudlin foolery. Instead he closed his eyes and listened, *really listened,* to the underlying music of the world. The pounding beat of the correct people's festival-rite only served to make that underlying music clearer. It seemed as though it provided a texture richer and thicker than any silence against which the world could make itself heard to him.

The beetles buzzed like tiny spring-wound toys. The fire's crackle was the disjointed fall of a box of small brass parts, tinkling forever. The correct people moved and spoke and sang with a precision fit for any ship's clock or astronomer's timepiece. Even the smells seemed composed of smaller and smaller mechanisms, each one's parts themselves assembled from tinier parts, as if all of Creation held a myriad more Creations nestled inside itself.

As each man was a Creation of his own, a mind unique in God's world.

The words began to come to him.

"No . . ."

". . . yes . . ."

". . . three orange and . . ."

". . . feet . . ."

". . . he loved her once . . ."

". . . I am whole! . . ."

". . . have a care . . ."

". . . joy . . ."

". . . we walked for seven days before we found water . . ."

". . . he is one of the grub-men, but God has still seen . . ."

". . . golden plate, words upon it . . ."

They were talking about him. Hethor was hearing the correct people speak, building their words back up from the clicks and whirrs of God's tiny gears within them.

". . . Arellya says . . ."

Arellya says what? The memory of her touch, her eyes locked with his, was a sudden surge in Hethor's gut.

"Kalker knows better. But he won't tell."

"Look at that one! Green as any crocodile, and I'll wager it's . . ."

". . . no good. Never any good when God . . ."

"Hot! Hot! Hot!"

She touched his arm, and Hethor opened his eyes to see Arellya, whom he already knew was there, offering him something baked in a banana leaf, smiling with all her teeth. He took the food. Amid the buzzing of the beetles and the deep, roasting smell of the festival-rite fire, Hethor greeted her in the language of the correct people.

"Hello, Arellya, and my thanks."

She wasn't the least surprised. "Why did it take you so long to find our words?"

MORNING BROUGHT a red-stained sun, a clearing full of gently snoring correct people, and the heavy, breath-choking smell of ashes. Hethor awoke sprawled on the ground just outside his hut, mere feet from his cot. His body ached due to the roots and rocks on which he had slept. He itched from the attentions of various night-dwelling insects. He wished he had William of Ghent's razor to set upon his face.

He didn't mind.

At this moment, Hethor was satisfied. He felt as happy as he could ever remember feeling in his life. Arellya slept nearby, curled up like a cat. The correct people woman was not someone he could court, or even love, but there was a species of affection between them previously unknown to him, all the more so as it had developed in the absence of words. They had talked for hours of small things—the beauty of the beetles, the colors of the jungle, the height of the Wall, how well this one danced and that one drummed. All that sort of idle chatter that had always eluded Hethor, tying his tongue, in the days of his youth back in New Haven.

Last night, somehow, he had found a way of listening to the world that finally allowed things to make sense once more. Not only was he happy, but he felt centered, like he belonged. Not since Gabriel came to him had Hethor known that kind of peace.

The thought of the archangel made his right hand itch. Hethor looked. The little key-shaped scar was prominent once more, standing out from the more recent wounds and insults that limned his palm in angry red and callused white.

"It is not my place to be happy, is it?" Hethor asked his hand, speaking to the uncaring scar. The Key Perilous awaited.

Arellya awoke at the sound of his voice, as did some of the other correct people. She smiled at Hethor. "Good morning, Messenger."

Last night she had told him her people thought "Hethor" was his word for "Messenger." She had insisted it was his name, even if Hethor himself did not know that.

"Arellya," Hethor said, somewhere between politeness and affection. The clicks and whistles coming from his own mouth still sounded and felt strange, but in his head the correct people's language was already as natural to him as his own Queen's English.

Her name, of course, sounded very different in her own language than it had in his mouth when she first taught him to say it. Sort of a rising whistle, with a silent pause at the top, and a liquid ell sound that was also a click.

Hethor liked that version better than his Anglicized "Ar-el-yuh."

"When will you take to the water road?" she asked.

"Pardon?"

"The river." Arellya's voice was patience itself. "When will you take to the water road?"

"I'm not sure what you mean," Hethor said.

"You already know the perils of walking in our jungle. The water road is the only path that can carry you as far as you need to travel."

Hethor sighed, smiling. "I don't know if I want to leave. Your jungle is hot, the air heavy and dense, but this is a kindly place to those who know how to live in it. I would guest as long as you allow me to."

"Messenger, God did not send you and your wonderful gold plate to us." Arellya managed to sound exasperated, even through her clicks and whistles and the underlying clatter of gears. "He intended something else. The correct people are like the ants beneath the jungle floor—we are a part of our place, and neither we nor our place would survive without one another. God does not send us messages except in the fall of rain and the heat of the sun. Your message, it is for something grand, for someone in a distant city of stone and colored wood."

"I . . ." Hethor knew perfectly well that Gabriel had not sent him on a quest to find a jungle home south of the Equatorial Wall. Even if he was tempted to be faithless to the charge that had been laid upon him, the resurgent scar pulsing on his hand was reminder enough of what was at stake. "You are correct, Arellya."

"Of course," she said with a small smile.

"I must go on."

Kalker settled next to them, groaning his age. "May you both dance in the shadows of the sun."

"Good morning," said Hethor. Arellya nodded.

"So you have found your spirit-magic," Kalker said to Hethor.

"No . . ."

"Yesterday, we were so many whistling savages. Today we are the correct people, with a different standing in your eyes. Did you come to wisdom on your own in the dark of the night?"

"Magic is . . . ungodly."

"Magic is." With that, Kalker was content to sit and gaze at Hethor, neither worshipful nor confrontational.

"I need to take up the golden plate," Hethor said, nodding at the group of guards sleeping in a circle, sitting each with their backs to the thing, spears on their laps. Even in the height of the previous night's frenzy, there had always been a watch. "I must carry it toward the sea and find a man named Malgus. Then together we will seek other men of greater wisdom to direct me."

"Wisdom is," said Arellya.

This time, Kalker nodded.

"Can you put me on the water road?" asked Hethor.

At his own question, he shuddered. Already the day was growing hot. Mosquitoes and blackflies whined; larger things rustled in the trees. The thought of the river was more threat than comfort, dangers in the water, falls and floods and huge crocodiles lurking in the muddy depths.

"The young males have been working," said Arellya. "In the woods, they have been making barkboats and rafts, carving paddles and steering oars."

"There is only one of me," Hethor said mildly.

"Many will come."

"I will not take them."

Kalker frowned. "You cannot refuse."

"Who speaks for the correct people?" Hethor asked.

"I do," said Kalker, "those times when it is not sufficient for each correct person to speak for themselves."

"You are the headman?" Somehow, this was not surprising.

"No, but I speak."

"The correct people have no headman," said Arellya. "Each is their own."

"Well, Speaker," Hethor said to Kalker, "tell your young males that they are brave and full of fire, and my respect for their dedication knows no limits. But this is my journey, and I must undertake it alone. So far my travels have not been lucky for those around me. I do not expect improvement."

Arellya touched his arm, her grip firmer, more possessive, than it had been. "You cannot stop them. If you take to the water road, they will follow. If you stumble into the jungle, they will follow. It is not you, Messenger. The word of God passes by not once in a dozen generations, perhaps not a dozen of dozens. Let them follow the word. If the word leads them to the limits of their life, that is their choice."

"So it is to be a river progress?" asked Hethor. "With the correct people in the flow?"

"By the will and want of everyone who comes." Kalker reached out, touched Hethor's knee where he sat. "Most of all, your will."

AS THE days passed, the correct people assembled a flotilla of canoes and rafts. They tied each little craft to the knobby knees of trees that grew out of the water like amphibious sentinels. Vines hung heavy there, and monkeys with green-tinged fur prowled close by to watch the correct people launch their fleet. Logs in the water moved against the current, crocodiles, a great gold-brown eye rolling open from time to time, but they did not approach the impromptu port.

Standing on a mound of clay to watch the effort, Hethor found that the river smelled much different from the jungle village nearby. More of mud and less of growth, with an unhealthy reek as if great monsters rotted in the watercourse's dank bed. The flow still had the coffee-colored, flooded look Hethor remembered from his first encounter weeks ago.

He discovered that though his sense of the passage of time moment to moment was as strong as ever, his sense of the days had vanished somewhere on the Equatorial Wall. It had not yet returned to him. Hethor shrugged—he was moving as fast as he could, at least while maintaining life and limb intact. The world would fare as it did until he could unwrap Gabriel's mystery.

Not for the first time, he wished the archangel had gone straight to the queen and all her armies. On the other hand, all her armies would not have been enough to pass over the Wall.

All of life was a puzzle, Hethor thought, *his own no more or less than anyone else's.*

The other thing he had lost, besides his sense of the passage of days, was that feeling of happiness with which he had awoken after the festival-rite. The Key Perilous was back in his thoughts, itching in the scar on his hand.

"I am ready," Hethor said to Arellya suddenly. "Tell the young males to take up their spears and supplies and join me on the water road."

Though she was only chest-high to him, Arellya reached up and hugged Hethor, placing her arms around his neck as she hitched herself higher to kiss his lips. The closeness of her face made his new mustache prickle and fold, while the pressure of her lips was something entirely new to him.

He stood, the taste of sweetgrass and clay in his mouth, and marveled at what he didn't understand while shouts and calls echoed around him. The correct people moved to their watercraft.

THE FLOTILLA of canoes and rafts put out into the brown flood accompanied by little banana-leaf boats filled with flowers, spice, and even tiny oil wicks aflame. Hethor sat near the back of the largest canoe, a steersman behind him, six paddlers before him, his feet overrun with blossoms. He held the golden tablet upon his lap, but today there was no nonsense of worship or chanting. Various of the correct people had bowed to it, or him, loading up their boats, but all the ceremony of his first days among them had given way to an almost anarchic sense of informality.

Most importantly, Arellya sat just before him, her hips buried in the flowers. Hethor had lost that argument before it ever started. She had simply looked at him and said, "You follow the message. I follow the Messenger."

Hethor was relieved that old Kalker hadn't thrown himself into the canoe as well. "Someone here is sane," he had grumbled on boarding, but Kalker had just shaken his head, mimicking one of Hethor's gestures.

"Old age is not sanity."

With that, they had pushed away.

Now the sun was high, morning already lost to their journey in the course of Hethor's early vacillations and late decision. The water road was more humid and miserable and insect-ridden than even the jungle, making Hethor wonder what it was he had seen in this place.

The little banana-leaf boats made more sense now, their odors of fruit and spice drawing some insects away from the travelers, while the trails of guttering oil smoke drove others off from the area. But the little boats spun away on every whim of the current, so their utility was limited.

Still, it was a proud flotilla that headed downstream to the dip of paddles and the ragged airs of singing and drumming on hulls. Hethor might have lost his sense of profound happiness, but this was no mean substitute.

He took the golden tablet from beneath its bed of flowers and studied it, trying to hear the language of Heaven beneath the clattering gears of all the world in the same manner that he had managed to hear Arellya's language.

The difference was, he feared, that Arellya had wanted him to understand, and the tablet was at best indifferent to him.

Spirit-magic, Kalker had said.

Hethor only wished he had such a thing, to ease his path and make him a happier man every day.

THAT NIGHT they did not stop to camp as Hethor expected. Rather, Arellya called the boats together with a series of nonsense cries that must have been some code Hethor did not yet understand through the secret of his spirit-magic, or the gift of divine hearing, or whatever he had been blessed with. Slowly, almost effortlessly, the flotilla drew together, closing up to a sort of floating island of wood and bark. A surprising number of the little banana-leaf boats were still with them.

Lines made of dried and woven vines were drawn through little knots in the wood, or even oarlocks, though Chief al-Wazir would have been appalled at both the indifferent discipline of the flotilla's sailors and the almost aggressively random result of their labors. The thought of al-Wazir brought Hethor's mind whirling back to *Bassett*.

Who among the ship's company yet lived? Did they realize that Gordon's expeditionary force had met ruin in the landslide, even while the poor bastards were already falling at the hands of the crystal automata? Hethor wondered if he had been memorialized with some impassioned speech, the way the other dead and missing were.

Or perhaps Smallwood had exercised the only sensible judgment and turned his course from the impossible, overwhelming vastness of the Wall and sailed for England, away from tumbling death and monsters out of legend. Somehow, Hethor doubted that pleasant outcome.

He sent a moment's good thought to al-Wazir and the others who had favored him, then returned from his contemplation to watch the correct people finishing their bivouac on the water road.

Young males now swarmed over the lashed-together craft, butting spears down to make poles, stringing yet more vines, arranging the shelter of woven reeds and even bolts of colored cloth—the first such that Hethor had seen among the correct people. Soon the mass of boats had more the air of a village market in the summertime. It was almost festive, with the floating equivalent of stalls and booths, the people swarming back and forth to trade gossip, or hugs, or share songs they had perhaps invented that day.

Hethor found that he was happy again. The sense of belonging amid the rising mists of the river at dusk, the songs of the correct people singing the night into its rightful place as the foetid scent of the river gave way to a sudden and unexpected freshet. Hethor roused himself to pound some waxy white root in a little bowl. Fruit juice of various colors was added, after which he passed something red and spiky to a young male with a flint knife who diced it and shared the results out, one fresh-cut sliver at a time.

It was a different kind of feast, quieter than others, prepared and eaten cold, in the spirit of the place and the moment. Absent flame on the wooden boats, the correct people sang up the moon, greeted the glimmering trails of the orbital tracks of both Earth and her satellite, and laughed their way to sleep.

Hethor soon followed. He found himself trapped in dreams of William of Ghent wielding a silver feather large as a broadsword, cutting slices from Hethor's flesh just as the young male had cut the red fruit, so that the gobbets might be served out to the viceroy's court in Boston. The clattering music of midnight woke him, audible as always to his inner ear, but also to his outer hearing. Though they were not so close to the Wall, it was perfectly visible from the river, looming over the roof of the jungle on the north bank.

The sounds were four seconds late.

Midnight's mechanical call, so familiar, brought Hethor past *Bassett* all the way back to New Haven. He found himself assaulted by a bout of homesickness. Not that Master Bodean's attic was anything to cry for, but he was so utterly lost to anything familiar, anything he had known in his younger life. Floating down a brown river on a bed of canoes surrounded by tiny, hairy people was beyond any sense he'd ever had of himself.

Arellya's fingers found his in the dark. She twined their hands together, humming a soothing little song that returned Hethor to his rest.

AT DAWN some of the young males fought off a crocodile longer than Hethor's great canoe, managing even to kill it. There was a terrific hooting and yelling, followed by a decision to make land and slaughter the catch.

"Such a wealth of meat and skin is not to be wasted," Arellya explained to Hethor.

After his dreams and wakefulness of the night before, Hethor was less forgiving than his normal wont. "We were all in a hurry to follow the word of God, now we stop to kill lizards?"

She just smiled, an expression he'd learned to interpret as sweet. "Each travels his own road. You can go on alone if you wish. But not every step of yours has been hurried before now. Do not begrudge us this."

So they spent a day on the riverbank. The correct people exchanged thrown rocks and mud with monkeys. They snuck up on great overhanging trees of a type Hethor had not seen before, like green castles with twiggy battlements, in order to startle scarlet-plumed birds from the endlessly ramified branches. Between mischiefs they foraged for fruits. An enormous snake was caught, thick around as Hethor's thigh and longer than he could guess at, which was gutted and sliced for roasting with the croc, as bacon might be placed with a turkey in the oven.

Hethor intended to study his golden tablet again that day. He thought to commit each sigil to memory in the hopes of once more reaching that evanescent place within his mind where the wheels and gears of the universe had meshed for him. Instead he found himself constantly drawn off into small adventures and chores—most of the latter more than a little bloody, given the nature of the flotilla's distractions.

After fighting with his sense of duty for several hours, Hethor finally gave in and spent the balance of the day playing with the young males. He lent his strength, and even once or twice his practical experience, to the game that they made of every duty and needful thing.

It was a different kind of happiness, he realized, to be at play in the jungles of the world.

That night they lit another bonfire on a bar in the middle of the river. The correct people chanted and sang and roasted the great chunks of meat coiled in the flames, so that even the smoke was delicious. The world's problems seemed far away. Late in the evening, as he listened to the travelers trade stories about the Snake That Ate the World, and the Great Tapir, and other heroes, the trees around them began to sway with a vigor far in excess of the night's wind. The correct people fell silent as Hethor cocked his ear to the music of Creation and heard discord, a stuttering like a gear with a burr in need of filing, hanging up inside some precision mechanism. Though the ground they sat on felt little different, the river slopped its banks as the day birds awoke screaming to take whirring flight in the dark.

After a time the earthquake passed, the river quieted, and the birds returned grumbling and calling to their roosts. The correct people all looked to Hethor, the Messenger, for some comfort.

"I do not know," he said slowly, "stories like yours of the Snake or the Great Tapir or your other heroes and challengers. But I can tell you of the Student, the Master, and the Angel."

Hethor wiped his eyes, took a deep breath, and tried to find a way to make his experience sensible to them.

"Once," Hethor continued, "there lived a Student. He was poor and without aunties or fellow males or a headman to advise him in his life. With his last few gourds and flints, he bargained for a place in the clan of a great . . . a great headman of a kind. Only this headman was a master of things of metal, not of a clan of people.

"The Student called this man Master. He lived among the Master's groves and game trails, taking meat that the Master gave him, and warming himself by the Master's fire. The Student gave to the Master all of his time and effort in service, doing as the Master bid, laboring as the Master saw fit.

"In return, the Master taught the Student the lore of things of metal, their making and their keeping. Things of metal were important in the place where the Student dwelt. They were prized by all the people. The things the Master made and kept, and traded away, were meant to count the motion of the heavens so that a man might always know the day and moment in which he dwelt. These were among the things of metal most prized, so the Student had promise of great success if he were ever to become a Master of his own.

"One day, an Angel came to the Student while he slept in a dirty corner of the Master's grove. The Angel said, 'Be the Messenger, and pursue the word of God to the place where the world has a hurt. There you must stanch that hurt.' When the Student told the Master of the Angel's words, the Master's sons were jealous, and called him liar and thief, and cast him out. The Student became the Messenger, and wanders God's world seeking to stanch its hurt, which causes the world to twitch in pain."

There was silence for a while, and the crackling of the fire. One of the young males finally spoke up.

"A question, Messenger. Why would anyone need to ask the day and moment from a thing of metal, when the sky freely tells this to anyone with eyes to lift upward?"

"I don't know," said Hethor with a smile. "Once, I could answer that question, but the correct people have taught me that I was wrong."

This answer pleased them, and a murmur ran among the hairy men.

Another spoke. "Why did the Student place himself beneath the Master? No person needs to be other than what he is."

"Another question I can no longer answer," Hethor said, "except to say that you are wiser than my old Master and all my teachers together."

They laughed then, and began to trickle away to sleep, each spitting in the fire to douse their little part of it. Hethor sat until the flames reduced themselves to embers, listening to the whirr of bats and thinking about his own story.

THE NEXT day the flotilla resumed its trip down the river. The bloody-damp snakeskin coiled over two rafts, while the crocodile had been sectioned out among those who had slain it. Dragonflies appeared on the water, with wings longer than the span of Hethor's open hands. The trees grew denser and darker.

The character of both the jungle and the river was changing.

Hethor sat among fresh-cut leaves with the golden tablet balanced on his knees, but it was the deepening shadows of the daytime jungle that caught his eye.

"What does it mean?" he finally asked Arellya, waving one hand toward the changing foliage.

"Kalker warned me that our water road eventually

comes to the Great Salt River. In that water a correct person would swim, or even merely drink, in fear of their life. Perhaps these are the first encroachments of the Salt."

"That is the sea," said Hethor, "and I have sailed over it in a boat of the air. Like a wooden bird with woven wings. It may be safely swum in, at least when the sun is bright and the air is calm, but Kalker is right about never drinking it."

Saltwater marshes, then, he thought, and turned his attentions back to the tablet.

It was different somehow, this day. The word he suspected of being the Tetragrammaton was more familiar, possessing something of an aura of holiness about it. Hethor had no sounds for it, so he simply said, in English, "God."

Three times, then: God, God, God.

He traced his fingers over the words. His fingertips felt the tiny clattering hum of the gears within the gears within the gears—that same sense he'd had the night of the festival-rite, when the tongue of the correct people had come to him.

This was the word of God. God's words spoke of Him.

What did God have to say? This message must concern the world—that was, after all, Gabriel's errand for him.

"World" leapt out at him, an echo of bird-screaming jungles and the cold air high atop the Wall mixed together in the touch of Hethor's fingertips on the metal. God . . . world, then God, then God . . . world again.

He was almost willing to believe Kalker now, that there was such a thing as spirit-magic. Hethor closed his eyes, tablet still in hand, and prayed. He sought not the arrogant, intellectual God of Pryce Bodean, but rather the God whose voice Hethor had heard echo through the world during the correct people's festival-rite.

You are there, he prayed, *in the ticking of every clock, in every spring that coils to store energy for the further*

*powering of Creation. Every leaf is a spring storing the
sunlight; every fruit stores the tree. The soul of man stores
You, doesn't it? You are—*

Then the canoe tilted as the paddlers shrieked and
Arellya shouted his name. Tumbling backward, Hethor
saw water *above* his head, and jaws longer than his legs.
Raddled teeth in lengthy rows aiming for his face. Scarlet
gobbets already clung to them as the steersman bobbed in
two surprised, bloody halves in the water.

Hethor slid into the jaws, his legs splashing into the
river. The mouth around his chest was pale and mottled
with gray, the stench of the crocodile's breath appalling
almost beyond measure.

I die, Hethor thought, *taken by a bandit on the water
road.*

His hands flew of their own accord to flip the tablet upward and snag it between the teeth to his right, near to the
back of the jaws. The crocodile's mouth closed with a
creak until it caught on the tablet, which wedged between
upper and lower teeth, stopping the bite. Definitely plated,
some detached part of himself observed. Real gold was
too soft to take such strain. There was still pressure on
Hethor's solar plexus, and death perilously close to his
neck. He remained trapped but whole.

"Messenger!" someone shouted in the speech of the
correct people as the crocodile thrashed.

He was not dead yet, but escape was denied to him.
The crocodile slid backward into the stinking water,
pulling Hethor down.

The music, he thought, hearing the music of Creation.
Change the gearing. Help me, God.

Hethor reached for that sense of hearing everything at
once. The water in his mouth and nose distracted him, as
did the thrashing of the beast that still held him in its
jaws.

He closed his eyes, thought of the midnight clatter he'd
always heard, reached from that to a sense of the crocodile as a made thing of gears and springs. Air pounded in

his chest, his lungs going hot and sour, while his mouth fought to hold back the river, every reflex screaming for a gasp on the very slightest chance that air might come with it.

Something bit his feet. Hethor's concentration shattered, he screamed; the water rushed in along with his comprehension of failure.

I am dead.

Something else struck his head. Not the crocodile, but another combatant in the river. Hethor tried to hit back, but his arm was seized. He grabbed hold of the golden tablet with his free hand, determined to die with the words of God close by.

Then there was propulsion, a sense almost of being thrown. Hethor leapt from the water, breaking the air like a fish striking at dawn's first flight of insects only to fall back down again and be caught by the hands of the correct people.

They pulled him onto a raft. He vomited river water and fear, the tablet still in his hands. Hethor was afraid to look at his feet, afraid to see what might be missing at the end of his legs. The misery in his lungs and head was sufficient distraction.

"Messenger!" someone shouted in his ear. "Do you live?"

He threw up again, gasped, and managed a "yes" in English. Hethor rolled onto his back, opened his eyes, and said, "I have no spirit-magic."

"Life is magic," someone said, sounding much like Kalker. Hethor became lost in a maze of coughing and wheezing and fighting for air as a white bird flew close by overhead, just at the edge of his sight.

HE CAME to sensibility sometime later, still clutching the tablet, curled on the deck of one of the largest rafts. Arellya sat next to him. Her left arm was wrapped in leaves, while her free hand trailed through his hair.

"Of course you live," she said softly when she saw his eyes focus on her.

"The steersman did not."

"No. There are four dead, including him. The other three were lost saving you."

That pained Hethor's heart in a way that the deaths of various of *Bassett*'s people had not. He was, in a sense, captain to this crew. Their lives were his to save or spend. No matter the cost of the spending.

"I'm sorry," he whispered.

"It was where their way led them. They walked along the water road a while in company with the Messenger. None protested his passing."

That seemed a strange way to think of it, as far as Hethor was concerned. Who would have time to protest being eaten by a crocodile?

"I was not paying attention," he began, but Arellya's free hand touched his lips.

"You pursued your spirit-magic into the Message, Messenger. Do not fault this old half-salt river if its small gods fought back. Even the crocodile only follows his nature. You must follow yours."

"Where is the plate now?"

"In your hands, silly little monkey." She leaned over and kissed him, lightly brushing his lips. "Take some fresh water, eat a bit of fruit, and rest. It will still be here when you are better."

LATE THAT afternoon he took up the tablet again. There was slime crusted on it, and blood, but he didn't try to clean the filth off. His heart was sore, his faith in the spirit-magic, whatever it was, bruised by his failure with the crocodile.

"God . . . world, then God, then God . . . world," Hethor said.

Heart, heartsore, the heart of things. With a whirr, another word came to him.

"Heart. The heart of God is the heart of the world." Hethor looked up and shouted, "I understand!"

There was a rippling cheer from the correct people, but nobody asked him what it was that he understood. Instead they busied themselves lashing their flotilla together again. No one had the slightest desire to put ashore in the salt-raddled forest, dark and dank as it was. Better to risk crocodiles in the night than to crouch in those horrid, stinking shadows.

He took up the tablet again, willing the words to come to him. There had been life and death in these tablets already, all three of them now. He knew he would not get a fourth.

"The heart of God is the heart of the world." His fingers traced the first two lines. The third and fourth were harder, but the last two almost came to him. ". . . God . . . the world. As . . . God, so . . . the world. God in the world. God of the world. God begat the world."

Hethor closed his eyes, let the metal under his fingers reveal the fine and finer structures that whirled within its form. The form carried the ghost, so to speak, of what the words and letters had meant to their author—be that Gabriel, God, or some other divine agency. Clockmakers, even, he supposed.

"As God lives," Hethor said, "so lives the world."

It was like a bell tolling in his head. He eagerly looked at the middle lines, that would join them together.

"The heart of God is the heart of the world.

"As man lives, so lives God.

"As God lives, so lives the world."

That was it. The divine message that he had been pursuing since the first golden tablet had come to him in the vertical city.

That was it?

He'd chased across half the world to hear something almost scandalously heretical, and nonsensical to boot. Comparing man to God, as if they were complementary terms in a syllogism, was just wrong.

Or was he focused on Pryce Bodean's God, the God of his childhood churches, rather than Arellya's god, who breathed with the continental green lungs of African jungles?

"Arellya," Hethor said quietly.

She stepped over a tightly lashed pair of canoes to sit with him. "How goes it?"

He read her the message on the tablets.

She smiled. "I worried that you might never understand the words, Messenger. You make me proud."

Though Hethor wished for it, she did not kiss him that time.

NINE

MORNING BROUGHT panic of another kind. They awoke just after dawn to find themselves still drifting among the brooding salt jungles. A distant roaring or booming could be heard. If it was a beast, it was huge. To make such a noise would require a mouth large enough to swallow one of the river's killer crocodiles.

The flotilla scrambled to cut free its member vessels, the better to pull apart and fight or flee as needed. The correct people did very little talking under this threat, far different from their usual chattering joy in almost every aspect of life.

"What comes?" Hethor asked. His heart raced, and though he hated the brand of coward, he could taste coppery fear in his dry mouth.

Arellya shrugged, a gesture she had copied from him. "We do not know. The birds are not fleeing, and nothing in the jungle screams, so perhaps it is not so dangerous."

Or perhaps it has driven everything else off, Hethor thought, but he did not want to say that.

The monster approached them in a rush of water, a wake or wall perhaps a yard high. The booming noise was the sound of the water racing upriver, echoing off the trees on each bank to be magnified. The correct people shouted and whistled, some few casting their spears, but Hethor began to laugh.

"It is a *tidal bore*," he said, using the English words for the thing, "a rush of water from the Great Salt River."

"The river itself attacks us?" Arellya shrieked.

"No," Hethor said as the water hit the boats and rafts, scattering them further and turning more than a few over. Correct people tumbled in the air, splashed yelling into the water, clung to each other and their boats.

It was gone within a minute, even the noises. Those who had tumbled in were helped out, and boats were righted. No one seemed to be missing or badly hurt, though some belongings were lost.

"If that is a peaceful *bore*," said Arellya, imitating Hethor's English word, "I fear to ever see an angry one."

"That is like a rain within the river," Hethor said, trying for a better explanation. "It is of the river's nature, but only near the Great Salt River."

This information was passed around among the boats to much nodding and chin-scratching. They shortly reformed the flotilla to collectively pole and paddle their way downriver again. Even the air reeked of salt, and what Hethor thought was the medicinal smell of seaweed. Everyone agreed they were close to their goal.

"The Great Salt River," Arellya told him. "That will be a sight to delight the soul."

"*Surf.*" Hethor once more of necessity used the English word. "Ripples in the Great Salt River, very big ones that fold over on themselves. They are beautiful."

As the day went by, the water road grew wider and wider, until they lost sight of the northern bank. The flow shifted from brown to a murky olive color, but it still seemed more river than sea to Hethor. They had not crossed into what he thought to be ocean, so he held his counsel even as various of the correct people dipped their hands in the water to taste, debating saltiness. Would the

Great Salt River be pure white, like actual salt? Would it be brown, or green, or some color known only to God?

Sometime after noon, the question answered itself. Streams of white foam, or perhaps little bubbles, appeared in the water. Up ahead the water looked choppy, surging rather than flowing.

"That," said Hethor, "is the Great Salt River."

Eager to be on the sea itself, the correct people paddled furiously, crossing rough water and a great bar to struggle among the waves. They screamed with delight as they were tossed, then dropped.

"South," called Hethor. "Turn south. Do not go out to *sea*."

Arellya joined him in calling to the excited correct people, but not all heeded the direction. At least three canoes and two rafts paddled enthusiastically out onto open water, far past range of voice.

Hethor despaired of ever seeing them again.

"It is their road, their way," Arellya shouted over the splashing of the waves.

They struggled south behind the line of breaking waves. Hethor scanned the shore. As best as he knew, Malgus had come to earth somewhere along this coast, but finding the man by simply casting about would be like searching all of Connecticut for a missing house cat.

Hethor scanned the jungled shore. Here, just as along the river, the trees came right to the water, omitting the usual courtesy of dunes and salt marshes, or decent rocky headlands—the sorts of geography Hethor was accustomed to along Long Island Sound. The jungle didn't even rise to the horizon. In his entire journey from Arellya's village, Hethor had been journeying across a great, low plain.

He finally spotted something out of place—a spire or spar that rose high. It glinted in the afternoon sun. Hethor stared, then waved for Arellya and some of the other correct people to look where he pointed.

"It is stone," Arellya said. "With a great fire atop."

A lighthouse, thought Hethor. Which implied a port of substance. "A large village awaits us," he called out. "A village of boats, and stones, and rock roads such as you have never seen."

On a great adventure, clearly ready for anything now that they had seen the sea, his correct people cheered.

They worked their way southward for another two hours, the lighthouse growing more visible, other towers rising beyond it. At the same time, the chop whipped up on the sea. It was clear to Hethor that a storm was working in from farther offshore. Though they had not yet reached their goal, he finally decided that the flotilla must move ashore.

"Land," Hethor shouted through cupped hands. "We must make our way to land."

The rising wind stole his words, though he stood in the dangerously rocking canoe. He milled his arms, trying to attract attention, Arellya yelling with him.

Some of the flotilla saw Hethor's signals, some did not, or perhaps chose to ignore him in their eagerness to reach the lighthouse. These people had never seen the sea, did not understand storms or open water, he realized. He wished mightily they had landed at the mouth of the river and walked south. Certainly the correct people would have known how to conduct that march, and they could have safely admired the sea from the shore.

As it was, Hethor and Arellya and their paddlers beached themselves unaccompanied. They glimpsed other canoes and rafts fighting the swells farther south, trying to come ashore in the wind and rain that had come up with the dusk. The oncoming storm in turn drove the surf harder.

Ten of them gathered in the slight shelter of a stand of palms. "We have to help the others," Hethor shouted.

"None can move in this weather," someone shouted back.

"Shelter," said Arellya.

He could not persuade them to do anything more.

Hethor felt a terrible guilt as the correct people wove a covering into the root balls of some enormous cypress-like trees just inland from the palms. Some of his flotilla was surely lost at sea, and more would drown. Arellya seemed less concerned, mostly sharing in his anxiety rather than the reasons behind it, while the erstwhile paddlers worked with almost their usual cheer.

Later, as they huddled under shelter with no light, and only a little cold food in their bellies, Hethor curled up between Arellya and one of the other correct people. The rest gathered around them in turn. "Why is death so easy for you?" he asked, whispering fiercely to her.

She half turned, so he could smell her sweet breath, and whispered back. "Death is never easy for the one whose path it is."

"But your people, you are not afraid. You almost rejoice in it."

"They came because they would; they died because they were doing what they chose to do."

He could see her teeth gleaming even in the dark of their shelter, punctuating her smile.

"They are gone now, too many of them. This hurts my heart," Hethor said.

"Mine, too. But what do you think death is?"

"At death we . . . we go to God." Hethor wasn't sure he actually believed that the Christ would return someday to restore everyone from their graves to a gleaming clock-work Heaven, though he had certainly heard enough sermons on the subject. The Winding of the Souls, many people called it. The enrapture was an article of fervent faith among some sects of Christians. It always felt like arrant wish fulfillment to Hethor.

What God wanted was for people to live well—that was clear to Hethor both from the Bible and from common sense. The rest of what people chose to believe was churchiness of various degrees.

"When correct people die, we become part of the world," whispered Arellya softly. "When we die in a beautiful place, we share that beauty. When we die in strangeness, we become strange. When we die in hunger, we are part of all hunger. So there is joy in dying where and how you choose."

How different was that from the teachings he had heard all his life?

That night Hethor dreamed that the Earth was a giant raft sailing a brass sea. Smallwood commanded everyone, giving rambling funeral sermons as people fell off the edges in never-ending waves.

HE AWOKE before dawn to quiet and an absence of dripping water. Extracting himself from the great, hairy pile of correct people, Hethor took his golden tablet and slipped from the shelter to pick his way to the shore.

There was actually a little bit of muddy beach beyond the brambled palms, which he stepped out onto. Looking south, he could see the lighthouse gleaming like a star fallen to Earth. The glow was pale and steady, which implied electricks rather than the more old-fashioned kerosene lamps some New England lighthouses still used. Hethor was surprised that there should be electricks in the Southern Earth.

Arellya joined him, slipping her arm around his waist. "We will look for our males as we walk south today," she said. "We will rejoice in who we find alive, sing the deaths of those we find beyond help, and honor the memories of those we never encounter at all. This is our way. Can you follow our way, at least on this day, Messenger?"

Hethor loved the feeling of warmth where she touched him, the gentle pressure and silk-fine texture of her hair. He was afraid to speak, afraid to spoil the moment, but she deserved an answer. "Yes," he said. "I can follow your way."

Together they watched color steal into the sky as waves

rushed at their feet and mists rose from the jungle bearing the stench of life. Her touch lingered long upon his wrist.

AS THE day wore on they made a slow pace of walking. Scouting ahead of Hethor and Arellya the correct people quickly found wreckage, but it was their own canoe, shattered in the night by the storm.

After a time they found a raft, mostly intact, but no sign of any more correct people. Arellya stood knee-deep in the ocean and sang for a while, free-form poetry about the Great Salt River and souls riding the waves. Moving on, they found a dead correct person, crabs gnawing at his body. Arellya and the others refused to bury him. Instead they sang another version of her earlier song, all of them together this time.

Farther along they found another canoe with six correct people dancing around it.

So the day went—the living, the dead, and the missing. By dusk they were perhaps three or four miles from the lighthouse, which seemed to be the northern end of the city. They had found twelve canoes and rafts from the flotilla out of the more than thirty that had originally departed on the water road. Some were missing their crews.

Hethor counted Arellya and fifty-three young males of the correct people with him at sundown.

"When we are again home," said one of the males, "I will make a story of the Great Salt River."

Arellya chittered her laughter. "We will all make that story. Like good shelter, the stories will weave together."

Hethor sat silent into the evening. He was sad despite his promise to Arellya. He turned the golden tablet over and over in his hands while the correct people began to try out different versions of their story. They ate grubs and shoots foraged raw from the swamp and whistled and clicked far into the night.

"As God lives, so lives the world," Hethor said to himself quietly. He had no stomach for the uncooked grubs, but sidled off munching on some shoots to watch the star-lit surf and think further on his golden tablet. What did it mean, then, that the Mainspring was running down?

Were the earthquakes the nightmares of God?

Or His palsies?

THE NEXT day after breaking their way through more jungle and mud, they had to swim two miles of swamp, clinging to driftwood, to reach the sandy beach at the base of the lighthouse. By some miracle all the correct people made it, though Hethor expected crocodiles to leap out at any moment.

The lighthouse itself was of a cyclopean architecture Hethor had never seen outside of fanciful paintings, though it did resemble William of Ghent's jungle fortress. The building appeared to have been raised in solid rock, towering perhaps a hundred and fifty feet from the sand around its base, and hexagonal in cross-section. The base in turn simply plunged into the sand like the blade of a sheathed dagger, rather than revealing any-thing that might be considered a foundation. At the top each of the six faces branched out in a prong to support whatever mechanism generated the light. The whole structure was seamless, a deep uniform brown. There were no doors or windows that Hethor could locate.

"Is this how the huts of your village are made?" Arellya asked him. Unlike Hethor, she did not seem par-ticularly awed by the lighthouse.

"Not at all," said Hethor. "In fact, this challenges even my imagination."

She smiled sweetly. "I find that unlikely."

There must be a great race abiding here, Hethor thought, *to make such things.* It was like reading Plato discussing Atlantis.

Past the lighthouse, the beach ran along another mile or so before reaching a breakwater and a city wall. Both structures were built of the same smooth, featureless brown stone in a scale far outsized to the needs of ordinary men, let alone the little correct people.

Though the wall was vertical, shielding the bases of the towers behind it from view, the breakwater had angled sides. After some confusion a mission was dispatched to cut vines and sticks for a ladder. Once that work was done, Hethor and his band climbed the breakwater for their first real view of the city.

There were rings of walls, walls within walls partially visible because of the high arched gates that opened between them. Towers of construction very similar to the lighthouse scraped toward the sky. Some were topped with orreries or great wheels of brass in apparent imitation of God's design for the cosmos.

These towers within the walls had windows cut into them, though few and widely spaced. The effect was that of a race of giant children who had built with crude blocks, rather than the rational designs of man.

Only the harbor looked familiar. The sheltered water hosted a dozen sailing and steamships, and three airship masts. One of the airship masts was occupied, though by an airship of a design completely alien to Hethor's admittedly limited experience. Its gasbag was narrow and wide, almost like a manta ray's body. The hull beneath seemed shallow and wide to match. It stood peacefully at the mast, though Hethor imagined just from the shape that it would be quite fast. He also noted that unlike *Bassett,* it had no steering oars or stuns'l spars.

He was not here about ships. He was here to find Simeon Malgus. Hethor turned to Arellya and the other correct people, who were seated, staring across the breakwater at the harbor and the city.

"We have died," one of the males said. "This is a place beyond the world."

"I have never imagined a village so big," said another.

"Or even stones of such a size," added a third.

"This is as great as any of the cities of men where I come from, beyond the Wall," Hethor said. The correct people's language had no word for Northern Earth. "But still, these are just men. I mean to enter the city and search for the guide I lost before I met you."

"You could spend a lifetime looking through such huts," Arellya said.

"Well, yes." Hethor didn't really want to consider that too carefully. "But I think it will be easier than that. I found him once before, atop the Wall, the previous time when I thought I had lost him."

"And you claim that *he* is the guide?"

There was something dangerous about correct people logic, Hethor decided. "Let us be on our way, then."

"This is truly the stone road," said one of the correct people.

"Truly," they all murmured.

IT WAS not hard to enter the city—the walls, while high and steep, were unguarded. The gateways lacked even gates to shut. These people did not fear, Hethor realized. Perhaps their walls were there more because some among the inhabitants believed a city *should* have walls than because they needed them for any particular reason. Ornaments for a metropolis.

The breakwater led them to a boulevard that passed through one of the empty gates; then they were among the people of the city, Hethor and his whole crowd of correct people.

These folk were impossibly tall, legs like storks' with arms to match, their bodies thin as knives. None of them were as short as six feet, and Hethor would have put most of them closer to eight. Their skin was coffee-dark, their features their own rather than resembling any race Hethor had ever seen. Noses were long and angled, ears had enormous lobes, and their brows were ridged as if all of them frowned with the labor of constant great thought.

They were all dressed in fabrics of a hundred colors. Each robe or sash or blouse was dyed to shame any rainbow. Most of the colors jarred the eye, inharmonious compositions laid over contradictory essays in hue and tone. There were animal skins and chains and other accessories in abundance, and most carried thuribles or wands, as a gypsy fortune-teller might.

Hethor even saw one fellow of middling height, about seven feet, made up with a white face and ruffed tunic, looking like nothing so much as a clown, walking a goat on a leash. Others had animals as well. Familiars, perhaps.

Every man was a sorcerer, every woman a witch. What else could they be? Not a single one of them seemed to notice Hethor or the correct people. This was beyond haughtiness or indifference—though no one collided with them, none made eye contact, none stared, none stopped them to ask what they were about.

Hethor could not even imagine walking the streets of New Haven or Boston with a mob of hairy little men carrying spears. There would be riots or arrests, or both, in very short order. Here, they might as well have been ghosts.

The strangest thing was that the clicking sound of gears, Hethor's gift from his deafness, was almost overwhelming with these sorcerer-folk. Among the correct people, he only heard the inner sounds at the height of emotion and sensory stimulation or on the edge of sleep. Here, just walking down the smooth-slabbed street, each of the witches and sorcerers he passed thundered like the works of a church steeple clock in need of lubrication.

Either the residents of this city were much closer to God or much farther away from God than most folk. Hethor would wager on distance, not nearness, but perhaps that was just his prejudice.

"These are a strange race," Arellya said to him. "They make even you seem ordinary."

He had to laugh, though somehow, she pained his heart at the same time.

THEY SEARCHED through the city most of the rest of the day, weaving their way through the circled walls and towering gates.

"What if we are lost?" Hethor asked at one point, looking down yet another curving street of oversized brown buildings.

"Correct people do not lose their way," said Arellya. "If we walk somewhere, we can always walk back."

"I'm glad some of us can do that," Hethor muttered.

The inattention of the residents continued to grate on him. It really did seem as if Hethor and the correct people were walking dead. Did this foretell some horrible doom at dusk, as in an E. A. Poe story? Or perhaps it was something else, some aspect of their bodies and their minds, strange physiologies suitable for life under the African sun and the practice of magic.

Not that he really believed in magic. But Hethor had seen, and done, too many strange and wondrous things the past few months since leaving home to be so certain of his doubts, either.

In the late afternoon the party made their way into the city center, where there was a great square. More accurately a round, as it were. This was bordered by the smallest stone structures Hethor had seen so far in the city, low-walled rectangles that looked as though they might have been intended for market booths or stalls, though there was no market here.

A few dozen of the local citizenry passed through the square, colorful as ever. Just like the rest of the city there seemed to be no idlers. All of these magical folk walked briskly on their missions, having scarcely more time or recognition for each other than they did for their uninvited visitors.

At the center of the square was a pillar shaped much like

the lighthouse, though smaller, perhaps fifty feet in height. Chains dangled down its sides. At the top a man was bound.

Simeon Malgus, Hethor realized with a chill in his heart. He knew now where the navigator had landed in his fall from Heaven.

"There is my guide," he told Arellya, pointing upward.

"Do you plan to follow him there?"

"No." Hethor's mouth set, grim and firm. "Is there any way to fetch him down?"

"Certainly."

Arellya went into a whispered conference with the other correct people. The males gestured and made hand signs. The whole group of them except for her scampered away, swarming about the base of the tower.

Hethor watched in some amazement as the correct people formed a mass, climbing on one another's backs and shoulders, until the leaders could reach the hanging chains. They shifted to a sort of hairy-man ladder that would be the envy of any troupe of acrobats, and passed some of their smaller members up to the top.

The result of this effort was that four correct people stood around Malgus on the crown of the pillar. Each carried a flint or bronze knife with him. They went to work undoing his chains, breaking the bonds by dint of slow, careful effort rather than the brute force that was lacking from both their materials and their slight frames.

Some minutes passed; then Malgus was handed over the edge. They lowered him past the stone talons of the top of the tower and into the arms of the correct people straining just below.

But his weight was too much. Hethor watched with dawning horror as the acrobatic ladder swayed, correct people scrabbling for purchase against the stone or grasping onto the chains.

The collapse came with the awful inevitability of the toppling of some forest giant. Correct people leapt or fell away from the tower as Malgus slid free. Tumbling as he fell, his body took one horrible bounce on the stone.

Hethor sprinted toward the tower base while correct people screeched and thumped down onto the plaza. Some of the hairy men seemed seriously injured, but Hethor's only focus was on Simeon Malgus.

Malgus had landed just against the base of his prison-pillar, lying on his left side facing out. His left arm was folded out of sight behind him, in what had to be a horrible fracture. His legs lay unnaturally still. They did not even shiver like the rest of him. Blood seeped from his nose and pooled at the lower corner of his mouth. His rounded face was drawn and chapped, and when his lids fluttered, Malgus' brown eyes seemed clouded.

"My apprentice comes," Malgus said in a weak voice. He gave a shuddering gasp. Then, "Ill met, Hethor."

"Navigator Malgus." Hethor reached down, took the dying man's right hand. It shuddered. Even within the skin Hethor could feel a movement that seemed to correspond to the gears-within-gears sounds he had been hearing. He had an intense sensation of Malgus as nothing more—or less—than an assemblage of tiny machines, tinier machines within them.

"You are a fool," Malgus said, his eyes fluttering shut again.

"I have killed you when I meant to save you." Hethor turned Malgus' hand over within his own, his heart banded tight with pain. "I am the fool."

Malgus' breath hissed hollow and loud like a bellows within his chest. He ignored Hethor. Around them, correct people keened and chattered over their wounded. Speaking English to Malgus, Hethor found the language of his helpers to be just so many clicks and whistles again.

"Nothing is . . . ," Malgus began, then stopped. He opened his eyes. "Do not believe."

"Believe what?"

"You take the . . . clockwork of the universe . . . as evi . . . evidence of God's plan." Malgus' breath hissed some more as he fought pain and gathered strength to speak again. "It shows only . . . the mechan . . . istic universe. Uncaring. An illusion. Even the Clockmakers have turned . . . their faces . . . from the world."

"You and I crossed the gear atop the Equatorial Wall," Hethor said, almost wringing Malgus' hand in his. "That was no illusion."

"God's love. God's plan." Malgus tried to sit up. "Your belief will doom you. Trust William of Ghent. The white bird. It . . . he . . . he . . . he will call back our—" Malgus coughed, then vomited blood.

William of Ghent? Too late for that man. For good or ill, Hethor had struck a blow against the sorcerer, though he doubted a fall into the brass had killed such a powerful man. More the pity that was. "What of William?"

Malgus' breath heaved; then his body stilled. A little brass spring popped from his mouth to strike the stones with a high ringing before it rolled to a stop in a pool of the navigator's blood.

Arellya squatted next to Hethor. "Your guide is dead." Her whistling clicks coalesced into language for him even as she spoke.

"Yes." He still held Malgus' hand, which was already cooling. He was afraid to think overmuch on what the spring meant.

A mechanistic universe was the ultimate extension of Rational Humanism, excluding the absent God, or even His indirect agency in the form of the Clockmakers. It was the most arrant heresy to think that the gears that drove the world were in no wise of God.

Wasn't it?

Arellya tugged on Hethor's arm. "We should go."

Hethor looked up, his eyes blurred and peppered by tears. Around the edges of the plaza, the tall, proud sorcerers and witches of the cyclopean city paused in their circlings. The locals, who had before gazed through Hethor like so much air, now stared at him and his correct people as if they were live coals on a sitting room carpet.

"The harbor," said Hethor. "There is no help for me

here. Either the Jade Abbott was mistaken, or Malgus was." Alternatively, Malgus had turned traitor—the name of William of Ghent the last words on the late navigator's tongue. "No matter. There are no Sages of the South who will advise me."

"To the harbor we shall go," Arellya replied. "But we must move soon." She called the young males together. Two were badly injured in their fall from Malgus' pillar of punishment, several more limping and stumbling. "Kiklo and Barshee must be carried. The rest of you ready your spears. We take the fighting road back to the harbor."

Hethor stirred. "Malgus. We must take Malgus. Hero or traitor, I will not leave him lie here."

"This is a strange and wondrous place," Arellya said, urgency in her voice for the first time since Hethor had come to understand her speech. "In death he will be strange and wondrous. We must move fast, Messenger."

"Malgus and I are not correct people," Hethor said, picking his words carefully even among the rattling of spears as the young males formed up around him and Arellya. "God has asked us to care for our souls in our own way. I will bury him, and say a memorial prayer."

Arellya held his gaze for a moment. She then shrugged and counted off four more males to carry Malgus' body.

Running in a mob, they jogged toward the gated exit from the market. The folk of the city lined up along the route Hethor and the correct people must take, but did not move to interfere.

We made this thing happen, Hethor thought. *Our choices continue to drive us forward.* He did not rightly know what they would do upon reaching the harbor. Take to a ship, perhaps, or even that airship, though he despaired of working any such vessel with this correct person mob trying to serve as crew.

They passed out the gate and into one of the curving streets. The correct people headed left without hesitation. Hethor was unsure of even that choice. Glancing back, he saw Malgus' body following him, chest high as the dead navigator rode on the shoulders of the correct people. Beyond Malgus and the last bobbing spears, the tall sorcerers followed. Their pursuers poured out of the gate at a quick pace that managed to still seem unhurried.

Hethor could have sworn he had never seen this street before, that this combination of buildings and alleys and tall, narrow doors was novel, but he had to believe Arellya and her people. They jogged, humming in time to their steps, all of them watchful.

The next massive gate approached on their right. The sun was westering over the ocean. Hethor's little band ran through blocks of shadow from the taller buildings. This gate's passage lay in deeper shadow, and as they turned into it, Hethor thought for a moment he saw the gleam of watchful eyes waiting in that temporary darkness. But they passed through unmolested, though the locals following behind continued to swell in numbers.

Running down the next avenue, Hethor sensed the pace of the correct people faltering.

"What is it?" he asked Arellya.

"The gates have moved," she said. "We will keep following this road, for there is no other."

The gates have moved? How was that possible? The whole city was built in circles, like an archery target, but it seemed inconceivable that it could somehow rotate on the central axis.

Sorcerers, Hethor thought. He had already been convinced they were sorcerers and magicians in this city. This was proof that eldritch power was at work here.

Another gate loomed on their left, this one completely unfamiliar to Hethor. Arellya and the young males took the turn without hesitation. These shadows were even darker, filled with sufficient menace to give the correct people pause, though even as they missed a step or two, they surged on through. The gateways were ten paces wide, enough for the group of them to pass, but still a funnel to choke and slow their progress.

Nothing substantive lurked there either, but a mob of the locals waited on the next street to block their passage left. Arellya swung right instead. Another mob waited there. She did not break her stride, but shouted something Hethor found unintelligible. The young males lowered their spears and bent their bodies, racing to surge around Hethor and Arellya to place them in the center of the correct people's charge, next to Malgus' body.

The sorcerers and witches were still silent, silent as the stones of their city, and their line stood unflinching as the correct people charged. Hethor wanted to shut his eyes, to hear the eerily quiet rush forward, the slapping of hairy feet on stone opposed only by the faint rustling of robes, counterpointed by the combined clockwork of a thousand hearts. The sight made his heart quail. The silence terrified him. He expected to hear the shrieking and screaming that any European charge would have entailed.

The correct people met the sorcerers' line, spears flashing off a brilliant glare, the first few of the hairy men screeching and collapsing. Their momentum carried them through a sheet of fire more like lightning than flame.

The stench of burning hair and coppery blood flooded Hethor's nostrils even as he stumbled over bodies large and small.

The mob flowed backward, away from their line of advance, the correct people still not slowing their pace. Hethor knew they were lost, that the moving walls or gates had defeated even the unerring sense of direction of Arellya's people. But he could not tell that from the behavior of those around him.

Four, perhaps five, correct people had fallen at the hands of the sorcerers' fire. The rest seemed unconcerned, almost as if they had not noticed. They had not lost hope. Hethor had been told why this was, how they saw death, but still he did not understand it. He continued to run with them though his lungs were beginning to burn and his legs ached with the pace.

Another gate, the shadows deeper this time. Eyes gleamed within that darkness as well, large and yellow. Fangs glittered beneath some of those eyes, crystal knives waiting for Hethor and his escort.

This time the guardians were real, or at least more real than before. The first rank of correct people shrieked. Some threw up their spears to ward their faces, but the mass pushed on through with dogged momentum. Eyes leered, fangs slashed, and a foetid breath, rank as the crocodile's or the night wind off the salt jungle, blew through the gate. Hethor had the impression of some vast strength, a beast with a hundred heads coiling throughout the dark of the world; then they were back in another street.

From here he could see the lighthouse. He knew that the harbor lay close to hand. The sorcerers and witches were spread out again along their line of retreat, no longer blocking the road as before. They seemed willing to let fear and darkness do their work.

Arellya barked out another command, and the correct people picked up their pace. Hethor stumbled, but caught himself, and broke into a sprint. Though his legs were twice as long as theirs, they moved with an economy and strength that he could not match. His muscles burned.

A last gate lay ahead, one more turn to reach the harbor and the escape of a boat or the airship. Even without the pursuing mob on their heels, Hethor would not have cared to remain anywhere near the city after dark. The great, terrible things that lived in the shadows would take form and pad the stone streets, hunting any who did not belong.

He had a sudden vision of the city as a living creature, its daytime people no more than fevered dreams of the thinking stones, its nighttime terrors the true embodiment of the spirit of the place.

Then they were in the gateway. Though they had passed through nothing like this on the way in, the tunnel was much longer than any of the other gates, the setting sun a gleaming, distant dot. An army of the shadow creatures stood between them and the sun, eyes and teeth gleaming, bodies just wavering into being.

"Light," Hethor shouted. "Run into the sun! They are only darkness!"

With a ragged shout this time, the correct people again leveled their spears and charged the angry shadows.

It was a terrible race, full of screaming and blood. Hethor's heart seized with terror, his veins turning to ice as his boots changed to lead. This close to sunset, the monsters in the dark found their voices and roared like all the cougars of New England massed on a single hillside. It was worse than the sounds of the night jungle, worse even than the attack of the crocodile on the river, though no claw or tooth touched Hethor. Many of the correct people suffered.

They must have hope, to reach the sun, Hethor thought furiously. His soul-magic had failed him with the crocodile, but he *was* the Messenger. "The heart of God," he called out to the correct people, "is the heart of the world."

"Heart of the world!" they shouted back.

"As man lives, so lives God."

"So lives God!"

"As God lives, so lives the world."

"So lives the world!"

The words seemed to have little effect on the shadow monsters, but they propelled Hethor's feet and the steps of his little war band on toward the reddening sun, until they burst out onto the dockside. The breakwater stretched to their right, the docks and airship masts to their left. The sun was a receding glare touching down on the horizon, pressing the ocean down with its weight.

Arellya raised her hand, and the correct people slowed. Hethor looked around. Where earlier they had been fifty and more, there were perhaps three dozen left. Malgus' body still rode on their shoulders. Fifteen or so dead, in the race from the central plaza to here, and even outside the concentric walls they were still not safe. He stifled a sob.

"The boats," he called out. "To the boats."

Down the docks they ran, even the seemingly tireless correct people slowing with the burdens of their wounds and fear. Night was approaching with an almost audible rumble, the city's denizens readying themselves to strike their greatest and final blow.

The sun was a glimmering paring when the correct people reached the first of the moored ships. They were small, fishing boats or shallow scows, Hethor realized. He had no knowledge of sailing, and though the correct people were apt boatmen, they knew less than he did about the sea—their Great Salt River.

Running on into the fall of night, they reached a larger ship, a wide-bottomed trader like a modern version of a European trading cog out of history. Too many sails, too many skills none of them understood.

It had to be the airship, Hethor realized.

The mooring masts were at the far end of the docks, and the sun was vanishing with an air of finality. "The trees," Hethor said, "at the end of the road." He had no correct people word for mast or dock.

The fanged shadows boiled out behind them, howling for blood, their voices creaking with the sound of snapping bones. The fallen of Hethor's own party seemed to be swept up in the pursuit, dead correct people on their trail, keening, crying, blaming. Rivers of red flowed rapidly across the stone dock in the twilight, slippery sticky blood overtaking their flight to make them trip and slide headfirst into stone bollards or pitch screaming into the sea.

The first of the correct people reached the mast where the manta-shaped airship was moored. Startling a pale bird that had been roosting there, they swarmed up the mast much as they had swarmed up the pillar in the central plaza—in groups and ladders and chains, some on the rungs, some on the chain, some grasping the edges of the stone mast with panicked fingers and preternaturally agile feet.

Hethor stopped and turned to look behind him. Though the reeking breath of shadow had been on his neck a moment before, rivers of blood tugging at his ankles, the dock was clear. It looked peaceful and deserted as it had when they first spied the city from the breakwater by the lighthouse.

"No," Hethor whispered. "You will not gull me with silence. You will not take me in the back."

He picked up a dropped spear, the haft of some wood so dark as to be black in the twilight, a bronze point gleaming even now. As the last few of the correct people flowed around him, Hethor swept the spear back and forth, seeking to block whatever followed.

For a moment, despite his instincts, he felt foolish. Then the air seemed to thicken like a soup stock on the boil. He didn't see the shadow monsters, but he *felt* them in the prickle of his hair, in the sickness of his gut. The gears-within-gears sense he had of hearing the universe was whirring loudly now, at a manic pace that threatened to strip the cogs of reality around him.

Hethor stabbed out, and the bronze tip vanished into thin air. He jerked the spear back with a gout of thick, black blood flowing from an unseen wound. Switching his grip, Hethor swung the spear again, once more striking something. It was like dragging a knife on carpet. Still invisible, the monster was as wide as the docks on which it stood.

He could not fight such a great thing, but he was slowing it. Hethor glanced over his shoulder at the mast. Malgus was rising upward, in a slow, steady parody of his fatal fall, the last of the correct people pushing the body from below. The sight reminded Hethor of so many furry roaches swarming a vast stone rope.

No matter, he thought. They were up, they were safe— safe as they could be on the airship.

He turned and stabbed again, the spear striking something so close Hethor could have reached out and touched it without a stretch. Time for him to go. Another hard stroke with the spear, this time leaving it hanging in the invisible monster, and he turned and raced to the mast.

Once his back was turned, the ravening horrors returned to his mind, his ears, the prickling skin on the back of his neck. "You can be killed," shouted Hethor, "and I left a spear in you to prove it!"

Hand on rung, hand on the next rung. Climbing as he had within the gasbag of *Bassett,* mindful of the fatal dangers and moving as quickly as he could.

Something grabbed his leg, a tentacle or claw. Hethor tugged, trapped; then several spears showered past him from above and the grip broke. He sprang up the ladder again until hairy little hands pulled him onto a small platform where ropes led to the airship.

"The great boat of air was empty of persons," said one of the males. "Quickly, across the vines."

Though they were a hundred feet above the stone dock, Hethor scrambled along two of the ropes like a monkey in the jungle. His fearful days on *Bassett* were behind him, while the possibility of falling from the lines was the least of his troubles here.

Another set of hands pulled him over the rail. A last few correct people followed Hethor. Lying on the deck, he looked up at Arellya and gasped, "How many?"

"We have lost twenty-one. There are thirty-two left, plus you, me, and the dead navigator." Though she did not seem angry, as a human would have, there was still a tension in her voice.

"Cast off." Realizing he had spoken in English, he said in the language of the correct people, "We must be free of the tree."

"Throw down the vines," Arellya called out.

The manta-shaped airship bobbed, then began to turn into the wind. Hethor wondered who was at the steering, then realized the unusual design of the gasbag was like the body of a bird—it would naturally face that way.

Could they drift this night, while he and the correct people recovered from their run? Around him the little hairy men couched or sprawled on the deck, most tending wounds, all gasping for air, soaked with sweat.

His sense of fear was gone, too. Hethor pulled himself up to the rail and looked overboard for the city of sorcerers and shadows.

It was below him, drifting toward the stern of the airship. He could clearly see the circled walls, as the streets seemed to be glowing with the same fixed light as the lighthouse had. It was a vast eye scanning the night sky for sin and villainy.

Or stolen airships, Hethor thought with a bitter smile.

Unblinking, bright, armed with the terror of every childhood shadow, viewed from above, the eye of the city still seemed blind. It was a genius loci, Hethor realized, the power of a place that did not extend beyond its bounds.

He badly wanted to drink some water, and then to sleep deeply, with a need as strong as any he'd ever felt. But this night brought one other duty first.

"I will commend the navigator's soul to God now," he said to Arellya when he found her on the foredeck. "It is mine to do, but you and any of the correct people are welcome to join me."

Trembling with fatigue, she nodded. Another of the habits she'd learned from him.

"I ONCE heard the headman of a boat of the air say that a great village of past times burned," Hethor said to the assembled correct people. Wrapped in some hastily located silk from belowdecks, Simeon Malgus lay at his feet, three spears beneath him for a pall. Somehow "Rome burned" had sounded better in English.

He went on.

"The past times of my people are full of fire and fear. Villages and villages of villages fought one another, the way monkeys will fight for scraps. This even though my people dwell among riches.

"The navigator was one of my people who heeded the word of more than one headman. Though all of us are free to follow different voices, it is thought poorly done to hear first this one then another by secret ways, pledging loyalty all the while. The navigator did these things.

"He was still a good man.

"The navigator treated me as you might treat a strange animal, or worse. He took my art from me, and destroyed it. He drove me away with shouts and threats, and avoided me thereafter.

"He was still good to me.

"At the last the navigator was set to be my guide against his will. He led me through a valley of danger, drove me over a cliff to fall forever through the sky, lost me and his own way, and came to death finally at my hands in a city of stones and magic.

"He still showed me the way."

Hethor stopped, bile in his mouth and tears once again stinging his eyes. He wanted to shout, rail against Malgus and the poor judgment of the Jade Abbott in setting the man as Hethor's guide. But was either of them wrong? Was Hethor wrong?

Under the night sky and God's brassy regard, he did not want to utter maledictions against the soul of Simeon Malgus. His words were not lies, his eulogy not a fraud. Just a way of thinking.

"The navigator made my way possible. The navigator brought the Messenger to the correct people, though his methods seem strange to us. The navigator died with the name of God upon his lips."

A lie, thought Hethor, but the right lie.

"With the navigator's name on my own lips, *Simeon Malgus* in the tongue that he and I share, I consign him back to God, who first created him."

Hethor nodded, and six correct people stepped forward, took the spear handles, and sent Malgus' body spinning into the blackness. Hethor stepped to the rail to study the starlit waters shimmering far below the airship. Though he watched a long time, and listened carefully, he never saw or heard a splash.

Finally he looked up at the orbital tracks gleaming like brass threads in the night sky. The music of Creation was still loud in his ears, though back to normal from the chattering chaos of the dockside monster.

"Thank you, Simeon Malgus," Hethor told the stars.

He found a place on the deck to sleep, trusting luck and decent weather to keep the airship in the sky until he woke to consider what to do next. Arellya stayed far away from him that night.

TEN

CLOUDS TRAILED themselves across the sky like regimented sheep marching to some distant war with the wolves. The Equatorial Wall loomed to the north, though it had already sunk noticeably toward the horizon since Hethor's last view of it in the great stone city. The moon's thread shone in the sky with Luna herself pale and blotchy amid the blue of the day. The sea below was patchy in color—irregular zones of purple, gray, blue, and where they passed closer to shore, the green of an old Mason jar. At this altitude, perhaps a thousand feet, the air was fresh and fine, scented of salt and sunlight.

All in all, it was a glorious day. Especially since no mute mages or toothy shadows stalked them.

Hethor stood at the stern of the stolen airship. A few of the young male correct people nearby watched him curiously. Since their escape the evening before, the ship had steered itself. As best as he could determine, their course had described a long loop out to sea during the night, and headed back toward shore with the dawn.

Which seemed to make some sense, given his basic understanding of meteorology.

The weather was good, the trim of the ship was stable,

and he was in no hurry to find new ways to drop himself out of the sky. Besides, even if he had known how to control the ship, Hethor had yet to set a course.

Dark shapes swirled in the air farther out to sea. Whether they were gulls, albatrosses, or something larger and strange, he had no way to tell. Still, the distant fliers prompted Hethor to think on the archangel Gabriel and Hethor's duties to Heaven.

"I still know nothing of the Key Perilous," he told his scattered onlookers, "even after all this time and trouble. But the Mainspring I could perhaps find."

The Earth orbited on brass tracks—a ring gear of planetary dimensions. The planet had an axis of rotation. That meant that there had to be a spring coiled around that axis to drive the rotation. The axis, of course, would meet the surface at the poles.

Hethor knew very little of the pole of Northern Earth, and absolutely nothing of the Southern Pole, except for the presumption that it was icy as well. But he knew perfectly well where it lay. The coastline below him ran roughly southward. If he could find the tiller of this airship and drive it to his whim, he would head south as well, making for the ice that surely lay at the bottom of the world in frigid mirror to the top.

Which meant he had a course to set after all, Key Perilous or no. Perhaps there was another way to fulfill his quest.

With that thought, Hethor began to walk the deck. What was the motive force for this airship? Though the gasbag was shaped like a wing of sorts, there were no spars or sails. Nor did he see engine nacelles such as *Bassett* had employed with her compact yet productive steam power plants. He walked along the starboard rail, noting that the bag was much closer to the deck than *Bassett*'s had been. There were struts rising every eight feet or so, multiple connections each lighter than the stout masts of his former ship, each carrying a smaller load.

This airship had a clearer deck as well. It was devoid

of the rope lockers, lines, and shrouds that had hung *Bassett* like a wood-bellied fighting ship of Admiral Nelson's fleet. More evidence, Hethor thought, that sails weren't simply stored away.

He reached the bow not much wiser. There he turned to head aftward again along the port side. By this time he trailed a whole parade of idle correct people—not jeering as the folk of his native New Haven would have done, nor questioning, just following. They were possessed of a wide-eyed curiosity that opened their small hairy faces so that his entourage resembled a mute choir of unfortunately hirsute children.

At midships, he stopped. There was a grumbling or hissing noise audible there, that he'd missed on his walk forward. Hethor leaned against the rail and stuck his head over the edge. The noise grew neither louder nor softer. He looked up along the strut nearest him and began inspecting closely for access to the gasbag.

There was a little section with separate, laced hems two struts aft of his position.

Hethor removed his belt and shoes. Unlike the access aboard *Bassett,* there was no ladder here. Rather he reached just over his head and unlaced a square of the gasbag material. It was not so different from the gutta-percha coated canvas of *Bassett*'s gasbag. Hethor pulled it open to peer inside.

Apparently one simply swarmed along within to wherever it was one wanted to go. There was no rope ladder inside, nor any obvious means of access except by exercising the main force of his arms to lever upward. Hethor reached in, steeled himself, and began to pull up, when he suddenly found that he was floating.

Hethor glanced down to see a dozen pairs of hairy hands on his legs and feet, lifting and pushing him in.

"My thanks," he told the correct people as they strained to loft him to his goal.

Inside, the gasbag stank of gutta-percha, canvas, and mold. The grumbling whisper was louder, almost a whickering noise. The gasbag was laid out quite differently from *Bassett*'s. Lightweight beams crossed the width of the ship, tying the vertical struts together, with more beams rising, like a very large, open-weave basket. Where *Bassett* had great huge cells filling portions of her bag, this airship had many small cells shaped like oversized bolsters set on end.

A more intelligent design, Hethor realized. This layout would economize on hydrogen and reduce the risk of fatality or sudden loss of altitude were one of the cells to rupture.

Picking his way along the narrow ribs and staves in nearly total darkness, Hethor followed his ears. He came to an odd shape as the source of the sounds. Careful exploration by touching revealed it to be a long cylinder wrapped in more of the gasbag's fabric, the concentration point for a maze of flexible pipes he had not noticed in the darkness.

An engine of sorts, Hethor realized, though what it was and how it ran was not readily apparent to him. There was certainly another one balancing it on the starboard side, and perhaps more fore and aft.

He only wished he understood the principles of its operation and function.

"Enough," he told himself aloud, the soft-walled darkness swallowing his voice in an absolute absence of echoes. "Back to the deck."

The faint gleam from the open access way guided his return to sunlight without particular mishap.

ARELLYA WAS on the deck, having appeared from wherever she had hidden herself away the evening before. Hethor didn't know why she was avoiding him. At the sight of her he realized how much he had missed her in their night apart.

In New Haven, he thought, *she would have been caged*

as a monkey. How was it that he had now come to see her as a woman?

No matter. Somehow, she did stir feelings in him that had been the subject of schoolboy gossip and a few blushing accidents—Darby the drover with the hearse came to mind. But this was nothing he had before experienced to any full or logical conclusion. Or, perhaps, been permitted to experience.

"Greetings," he stammered in the tongue of the correct people. Stammering was a human speech problem that they seemed to find tremendously amusing.

"We are in a wondrous place," she said. "None of my people ever thought to fly. It would be a gift to die here."

"Of course," he said. Sometimes it was very hard to see the world she lived in, even though they stood right next to one another. Hethor cleared his throat. At the moment it was more important for her to see his world. "I need to understand what guides this boat of the air, or we may be thinking of the ground all too soon. Would you walk with me?"

She went with him, though today she did not loop her arm in his.

There was a little shack or locker between the waist of the ship and the stern. It was one of the few deck structures. Hethor had passed it on his walk forward without much consideration. Now that he realized in broad daylight how sparsely furnished the deck truly was, he was far more curious to see the locker's contents for himself.

About four feet high, with a base three feet square and an angled top, the locker seemed to be an affair of folding panels or shutters. Hethor was at a loss as to how to open them. Obviously, if one knew the secret, they would flex in some well-crafted fashion. He had the clear image of a square-petaled wooden flower in mind.

The mechanism, however, was not apparent.

Hethor tapped and pushed at the shutters, or panels, or

whatever they were, for a while. Nothing came free. His frustration began to mount even as the correct people chattered quietly amongst themselves. Hethor wondered where the axes were aboard this vessel.

As he grunted and chuffed in his frustration, Arellya finally tugged Hethor's elbow. "Salwoo is a monkey-puzzler. Permit him to try this little hut of the boat."

Hethor stepped away with a wordless nod. One of the correct people males scrambled over to the shuttered affair, began running his hands over it, barely touching the surface but never quite losing contact either. He circled as Hethor and the others watched, one or both hands always on the wood. After perhaps ten minutes of this, a time that was almost as frustrating to Hethor as his own lack of success, Salwoo pressed on two shutters at once, one on each side. He then jumped back as a clever series of springs and hinges flipped and folded the panels into a small box below a shelf. It looked like nothing so much as a podium or lectern.

Hethor was impressed. He bowed to Salwoo. "My thanks."

The correct people all laughed at this, then with much chattering and waving of hands urged Hethor to the newly revealed station.

There was a dome or hemisphere set there, brass, with the shapes of land and sea etched on to it. A demiglobe. A bright gleam winked near the base of the dome—their current position?

Impressive as the folding box was, it was basically a cabinetmaker's trick. The brasswork map was something else entirely. Hethor could not conceive of how it had been crafted or made to work.

Still, the airship *had* come from a city of sorcerers and witches.

A stick stood up from the lectern, perhaps a foot high. Several levers were set along the shaft. He tugged lightly on the stick.

The airship shuddered.

Hethor let go quickly, and the airship resumed its stable flight.

So this is where the mysterious engines are controlled from. Presumably along with altitude, trim, and rudder. It even had its own map of the Southern Earth. He turned to Arellya. "I must work with this a while, which may cause the boat to spin or rock. Please, there is no cause for alarm among the correct people."

"Shall we stay away from the edges, then?"

A very practical question. He should have thought of it. "Yes, that would be well. Perhaps some below the floor, if there is any ease to be taken there. The rest may shelter in the middle up here."

She herded her fighters into two groups, and dispatched them to their places of relative safety. Hethor noted that Salwoo stayed above, to watch the experiments with pointed interest and a certain pride of ownership.

Fair enough, he thought. His own efforts would take longer, though.

HE KNEW little enough about the principles of flight. Even so, this airship was built to be operated by any man fresh off the docks. Over the course of several hours of cautious experimentation, Hethor found that not only could he direct the airship, but it followed a course once he had set it.

The vessel was a marvel of engineering. He could not imagine any British or New England engineer even conceiving of this sort of self-operated machine, let alone dedicating such a great resource of intellectual and mechanical design to the use of casual passersby.

Gabriel's hand was once again visible to Hethor.

Though still lacking the skill to land the airship, he could certainly direct it. Hethor set it on a southward course and stepped to the stern rail. He wasn't prepared to leave the command lectern completely abandoned, though perforce he must trust the unknown engineers who had made this thing.

Africa lay below, to his right. White foam met dark beaches lined with more jungle. The land rose slowly under the carpet of complex green, lacy geometries of treetop and vine lending texture still alien to Hethor's eyes. A line of stony hills erupted in the distance, their heights creating an eastern horizon.

To his left, the ocean. He supposed it was the South Atlantic, though the only name he had heard for it in the Southern Earth was the correct people's Great Salt River. The unknown birds still circled in the distance, though they seemed closer, bigger. He studied them a while.

Winged savages.

The rangy angel-bodied creatures had both threatened and saved him, their rude aspects a weird echo of Gabriel's beauty and power. The Jade Abbott had implied they were a lesser Creation. Did the winged savages serve God? Or some other master, such as William of Ghent?

Hethor felt a pang of guilt, then, at his precipitous action in shoving the sorcerer into the whirling brass bowels of the Earth. He'd had no other choice, he told himself, not as prisoner in a strange land. The traitor had to be dealt with. Hethor had seized his chance.

"I must carry on my quest," he told the distant fliers. "Southward I go and southward I shall discover myself."

He turned back to the deck to find the correct people all along the rail, staring down at the ocean and shouting to one another at the sighting of a particularly interesting wave, or the passing shadow of a cloud. Arellya had lost herself among the war band, so Hethor went forward, to where he had slept. There he sat with the golden tablet in his hands.

"The heart of God is the heart of the world.

"As man lives, so lives God.

"As God lives, so lives the world."

He now understood what the words said, but what did

they *mean*? How would this message from Heaven help him find the Key Perilous?

The airship passed then into the shadow of the cloud, light leaching from the deck and darkening the tablet. "Perilous" was right, Hethor thought. That part of it he understood. It was the key itself he did not understand.

He looked at the scar on his hand. The mark had reemerged after all the other insults done to his body, still in the shape of a key. Was the Key Perilous somehow within him, the way the heart of God was within the world?

Hethor became very afraid that if he failed in his mission, failed to wind the Mainspring of the world, the heart of God would stop when the world ran down. Which could not be possible, of course. God encompassed the universe. He was not subject to it.

It all made Hethor's head ache, so he set the tablet aside, rubbed the scar for a moment, and went to look for food and water.

He would have much time to consider the mystery before they went so far south that urgent action would once more be required on his part.

ALL DAY Arellya kept her distance from Hethor without ever quite managing to disappear from sight. If he went aft, she idled amidships. If he went forward, she stayed at a rail somewhere nearby. The few times he had headed straight toward her, Arellya walked briskly away.

He looked down on the folding waves. The wind whistling around the gasbag merged with the distant rush of the surf below, but inside both noises, Hethor could hear the clattering of the tiny gears-within-gears. He was hearing the sounds of Creation more and more often now, not just under distress or fear. It was becoming an ordinary background to his everyday life.

Hethor could not decide if that was a frightening thought or a comforting one.

He pushed away from the rail to look for the water that Salwoo and his fellows had reportedly found belowdecks. As he walked toward the companionway, something made Hethor stop.

It was a change of wind, perhaps. Or a shift in the water below.

He cocked his head, listening carefully. How far away was the sound?

Then Hethor realized that he was hearing a shift in the gears-within-gears noise of the universe. There was a clatter, like a slipping clock, out of time and out of rhythm. He ran back to the rail and stared down at the surf.

It was hard to see if anything was different. The surf rolled; the trees along the shore swayed in the breeze. The world looked as it had a few minutes before.

The noise grew louder to become an intrusive rumble. The surf receded quickly, as if the tide were running out at terribly high speed. The trees swayed against the wind now.

He ran to the other rail and looked west farther out to sea. Even from a thousand feet up in the air, the approaching swell was clearly visible. This wave had robbed the shore of its water.

His heart plunged, tight and cold. It was a terrible sight, driving fear through Hethor's entire body. But fear would change nothing. "Look!" Hethor shouted to the correct people, pointing.

"A monster," one said. "A spirit," said another. "The Great Salt River is angry." They chattered, excited again rather than sharing Hethor's sinking spirits.

He crossed the deck again to watch the wave strike shore. Strike it did, the swell curling over as it approached to form a giant wall of surf. Hethor guessed it was close to a hundred feet in height, a wet cliff advancing on the jungle.

Birds shrieked into the sky ahead of the roaring water, streams of irregular color streaming away from the treetops. He had seen this before. Some of them were already too late, Hethor realized. He wanted to reach out, pluck them from their jeweled flight to doom, and set them safe much higher in the air.

The wave swallowed the shore, collapsing across the leading edge of the jungle. A riot of water ran through the jungle, almost as high as the treetops—white foam, blue sea already staining brown with mud and soil, the boles of enormous trees tossed upward like kindling in a gutter.

The noise was horrendous. Hethor could hear it all— the heartwood groaning as the trees snapped, the cut-off screeches as animals of ground and treetop drowned, the fluttering slap of birds caught in the flood. Water roared, advancing inland in an increasing front of chaos, pushing roiling debris ahead of it.

Oddly, the wave stank of mud, and rot, sea stench and jungle reek all mixed together. Why had he ever thought the sea smelled fresh?

"The Great Salt River punishes the land," said Arellya, next to him again.

"The world hurts." It was as close as he could come to explaining what was wrong. The gears clattered and ground somewhere at the edge of hearing.

They watched the water flow back out of the jungle, carrying thousands of trees with it. Great furry corpses followed along. Three more waves came in, smaller than the first but each terrible in its own right. By the time it was over several hours later, the coast looked as though all of God's artillery battalions had taken practice. There was only a tangled mass of broken greenery, standing rocks, and slumped, steaming mud.

Hethor went below, stumbling until he found his way to a cabin. None of the correct people were within, so he lay on the bunk and stared at the planking of the ceiling, wondering why God's design encompassed so much blight to the world.

"What causes it?" Arellya asked from the hatch. "You said the world hurts. What hurts the world?"

"William of Ghent," said Hethor with a flash of re-membered anger. "A man of my people."

But that was not true, he thought.

"Who is this William to hate the world so much as to hurt it?"

"I spoke hastily." Hethor tried to frame his words, picking through Arellya's language. It was so much less precise than English, at least for matters of theology and things mechanical. "When God made the world, He made it with a . . . a . . . flaw."

"Everything has a flaw. Only God can be perfect."

Hethor hadn't thought of that. To his experience, the perfection of a thing reflected on the worthiness of its creator. "Yes," he said. "Yes. The world must be, well, turned, from time to time."

He could not find a word for winding a clock in the speech of the correct people.

"Turned?" She laughed her soft chittering laugh and sat on the edge of his bunk. The almost-touching warmth of her body was an electrick spark to him. "Like a yam on the fire coals? Surely the world turns itself."

"No, no." He laughed, too, now, washing away some of his grief and fear. "There is a heart inside the world, like the heart inside a man. It beats in rhythm with the world."

"That seems like a sensible way to arrange things," she said.

"Well, yes. But the world is a made thing. The heart must be turned once every few lifetimes, so that it will continue to beat. My people call that turning *winding*."

"So this heart of the world must be *winding*?"

He thought of the words on the golden tablet, recited them to her.

"The heart of God is the heart of the world.

"As man lives, so lives God.

"As God lives, so lives the world."

"The heart of the world is our heart, and God's," Arellya said, sounding satisfied. Then she took his hand in hers. "How is your heart, Messenger?"

His heart raced, actually, his hand prickling at her touch. "My heart is well, Arellya," he said softly.

"Is it full already?"

"Full?"

She pulled herself close and kissed him on the lips. The fur of her face tickled his moustache and rough beard. He had not shaved since his time with William of Ghent, and did not realize how far his facial hair had grown till it rubbed together with hers.

A few months ago, he could no more have grown a beard than grown wings. Of course, since then he had flown from the Wall, too.

He found her lips on his again, and set himself to kissing her in return. It was not a subject of which he had knowledge or experience, but she seemed willing to let him practice. Her lips were firm, fringed with hair, and the tip of her tongue darted into his mouth like a little snake.

It was a thrill he'd never felt, the electrick feeling coursing through his entire body. He opened up his arms and she settled onto his lap, so much the smaller that she fit. His personal parts stirred, stiffening, which caused him to blush hotly. Hethor tried to shift his hips and pull the embarrassment away from the weight of her little buttocks.

She broke away from the kiss and took his cheeks in her hand.

"I am sorry," he gasped, mortified.

Arellya wiggled her bottom. "Don't you run away from me," she said with a grin, then came to his kiss again. Her hands explored his hair, his neck, loosed the upper buttons of his ragged linen shirt.

He rubbed at her hairy back, enjoying the silky smooth feel, like petting a giant cat, until she broke away from the kiss again. Fumbling, she opened the rest of his buttons.

"It's a sin," he gasped in English, thinking back on sermons and alleyway gossip and what Pryce Bodean might have said.

She took his hand and placed it on her chest. Through the silky hair she had a tiny breast, with a perfect little nipple like a miniature cherry. The mound neatly filled the palm of his hand. A warm, wet feeling shot like a bolt through Hethor's personal parts at that touch.

He had found his own heaven, right here.

Then she pushed him down onto the bunk and climbed forward, lowering the little pink nub of her nipple to his mouth. Hands around her back, he gave suck. It was like nothing he had ever felt before. His mouth had come home.

THEY WERE locked together in sweet embrace in the little cabin for hours. She soon fumbled him out of his trousers, marveling at the size of his penis. He was torn between embarrassment and fascination.

He had already made his drawers sticky, but she licked him clean. Then they spent quite some time making sure she could open up sufficiently to take him. Her tight little womanly parts, furry as he had heard human women's were, responded to her own fingers first. Then she guided his into her. After long and gentle persuasion, she pulled his mouth down there. She called it the "Little Salt River kiss."

Later, after he had been inside her face-to-face, she rolled over and showed him where else to kiss, where else to use his fingers, where else to enter her with the aid of her natural juices spread liberally. In between times, they touched everywhere with lips and fingers, traced designs with each other's toes, sampled every flavor and scent and combination that they might share. Then over to the front once more, until he was so exhausted he could not move, except for his lips, which she continued to employ to her own benefit and his.

This was what everyone was hiding, Hethor thought. This was what had the New Haven fishwives smiling in the morning and the preachers in red-faced anger on

Sunday. God's greatest gift to man, and it was locked away in scorn and shame from young folk like him who could use it best.

As if he'd never before encountered the perverse nature of the world, Hethor marveled once more at how unfair it all was.

Then he kissed Arellya all over again, from the soft spot behind her ears to her tiny little toes, paying special attention to the secret, lately forbidden places along the way.

HETHOR AWOKE in the little cabin alone. His groin ached, in a pleasant fashion. His inner sense of time told him it was morning, though in the windowless cabin it could have been any time of day at all.

Arellya was . . . He concentrated, listening to the clattering music of the universe that always lurked just at the bottom of his hearing. There was a particular combination of notes and rhythms that comprised Arellya, a combination with which he had become much more familiar in the course of the preceding night.

Even in the dark of the cabin, Hethor felt himself blush. With the blush came shame, like Adam after the fall. Could he look her in the eye? Would he have to fight the correct people for her honor? Or his?

"This was a terrible mistake," he groaned aloud, seized by conscience. He had taken advantage of her, cowed Arellya with his superior size and force.

But his body argued otherwise. As did his memories of the previous evening.

Hethor stood up from the bunk. Not able to remember where or how the lantern was lit in this cabin, he found his clothing in the darkness before stumbling out the passageway. There was a little galley aft, with fruits and breads and water in blown-glass bottles, though he was sure the food would not hold out for so many of them.

There were a number of problems to solve—correcting the course of the airship, finding fuel for her mysterious engines, finding food and water for the correct people. His actions of last night. He would have to be manful with Arellya, and take responsibility for his deeds and misdeeds.

Up on deck everything seemed less serious. It was another glorious day, warm and breezy even under the shadow of the gasbag. The coast was farther to the east this morning but still visible, brown rather than green. A sere line of hills ran behind a coastal plain characterized by dunes and struggling grass. The great waves of the day before had been smaller here, smashing the beaches with wrack, but not running far inland. Farther out to sea, winged savages again circled with apparent aimlessness, yet somehow never out of view.

Arellya was up in the bow, staring out across the ocean.

He went to her and stood nearby watching her stretch out on the deck with her face pressed against the rail. Hethor admired the shallow, perfect curve of her buttocks. What she had shown him last night was beyond even sin, he decided. It was a different world here in the Southern Earth.

"Luck of the day to you, Messenger," she said without turning around.

He smiled. "And good morning."

Then she looked over her shoulder at him, smiling as well, her lips just a bit crooked. She patted her rear quarters. "Come for more already?"

He blushed deep red. "Here?" asked Hethor, spluttering like Master Bodean might have done in spite of his resolve to accept the miracle that was Arellya. "Now?"

"The correct people celebrate each other when and where they will," she said, almost primly. "The young males would cheer you on, and be impressed to see your—"

"*No!*" Hethor shouted. He had seen them doing that at the festival-rite, back in her home village. And sometimes since, young males pairing on the journey—Hethor had no idea what to make of that. In any case, he had no desire to be a part of such display. He collected his thoughts.

"Among my people, this is a solitary act, not for public viewing or comment."

"We are not among your people," she said, smiling. "And last night was far from solitary. Twice as far, I believe."

"Food," said Hethor, trying to find a way out of the conversation. "We must have food. I worry there is not a sufficiency aboard."

"Salwoo and some of the others report considerable feasts laid by." She paused. "If the journey is long, you may be right. Already you have led the correct people farther from home than ever we have gone since Creation began. We follow, but hungry followers gossip and fight. It may be that Salwoo's feasts will not be enough."

"If we can find . . . vines . . ." Hethor struggled for a better word. "Narrow strands of great length, rather, I can lower the boat so that we might fish in the waters."

"I will set Salwoo to the problem," Arellya said. "Are you well this morning? Did I strain you?"

"I . . ." He blushed *again*. Hethor was rapidly becoming resentful of his own body.

"You are much bigger than any other that I have celebrated with," she said politely. "I thought things might be more difficult for you."

"Other . . . ?" Now he was embarrassed and angry both. She was not a virgin! He had lain with a fallen woman, and was fallen himself. "I—"

Then Hethor had to laugh.

He was thinking like Pryce Bodean, as if he were back in New Haven. He was no sailor and Arellya was no whore, but he was at sea, in a different sort of port.

A half-guilty, half-relieved thought darted through his mind. *She isn't even human.* He knew boys at New Haven Latin who'd had the pleasure of sheep, and even Grotty Matthews who everyone said had mounted his father's mare. No one thought them sinners—ridiculous, to be sure, but not fallen.

Enough.

"Food," he said firmly. "I will steer for the shallows and take the boat down low. Have Salwoo and other young males find ways to secure the fish."

THAT AFTERNOON they cruised perhaps a hundred feet above the water, keeping close to shore. Hethor would take the airship no lower. He was not confident of his ability to land the vessel. He was even less confident of his ability to lift off again. The near-magical controls were wondrous, but his grasp of the principles of operation was tenuous.

Salwoo and the others had found both lines and nets. They were happily experimenting with different ways to catch fish.

"We use spears in our home," he explained to Hethor. "But we have seen the Ivory-Eyed Tribes cast nets from their little boats, so we know it can be done."

Below, fish flashed silver in the shallows. The pale shapes of sharks moved among them. Hethor realized that there must be almost no fishing fleets on this part of the African coast, for he had never seen such schools from *Bassett,* which had sailed over waters of Northern Earth well traveled by fishers and traders both.

Shouting erupted, screams and hoots and laughter all mixed together. Hethor ran to the rail to see what the commotion was about.

One of the males—Kikiowo, he thought—wrestled with a rope, which jumped in his hand like a thing possessed. Half a dozen more of the correct people grabbed Kikiowo's arms and legs, or tugged on his rope, while many others lined the rail.

"Messenger, come look!" they shouted.

Kikiowo had caught a shark, a large wicked shape that leapt and turned in the water. It was enormous, at least twenty or thirty feet in length.

"He had a big fish," said the correct person next to Hethor, "and a big, big, big fish took the big fish."

"Cut the line," Hethor shouted, "before he drags you under."

The correct people laughed. More of them grabbed on to Kikiowo in a great crowd. The struggle was so violent that the deck actually rocked, straining against the stabilizing influence of the huge gasbag.

"Let it loose," Hethor shouted again.

"It is my Grandfather Fish," Kikiowo called back above the yelling of the crowd. "His soul is mine; my soul is his."

"He will kill you!"

The rail dipped just then, Kikiowo going over with his rope, pulling a chain of correct people with him. Hethor dove for the screaming mass of hairy legs and arms and began hauling backward.

The young males swarmed aboard again, climbing on one another as they had to ascend Malgus' column back in the great stone city of sorcerers. Even Kikiowo made it back aboard.

"My soul has fled for deep water," he said in a serious voice, his pale eyes narrowed in thought.

"Ho! There are still two of us left behind in the Great Salt River," someone shouted.

So for a little while they fished for correct people while Hethor steered the airship around, beating across the wind to stay near the lost. Hethor had to talk hard to keep others from jumping to their aid. He explained that the shark was a grandfather crocodile that lived in the deeps of the Great Salt River. The correct people humored him as they brought up rescuees and fish alike, until there was a sufficiency of wriggling silver marine life for a true feast that night.

THE DAYS PASSED and so did Africa. The coast, always to their left, trended east of south. Hethor kept the airship on the same course. He felt more comfortable following the line of the continent than striking off across the open ocean. Were the airship to run out of fuel or be forced down by weather, the advantages of a terrestrial landing over a marine landing were both obvious and considerable.

At the same time the ocean continued to provide food in deck-slapping abundance. Several days after Kikiowo's attempt to land the enormous shark a group of correct people and Hethor managed to bring up a small one. It thrashed about the deck, biting and snapping for quite a while, but the steaks were delicious.

The land below became progressively drier and more desolate as they passed southward, the scents on the breeze changing. The jungle foetor slipped away, followed for a while by the crisp smell of dry grass, which in turn melted into a salty dirt smell. Hethor sighted no cities and very few villages. A fire glinting in the night was rare. After the sixth or seventh day, they saw no more signs of settlement at all. Malgus had been right about the Southern Earth being a paradise of sorts, at least if one defined "paradise" as nature in the absence of the hand of man.

The only thing that disturbed this quiet paradise was the fact that midnight came a little later each night. The Mainspring continued in its progressive failure, even as Hethor journeyed ever southward.

But Arellya met him in the evenings in the little cabin, driving all cares from Hethor's thoughts. They explored the hours together with hands and hearts and tongues. This was Hethor's definition of paradise, a loving and joyful partner in the sharing of bodies. It bothered him that the correct people speech had no word for love. He wanted to explain to Arellya about the swelling rush of warmth in his soul, the half-weary longing he felt through the day, the pride with which her every word and action filled him.

"I love you," he whispered one night, using the same word that would have meant he favored papayas over guavas.

"Mmm . . . ," she'd said to his roaming hands. "Your taste is good, too."

"No, no. My heart aches for you."

"You should drink a bitterbark tea. One of the young males may have brought some onto the boat."

"Not that kind of ache!"

"What ache, then?" She giggled. "You are trying to tell me something of your kind, are you not?"

"Yes . . ."

"I am of the correct people. You can tell me anything of my kind. Your kind, they are beyond the Wall. Leave them be there, that you might someday return to them with your words of their tongue intact and unflavored."

He didn't expect to return. If by the grace of God and the help of the archangel Gabriel he survived this trip to the Mainspring, Hethor wanted to stay with Arellya. Giving up on his language and hers, he proceeded for a while to demonstrate the thrust of his devotion in a firm manner.

Back on deck, away from the pleasures of the evening, among daylight's concerns, it was Salwoo who turned the journey's last great worry to a species of almost-joy. Hethor was down in the galley inspecting the water barrels and wondering if he dared land the airship at the next river they came to along the increasingly sere coast.

"I have found the tits of the boat," Salwoo announced to Hethor. He was grinning even more than usual.

Hethor held in his surprise. "I'm sorry; that didn't sound quite right."

Salwoo grabbed his own chest, mimed squeezing with his hands while favoring Hethor with a salacious wink. Hethor's blush came back, making his skin prickly and hot. His embarrassment raised his temper along with it.

"I don't think—," he began, but Salwoo held out a palm. "Come with me, Messenger."

Hethor followed Salwoo aftward down the passageway, seeing by the light of one of the airship's little lanterns that the correct person carried. They came to a stowage locker he had inspected in one of his early tours of the ship. Salwoo had dragged the collection of tools and small lumber out to reveal a hatch in the floor that Hethor had missed.

"The boat of air," Salwoo said, "her belly has more shape than these huts within show us. So I looked, as I have become your finder."

Hethor looked down. It was cramped below, where the bilges and ballast would be on a surface vessel. *Bassett* had stored fuel there for the steam engines. There were bladders and pipes down beneath the deck, much as *Bassett* had held.

"Look," said Salwoo. He gently nudged Hethor aside, then dropped below. The space almost accommodated the correct person. There were a series of stopcocks of odd design on the port side, now visible in Salwoo's lantern. He set the light down, opened a stopcock, and let a fluid splash into his hands.

For one startling moment, Hethor thought Salwoo was letting oil flow free next to open flame. He yelped, then caught himself.

Salwoo was drinking the fluid.

Hethor cupped his hand, leaned into the darkness, and captured a little.

It smelled like nothing. The stuff was oddly flat, in fact. When he put it to his lips, it was water. Clean, in a sort of stale, aggressive manner, as if it had been scrubbed by the most determined of housewives.

"Water," said Salwoo. "From these tits. No flavor. It must be Messenger water. Correct people would not favor this."

Looking at the piping and bladders in the bottom of the hull, Hethor realized that the eerily clean water was connected to the mysterious engines. It had to be. They either ran on water or exhausted water as waste. Neither seemed likely to him, but he had no better theory.

"My worries are fewer," Hethor said. "And you are my hero, Salwoo."

That night on deck they feasted. For the first time a stew had been made, a fish stock being boiled down in the galley from the now freely available supply of water. Hethor wondered if he was imperiling the airship's range or fuel supplies, but evidence so far was that it had been designed and built for far lengthier journeys away from a friendly port than *Bassett* or any of her similars in the Northern Earth.

Correct people danced and sang on the deck. In the skies around them, a few of the winged savages circled closer, attracted by either the cooking or the noisy revels. Hethor watched the moonlight on the water. He even managed to trace the fine golden line of the Earth's orbital track where it reflected in the night's desultory chop, though the moon's more delicate trace was lost. Arellya stood in the circle of his arms, her narrow fingers reaching up to stroke his hair.

"I think we shall make it to the southernmost part of the world," Hethor told her. "Since Salwoo found the water, the air boat seems secure."

"Messenger," Arellya said formally, "we are all passed out of life already. Your world is our world now. I look forward to this south."

"Thank you. But there is a custom among my people I would like to bring to us here."

She rubbed tight against him. "Some of your customs have been adaptable."

Not customs, Hethor thought, *but rather improvisation.* Still, he took her point and the compliment that came with it. "Our boat of the air requires a name."

"Really? We do not name our canoes."

"We do," he said shortly. Then: "May I name it after you?"

She laughed. "No, you may not. My name is my own, not to be bestowed on some great bird of artifice."

"Oh."

"Do you have another name to hand?"

"We often name boats after people, but since this is

your side of the Wall, I will follow your custom of the names. I think perhaps instead we should call it *Heart of God.*" Pryce and his fellows would have hounded Hethor out of Connecticut all over again for such a blasphemy, but high up in the African night, it seemed right.

"*Heart of God.* A good name."

"We should have a ceremony. A feast in honor."

"Every day is a feast in honor."

They went to tell the others, who danced the night away, hairy feet slapping on the wood until the moon was long gone and the east glowed with the fire of the impending day.

SIXTEEN DAYS out of the cyclopean city, Hethor was awoken in his cabin by a panicked Salwoo. The correct person flung open the hatch, shouting unintelligibly.

He was glad Arellya was gone already—as often was her habit—though he knew Salwoo would have had nothing to say about it even if she had been present. "What is it, man? Slow down."

"Jewels," Salwoo said. "There are jewels on the ship! And the sun has died."

He had failed! Or did the Southern Earth somehow have different eclipses than the North?

Hethor leapt to his feet, tugged on only his linen underclothes, and followed Salwoo up to the deck. Some of the correct people were wailing. Others huddled in the waist of the airship. Arellya moved among them, talking, reassuring, her hand brushing across miserable shoulders.

Heart of God was fogged in, completely embedded in a frigid cloud. Hethor couldn't make out the stern at all. He could barely see the bow from where he stood. It was dark, too—a deep, thick cloud. And the cold had condensed into droplets of ice along the seams in the gasbag, on the struts supporting the deck, on the rails of the ship.

He was mightily glad of his thickening beard even though his breath was crusting on it.

Then Hethor understood Salwoo's panic. There was no word in the correct people's language for "ice." They had never seen such a thing.

"Is this what comes after life?" Salwoo asked in a still-frightened whisper.

"It is but water," Hethor said. "Great cold makes water turn to a kind of rock. It flows free again when warmth returns." He stepped to the rail, picked off a little icicle, held it in his hand to show to Salwoo. "Look. See, already it runs away from the warmth of my touch." It was cold, painfully cold on his skin, but he wanted to make his point.

"So we are inside the Great Salt River?"

Hethor laughed at that, though he tried not to. "No, no, we are inside one of the clouds of the sky."

"We have been in clouds before," Salwoo objected. "They were like mist on the water. This is thick and cold enough to kill."

"South," said Hethor. "The south is cold." *We must be closing in on the pole,* he realized. But that made no sense, unless they had been blown very, very far in the night. "Let us check the helm."

He and Salwoo unfolded the casing of the navigation station. The glowing dot on the little globe showed them still off the African shore, a long distance of water separating the land that capped the pole.

Winter? In July?

If so, Southern Earth was indeed a different world.

Hethor walked back to where most of the correct people were huddled together. "Among my people," he began, speaking loudly so the whole ship's company would hear him, "in our land, we have a season that brings cold weather. Very cold, so that water turns to this jeweled rock you see around the boat of air. Our word for this is *ice*. It will not hurt you, except if you allow your bodies to become too cold. *Ice* can be touched and eaten. It is part of God's world. There is nothing to fear, not here, not now."

At his words, the correct people chattered a bit, then stood up and began exploring the possibilities of frost and ice. That was it—their fear had left with his words.

Arellya came to him. "You did well to speak out."

"I did not at first understand the problem," Hethor admitted. "But your folk live near the Wall, where the sun is always warm."

"If your home is like this from time to time," said Arellya, "I would not care to visit. Why anyone would live among this cold is beyond me."

"In reaching my goal, there will be more cold to come."

And how would they survive it? The correct people had no woolens or heavy coats or boots. Neither did he. Miraculous as the airship's provisioning and controls had proven, it had obviously been built and run by people of the tropics as well. There would be no hidden hold full of furs, Hethor was certain.

He would find a way, though. He had found a way to pass every other obstacle that had impeded his progress toward his charter. This would be no different.

THE SUN failed them for days. Africa continued to crawl past unseen far below the port-side rail. Once, something howled from the waters, a voice as great as Leviathan, but there was no telling what it was. Their fishing was more difficult, but when the catches did come they were greatly increased.

Hethor watched the brass globe with its winking light as Africa first narrowed to a point, then passed completely by to their east. He wondered at the weather—it was not much of a hindrance, but the chill clouds depressed the correct people. The cool damp kept them huddled in miserable heaps or hidden reluctantly belowdecks. The days grew colder and more ice appeared on *Heart of God,* especially in the mornings.

Then one day the sun returned. Hethor came on deck to a brilliant glare that narrowed his eyes while giving him an immediate headache. The light seemed so bright it was almost like being stabbed, yet the air was chill as ever it had been inside the icy fogs.

Below there was ocean. Enormous swells rolled by larger than any he had ever seen save for the earthquake-spawned monsters that had swamped the coast early in this journey. There was water from horizon to horizon. The Wall and the land below it were long gone except for large white rocks studding the sea.

After some scrutiny, he realized the rocks were ice. Enormous chunks the size of cities, or even counties, floated below him.

How cold *was* the water?

He was still far from the pole and the Mainspring. If *Heart of God* was forced down here, Hethor and his correct people would die in minutes of sheer exposure. They were very far from God or man, and his quest was still far beyond the curve of the world.

Even with Arellya nearby and a ship full of her brethren, Hethor was suddenly as lonely as he'd ever been.

ELEVEN

THE COAST of the southernmost continent slid by several thousand feet below *Heart of God*. Nights were much longer and colder over the Southern ocean, and when morning came it brought a short-lived day. This made sense to Hethor, as he had read much the same of the North Pole. Clearly the Southern Earth was in the grip of winter despite the time of year. Perhaps there was a balance of nature between the sides of the Wall.

The sun that greeted them was wan. The light possessed an almost tinny quality. The wind carried a chill as bone-wrenching as any Hethor had ever felt in the depths of New England's hostile winters. Even this high up, the rot-and-wrack smell of the frozen coast was discernible—all of the bird droppings, seaweed, and who knew what else crusting the shingled beaches undisturbed for the six thousand years since Creation began.

Even in the midst of this frigid, forbidding territory, there was beauty. Ahead some distance, Hethor could make out glinting towers that seemed to be made of ice— sister cities to the crystal metropolises he had seen in his ascension of the Equatorial Wall. It made him wonder why the exotic only persisted at the boundaries of the known. Or was it that the familiar was incapable of seeming exotic?

The towers were studded along a coastal highland, catching the pale sun in their peaks only to throw it back again diamond-bright. Lower domes clustered about their bases. What commerce or industry sustained them was impossible to determine from a distance, but simply to live among such beauty would steal his heart away with each rising of the sun.

"Messenger."

Hethor turned from his reflection. Arellya had taken his hand, stood beside him now accompanied by Salwoo. "I'm sorry," he said with reflexive politeness. "I was paying no attention."

Arellya nodded, both acknowledging and dismissing his apology. "The correct people are chilled. They will be unwell. Can you bring back the true sun? This pale cousin haunting the sky is worthless."

Hethor stifled a laugh. "No. Only through travel back to the north, which I cannot do. There are blankets in the ship's stores. We should have a work party to parcel them out."

Salwoo looked miserable. "You cover your full self in plant skins in the manner of your people. Correct people do not do such things."

"Then correct people will die of cold," Hethor said. He squeezed Arellya's hand. "Do you want your souls to be cold forever?"

The two correct people nodded, then walked away conferring.

Hethor turned his attention back to the coast and the distant towers. *Heart of God*'s course was taking her farther inland. Immediately below were long, graveled valleys dotted with humps of ice or snow. The rotting smell of the coast was not yet gone.

There was a groan, almost a screech, that echoed through the whirring sound of gears that always hung on the edge of Hethor's hearing. *Earthquake,* he thought. He looked down carefully.

It was hard to tell for sure what was happening. The valleys below did not seem to jump or ripple particularly, but from this height their graveled landscape was little more than a texture. He looked over at the towers.

They swayed.

The winking diamonds of their mirrored sunlight danced in the sky like a swarm of fireflies. Even as he watched, one of the towers shattered, a glistening spray of splinters erupting to make a brilliant, deadly fog around the tower's mates. Two more toppled. All this occurred in an eerie silence, until like thunder following lightning, the ringing, clattering crash of their demise was clearly audible from the deck of *Heart of God.* The rising fog from the wreckage obscured his view, turning the icy city to a rainbowed cloud glittering just above the frozen Earth.

Amid the whirring of the world's gears, he heard stuttering, like a great escapement retarded in its travels. The day was slipping, and the Earth was once more missing her time. The slippage in midnight had increased from the three seconds or so he'd noted back on *Bassett* to almost fifteen seconds. Every time one of these terrible earthquakes happened, the Earth's rotation seemed to slow a bit more.

The key-shaped scar on the palm of his hand flared an angry red. It ached in sympathy to the wretched destruction below. Watching the glimmer of the ice city's death, Hethor felt moved to offer some epitaph, some comment to mark the passing of such a wonder from the world. He could only think of one set of words that would fit.

"The heart of God is the heart of the world.

"As man lives, so lives God.

"As God lives, so lives the world."

FARTHER INLAND they passed over the ruins of another frozen city. Judging by the clouds of icy mist that shrouded the shattered tower bases, this one had also toppled in the recent earthquake. The long night had already come, after a day measured in minutes rather than hours, lit by a pallid sun that lurked far to the north. The starlight was so cold the air seemed to creak, though the heavenly glimmerings lit the ground well enough. Great cracks ran across the surface of the snow and ice that covered the land here away from the coast, several of the cracks meeting amid the jumble of toppled towers. Hethor could see no streaming refugees or folk straining at the rescue—these places were as abandoned as the vertical city had been back on the Wall.

Who lived in them once? Angels? Or perhaps other kinds of men, as the correct people were another kind of man designed by God to favor the green depths of the equatorial jungles.

He wasn't sure if he preferred to have the heaving chaos of the ocean beneath him or this crystalline killing field of ice. Were *Heart of God* to put down here, Hethor and the correct people would be dead in a matter of hours. If they lived even that long. As it was, today the last of the correct people had abandoned the deck for the misery of the cabins below, crowded five and ten to a cubby. The cold had finally overwhelmed their resistance to suffering the rigors of enclosure.

Hethor prayed that they would find the South Pole without further setback. There was no edge left, no margin for another miracle.

At least *Heart of God*'s mysterious engines continued to work, even here in the frozen misery of the deepest south.

He didn't have the courage to wait for midnight, to see how late it might come. Instead, Hethor went below to wrap himself in Arellya and the cold comfort of his dreams.

MORNING BROUGHT only more darkness—this far south dawn was a time of the soul rather than a moment in the sun's transit across the sky. Wrapped in half a dozen blankets, Hethor went up on deck to check the course with the magical globe and see what there was to see.

As he stepped up out of the aft ladder Hethor was immediately aware that something was different on the ship. The mysterious engines thrummed in the surrounding darkness. *Heart of God* still traveled through the night. Their course remained true to the southward heading, as best as he could tell without studying the stars or the globe in its little shelter.

What, then?

The shadows, Hethor thought. *The shadows are wrong upon the deck.* It was far too dark for a cloudless night.

He looked around at the rails.

There were winged savages crowding the ship, occluding the night sky and the silvery gleam of the ice below. Now that he could see them, Hethor realized they were pale in the gloom, like so many white birds.

"Get off!" Hethor shouted, startled and angry.

He was answered with the twang of bows.

Hethor ducked back down the aft ladder, screaming for Arellya, Salwoo, Kikiowo, any of the correct people. He stormed toward his cabin, intent on retrieving the golden tablet that had served him well with the winged savages in the past.

Correct people emerged into the narrow passageway clutching spears and sticks. "What dreams, Messenger?" one called.

Hethor stopped at his cabin door. "Our boat of the air is attacked," he said. Then, shouting: "There are bird people on the deck, with bows and swords."

These often silly, often strange young males of the correct people were all hunters and warriors, survivors of an expedition that had taken them farther from their homes than any of their ancestors had ever dared venture in the entire history of Creation. Roaring with pride and anger, they flowed past Hethor to meet the threat.

He ducked into the cabin to be nearly skewered by Arellya wielding a stone knife.

"Hai," she shouted. "Be careful, Messenger."

Hethor kicked a bolt of canvas aside, looted by Arellya from ship's stores for some unknown purpose. "My golden plate, the words of God. Where is it?"

She reached under the bunk, pulled the tablet out, and handed it to Hethor.

He took it with a desperate grin. "Stay down here. Please."

"No," she said.

There would be no discussion, he knew. "At least stay behind me."

Arellya pulled him close, kissed him tight. After a moment, they separated, gasping. "Remember me in the next world, if needs be," she said.

As they ran for the deck ladder, Hethor realized that she meant that either of them might die.

THE DECK was a freezing hell of steaming blood, screams, and the heavy, ragged thumps of butchery. At first it was impossible for Hethor to tell who had the advantage in the battle, for the combat was everywhere. He brandished his golden tablet like a battle standard and rushed into the fray, screaming, "Stop! Stand down, I tell you."

Most of the surviving correct people tried to pull back from the fight. The winged savages ignored him and pressed their advantage. Hethor quickly realized that it was the correct people who were being butchered—the winged savages fought with the same rangy strength and eerie precision they had shown aboard *Bassett* when kidnapping him.

It was not their blood and limbs that littered the deck.

Waving the tablet wildly, Hethor rushed to catch a winged savage alongside the head. Another swirled, swinging a glittering bronze sword that took Salwoo in the side just as the correct person stepped in with spear in hand to help Hethor. The winged savage's blow split Salwoo in half, showering blood and offal over Hethor.

He drove the golden tablet edgewise into the face of Salwoo's killer, who fell back clutching at his eyes. The tablet itself was bent nearly double with the blow, so Hethor dropped it to the blood-slicked deck, grabbed up Salwoo's spear, and gave chase.

The fight raged on, unequal as the invasion of *Bassett* had been on the other side of the Wall. Correct people were slaughtered like conies on a cricket pitch while the winged savages danced among them.

Hethor continued to fight for his ship and his people, taking blows that stung and burned double or treble, thanks to the terrible cold. The entire time, he wondered desperately where Arellya was. He had lost his sense of her in the confusion of the battle. That delicate touch inside his head and heart was drowned out by the shrieking chaos.

The deck heaved, bouncing for a moment before listing to the port. Hethor whirled, spear braced outward.

Winged savages on the port rail were cutting away the stanchions that attached the hull of *Heart of God* to the gasbag.

In the terrible dark of the ultimate south, being forced down unprepared to the surface was a death sentence surely as any sword sweep to the gut.

"To the left edge," he shouted, trying to rally the correct people.

There was a movement, but by no means a rush. So many had already fallen. He charged anyway, screaming incoherently, the air burning his lungs with cold flame.

The winged savages grinned and tumbled over the rail where Hethor could not follow. With a sickened suspicion, he spun around to face the starboard rail. A moment later a group of the fliers appeared like mechanical jacks parading the hour before a cathedral clock. They immediately began to cut at the stanchions on that side.

Hethor glanced over the rail. The moon was only a glow in the north, providing vague illumination. A thousand feet or more of air lay between him and the killer snow.

He had never seen a parachute on this airship.

"We are lost," he called, letting his spear drop to the deck.

A small crowd of correct people huddled around him. Their wounds steamed in the chilly air. The airship was suddenly quiet, except for the harsh breathing of the winged savages as they continued to hack at the stanchions.

The deck lurched again, dropping Hethor to his knees. The correct people swayed like treetops in the wind.

Hethor set his mind to the wheels that lay hidden behind everything in the world. He set his mind to God's clockwork and the miracle of brass and design that kept the Earth spinning round the life-giving sun.

"The heart of God is the heart of the world," he said.

The correct people muttered along with him, picking up the prayer. The gears clicked in his head, loud as ever.

"As man lives, so lives God."

The winged savages left off their hacking and sawing to stare at Hethor, so many long-muscled killers suddenly at their rest.

"As God lives, so lives the world."

The savages leapt over the rail in a single wave of flesh and were gone.

Hethor breathed a heavy sigh of relief, immediately regretting it as his throat was seared anew by the cold. He and his followers stood in silence for a moment, torn between relief and horror at the sight of so much blood, so many bodies, so much life lost in the night.

The deck lurched once more, nearly spilling them all over the rail in a wingless counterpoint to the sudden departure of the airship's attackers. There was a rattling noise from above as one of the quiet engines strained at the shifting load before it surrendered with a horrendous roar that bespoke futility of repair. The deck lurched again, and Hethor's stomach rebelled as the airship lost altitude far too fast.

"We die now," said one of the correct people, echoing Hethor's own horrified thoughts.

"No," he said. Could it truly end like this? Gabriel had intended more for him. "We are not finished yet." All evidence was that he would too soon be made a liar.

"Messenger has spoken."

It was Arellya! She lived! In that moment, Hethor found hope, though he did not know how it might play out. "Arellya, open the navigator's station," he ordered. "I will take the helm and see what is possible. The rest of you, gather any cloth or padding from your sleeping places below and make the tightest nest you can. We will survive the breaking of the ship."

Given purpose, they ran, treading heedless on the faces of their own dead. It was too dark, too late, too hopeless for anything but whatever might grant them all a few more minutes of life.

Hethor struggled to the helm. Once there he unfastened the catches that kept it in the hands of the magical, invisible pilot. *Heart of God* listed hard to the port now, so he steered into the list, trying to make a virtuous spiral of the airship's vicious, dying necessity. There was no need to pull the levers that controlled altitude—the airship already had more descent in her than he would ever have cared for.

Within moments only he and Arellya were on deck. Hethor fought the wheel as he tried to keep the ship heeled over to port. Arellya clung to the navigator's station, but turned to face him. "We are still far from your goal, Messenger," she shouted, "but it has been a good journey."

"We are not dead!"

He could hear the smile, even in her answering yell. "Certainly we are. It is only that our bodies have not yet learned the truth."

The other engine began to strain. The gasbag shuddered in threatening sympathy. The deck had slanted over so far as to be useless for anything but a death trap, but the trim levers were worthless. Hethor reluctantly pulled the wheel back to center.

Their only remaining advantage was that the hull still retained sufficient connection to the gasbag for the airship to fall slowly. Had the winged savages done much more of their work, even that solace would no longer matter.

Hethor looked to his left, over the angled deck at the ice and snow below. It was much closer and moving too quickly for what an airship's earthward progress should be.

"Brace!" he shouted, just as the remaining stanchions ripped free in a series of popping noises. The seams on his life coming loose, Hethor realized.

Then there was no deck, only falling. Then there was no falling, only deck. Ice and snow exploded around him, filled with splinters and planks and cold so sharp that its mere touch might snap bone.

His last sight was the gasbag tumbling free, shapeless and eager for independent flight, a second, trackless moon rising in a sky dominated now by bright, uncaring stars.

SOMEHOW, AGAINST all logic and memory, Hethor was warm. Not comfortable, but warm. He wasn't ready to look. There was a carillon of pain in his joints and chest, and his head hurt as badly as he could ever remember. He smelled blood, sweat, and water, all overlain with a crackling smoke.

Fire.

Hethor opened his eyes with a sudden panic.

The hull of *Heart of God* rose before him, broken-backed and partly shattered. The airship burned, sending gleaming smoke into a night sky that was still free of clouds. Stars surrounding the moon's thread glittered like the points of blades as his eyes stung with smoke.

A dozen correct people huddled with him or near him. Perhaps fifteen. Hethor was having trouble counting.

"We are all that remain," croaked one. Tiktiktee? Hethor could not recall the name. "Welcome to the end of worlds, Messenger."

"It's not the end of the world," Hethor said. "It's the bottom." Though what difference that made, he could not think. "We must make a trail south."

Tiktiktee sighed. "I would rather perish in the warmth here by the fire than march into the cold darkness to die. My soul would prefer it, too."

"Then I will go on alone."

"No." It was Arellya, though he could not make her out through the blur of the smoke.

Or was the blur in his eyes? "I ask no one, not even you, love," Hethor said. "You have brought me farther than I ever thought to go. Stay here with the flames if that is your desire. But I have a mission to discharge."

He tried to stand. Amazingly, he succeeded. Hethor's knees burned with cold and pain almost as badly as his lungs. He found he was already wrapped in blankets, so he turned slowly, his feet mashing deeper into the muddled snow until he found what he thought was south.

"You will not last an hour," Arellya said. She wriggled free from the huddle of her people and stepped across the snow to take his arm.

Hethor realized that Arellya wore far fewer blankets than he did. "How can you stand the cold?"

"It is just a different sort of jungle. Now stay here until the fire is almost gone. The heat will help, and you can sleep with less fear of being taken unawares by the chill."

So he sat again, surrounded by hairy bodies, watching this fire on the ice. It was so different from the fire in the jungle where he and Arellya had first met. No insects flew here; there was no food or water or dancing. But he was still with her and the correct people.

"I have brought you too far," he said. Tears stung his eyes, driving out for a moment even the smoke. "You came to help, and I have caused your people to be slaughtered. You will never see your jungle again. I apologize to all of you, to your dead, and to your tribe."

"You are the Messenger," said Tiktiktee. "This is what had to be."

Hethor watched the ship burn for hours, until sleep took him. He had a real rest this time.

HE AWOKE again not knowing the hour, his muscles stiff nearly to the point of immobility. It was hard to know the time so far to the south. *Heart of God* still burned, though the airship was now little more than a line of coals and glowering ash. Their respite from the cold was at an end.

Around him the correct people, led by Arellya, were organizing themselves for a trek southward. Even his own experiences with the New England winters told Hethor they would not last a day, not without food or decent coats and hats and boots. What else was to be done?

He would die with his face pointed toward the pole.

Noticing he was awake Arellya brought Hethor more blankets. "Wrap your arms and legs," she said. She tossed some rope at his feet. "Here are vines, too."

"Thank you." What else was there to do?

Hethor armored himself against the cold as best he could, swathed in folds and layers. He tied off his sleeves and waist and neck. There was little he could do for his feet. The leather boots he'd worn since leaving William's fortress were almost worn to shreds, but Hethor could not imagine walking any distance at all with his feet shrouded in cloth.

All too soon they formed up into a marching line. The correct people looked so different from the happy band paddling the fleet of canoes that had set out so long ago, Hethor thought, but Arellya's people still stirred him with pride. It was not that they were loyal to him. They were loyal to their own commitments. As he was to Gabriel.

"You'll just have to find another hero," Hethor whispered.

They began their straggling march, leaving the last of the fire for the deadly cold of the road south.

HETHOR LED in order to break a trail in the snow for the rest of his party. None of the correct people were large enough to serve, but they were too heavy to scamper over the top. It was not a deep snow—just a layer upon tougher, slicker ice, and sometimes gravel at the ridgetops—but where there were ripples or dips, the snow could go from inches to feet deep in a step. The correct people would have been lost immediately.

He set his pace with as much dedication as he could summon, though his feet were heavy as clock weights. "One." Huff. "Two." Puff. "Three." Huff. "Four."

Pause.

Rest.

Do it again.

There was nothing else, except perhaps to lie down and sleep.

On he went, breaking the trail in a private universe of stinging pain and, strangely, hope. He was still alive, after all. That was a miracle, however temporary. He had fallen from the sky yet again and once more lived to tell of it.

Behind him, Arellya also lived. Her whirring clockwork presence was audible to him. She had become a chain of love and desire wrapping his heart. He had been blessed by her before coming here to die.

To hell with Pryce Bodean, Hethor thought. *He can have his New Haven society girls and his future bishopric. I have lived.*

But the snow ate at his strength; the cold ate at his endurance; his feet had numbed to blocks. A glance back showed correct people straggling far behind, an irregular line of fur-bodied suffering. One dropped as he watched. There seemed to be others missing. He could not stop, though.

"One." Huff.

"Two." Puff.

"Three." Huff.

"Four."

Could he do this, for days without food or water or rest? Would God lend him that much strength?

His foot slipped, catching on a little ridge just beneath the surface. Hethor fell. He slid downhill into the snow ahead until he was engulfed in frozen darkness. He tried to scream, but his mouth was blocked. He tried to push it away, but it was like pushing the ocean. He closed his eyes, reaching for calm and the eerie false hope he'd felt moments before. All he could find was the rustling of the tiny ice crystals in the snow as they settled in to compact around his ears.

This is where I die, Hethor thought.

Little hands plucked at his blankets, reached under his hood to tug at his hair and shoulders. Hethor was hauled slowly out into the moonlight. There Arellya kissed him.

"You will not die alone," she said.

"Hope," croaked Hethor.

"We sit now."

"Keep on. Huff and puff."

"We sit."

"No."

"Sit."

And so they sat, in a tight circle, leaning inward, nine hairy faces and Hethor arranged in a funereal tentwork of bodies. A gentle snow began to fall upon them. He wondered how they would look to some future natural scientist exploring the ice. That is, if the nations of man survived what was coming well enough for there to *be* future natural scientists.

The Mainspring of the world ticked in his heart.

"I shall pray," Hethor whispered. He tried to recall the

day when the correct people's clicking, whistling language came to him. He fastened his attention onto the ticking of the Mainspring, imagined the massive escapements and gear trains necessary to turn the vast Earth. Counterpoint to that, he fixed on Arellya's whirring, the sound of her nature that he almost always heard now.

There was music beneath Creation. It was the clangor of brass and springs and pawls and stops and jacks—the greatest clock ever built. Every man and woman of any race was just a movement in the music, a tiny assembly within that vast train of clockwork.

Hethor let the clicking build within his ears, drawing from both the great unwinding of the world and the feverish little rattle that was Arellya, filling in all the things in between.

The stars had their own brittle, brilliant music. The moon hummed on her track, a silvery rattle much lighter than the roaring of the Earth's passage. Night's air was soft and vast. Snow scattered pin-bright upon the ground, a carpet of bright pain upon the slower-moving Earth. Each of the correct people surrounding him was their own song. All of them were in tune to one another, all their gear patterns closely allied.

His ears lost the sound of breathing, lost the worrying whistle of the wind, heard only the gearing of the world.

Everything was clockwork now, a vast sea of gears and springs and arbors and escapements and detents and shafts and wheels. Even his memories were of such things.

Hethor had good memories.

So he reached out to touch the world before him. The South Pole was a looming presence in the distance. Hethor faced that, made to part the way. A road was what he needed—a road of memory.

He stopped some wheels spinning, reset some gears, bent some escapements back, changed the length and period of certain pendulums. He made a smooth, shining road of his memory that cut through the brass jungle of cold death.

He closed his eyes, thanked God, and thought of Arellya.

HETHOR STOOD in a field of brilliant flowers, poppies and marigolds and all the things that bloomed in a New England spring. Though there was no sun in the sky, the field was bright, and warm. Snow swirled in a deadly darkness a hundred yards to each side.

Arellya limped from the still-huddled circle to hug him. "Messenger, you have done this thing."

"I . . ." Hethor didn't know what he could or should say. "God did it."

"*You* did it."

Though he was in a field, the grassy marge stretched away south, topping the ridgelines and plowing through the snow in a bright band of warmth and color. A spring glistened nearby. Conies leapt and played.

"We shall drink, and eat," he said. Or was this his dying delirium?

"To the hunt!" Arellya cried.

Though they groaned out their pain, the eight surviving young males were happy for the warmth, and desperate for the food. They ran the rabbits down.

"I WONDER how long it will last," Hethor said, wiping blood from his lips. They had not been able to make a fire to cook the conies.

"Do not think of that," Arellya said. She glanced at the nearby wall of swirling snow. "Each breath here is a gift to our souls. A scrap which you were able to beg for us from God's campfire. I will live with it as long as I can."

"Am I a sorcerer, or is God?"

"Are you concerned with the evil of other men? Do not be. Messenger, you are who you are."

She took him by the hand, and the two of them found a gentle slope a small distance from the young males.

There they lay among the poppies and had the joy of each other's bodies one last, unexpected time.

HETHOR AND the correct people walked for days, eating flowers, hunting small animals, and drinking from springs. Where the meadow-road met an escarpment, it snaked around, up hidden ravines and sly valleys, but otherwise their progress was steadily to the south. The polar winter was always just a few hundred yards behind them, the road vanishing as they progressed along it.

Each step was a cheat of death. Each breath was borrowed life. The smell of the flowers crushed beneath Hethor's feet was like stars burning in his head, each tingle a bright light. The gears were never far away either, echoing in the buzzing wings of the bees that tended the flowers, gleaming in the strange light that lit their path though all around them was howling polar darkness.

Two weeks after they had set out walking, Hethor began to hear a deep rumble underneath the whisper of the storms and the endless chatter of gears that had captured his hearing. This new noise was more measured, slower, and somehow bigger than any sound he'd heard since the great gear atop the Equatorial Wall had stolen his hearing. And perhaps his mind, Hethor had to admit.

"Do you hear it?" he asked Tiktiktee.

The correct person shook his head, a gesture copied from Hethor. "No. You have the hearing of the world, Messenger."

"I think it is the South Pole. We approach the axle of the world."

"Your journey is almost over."

"Or just begun."

THREE DAYS later, cresting a rise, Hethor and the correct people saw the South Pole.

Perhaps two more miles of the flowered highway

stretched ahead. It was lit as always by some milky version of Heaven's light though the storms and darkness swirled around them. The highway ended in a great circular meadow. In the center of the meadow a brass shaft erupted like a javelin stuck into the unyielding earth. It was about a quarter mile in diameter, and rose to vanish frost-rimed into the dark sky above.

Perhaps a hundred yards up a collar was set that extended to a four-footed frame grounded at the edges of the meadow. Another hundred yards above the collar, just below the frost line where the air changed, whirled a set of weights. These were four brass balls, each larger than Master Bodean's shop building back in New Haven, which must serve to balance the shaft.

Hethor could not see upward past the weather, but he could easily imagine the shaft towering as high as the Equatorial Wall. In the endlessly bright polar summer it must be a brilliant reminder of the last withdrawal of God's finger from His Creation.

"We are here," Hethor whispered.

"This is the end of the world?" asked Arellya as the few surviving correct people crowded around them.

"The end, the beginning." Hethor shrugged, feeling the weight of his borrowed days of life as though they were years. "God has spared me to come to this place that I might descend beneath the Earth and pursue my errand." The thought filled him with dread. "I . . ."

"No one ever wants to walk into the fire," Arellya said softly, her fingers entwined with his. "But someone must, if only to save the ashes."

Hethor had to laugh. "What does *that* mean?"

Arellya laughed as well, the correct people joining in. "It is something mothers tell their children to quiet them."

"Mothers are fools, too," said Hethor, but his fey mood had broken.

Then the correct people began to run, eight young males who had voyaged to the bottom of the world for him, a stranger, capering and shouting as if they had come home. They raced for the shaft. They bounded through the flowers. They stumbled together to wrestle and push in the manner of young men of every race and species.

Hethor stood with Arellya and smiled. He might in that moment have been a little specimen of God, and these his little men.

"We are old," she said.

Had she read his mind?

"Your stories of the garden and the snake, these are the history of our people."

"God created you first," Hethor said.

"Perhaps. We do not tell it that way. You might, were you to write our words in your tongue."

"What of the giants in the earth that the Bible speaks of?"

"The other hairy men. The ones who live upon the cliffs of the Wall. Brothers to you, almost, save that they think with their noses and eat like antelope."

"We of the Northern Earth think with our manhood and eat like wildfires," said Hethor.

She poked him in the hip. "That is not all a bad thing."

Hand in hand, they ran after their little army of boys, Cains and Abels dancing in a flowered Eden in the dark heart of winter.

THEY CAMPED near the shaft. This was the end, in more ways than one.

"I fear we shall·not return from here," said Hethor.

"Surely you are not surprised in thinking that, Messenger," replied Tiktiktee.

"Do you want your soul to linger at this pole, once the snow closes in again?"

Tiktiktee ate a mouse, thinking over the question. As he swallowed, he smiled. "If your stories are true, there is a paradise of sunlight and beauty here half the year. What is this but the long night that comes before the bright day? My soul would rejoice for the change."

"Every season a day," said Hethor, "and every day a season." Not that it was that simple, but Tiktiktee was not far wrong, either. Hethor went on. "I must carefully examine the shaft, and possibly the legs of the collar. Somewhere here there will be a route downward into the heart of the world. This is where my journey takes me." He looked significantly around the circle of correct people, finally resting his gaze on Arellya. "I will go alone."

She simply smiled at him. The other correct people nodded or grunted.

"I cannot counsel you further," Hethor went on. "There is no return from here." The last of the flowered road had closed behind them when they entered the meadow around the shaft. "When I descend, the snows may come immediately. Or if I am killed. Even if I survive and make my return to the surface, I do not know how to leave this place."

Tiktiktee touched Hethor's arm. "Enough, Messenger. We know these things. You owe us no apologies."

Hethor glanced down. "It is the custom among my people to make a speaking when we set out for great danger or certain death."

"Then speak all you want," said Tiktiktee. "We will listen. But it is for you, not for us."

"And I am going," said Arellya, "though the others will stay here and watch for us until the snow takes them."

"No!" Hethor jumped up. "It is too dangerous!"

Arellya looked around at the wall of dark and freezing night bordering the meadow. "More so than here? Our place is with each other, Hethor."

"I won't have it." He began to pace. "The Key Perilous is my business, the Mainspring a job given me by Gabriel. I know it will end badly. I can't be responsible for what will happen to you."

"The time for avoiding responsibility passed many days and miles ago," said Arellya.

"There may be fires, devils, or demons. Winged savages." Hethor could feel his voice rising, pitching toward stinging frustration and the tears that had brought him only ridicule at New Haven Latin.

"I have faced all those things with you already on this journey."

Arellya's calm reminded Hethor of Librarian Childress. The old woman had been unyielding in a strange way, something that still bothered him. She had upset his sense of the female kind for good, it seemed. Here Arellya was bent on shattering what remained of that upset sense.

"No," he said. "There is no more arguing."

She just smiled.

He lay back in the poppies and stared up at the sky. What was left to argue?

"I rest now," he announced, meeting no one's eye. "To be ready for my journey below." He lay for hours, flowers tickling his face, as the correct people moved around him, murmuring among themselves.

"THE YOUNG males have found your entrance." Arellya lay in the poppies next to Hethor, tickling his face with her hairy fingers.

"I told them . . . ," he began, then stopped.

Had he slept?

He must have.

"You told them not to come below with you. Not a one of them has set a foot upon the stairs that lead beneath the world. They merely found it for you. Are you rested, Messenger?"

"Yes," he said, surprised to find that it was true.

She handed him the bulb from some unlucky flower. "This will help hunger. I have meat for later."

Meat meant mice, and an occasional rabbit, but Hethor had long since lost any pretense of being fussy about his food. "Thank you," he said. Sitting up, he split the bulb. It tasted like a mild cousin of garlic or onion, with little strips of fiber that caught between his teeth. The food made his lips and tongue tingle as well. He paid that no mind.

It was a short walk across the poppy meadow to the shaft. Up close, the brass was like a wall. The curve was so large that it was shallow almost to the point of flatness. The shaft spun with a whirring noise that was much quieter than he had expected from the rumble he'd heard several days distant. Rotating rapidly, it stirred the air like a spring breeze. There must be a massive reduction gearing deep within the world, he realized, to translate that speed to the stately revolutions of the Earth in its orbit around the sun. Cold radiated off the surface before him, doubtless conducted downward from the immense length of the metal that protruded into the long polar night not far above his head.

Hand in hand with Arellya, Hethor followed the shaft clockwise around its curve. The great column of metal fit into a little lip of rock where it emerged from the flower meadow. Given the immense size of the thing the tolerances were miraculous. Which by definition had to be true.

Hethor smiled upward as if God or His angels were watching.

A cluster of the correct people waited ahead of him, Tiktiktee and the other young males crowded around the entrance. As he approached they stepped back, flowing away in a hairy tide.

The stairs were simple enough, descending into a hole in the flowered turf that resembled an open grave. It was set a few feet back from the shaft. *Perhaps to provide clearance,* Hethor thought, though why divine Creation would need an inspection access was beyond him.

There was no marker to indicate the access way, though with the shaft close to hand, one was not needed. He stopped at the head and stared downward. Stairs led into the earth, their well gloomy but not impossibly dark as it curved to follow the shaft. The spiral ran counter to the rotation of the axis, heading to the left. Hethor could see where it bent out of his vision, following the curve.

"This is it," he said, resisting the urge to make another speech.

One of the young males stood and walked over and touched Hethor's hand. "Luck, Messenger," he said, "and may your soul rest in the easiest of places."

"And yours," he said.

Then another, with a simpler message. "Luck."

Tiktiktee hugged Hethor, the correct person's strong arms tight around his waist. "Our world is yours, Messenger."

One by one, the rest of Arellya's eight surviving tribesmen came forward to Hethor. Each had a word or two. Each took a moment to let their touch linger. Each walked away into the flowers without a second glance.

After a few minutes, only he and Arellya remained. She held one of the last of the correct people's spears in her hand.

"You cannot come," said Hethor.

"You cannot stop me."

"Don't. Please."

She smiled again, though the smile wavered. "I will not stay here to die of cold, wondering what finally became of you."

Hethor didn't want to be apart from her, not for a minute, but he couldn't take her into the Earth. It was akin to inviting her to stroll with him in Hell. "The men of your tribe will protect you."

"From the storms? No." She tugged free of his hand to set foot upon the first of the steps. "I can run ahead of you to make you chase me." She pulled her foot back up. "I can hang back to follow you like a shadow cut free from its source. Or we can walk down together. Partners. Mates. Woman and man."

"You are from Creation's dawn," Hethor said. "I am from its noontime."

"Or sunset," she replied, "if you fail. That is no argument against me."

He opened his arms and she stepped into them. They hugged for a long time, him breathing in the sweet scent of her hair, mingled with poppies and the tingly bulbs they had eaten and the slightly raw odor of mice. Hethor imagined the world shuddering to a halt on its track, the sun's light boiling some oceans while others froze in eternal darkness. Would the Chinese Empire suffer in eternal night? What if the turning of the Earth stopped on the other side, with London facing the stars? Would anyone's interests be served?

Master Bodean, Librarian Childress, the farmers who had helped him, that girl with the hearse, even the crazed and foolish candlemen, Her Imperial Majesty's sailors, the Jade Abbott—all their lives hung on him. If Arellya chose to walk by his side, who was Hethor to deny her? Perhaps she, too, had been called by God. Perhaps he was her angel, her Gabriel come from the sky to awaken her people to their peril.

Just as someone else might have sent Gabriel to him.

Hethor felt an unaccountable longing for the late Simeon Malgus, though the man was half a traitor and fully arrogant. The navigator had possessed a way with words and a willingness to explain things. Sometimes, at least.

Hethor could no more explain the world to himself or Arellya than he could explain love.

Arellya shouldered her spear. Hand in hand, facing the darkness, they descended beneath the Earth little more than an armspan away from the spinning wall of brass that drove the world.

TWELVE

THE BRASS stairs spiraled slowly through layers of rock. The wall of spinning brass that was the main axle of Earth's rotation was always on their left. Hethor could glance over the brass rail of the stairs and see something like infinity receding until perspective folded the view into itself. On the right, the differing strata. They told a history of the Earth's Creation, the careful folding of layers into one another by the hand of God.

Always there was light. Vague, sourceless, as though stars shone overhead even in the depths of the Earth.

"How deep do these stairs descend?" Arellya asked as they made their way downward.

"Farther than we can journey before we starve, I fear," said Hethor. The mathematics were simple enough. If he truly had to descend into the clockwork heart of the Earth, it would be a walk of thousands of miles spiraling ever downward. No man, or correct person, could survive that. "We must as always trust to faith."

"You have come far on trust until now, Messenger," she said with a squeeze of his hand.

After a time the rock gave way to gear trains and layers of metal clattering just to their right as they descended.

Walls of machinery and spinning fields of brass extended into the gloom. They walked among it all like flies on the windowpane of a machine shop.

This was the balancing mechanism within the Earth, part of what kept it on God's track. Hethor tried to imagine what sort of interrupter gear would allow these devices to function tied to the central shaft, while also permitting his descent via the stairwell. Perhaps there were spiral reliefs cut through the shells of the inner spheres of the Earth. Or the stairway itself was discrete, a section that descended like a worm gear regardless of how rapidly or slowly he and Arellya walked.

As well to imagine flights of angels buoying them toward their destination. Yet this was all the work of God, somehow.

In time, the gearwork gave way to crystal caverns extending into the depths of the Earth. These spaces glittered like the captured stars of Hethor's imagining. Their right-hand wall vanished utterly, so that the brass stair wound onward seemingly unsupported. On the one side it wound around the spinning shaft like a lover's hand. On the other, empty void, their clanging footsteps echoing from the star-speckled depths. Everything had the clean, cold smell of an icehouse in winter.

It was here, lulled by hours of walking without need for rest or food, that their first test came. Wooden statues tumbled out of the surrounding darkness—the tall, flat-faced servant-automata of William of Ghent. In a clattering moment, Hethor and Arellya were trapped upon the stairs. Two wooden men blocked them below. There were three more above.

Hethor had no fire with which to fight them this time. No weapon at all. He had not thought to need one here.

Of necessity, he raised his fists. "You will not bar me from the heart of the world!" he shouted.

Then the creatures were upon them. Splintered arms slashed toward him only to bang against the brass rail of the stairs as Hethor ducked the blow. Arellya slipped to his back, shrieking a ululating war cry of the correct people. He felt her move, bumping against him as she jabbed with her spear.

It was like fighting a house. He would land a blow only to shock his knuckles. One of the wooden automata would strike back, nearly shattering bone in Hethor's shoulder or arm. All that stood between him and final ruin was the crowding of the stairs. Only two at a time could face him.

Behind, Arellya shouted and jabbed some more. She did not scream in pain or fear. He trusted her and instead concentrated on what stood before him.

You've been among sailors and tropical warriors, Hethor told himself. He must have learned something. He stepped into an incoming blow, set his weight against the wooden automaton's chest, and shoved it into its neighbor. The two toppled and spun, trying to untangle and carry on the fight, until one tipped against the rail and fell silent into the pit that spread below them.

Hethor rushed the second, which was still off balance, before its fellows could close. He got it over the left-side railing. There he pressed his advantage to slide its head into the spinning brass wall of the axle. Splinters and sawdust flew amid a burning stench and a strange buzzing noise. Blows rained down upon his back in a sort of vengeance.

Arellya screamed.

Hethor heaved the suffering creature over the side, where it would bounce splintering against the whirling shaft, and turned to duck another swinging blow. Arellya lay on the stairs. Her spear was braced to keep two of the wooden attackers at bay. They loomed over her, jostling one another for the chance to stomp her.

Hethor tried to leap, but the one survivor above him grabbed at his ankles. He fell, striking his face against the wrought metal of the steps.

In a moment his legs would be smashed. Just ahead of him, Arellya cried out again, blood matting her lovely, lovely fur.

It could not end like this.

Hethor closed his eyes and reached for his sense of the underlying reality of Creation. The wooden automata were masses of gears, eerily regular in their formation when compared to the wild naturalistic designs within Arellya or himself. He reached back with his power, working against the pain in his legs, to crumple and scatter the gears of one of his tormentors.

His ears reported an explosion as splinters hammered into his body. He turned to face Arellya's attackers. The image of fire came to his mind. In his holy sight it was an unbound chaos in this version of the world, a chaos that destroyed through reduction, making unstable structures of breathtaking beauty that collapsed in a moment in a shower of springs and parts, each in turn another world of complexity.

Hethor made a gift of this chaos to Arellya's two. They each erupted into billowing heat and flaring madness—an unraveling of the orderly world of Creation.

Setting aside his holy sight, Hethor knelt beside Arellya. She still clutched her spear. Her eyes were filmed over and she was whimpering. Blood matted the fur of her neck and shoulders and chest.

"Can you hear me?" Hethor asked.

Arellya nodded.

"Will you live?"

She just stared.

He reached for her then, trying to find the mainspring that drove her body without disturbing her essence. There were patterns of chaos, or worse, silence, in the tumbling assemblage that was Arellya. She had taken a sharp blow to the head. He caressed her there, his fingers feeling matted fur over shifting bone even as his eyes saw more of God's favored brass.

Though Hethor could not make her whole all at once, he could smooth out the chaos and set gears spinning within the silent places of her head. As he bent to do that an unexpected blow struck his back as an ax strikes a sapling.

There had been another attacker.

He collapsed on the stairs, still seeing the underlying world as he slid past Arellya. Hethor's hand reached for her spear even while he rolled away from a further blow that set the stairs ringing. The spear was close, but not close enough as it brushed against his fingers, so he made his own, willing it from the fabric of the air. There was a rushing howl of winds and the sharp smell of a storm as he thrust his clockwork spear forward.

His holy sight was gone, stripped from him by exhaustion. The last of the wooden automata tumbled slowly away from him. Its flat face melted into the screaming visage of a dark-skinned man, much as William of Ghent's servants had done when his great jungle fortress took flame.

He stood to shake off his vision, soul-sick from the magic. His feet ached dreadfully. Blood streamed from a hundred splinters. Arellya clung to the rail two steps above him now. Her spear stood wedged into a stair riser. She smiled. "We live."

"We live." He shuddered. Hethor had never known he could absorb, or deliver, such punishment. He only prayed to God he would not have to do more, though he suspected such a prayer to be no better than vanity. "Onward."

"Messenger . . ." She sounded uncertain. Heartbreakingly so.

Hethor paused in the act of turning around, one hand on the rail. "What?"

"I am afraid that I cannot stand."

"Ah." He looked at his beloved for a moment. "Then I must carry you on my back."

THEY PRESSED onward. The diffuse light came to seem a despairing gloom. The endless echo of the brass stairs was a bell tolling out the last strokes of Hethor's life.

Each footfall was multiplied in weight, and pain. He had come so far. Hethor would not stop now.

He could do little to command his own slowing, however.

The crystal caves were gone. There was only an endless, echoing space with the shaft always to their left. The wind of its rotation plucked at them. The hum of it nagged at their ears. Arellya's weight on his back grew and grew, until Hethor felt as if he carried a draft horse into the nether regions of the Earth. Only her warm, shallow breath on his neck, the sweetgrass scent of her tingling his nose, reminded him of his true self, his true purpose.

After a while he became aware of a creaking noise in the shadows around him. Something large moved there. It made him think of *Bassett* under way, or perhaps how the chest muscles of the winged savages popped as they flew.

Then Gabriel alit upon the stair rail. The angel crouched to grasp it with its fingers, each hand set just outside the feet pressed together. The pose was odd, balanced by the wings, making the angel seem like a great turkey or rooster.

"Greetings, Hethor," said Gabriel. "You have come so far."

Hethor wanted to kneel on the steps, babble out his relief and pray for aid in this terrible place. Only Arellya's weight upon his back kept him standing. "I have done all that you asked and more," he said, "though it cost me dearly."

Gabriel nodded over Hethor's shoulder. "It gained you dearly, too. But you have not done everything. You have neglected the Key Perilous."

Hanging his head, Hethor said quietly, "I never came near it. Though I sought it far and wide."

"You turned your face south too soon." The archangel smiled, pity and love mixed together like a balm for Hethor's wounds. "Your errand is moot now. Another way must be found, though time before the end is very short."

"I go forward," said Hethor. "There is no turning back."

"No," agreed the angel, "but you can rest. You have earned it. Sit here a while. I will find some food and blankets for you."

Where would it find such things? Hethor wondered. On his back, Arellya stirred. Gabriel was right. He should just sit down and rest. He must set his load aside first.

"No," she whispered.

No, he thought. She was right. This made no sense, though it was hard to find the logic amid his fatigue. "Why would you have me abandon my quest?" Hethor asked. "Turn back perhaps, but why stop here?"

"You deserve your rest."

"No," whispered Arellya. "He plays you false."

Hethor considered. The wooden men must have been a sending from William of Ghent, still seeking an end to the world's turning. Allowing the Mainspring to wind down was freedom, perhaps, but Hethor could only imagine it as the freedom of death.

And now this. Gabriel had not spoken to him so, back in New Haven. Gabriel would not urge him to lie down and rest.

"The token you gave me," Hethor said, "the horofix that was taken from me in New Haven. What became of it?"

"It is in God's hand." Gabriel smiled.

"It was a *feather,*" Hethor shouted. "Not a horofix." He gathered his holy sight, made a fist of the power, and shoved the false archangel from the rail. Gabriel exploded in a cloud of clockwork, much of it tiny as the splinters of the wooden man had been, so that Hethor's clothes and skin were slashed anew.

He was so weakened by this use of his power that he slipped some distance down the spiral on his buttocks, dragging Arellya with him. They finally came to rest in a groaning tangle with Hethor's left leg jammed against one of the metal stair posts.

"Perhaps we should take our rest now," he said quietly.

"Up," she said. "I think I can stand."

She could not, so he took her on his back again and stumbled onward.

MORE WALKING. The minutes stretched like days while the hours passed in seconds. Hethor finally lost the sense of time that had stayed with him as long as he could remember. He surrendered it to fatigue, despair, and the endless brass coil of this journey, always an armspan away from the whirling face that marked the axis of the world. Even amid the loss and surrender, his feet kept moving.

The walls closed in again. Honest stone pressed tight. The space robbed the diffuse light of its power, so his descent became a winding tunnel that constantly seemed likely to pinch Hethor and Arellya within its rounded grasp. He considered throwing himself over the rail, wondering whether the quick, sharp fall would be better than the endless walk, but he was not yet so desperate.

So he walked.

Step by echoing step.

Downward.

His feet hurt.

His back hurt.

His head hurt.

His body stung from a hundred cuts.

Arellya was a millstone upon him.

Hethor made the inscription from the tablet his marching rhythm, stepping on every beat, saying the words with his breath. It was as if he could conjure strength and endurance by main force.

"The heart of God . . ." Step.

"Is the heart of the world." Step.

"As man lives . . ." Step.

"So lives God." Step.

"As God lives . . ." Step.

"So lives the world." Step.

It made of his entire body a prayer, and carried Hethor through his dark hours while Arellya quietly shuddered her pain on his shoulder.

HETHOR CAME round a turn in the stairs to see a whole new cavern extending below him. The light was brighter here. The walls seemed lined with fungus, an infinite folding vista of glistening color and sickly sheen. Ribbons of spores moved through the air like eels in tropical water. He stopped to look, arresting his pace for the first time in hours. Was there a city down there? Did people live here, even in the depths of the Earth?

There was no end to the wonder and manner of men to be found in God's Creation.

After an indefinite time, he met the third guardian of their descent.

William of Ghent.

The sorcerer had survived Hethor's push into the spinning brass fields of the underworld, but he had not survived them well. The old arrogance was gone—lost with the classic beauty of his face. The red-brown hair was now a dirty yellowed white that grew in patches. One ice blue eye was puckered shut. A livid scar seamed William's face below the missing orb. The other seemed clouded though a spark glowed within. He stood as though his body were a curse rather than a blessing.

But when he spoke, it was with the same honeyed tones of sweet reason and contempt that Hethor had first heard condemn him to death in the little room beneath the viceroy's court in Boston. "I see your persistence has outweighed the combination of your other virtues, young Hethor."

"William," Hethor said. He eased to a sitting position on the stairs. This was not a fight he could win at blows, or even with the magic of Creation. William of Ghent was taller, stronger, older, more experienced, and more powerful than he. Hethor was certain that was still true, even now when William was far from the height of his social position and physical grace.

Hethor concentrated on sliding a sleeping Arellya off his back and twisting so that he could hold her in his lap. As she was no bigger than a child, this was easily done. If he was going to die at William's hand here deep beneath the Earth, he preferred to see her face.

"A gentleman to the last," said William. "If only your reasoning had kept pace with your deeds."

"There is nothing wrong with my thoughts."

"Hethor . . ." William sounded sorrowful, just as Master Bodean might have done. "If you had listened, and considered the evidence to hand, we might now be standing in a very different place."

"I did what I could." Hethor felt his breath rattling in his chest. Was the infinite walk taking its ultimate toll on his body?

"But you did not do what you should." With a visible effort, William knelt to bring himself to Hethor's level. They were eye-to-eye now, William two steps down. "You were taken in by a tale told by an idiot, one of Heaven's castaways. Your precious Gabriel was no more than a winged savage gifted with speech. A genius of his kind. Still, he is nothing but a debased angel."

"No." Hethor refused to believe that, refused to countenance such an idea. He had come too far, seen too much, to believe an error. "The world does run down. It will be the death of us. The tremors of the Earth have already slain far too many."

"Of course the Earth is running down," said William. "God abandoned His Creation from the first, if ever it was His. The Clockmakers are with us, Hethor. They will see our distress and return to reset the clockwork of the world. Thus will man be free of the chains of Heaven and set into a state of nature so that we can find our own way."

"You have argued this before. You are no more sensible now." Hethor flapped his hands at William. "Begone."

"I am right. You are wrong. I have evidence, which you lack."

"The heart of God is the heart of the world," said Hethor. "As man lives, so lives God. As God lives, so lives the world. He has not abandoned us. He is everywhere among us."

"Everywhere and nowhere," William whispered. "Which is to say, He is absent. We must chart our own path free of the tyranny of Creation and invariant fate. You and I could have freed the world together, set it on a new path." William rose to his feet, his voice pitching higher. "Instead you seek a rewinding of the Mainspring, to do again what that fool Brass Christ did two thousand years past. Let it run down, man! Let the world run down so that the Clockmakers will return."

"We do not need the Clockmakers." Hethor was tired, so very tired. "We need a world that works. Following God's path, man can find his own way."

On his lap, Arellya opened her eyes and stifled a groan.

"You are a hopeless and venal fool," William said. "I cannot imagine why I ever sought you out. Heaven is a fraud and so are you."

Hethor hugged Arellya and stared up at the sorcerer. "I do not know what is fraud and what is not. I only know what I must do. Please, let me pass. If you are correct, and God has indeed abandoned His Creation, all I shall do is make a fool of myself. If you are mistaken, then you might be glad to see things set to rights."

"So pretty a plan. Such wise words." William shook his ruined head sadly. "The world needs to be set to rights. What if you are wrong, but your interference only makes it worse?"

"Faith," muttered Hethor, then struggled back to his feet. Arellya clung to his chest, her arms around his neck. "Have faith, sir."

"Never." The smile was unmistakable, even in the bloody violence of his face. "I am a Rational Humanist, perhaps *the* Rational Humanist."

"Then at least let me pass like the gentleman you are." Hethor bent to pick up his spear, and Arellya's grip slipped. She tumbled free from his neck. William reached to grab her, to stop her, and their hands clasped— Hethor's lover and his enemy, grasping one another's wrists for a moment before she overbalanced him and they both slipped past the railing into the empty air.

Hethor was halfway to vaulting the railing after them when he caught himself.

What could he do to save her?

He could never even catch them on the way down. Only fall and watch his beloved die in the arms of a mad, mad sorcerer. Who was the Rational Humanist now?

That thought almost sent him over the rail again.

Instead Hethor sat, Arellya's spear on his lap, to fold his face in his hands and scream his way to tears.

"THE HEART of God . . ." Step.

"Is the heart of the world." Step.

"As man lives . . ." Step.

"So lives God." Step.

"As God lives . . ." Step.

"So lives the world." Step.

The words had become more of a curse than a prayer, but what else could Hethor do? He had to go on.

If he could create flowers on the ice, he could raise his beloved from the dead. All he had to do was find her body at the center of the world and pour his holy magic into her.

Hethor imagined Arellya and William lying in a tangle on some great balcony. They would be surrounded by angels crooning a requiem. Heaven's light would play on his beloved, while William's body rotted in shadow. He would approach with the gift of life in his hand and bend to kiss her brow. At his touch Arellya would be restored. He would cheat death and ignore the old fraud that was God, all in one mighty kiss.

She would breathe. She would open her eyes. She would call his name.

Hethor stepped onward, clinging to a dream he knew to be as false as William's words.

THE DOWNWARD walk continued for what seemed a lifetime or more. Hethor passed through fire that raised blisters on his skin and set his clothes to smoldering. He passed through ice that cracked his lips and caused his hair to freeze and break off. He passed through giant gear trains of brass set so close to the stairs that to extend his hand would have been to lose his fingers.

Then he walked some more.

No further guardians troubled him. It was the distance itself and the tiny, private little hells of the journey, that should have persuaded Hethor to turn back. He needed Arellya, needed to see her face and touch her hair and leave one last gentle kiss on her cool forehead. All the rest of the world was dead to him.

When he came to the end, Hethor was surprised by it. At first he did not recognize what lay before him.

Stair and shaft emerged from another rock layer into a domed cave much brighter than he had seen since leaving the surface. Far below, miles perhaps, though perspective and distance had tricked him time and time again on this journey, the brass shaft plunged into the center of a wide, textured plain covered with curved scorings. The stairway ended in a catwalk that extended in two directions over the vast surface.

Which had to be the Mainspring of the world, Hethor realized. It was a steel coil spring set upon its side.

He was seeing it for himself. Something that perhaps no one had seen since the Brass Christ—the legendary Mainspring. And he still did not have the Key Perilous, though the scar on his hand throbbed piteously.

"Arellya, I am here," he shouted, then pounded down the stairs again. As he descended, he saw a small dot on the spring that must be the bodies of William and his beloved.

It is so huge, he thought. How would he ever have been expected to wind it with a key small enough to fit in his hands? The Key Perilous would have to be the size of Boston to even begin to have leverage enough to wind this spring.

On he plunged, racing from step to step. Somehow the spring did not get any closer, though the ceiling receded above him. He kept his eye on the spot that marked Arellya's passing. That was where he would fall to his knees. That was where he would cry out his heartache. That was where he would lay himself down to die, releasing all the fear and pain and suffering that was in his body.

Eventually Hethor stepped off the stairs onto the catwalk. It was like being born anew, to leave that winding path of struggle for a level place. He looked up. Shaft and stair vanished into a misty darkness. Perhaps he was at the center of the world. If so, God had made it much like any other cavern, save for its size and the vast machinery that drove Creation. No choirs of angels awaited.

Below his feet lay the steel with Arellya's body upon it. She had fallen straight and true to land near the base of the shaft. There was no sign of William.

He studied his beloved.

She sprawled broken-backed upon the striated lines of the Mainspring. There was no stirring of life. Blood stained the metal around her.

The lines he had seen proved indeed to be the edges of bands of steel set end-on. They could be a hundred miles deep for all he could tell. This close, he could see the metal flexing and loosening. The bands moved farther apart at a speed visible even to his eye.

Soon they would part like the thin lips of an angry master and her body would plunge again to be lost within the coils of the Mainspring.

"I am coming," he said, grasping the railing to step over it and drop the twenty feet or so to rest beside her.

"No."

Hethor looked up at the sound of William of Ghent's voice.

A shambling horror stood on the catwalk a few yards from him. Bare bones glistened; metal cables showed along its joints. Skin and cloth were slashed together as blood, oil, and shavings dribbled onto the catwalk's metal grid.

It was William of Ghent, recognizable only by the voice and the surviving blue eye that gleamed like madness in the spring.

"Let the world be," the William-thing said. "The Mainspring will fail as it should to call them back."

This was indeed a thing, sprung from darkest magics. No human, no creature of God, could have survived that fall to the center of the Earth to rise again.

"I no longer seek to repair the world," said Hethor mildly. He looked down at Arellya again.

The William-thing didn't seem to hear Hethor's words. "I am the guardian of the winding shaft. The Clockmakers will return." Ruined hands reached forward, sparks crackling on the fingertips as it shuffled forward.

"As man lives, so lives God," Hethor told the William-thing. "I will not fight you. I follow my heart."

Hethor flipped himself over the rail, hung, then dropped to the surface of the spring. The impact nearly broke his ankles. His feet stung like they were on fire. The spring edges flexed beneath him, making a perilous ground. The same depths that threatened to swallow Arellya threatened to take him as well, even before Hethor could reach her.

Balancing on the narrow edges, Hethor leapt from coil edge to coil edge. Above him the William-thing pleaded with him to come away.

As the spring creaked beneath him, Hethor reached his beloved and took her tiny body up into his arms. She was still warm somehow, not the cold lump he had expected. He ruffled her hair, feeling its familiar silkiness. All the nights they had spent together came rushing back to him. Her guidance on his journey. Her leadership of the war band of correct people even as the group eroded around him. Her simple patience and uncompromising sense of purpose.

"I hope your soul finds peace in this place," he whispered. "Surely no correct person ever journeyed so far to find life's end."

The spring yawned wider. He could have simply tipped forward and plunged into the metal crevasse and died with Arellya.

Something held him back.

There had to be more purpose to all of this. Gabriel had not visited Hethor in New Haven simply to send him out to die. He had survived ocean and air and frozen night and screaming fate. He had found unlikely friends and unexpected enemies and still completed his journey to this place.

If Hethor had wanted to lie down and die, he could have done so on the ice, in the poppies, back on the stairs. Even in the gutter in New Haven.

Why had he not?

Gabriel had said he could wind the Mainspring of the world. Hethor had the power. Whatever that power was.

He also had the choice.

Bracing Arellya on his left arm, he opened his right hand to look again at the key-shaped scar that had reasserted itself. He had never found the Key Perilous, not with the Jade Abbot, not in the jungles of the Southern Earth. The Brass Christ or the wise men who came after Him had hidden it too well.

Had it ever been there to find?

Above him, the William-thing continued to shout, about choice and freedom and betrayal.

Hethor had always possessed the Key Perilous, he realized. His journey wasn't to find the Key. It was to understand how to use it. Everything else—Gabriel's mission, the messages on the golden tablets, all his tribulations—were his schooling. With a far harder hand than Headmaster Brownlee would have dared extend even to him.

Well, perhaps he had learned something.

"The heart of God is the heart of the world," Hethor said quietly to his beloved. "As man lives, so lives God. As God lives, so lives the world. I choose to live the way I will."

He closed his eyes, summoned his holy sight to see the clockwork and gear trains of Creation. The room around him did not change much. The great spring on which he crouched was real here, too, though Arellya was merely a jumble of broken, inert mechanisms.

Hethor reached into the orderly workings of his own heart, trying to capture the rhythm and the strength of it that he might give that to Arellya. His body twisted with the springs, as though the leverage that drove the world were being focused through his joints and sinews. Fire ran across him.

He ignored the pain and continued to set his beloved's body to rights. It was the hardest work Hethor had ever done, a strain deeper than any study or argument. A journey longer and more dangerous than his descent into the Earth, for all that this lasted only seconds. His own heart slipped, skipping beats, as he tried to bring Arellya's back.

All the gears of Creation rattled. Hethor's head filled with light, a bloom of peaceful energy that drowned out the pain, his own attempts at holy magic, everything. He was for a moment the sole focus of God's kind regard. He was wrought of silver and gold, with crystal for his soul.

He reached out and made the greatest offering he could, passing that precious gift of God's attention to Arellya and to William as well.

Arellya coughed her way to life then as the Mainspring snapped shut. The motion caused Hethor to slip, tumbling into the closing crevasse so both his legs were trapped tight to crushing, just above the knees.

Even the pain was welcome.

His beloved was whole.

She opened her eyes and said, "Hethor?" just as the William-thing burst into light on the catwalk above. Not merely light, but the brilliance of chaos. All the randomness of fire mixed with odd shoots of Creation, flowers folding to buds, rivers running backward, islands sinking beneath the sea. The world itself stuttered in reverse among the glow.

Still touched with the holy sight, Hethor smiled upward. With the breath of God still upon him, he opened up his heart, plunged his hand into his chest, and withdrew a small crystal key.

It fit the scar on his palm perfectly.

"The Key Perilous," he said. "Love is the heart of God." He gave himself to the world.

The agony and bleeding from his crushed legs threatened to overwhelm Hethor then. He let Arellya gather him into her arms as she whispered questions he had trouble understanding. Above him, William's chaotic fires of life subsided to something cool and beautiful and quite surprised, while Arellya sobbed out her heart's pain to send Hethor to his rest.

HETHOR WAS amazed to find himself awake once more. He'd imagined death to be more like sleep.

He was in a curious place, too.

Something blue and brown hung in the sky above him. It was covered with white swirls. An orbital track stretched in both directions away from it, left and right, while a smaller brass ring circled it, rising like horns from the limited horizon of his view.

He looked at the Earth, safe among her gearing, high above in the noontime.

Which meant he was where . . . ?

The lamps of the stars were clearly visible beyond the Earth. He was surrounded close at hand by a few silver lights. Glistening forests of bamboo stood nearby, edging lakes of quicksilver that shivered slightly as if the land itself breathed. Pale deer darted through the brush while a flight of albino swans winged overhead. A white toucan watched him from atop a rock.

It had to be the moon. Was this where Heaven lay?

Hethor looked down. Though he thought he could feel his feet itching, he seemed to have no legs below his thighs. The bite of the Mainspring had been real enough, then. The sight should have gripped him with a hysterical panic, but Hethor was far too tired to scream now.

He sat propped against a boulder covered with silver lichen. A ewer of water stood near him, and a loaf of pale bread. On the boulder next to him, surely there the whole time though Hethor just saw him now for the first time, sat the archangel Gabriel.

Had he been a bird the moment before?

The real Gabriel, Hethor knew, was no more like the winged savage Hethor had defeated on the stairs than the monkeys of the Guyanan jungles were like him. The archangel sat with an air of simple confidence. It possessed an authority that no ordinary man or beast could attain.

"I have a question for you," said Gabriel in response to Hethor's attention. "One very few born of woman ever get to answer."

Hethor thought he already knew, but he asked anyway. "What is it?"

"Are you ready to go to God?"

Hethor took the question as seriously as life itself. Which it was. He had felt, for a moment, the soul-warming touch of God down in the heart of the world. But that was a reward, a finality. It promised an eternal haze of paradise, a summer day that never met its sunset.

Life was more than paradise.

Arellya.

Even if she was climbing up those endless stairs, doomed to die of starvation and thirst deep within the heart of the world, he wanted to be with her.

"I have a love, back on Earth," Hethor said slowly. "I want to live out my life with her."

"If I send you back, you will be a powerless cripple. At the mercy of every brigand or animal that might chance upon you."

"Then I shall have to trust in God as He trusted in me." Hethor smiled. "Send me back to Arellya."

The jungle spread around Hethor where he sat on the warm ground. Huts nested in and among the trees as hairy children threw fruit and played tag in the shadows of a hothouse sun. Kalker stood before him stirring a great clay pot. The old correct person glanced up.

"You have come back," he said.

"I am back," Hethor agreed.

"Would you like me to tell Arellya?"

Hethor smiled until his cheeks ached.

THEY FEASTED; then they promised themselves to one another in the manner of Hethor's people; then they went to live in a little hut overlooking the river. Legless, he could not use a wheeled chair as he might have back in New Haven. Instead Hethor fitted wooden pegs to the stumps of his legs so that he could walk with the aid of canes. At times of need he allowed himself to be carried. It was not such a trial, as much of his life there took place in the trees or on the water.

After he'd fashioned tools for himself with metal the correct people had traded for from distant tribes, Hethor carved a wheel-and-gear of the horofixion from jungle heartwood. He omitted the usual Christ figure. "Enough people have died for enough sins," he told Arellya. "It is time to get on with . . . well . . . time."

William of Ghent came after a while, clothed in light. Somehow he looked much as Gabriel had on the moon. The sorcerer and Hethor just stared at one another a while without speaking. William finally nodded, saying, "Perhaps 'Clockmaker' was just another word for 'God.'"

"Perhaps we were both mistaken," said Hethor kindly, though he was certain he'd understood all too well at the end. Not that he remembered those moments with much clarity now.

"The Earth still turns." William nodded to Arellya. "I must go to London. There is work to do in the world. I will see that you are remembered there."

Hethor reached upward to touch William's sleeve. Their hands met. "Do not tell them I yet live."

William shrugged. "You gave up your life for God upon the brass, and gave me back mine in the bargain. Who am I to say if you live? It is enough for me that you are here, and we have met this one last time."

He was gone, stepping away into more light.

After a few seasons Hethor took his wife as an apprentice in clockmaking, for all that he lived among a people who told time by watching the gears in the sky. It was enough to know that the Mainspring at the heart of the world ticked on.

Still, Hethor sometimes wished he could yet hear the clattering clockwork of Creation.

Turn the page for a preview of

ESCAPEMENT

JAY LAKE

Available in June 2008

TOR® A TOR HARDCOVER

ISBN-13: 978-0-7653-1709-4   ISBN-10: 0-7653-1709-5

Copyright © 2008 by Jay Lake

ONE

Paolina

THE BOATS had been drawn up in the harbor at Praia Nova when the great waves came two years past. The men of the village generally thought this a blessing, for that circumstance had spared their lives. The women generally thought this a curse for much the same reason. *A Muralha* remained silent and unforgiving as ever, a massive rampart of stone, soil, and strangeness soaring 150 miles high to separate Northern Earth from Southern Earth. In the shadow of the Wall, there was less food than ever until boats could be rebuilt and nets rewoven, but no self-respecting man would go without dinner. So the women quietly starved themselves and their babies to keep the drunken beatings away.

No one starved Paolina Barthes, though. Demon-haunted or touched by God, in either case she had saved Praia Nova after the waves. Still, she was boy-thin and narrow-shouldered, not yet to her monthlies though she wore the black linen dress that all the grown women favored.

The *fidalgos* spent every Friday night in the great hall

at the edge of Praia Nova. The building had been erected in an absolute absence of architects or—at least prior to Paolina—engineers, but instead with the dogged determination of the *fidalgos* that they knew best. Generations of pigheadedness had raised a monstrosity of coral cut from the reefs at the foot of *a Muralha,* granite chipped with slow, steady pain from the bones of the Wall itself, marble salvaged in furtive, fearful expeditions to the cities of the enkidus higher up. This resulted in something like a cross between a cathedral and a toolshed. Still, it had survived the quakes that came with the waves, where many of the traditional *adôbe* houses had not.

It was a harlequin of a building as well. The mix of materials and styles across the years made the thing a patchwork, a Josephan coat to shelter the guiding lights of Praia Nova in their wise deliberations.

This night, they were drunk and afraid.

Paolina knew this the way she knew most things. It was obvious from the scents in the air, the rhythm of the glasses pounding the table, the fact that another of Fra Bellico's children had been buried that day in the hard, thin soil on which Praia Nova huddled, 317 steps above the coral jetty and the unforgiving sea.

She walked toward the great hall on the path they called *Rua do Rei*—the King's Street. In truth only four men and one woman in Praia Nova had ever seen a street, and they had no king save the Lord God Almighty. *Rua do Rei* was just wide enough for two goats to pass, and had a rope strung to provide a grip during one of the great Wall storms off the Atlantic. One side opened into a ravine where the villagers threw what little garbage they were not able to intensively and obsessively reuse. The other passed close to a knee of *a Muralha.*

Juan and Portis Mendes had found a boy, but no one had brought him to her. Instead the fools had taken their prize to the *fidalgos.*

He was English, she'd heard, and had not come from the sea like every Praia Novado. Not from the sea at all, but down the eastern path through the countries and kingdoms of *a Muralha* toward mythic *Africa.*

Paolina hated, hated, hated being told things. All they had to do was let her see and she would find a way. When the earthquakes dried the springs that watered Praia Nova, she'd built the pedal-powered pump to raise water from the Westerly Creek down near sea level. When Jorg Penoyer got his leg trapped up on the coal face, she'd figured out the pressure points in the rock and set rope-and-tackle rig to get him out without an amputation. She understood the world, and when the *fidalgos* managed to forget Paolina was a girl, they remembered that.

Even more she hated being told she was merely a girl. Not even a woman yet. God had not put her on this Northern Earth to squeeze out some lout's get like a she-goat every nine months after being topped. Women lived only to serve, while the *pilas* of the men made them Lords of Creation.

To hell with that, Paolina thought.

She stopped outside the great hall and stared up at the sky. The earth's track gleamed, tracing a brass-bright line across the hemisphere of the heavens, that barely bowed outward from *a Muralha*. The Wall itself remained mighty as ever, the world's stone muscle, greater than any imagination could encompass.

Except hers.

Paolina smiled in the evening darkness. God could set His little traps. She would find her way out.

The rising blare of voices called her onward. She marched toward the doors of the great hall, closed now against evening's chill and the untoward attentions of people like her.

INSIDE, THE men did what they usually did, which was pretend not to notice her. Dom Alvaro, Dom Pietro, Fra Bellico, Benni Penoyer, and Dom Mendes were pulled close around a plank table in the main hall, a bottle of *bagaceira* between them drained down to eye-watering vapors and bubbled glass.

The English boy—a young man, really—sat on a bench against the west wall. Half a leering face, broken off some great enkidu carving, was jammed into the stone above him. He was sallow and burned by the sun, with greasy, pale hair and a tired look in his eyes. Their gazes met a moment. There was no spark of recognition, no sense of a kindred spirit close to hand.

Just another man, then, in love with his own *pila,* to whom she was nothing more than furniture.

Still, Paolina wished she'd gotten to him first, before the stranger witnessed the drunken anger of the *fidalgos.* He would think them nothing more than a village of fools. This boy, who must have seen London or Camelot once, now knew her people to be little more than asses braying in an unswept stable at the very edge of the world.

Paolina felt her anger rising again.

"We cannot afford him," shouted Dom Mendes. He was haggard, dusty to the elbows with the work of building new boats. Oh, they had not liked her opinion of that effort. "That old fool who lived among us before the waves came was bad enough, and we dwelt amid plenty then. There are too many mouths now."

"One less today," blubbered Fra Bellico, who had not missed a meal yet though he kept his Bible always close to hand.

"My boys hunt," Mendes hissed.

Penoyer snorted. "Yes, and bring back more mouths." No *fidalgo* he, his grandfather having come off an English boat by way of unsuccessful mutiny. Only quality took the titles of respect in Praia Nova.

Caught between anger and embarrassment, Paolina finally stepped up to their table. She shoved herself between Mendes and Pietro. "Do you suppose he might understand Portuguese?"

Bellico waved a pudgy hand. "He is English. The roast

beefs never speak anyone else's tongue, only their own barbarous barf."

"Then I shall speak to him in English," she announced. "Perhaps he brings knowledge or tools with which to feed himself and others."

Penoyer, pale as a grub with hair the color of fireweed flowers, shot her a glare before answering in that language, "No good will come of it, girl."

The boy perked up a bit, then slumped down as the words sank in.

"It can't possibly get any worse," she snapped, also in English.

Let Penoyer explain it to the *fidalgos*.

Paolina stepped around to the boy. "Come with me," she told him, in his language.

He stood and followed her out, without a backward glance. Nothing lost there, she realized. Outside she turned to him. "I am sorry." She paused to frame her next words.

"*Não faz mal*," he replied, surprising her. *It doesn't matter.*

Despite herself, Paolina giggled. "You understood everything they said?"

"Most of it." English again.

"My mother has bread." It was the kindest thing she knew to do for the boy. She took his hand and tugged him along the path that was King Street, back to the houses of Praia Nova and their quiet, hungry women.

TO SAVE the expense of the candle, they ate on the back step of the hut. Paolina's mother washed and swept the stone daily. She'd been sitting quietly, staring out at the moonlit Atlantic when Paolina came for the bread, and did not stir.

So it had been in the years since Paolina's father's boat came back without him. Marc Penoyer had been captain. He and his two brothers had sworn a tale so alike it had to be concocted—even at six, Paolina had known no two people perfectly agreed on anything. People didn't *see* what was in front of them. They saw only what was dear to their hearts.

After that, her mother worked her days and dreamt away the nights. Sometimes she spoke, sometimes she didn't, but Paolina always had at least one dress. She'd never gone an entire day without eating something.

It was the bargain of childhood, she'd supposed. As her cleverness had begun to count for something extra, Paolina had made sure there was always a little flour from the sorry mill above town, always a little dried meat from the line-caught fish the idled boatmen brought in.

The boy asked no questions about her mother, merely gnawing the crust with a gusto that betrayed how long it had been since he'd eaten decently. She'd spared him only two chunks torn from the loaf, and a handful of dried sardinella, but Paolina knew that offering food made her civilized.

He'd seen *London,* a voice within her cried. London. Even Dr. Minor had not been there.

In that moment, she hated *a Muralha,* Praia Nova, and everything else about her life. She stared up at the brass in the sky, wondering how to break it and set free the earth, and herself.

"Thank you," the boy said.

"Hmm?" She swallowed the harder words which lay too close to her tongue.

"Thank you. They were going to throw me out of the village, weren't they?"

"Of course." Despite her anger, Paolina laughed. "You might say or do something dangerous. News of the world helps no one, serving only to make us doubt our traditions. Besides, we are starving."

"So am I."

She looked over at him. The boy wore a leather wrap, something that had been tailored in a sense, but as if sewn by cats who had only seen paintings of real clothing. He had a grubby, torn shirt beneath that, and a pair of canvas trousers that must have once been white. Bare feet, which made her wince.

"Sure you did not walk here along the Wall?" she asked him.

"I fell from a ship."

She resisted the urge to glance toward the ocean far below, but there must have been something in her face. He raised one hand in defense. "An airship. I fell from one of Her Imperial Majesty's airships."

Despite herself, Paolina was impressed. "You look well enough for a man who fell to earth."

"I had a parachute."

She didn't know the word, but she was not going to ask him to explain. It obviously referred to a device for retarding the rate of fall. Cloth or ribbons could do that, though with his weight, it would need a wide spread to provide sufficient surface area for braking. In the back of her mind, she began to work out the formula for the relationship between the size of the cloth and the weight of the load.

"I am Paolina Barthes," she said. "This paradise on Northern Earth is Praia Nova."

He stood and bowed awkwardly. "Clarence Davies, late the loblolly boy aboard Her Imperial Majesty's airship *Bassett*." After a moment he added, "Very late, for it has been two years since I fell overboard and began my walk along the Wall."

Now she was very impressed. "You survived two years on your own?"

He nodded, still looking both hungry and hunted. It could not have been easy—Praia Nova barely clung to life, and that was with several hundred people who at least theoretically could coordinate defenses and share what they had.

"You must know how to live out there, then," she said.

"Knew how to live aboard *Bassett*." His head drooped lower. "Stay out of Captain Smallwood's way, listen to whatever the doctor mumbles when he ain't drinking, watch out for the clever dicks like Malgus and that boy of his."

"You're not a— clever?" She was disappointed. He was *English.* They were the genius sorcerers who ran the world. Dr. Minor had taught her that, before he'd fled into the wilderness.

She'd learned so much from the old Englishman.

"Just a boy, me," Clarence said. "The officers and the chiefs, they know their business. Al-Wazir, he was a magician, could make a man do anything. Need to, I guess, to work the ropes."

The power of compulsion. That explained a great deal about the British Empire.

The boy went on. "Smallwood, too. The gas division. They walk in poison, you know."

"This *Bassett* was a magnificent ship?"

For the first time, Clarence Davies smiled. "The greatest. Soaring through the clouds on a summer day, looking down on them whales and sharks and fuzzy wuzzies . . ." His head dropped again. "I want to go back to England, though. But 'tis too far to walk."

"You flew through the air to come here, and now you cannot find your way home." Something in Paolina's heart melted, that she had not known was frozen. "They'll grumble for a month, the *fidalgos,* and never come to a decision. So I decide now. I invite you in my mother's name. We will find a boy's family for you to stay with, and I will make sure there is a bit more food."

"I . . . I . . . have nothing to give."

"Nothing is required. Help where you can, lend your muscles, speak to me in English." She smiled, trying to coax another flash of bright teeth out of this Clarence. "There are few enough safe places on *a Muralha.* Stay here a while."

"Thank you." He came to some visible decision, a flash of relief and recognition in his face, then dug deep into an inner pocket of his leather wrap. Clarence shoved a little bag at her. "Here. I don't need this. Ain't wound it in months. Smart, clever girl like you maybe could use it."

The thing was heavy, a hunk of metal or glass. She pulled it out and corrected herself. A hunk of metal *and* glass. Round face, with hours on it like a sundial and a heavy metal rim containing more weight. The face was topped by three metal arrows. There were tinier faces within, with their own calibrations, and a little cutaway showing something behind the face.

She peered close and saw Heaven.

Gears.

It was God's gearing, the mechanisms of the earth and sky captured in the palm of her hand. Light flooded her head for a moment, the dawn of a new awareness. Paolina's stomach knotted in something between fear and fascination. She'd had no idea that a person could fashion a model of the world to carry with him.

"It counts the hours," she whispered, her voice and hands trembling in awe.

"Yes." He touched a little cap extending from one end. "See? It's a stemwinder. A Dent marine chronometer that needs no key."

Her fingers lay on the knurls of the cap. At his nod, Paolina very gently twisted it.

The tiny model of the world within clicked, just as the heavens did at midnight.

This was Creation in the palm of her hand. The English were truly magicians.

Much to her surprise, Paolina began to cry.

PRAIA NOVA had seven books. They were kept in the great hall, in an inner closet with the precious bottles used to contain *bagaceira* when Fra Bellico found the necessaries to distill more, or the wildflower wine the women made when Fra Bellico lacked materials, time, or ambition.

There was half an English Bible, the Old Testament through the middle of Ezekiel. It was water damaged. The New Testament, with its stories of the Romans and their horofixion of Christ, existed in Praia Nova only as a scrawled leather scroll reconstructed from the memories of the various shipwrecked sailors who'd brought their indifferent faiths to the village over the generations. It did not matter what she thought of the prophets or the inept copy work of recent times–the Bible needed no more explanation than a look to the sky.

The other books were a different matter entirely. Her favorite was *Fiéis e Verdadeiros Segredos,* a Portuguese translation of a book that claimed to have originally been published in French, written by a Comte de Saint-Germain. It was a magnificent volume, bound in a slick, smooth leather that she was fairly certain was human skin. The title was stamped into the binding with traces of gold leaf and faded red pigment. There were lurid woodcuts within, lavishly illustrating scenes of debauchery from the ancient days. She'd spent time studying those, but had not yet divined the meaning of most. In any case, Paolina found it difficult to credit what Saint-Germain said of himself and the world. The man, whoever he had truly been, was an extraordinary storyteller at the least. She hoped to meet a Jew one day so that she could pursue some of the questions raised in *Segredos.*

There was also *Archidoxes Magica,* by Paracelsus. It was bound in boards, and quite damaged by damp and age. Furthermore, no one could aid her with the Latin. She had no second text to compare it with in order to puzzle out the language. As a result Paolina had struggled mightily with the book. In *Segredos,* Saint-Germain claimed to have known Paracelsus as an alchemist and physic, but that only told her one thing–fraud or genius, he had seen into the heart of the world.

That inspired her.

Three of the other books were popular texts, two in English, one in Spanish: *The Mystery of Edwin Drood* by Charles Dickens, *Mathias Sandorf* by Jules Verne, and *Cartas Marruecas* by José Cadalso. There was also one volume in an alphabet that looked maddeningly familiar while making no sense at all. Paolina was surprised the last hadn't been burned for fire starter. She'd read through the English works many times, and puzzled through Cadalso twice.

She'd learned how strange the world was, beyond *a Muralha* and the goat-dung paths of Praia Nova. That, and how badly she wished she lived in a part of the Northern Earth where there were printing presses and libraries and bookshops.

Even Dr. Minor's visit to Praia Nova, while immensely improving her English and her knowledge of the world, had only deepened her dissatisfaction.

Now, though, now she had a treasure beyond price. She had a pocket watch. A stemwinding marine chronometer, to be specific.

Neither the Bible nor Saint-Germain had anything to say directly about watches, though both certainly discussed clockwork—albeit somewhat metaphorically in the Bible. Paracelsus was no help at all, and neither was Cadalso. Verne and Dickens, however, seemed fully in command of a world where pocket watches were ordinary.

In the days that followed, she reread both works carefully. The purpose of the watch would have been clear enough even if Davies had not explained it. Paolina was far more interested in the design and construction. She'd never so much as seen a clock. There were obvious inferences to be made about the mechanism from looking at God's design for the universe. He had written His plan in the sky, after all.

What Paolina wanted was a clear set of instructions.

THE STEMWINDER was heavy in the pocket of her homespun smock. She knew it was there the way she knew her heartbeat was there. Wound, it ticked. Ticking, it reflected the world.

Time beats at the heart of everything, she thought.

It was one of those ideas that pricked a spark in her mind, a little flare that staked a claim of importance.

God had made the universe of clockwork. The world ticked and turned. Two years ago, it had stuttered. The great waves and quakes came from deep within, she knew. Midnight had slipped by a few seconds. No one else understood, and there was no point in explaining, but she'd known.

Then the world had been fixed. Whatever time beat at the heart of the earth had been restored. Paolina wished she knew how. A question that ran through all the books (except the Bible, of course) was whether God acted directly in the world, or simply let His handiwork sort itself out.

Something had been sorted out.

And still time beat at the heart of everything. The stemwinder was a model of the universe, no larger than the palm of her hand, no thicker than two of her fingers, and it ticked away the moments and hours just as all of Creation did.

Paolina put it close to her ear, listening with the words of Dickens and Verne and the Old Testament prophets close in her mind. Ezekiel 24:6 suggested itself to her in the gentle ticking deep within. *Woe to the bloody city, to the brasswork in which there is verdigris, and whose verdigris has not gone out of it! Take out of it piece after piece, without making a choice.*

That was clear enough. God was telling her to take the watch apart.

PAOLINA'S MOST difficult problem was finding a clean, clear workspace. Whatever gears and trains lay within the stemwinder were tiny reflections of the brass in the heavens. She'd need a room sealed from the winds, relatively free of dust and dirt, where the complex work could remain undisturbed in her absence.

The inner room of the great hall, among the books and bottles, would have been ideal. But even Paolina couldn't quite imagine how to get the *fidalgos* to come around to that. They would beat her for a stupid chit and set her to scraping moss off the water stairs if she had the temerity to even ask.

She wandered the village, looking at the houses and storerooms that comprised most of Praia Nova. The ones that were not inhabited were tumbledown. Paolina didn't want to contemplate the patience required to clean up an abandoned hut.

On the Oporto shelf, the second ledge above town, where more of the thin wheat fields ran, she realized she was looking at her answer–the mushroom sheds. They were sealed with lacquered canvas, and they were quiet. It would be a month or more before another set of trays was picked. All she needed was a bit of light.

Best of all, the women of the town ran the sheds. Senhora Armandires was the dame of the mushrooms. Paolina had built a much improved chimney in the woman's house last year, once Senhor Armandires had finally moved out for good and the senhora could make her own choices. The lady would make no objection.

Light was still an issue, but it would take little enough to see the watch. Candle stubs were her friends.

Paolina went off to find Clarence. He could help her drag a table out of one of the abandoned houses and up to the Oporto shelf. And a cloth to cover it.

She would find a way. This was the solving of problems. She was good at that.

DURING THE course of the following days, Paolina opened the back of the stemwinder to observe the delicate movements of the mechanisms within. What she saw nearly turned her away from her project. She lacked the tools to grasp such miniscule things. She might be able to make those, in time, with scraps from the Alcides' smithy. She would need a lens, as well, scarcely possible here in Praia Nova. In any case, this was a task for the slow and patient. She stuck with picks and pries made out of hardwood splinters.

Clarence was something of a help, ghosting about and answering her occasional question. He spent time foraging, too, farther from Praia Nova than most of the locals would go. Of course, he'd walked the Wall for two years–the boy had survived far stranger things than the glittering, scaled cats that occasionally prowled the ledges here, or the bright, frigid rocks that sometimes bounded down from higher up.

He came running in the evening of her fourth day in the mushroom shed. Panting, sweating, as the whites of his eyes gleamed in the light of her little candle stub. "The *fidalgos* are looking for you!" he shouted in Portuguese.

"Someone is always looking for me." A tiny stab of fear stole into her heart.

Davies switched to English. "You have been summoned. Senhora Armandires argues with Fra Bellico down in the village."

Paolina sighed and put down the teakwood picks. She carefully covered the stemwinder with a square of pale silk, part of the bounty harvested from the body of a Chinaman brought up in the nets the year before the big waves. "What does the good father want of me?" She dusted off her hands.

Clarence looked down at his feet a moment. "The *fidalgos* are angry."

The answer was obvious now, but her rising irritation made her unkind. "About what are they angry, Englishman?"

Walking behind her through the canvas flap that was the door, he mumbled some answer she couldn't hear.

"Pardon?" Nasty now.

"That you were given the watch."

"That I was given the watch." Her singsong tones mocked him. What had she ever thought worthy of this idiot boy? "The heavens opened up and spat a watch into my hands, which by the grace of God should have been given to the men of Praia Nova, is that it?"

"I'm sorry," he muttered, but she already raced down the paths toward the shouting.

THE *FIDALGOS* were drunk and angry. The first thing Paolina realized was that they were into the wildflower wine. The *bagaceira* was gone, and Fra Bellico had not found any more of the wild grapes and plums from which to press his pomace and make more. No wonder they were upset, forced to drink a woman's swill.

The five were drawn up to their table again, facing her: Alvaro, Pietro, Bellico, Penoyer, and Mendes, who chewed his moustache and looked thoughtful. The rest merely seemed possessed by the same tired anger that had gripped the men in the village since the fishing fleet had been lost.

They badly missed the seafood trade with the enkidus and the down-trail tribes.

"You!" roared Bellico. "Thieving girl! We should sell you up *a Muralha*."

"I have stolen nothing," said Paolina. "I give you everything and more. What is it you want now?"

"What is our due," Mendes said quietly, casting a side-long glare at the others. "What the boy mistakenly set in your hand."

"What he *gave* me?" She let her voice seethe with contempt, though in truth these men scared her. Not for who they were, but for what they could do. The *fidalgos* in council, which they were now, were judges and swords of the law in Praia Nova. Never mind that no one owned such a blade.

This was as large a matter as they'd ever broached her over.

"The watch," said Penoyer. He was flush, even in the candlelight, with a graceless air of shame.

"You want me to give you my watch?" As with Clarence, she would make them say it.

"Yes!" It was Bellico again. "The village could do much with that wealth of metal. Trade it, keep it for a treasure. Not let it be greased by the clumsy hands of a youthful *Carapau de Corrida* with more ambition than sense!"

"Fra," said Paolina slowly and deliberately. "If you call me that name again, I shall make sure your still produces nothing but vinegar, and your *pilinha* will burn every morning for the rest of your days."

"She's a witch," muttered Alvaro. "Always was, little chit."

"Enough," said Mendes. He was not the bull among them–that was Fra Bellico–but he was the only *fidalgo* with enough sense that Paolina could consider having respect for him. "It does not matter. What matters is you took an object of great value, easily considered salvage and thus the property of all, and have hidden it away. That should have been the decision of the village."

"You mean your decision." Paolina just couldn't stop herself from speaking. The men didn't merely believe they were entitled–they *were* entitled. This transcended reason.

"Our decision is the decision of village." Mendes leaned forward, the room around him now quiet, the guttering candle filling his eyes with shadowed darkness. "Your decision is not."

And there it was. The truth of the matter. She might as well argue with *a Muralha* as argue with generations of tradition.

"No," Paolina told him. "You cannot have it until I am done."

"You will not obey the decision of the *fidalgos* in council?" Mendes asked. Slowly, carefully.

She was on an edge here. But she simply couldn't give

in. If she did it now, she was lost. "No." It was amazing how easy that word was to repeat.

Mendes glanced at Bellico in particular. The father took a deep, shuddering breath, then nodded. "Very well. At fifteen, you are old enough to heed the will of the village or pay the consequences. I only regret we did not take you in hand earlier."

They were getting up from the table, chairs scraping, feet shuffling as the large drunken men encircled her.

Paolina felt a stab of fear. She shrieked when they grabbed her, already clamping her knees together, but the *fidalgos* dragged her to the back room, shoved her in with the books and bottles, and shut the one door in all of Praia Nova that actually had a key.

It took her a while to cry, and longer to begin screaming, but the door remained thick, wooden and locked no matter how she pounded and pleaded. In time, they doused their candle and left. She didn't know whether the wine had run out or they had tired of the noise of her fear.

Al-Wazir

Threadgill Angus al-Wazir, formerly Ropes Division chief petty officer aboard HIMS *Bassett,* ship lost in service along the Wall, scratched at the starched collar. The civvie shirt cut into his neck like a dock monkey's shiv. "This is worse than a lashing," he muttered, though no one could hear him save the two lobsterbacks standing guard in front of the great double doors outside which he waited.

Royal Marines, in uniforms that could have been paraded in his grandfather's time. Insufficient to fend off a howling mob, and yet too much for the mere keeping of a door, no matter how many admirals and MPs sat on the other side of it.

Some days he almost missed starving on that dhow off the Mauritanian coast under the blazing Atlantic sun. That was an honest fate for a good sailor. Nothing like death by sweat and knife-edged crease.

Civvies, at that. Not even a uniform. He hadn't worn
civvies since he'd left short pants. Even on leave, it was a
tar's canvas trousers and some old blues.

The room was as bad as the clothing. The lobsterbacks
might as well have been furniture, bayonets silvered and
polished to shaving-mirror brightness. The walls were
done in some strange lumber, in them little panels like
pictures in frames except it was all the same wood. A
chandelier with far too much cut glass glowed with ill-
wired electrics. A big painting of the clockwork two-
decker *Vincent Leonard,* that had foundered under
Nelson and put an end to those old spring engines. Back
to sail, it had been, until they'd worked out the steam. Another big painting of the admiral himself, victorious at
Trafalgar with the head of Villeneuve dangling from one
hand. The old Froggie's eyes were as surprised as death
ever made a man.

Al-Wazir saluted the Frenchman. It had been near the
last gasp of their power.

Below the level of the paintings the room grew peculiar—delicate settees covered with paisleys he wouldn't
bury a dog in, tiny end tables bearing tinier silver dishes
of mints the size of biscuit weevils. Rugs on the floor
from somewhere far to the east, with the look of knotting
by little fingers. He'd seen enough posh in dockside
knocking shops to have an idea. All that bawdy house
stuff was just so much tinfoil and chintz imitation of this
room, where the Queen herself could have eaten off the
parquet flooring had she taken a mind to do so.

Being a chief petty officer, however discharged at the
moment, al-Wazir had to admire the obsessive attention
to cleanliness. He doubted even the most white-gloved
psychotic could have found fault on an inspection here,
unless one of the marines had soiled his linens. Knowing
that lot, their bladders were at firm attention.

He scratched at his collar again, grinning with evil intent at the unmoving sentries. *He* was out of uniform,
he'd by God scratch. Al-Wazir studied them intently. Yes,

the one on the left had a bead of sweat on the tip of his nose. He didn't quite have the kidney to give a good ribbing, not when yon doors could open at any moment and his undivided attention be required by Admiralty, but for now he could enjoy another man's discomfort with a genteel incivility.

Al-Wazir waited in an antechamber somewhere within the second floor of the Ripley Building, where Admiralty was housed. He was aware of the irony of finding himself in this elevated estate only after being discharged from the Royal Navy by an examining board at Bristol. The summons to London had been a surprise, to say the least. Al-Wazir had been on a train to Scotland with the last of the Queen's shillings in his pocket. A whey-faced lieutenant with a squad of Royal Marines in sensible woolens and hard hands had pulled him off at Pemberton. It was not arrest this time, as had happened when their dhow had finally creaked into Bristol harbor to the jeers of the dockside idlers. Rather, he was taken aboard a sealed first-class car, alone except for his escorts.

That had been all right with him. Al-Wazir hadn't really been looking forward to seeing his ma anyway. Besides which, he possessed no notion of what to do next out of uniform. Al-Wazir had figured on dying in the air one day, but when *Bassett* had gone down under the combination of monstrous attack and inclement weather, the Lord God Almighty hadn't seen fit to take him with the ship.

So now he was here, scrubbed and shaved and pressed and folded into a black suit and a little seat in a room where Prime Minister Lloyd George had passed him by an hour before.

Quality, his ma always said he was destined to hit quality. She'd just meant it in a different way.

AL-WAZIR STARTLED awake when the doors creaked open. A quiet little man in a suit much like al-Wazir's own nodded to him.

The Royal Marines remained a pair of silent logheads. This was no better than being called before the captain on account of some ropes idler going stupid while he wasn't looking. Admiralty, and even the Prime Minister, were nothing more than bigger captains.

So he followed the quiet man into a very large room, where older, heavier men with long muttonchops and red faces sat around a table the size of a longboat, nodding at a bloody huge chart of some islands. It wasn't anywhere al-Wazir had ever been; that was for certain. He adopted the blank look-at-nothing practiced by sailors in the presence of officers since the first reed boats had sculled along the Euphrates.

His escort faded into a number of similar men making notes and riffling through red folders along the dark edges of the room. There were no windows here, just as in the outer room, though a pair of frosted skylights admitted some gray from above. Otherwise the room was lit by electricks in sconces around the walls, giving forth a slightly scorched smell. Where there might have been more paintings of naval history, there were now charts or maps. Al-Wazir would be damned if he was going to stare.

Busy. The room was busy. In some indefinable way, it reminded him of a gun deck just before battle. Men were sweating and the air was thick with tension. Simply because no guns were in evidence did not mean there was no enemy at hand.

"Chief al-Wazir." He was being addressed by a broad-faced man with humor in his eyes, dressed as all of them were here in black. The Prime Minister, in fact–Lloyd George himself.

"Sir, yes sir."

"The man with the interesting name. You would seem to be as Scottish as the next oat-eater from Lanarkshire, I must say." The Welsh in Lloyd George's voice was almost absent, though the humor carried through. "You may think of me as the Member from Caernarfon Boroughs, if that helps. As for the rest of the gentlemen here, they are simply persons committed to the interests of the Crown. Their names and titles should not matter to you."

"Sir, no sir." Though he did wonder why a room full of senior men in the heart of the Admiralty complex should be so empty of uniforms. Including his own.

"Tell me, Chief . . ." Lloyd George's eyes sparkled. "Have you ever heard of the city of Chersonesus Aurea?"

Of all the questions Her Imperial Majesty's Prime Minister might have asked him, that was not one al-Wazir would have imagined in his wildest dreams. "No idea, sir."

"To be expected, I suppose." The PM sounded disappointed. "Neither had any of the rest of us. I daresay you know the Wall, and the Bight of Benin?"

Al-Wazir felt a smile cracking. "Thumping huge bit of rock, sir, far to the south. Been on her a bit, then sailed myself home out of the Bight by way of Dahomey and Mauritania."

"So we have been informed." He walked around al-Wazir, an inspection in all but name. "I shan't apologize for your discharge hearing in Bristol, Chief. Regulations are regulations." Lloyd George reappeared in al-Wazir's line of sight. "But would you be interested in going back to the Wall on Her Imperial Majesty's service?"

"At my rank and grade, sir?" The question slipped out.

"If that is what is required. Or as a civilian— No . . . I think not." Lloyd George nodded at one of the quiet men on the edge of the room. "I expect you'll be a chief petty officer once more by Monday next, if not sooner."

"Sir, yes sir." Al-Wazir could feel his sweat pooling now. He felt much like the marine he'd silently mocked in the antechamber.

"Kitchens," said the PM in a carrying voice. "The other map, please."

One of the quiet little men used a long pole topped by a metal hook to roll up the island chart. A moment later he replaced it with a chart of the Bight of Benin, the bulk of the Wall a dark line brooding at its southern extent.

"Your ship was driven down there, yes?"

"Sir, yes sir. Storm and enemy action."

"I've seen the report of your court-martial. Pity to lose Smallwood and so much of his crew. Experienced hands, the lot."

Al-Wazir held back a shuddering breath. They were long dead now, his old crewmates and charges, and nothing he could do for them or their memory from this distance. "I was rather surprised to make it home alive, sir."

Lloyd George gave him a long look. "I'm sure it's a fascinating tale, Chief, but I don't suppose I'll ever have time for it. However, your recent experiences have granted you the unique qualification of being the Crown's leading expert on survival at the Wall. We lost far too much with Gordon's expedition of 1900."

"*Bassett* foundered in support of that same expedition, sir."

"Of course." The PM seemed slightly surprised. "Yet the holocaust produced you, trained and experienced, annealed in the blazing sun of the tropics."

"Burnt red is more like it, sir." He wasn't sure about the annealed bit.

"There is a town, Acalayong, just above the foot of the Wall at the easternmost verge of the Bight. I would ask you to take ship and go there."

"Sir, if I'm in uniform again, I'm under orders." Al-Wazir could feel the trickle of his sweat burgeoning to rivers. Nervous, he was not nervous. A chief never was. "Her Imperial Majesty's Navy don't ask its sailors what they want to do."

Lloyd George gave him a long, thoughtful look. "In this case, I'd prefer to have your willing agreement, Chief al-Wazir. There's a scientific expedition being mounted, under qualified supervision. I've many men who will follow orders. I'd very much like an experienced man along for whom I can have some hope of personal trust."

"Sir . . ." Al-Wazir swallowed hard. "You do not know me in the least wee bit. I'm a sailor, a Scotsman, and quarter an Arab. Any Englishman will tell you that makes me a liar three times over. You've no cause or call to trust me. Not outside the following of orders."

"I said hope of trust," the PM reminded him. "Neither of us is a fool. We'd both have been cast aside or left for dead long ago if we were. I've good men and true in the expedition, both officially placed and otherwise. But they're each under orders in their way. You, sir . . ." He took a deep breath. "You survived, in a place where most men have perished without a trace. As did your father, it would seem, back in his day. That's a special quality in a man. Quite possibly incongruent with the quality of obedience."

Al-Wazir cut to the obvious point. "So you're not certain this expedition will succeed?"

"No. I'm not." Lloyd George turned toward the map. "I shouldn't think it prudent, or even possible, to claim certainty, no matter what drivel we tell the papers. It is a great hunt we're about, Chief. We're surveying to drive a tunnel through the Wall, to beat the Chinaman at his own game. Because regardless of whether you or I have ever heard of Chersonesus Aurea, the Celestial Emperor most certainly has."

"They're finding a way across the Wall?" al-Wazir asked. Might as well find a way to the moon. There were always stories, to be sure–*Bassett*'s lost navigator Malgus had walked amid some of the tales himself, and his poor, doomed boy Hethor–but it was one thing for some plucky hero to scale God's ramparts and look down on the kingdoms of the Southern Earth. It was far different for Johnnie Chinaman to do the same thing with his wizards and his priests and his coolies and his endless waves of marching yellow soldiers under their banners of heaven.

Al-Wazir found that thought horrifying.

Lloyd George cleared his throat. "Through the Wall, we believe. Which cannot be permitted. Should China gain a foothold on Southern Earth unanswered by Her

Imperial Majesty, our game of nations is at an end. There are no higher stakes.

"Her Imperial Majesty is sending a scientific and technical expedition under one of Her German subjects, the engineer Lothar Ottweill. Herr Doctor Professor Ottweill will have full command of the mission. It is my hope that you will accept responsibility for securing their survival. A thousand men and more are nothing but a mote in the grand design of the Wall."

The Wall. He'd hated it, feared it, lived on it, fled from it. It had eaten his da's wit in the years before. The old man was never the same once he'd come back. It had eaten al-Wazir's ship and most of his friends and mates.

It was the only thing besides the thought of serving once more in the air that might truly bring him back to life.

Al-Wazir dropped to one knee. "Sir," he said, fumbling for the words. "For the sake of that, I'll be your man to the Wall and beyond."

"Up." The PM was clearly uncomfortable. It was as if the two of them were alone, in this room of whispers and maps. "Mr. Kitchens will take you in hand. There's much to be learned about Dr. Ottweill and the expedition before you leave. I believe the next sailing is in less than a week."

Al-Wazir stood. Kitchens was there, though he hadn't seen the man move. These dark-suited men were the true heart of the Empire, not the braying asses in Commons nor the bright Lords in their formal estate.

He tried to take comfort from that thought as he was led away from the Prime Minister without a farewell.

Childress

Librarian Childress sat at her high desk in the Day Missions Library, the Berkeley School of Divinity at Yale University. Her heels hung nine and quarter inches off the floor when she used this stool. The height allowed her to look down at all but the lankest of the Yale boys. That in turn helped keep their worst tendencies at bay.

Most people had the sense to be afraid of an old woman with iron-gray hair and a long ruler.

The day had clicked slowly by, dust roiling in the shafts of golden light from the high windows, the ever-present smell of leather and glue and paper that made up the bellows breath of the library, the footfalls of students and porters, the gleam of the dark, ancient oak shelves under generations of oil.

She loved these autumn days when the semester had begun but the students were not yet consumed with research and the fear of their midterm marks. The trees were just turning outside, while the building within still retained a bit of the warmth of summer.

The clock on the administration building struck the third hour of the afternoon as a woman approached her desk. That was unusual—there were no women at Yale, save for a few specialists such as herself. The porters were ordinarily quite firm about not admitting the weaker sex.

This one was no student. Perhaps forty, with pale brown hair and an unmemorable face, wearing high button shoes and a sage-green silk dress that rustled of crinolines. She had a white sweater shrugged over her shoulders against the possibility of an early autumn chill.

The visitor's steps echoed with a controlled rhythm that set Childress' mind to racing. Her arms seemed a trifle thick, muscled even, through the silk. Her eyes were the same pale green as her dress. They tracked the room briefly, then focused on Childress.

This was a dangerous person, trained to violence in a way that Childress had rarely encountered in men and never in a woman.

"Emily McHenry Childress." Neither question nor greeting. Just a statement.

"You already know." Her voice was so soft that the woman had to strain slightly to hear her.

"As may be." The accent was London with a hint of the Continental beneath it. The woman reached up and touched the edge of Childress' high, narrow desk. Something clicked beneath her palm. "Tonight." Her voice was equally soft. "On the Long Wharf, at dusk."

A feather carved of delicate ivory remained behind when she walked away.

It reminded Childress painfully of a silver feather a boy had brought her some two years earlier. He'd stood here, holding back tears and wondering how it was he'd seen an angel of the Lord when no one else knew or cared. She'd sent him on in the name of the *avebianco,* the white birds.

She'd wondered, ever since the earthquakes stopped and time seemed to settle down once more, when her turn would come. She'd wondered ever since if she would go.

Even without the threat implied by the messenger, Childress knew she would have answered the summons.

THROUGH THE course of the afternoon, Childress walked the halls of the Day Missions Library. She made one silent excuse after another as she passed from room to room. Inspection . . . a lost book . . . reinforcement of her *ars memoriae.* Nostalgia, even, for the overwhelmed young woman first hired on sufferance during the labor shortages of the Loggers' Rebellion.

Childress was certain that if she went to Long Wharf at dusk, she would not be returning to the library. The messenger hadn't said so, but it stood to reason that the *avebianco* would hardly have sent someone all the way from Europe to New Haven for a quiet hour over tea and sandwiches. One had to look into the thing to understand it. The true powers in society were almost always invisible, much like God's messenger angels passing on a moonless night–sensed but rarely seen.

The sum of her days thus far had been little more than another round of days. Her greatest deed in life had probably been to send that young man on to Boston. She might as well follow the path and see where it led.

She'd sworn herself to this, after all, when she'd become part of the *avebianco* all those years ago.

Childress went to pack her desk. Though the entire building had in a sense belonged to her, there was little enough that was personally hers. Reverend Doctor Dunleavey was the head of the library, with his fur cap and tassels and seat on the faculty senate, but it had been Childress who sought out new works, accepted bequests and donations, cataloged what came in and what was found moldering in the basement storerooms, shelved and then reshelved books as times changed the needs of the students.

Other clerks had come and gone, pinched men of furtive habits who spent too long looking at the coltish boys playing rugby in the yard outside, and the occasional woman waiting for a proposal to carry them to maternal, married life. She'd remained here, married to the library, girl and woman, for almost four decades.

And still the white birds had held her. Childress remembered when the first feather had come, pressed within a slim volume of anonymous verse that arrived addressed to her. It had carried marks from Strasbourg in Her Imperial Majesty's Germanies. Her sixth year at the library, 1877, and old Master Humberto had finally allowed her the privilege of cataloging new works. In that same month, this had come as if by signal.

Which, of course, it had been.

To be a librarian was to know everything that was known. Not the entire sum of human knowledge literally at the command of one's thoughts–Newton had perhaps been the last to do that. But to know what *could* be known, understand the indices and passwords of all the secrets of Creation. The science of libraries was the science of the truths hidden within the world. She'd even learned the *ars memoriae* as first described by Simonides of Ceos, using the library as a locus to build a memory mansion.

The library and its work were her life, both within and without, but for where God dwelt in her heart. Into this world the white birds had spoken with a bit of doggerel about the vanities of creation and those who stood in the stead of God. Later, there were other books, letters, whispered words. The *avebianco* were in libraries the world over, from the emerald-hatted mandarins of Imperial China, to the rough-hewn keepers of shipping records in African ports, to the university librarians of the British Empire.

Childress looked up to see the head porter watching her. Cletis Barron's long, dark face was infused with concern. "No one said you was going away." His voice was as deep and gentle as a boat's horn on the foggy Sound.

She tried to smile. "No one told me, either."

"Woman put away her nibs and her cutting knife, she ain't coming back."

"I shall miss you," Librarian Childress said firmly.

"We too, ma'am. We too."

With that, he escorted her to the door. When she stepped outside, the evening chill was already descending. She'd forgotten her cloak, but Barron handed it to her. "Go with pride," he said.

She nodded, words flashing away from her like fish before a hand set in a stream, then set her heels to the street and the walk down to the Long Wharf. She wondered as she strode whether the Reverend Doctor Dunleavey would even notice she was gone.

And that, Childress realized with a sad shiver, was perhaps the truest sum of her life.

NEW HAVEN was dubiously blessed with shallow anchorages, a problem that had been solved with the Long Wharf. The structure extended from the west side of the harbor well out across the tide flats to where the deepwater channel lay. Six airship towers stood closer in to shore, along the waterfront itself among the dories and skiffs and shallow-draft fishing boats that plied the coast and crossed the Sound. Only at the Long Wharf could steamers and clippers and Royal Navy ships be found.

A few years earlier, a coalition of merchants and shippers had built a great pier out in the middle of the harbor, near the far end of the Long Wharf, to provide greater ease in unloading and transshipment. An effort was in progress even now to reinforce both structures so that railroad trains could reach every portion. This would remove the necessity and expense of horse-drawn drayage from the ships to the freight terminals along the shore itself.

The gulls wheeled in great gray clouds amid the gathering dusk. The scent of their waste filled the air like damp ammonia. *The waterfront is a giant midden,* Childress thought, but without the benefit of tillage being turned so it could rot decently into the ground.

It was simple foolishness to think she'd find someone, anyone, on the Long Wharf. There were hundreds of longshoremen out there even now in the decline of the workday, along with their carts and hand trucks, horses, dogs, sailors both merchant and Naval, errand boys, pickle sellers, women of questionable virtue, customs officers, deputy port-masters and the miscellanea that any great port drew into itself. Childress had known this all along.

She would not find anyone, but they would find her. It was a reasonable presumption that the white birds had a ship tied up among the several dozen vessels moored to the Long Wharf. There they would conduct the business of the secret empire of knowledge.

The *avebianco* all held a common goal—quiet advancement of the Spiritualist cause. The movement went by different names in different places, even within the British Empire, but the purpose was always the same: acknowledge and preserve God's work in the world, while advancing the labors of Man. The Rationalists dismiss that viewpoint as secular spiritualism, while the orthodox laughed them away as feeble in both faith and mind.

It was of no matter to the white birds and their allies. Only a fool could look at the brasswork in the sky and deny God's handiwork. Only an idiot could look at the brasswork in the sky and declare God immaterial. Childress and her sliver of the quiet wisdom of librarians had been content to nudge where nudging was called for, teach where teaching would be heard, and report that which was noteworthy.

This business came back to Hethor and his feather, she knew. That had been a time when the world shook, great waves striking coasts all over Northern Earth. That New England had been spared was nothing short of a miracle, but English and Colonial lives had been lost aplenty elsewhere. The boy had gone seeking William of Ghent and passed out of her view. She'd heard sufficient echo of his later effort to know he'd achieved something.

Success, evidently, as the world seemed to be yet turning, and the horomancers had settled down once more to casting lots and predicting the fevers of children. William of Ghent had left Boston on a mysterious errand, not yet returned to the courts of Empire even now.

She tried not to wonder if her own note to the man in Boston who ran his specials had made things worse for poor Hethor. Phelps was part of the *avebianco,* too, in his way.

As she reflected, her boots echoed down the wooden planks, past bales of cargo netting, cotton and canvas, as well as larger, bulkier containers–hogsheads and tuns and barrels. There was a profusion of practice around her that signaled a vocabulary of action and word. Every craft carried its own cant, librarians and libertines alike.

Men looked at her, too. Wondering. Childress knew that nothing of her appearance telegraphed any sense of belonging here. She was far too old to be a dockside hussy, or even a madam. Her attire, high-necked black in close semblance of widow's weeds for all she'd never married, was far too plain to be a captain's wife or widow-owner. In the rising dark of the evening, the torchlight and great storm lanterns would deepen the lines on her face to those of a children's witch.

It was no surprise at all when the *avebianco* found her. The woman who'd visited her at the library looked out from under a sailor's flat hat, just as Master Boyett of the University of Connecticut libraries stepped around a stack of wide, shallow chests.

"Good evening, Librarian Childress," Boyett said quietly.

She was aware that at least four of the sailors nearby were not moving about at their tasks, but rather focused on her.

Childress let her voice go frosty. Boyett had always been a bit of a sucking grind. "Something of a walk from Storrs, isn't it, Brian? Out for your evening constitutional?"

Boyett moved his hands slightly, the *v*-and-*x* signal of the white birds. "I'm here as witness. . . ."

She took satisfaction that he couldn't quite bring himself to call her by her Christian name. She still had the advantage of him. Her only advantage now, and not one she could see a way to playing. "Witness what? I have been called, I come. Most of us spend our lives watching and waiting without ever serving at all."

The sailor-woman's hand closed on her arm. "Time to go, Librarian." Had Childress not seen this woman in a dress some hours earlier, she would not have questioned that a man stood beside her now.

"Nonsense," Childress answered. "The tide's running for several hours yet. Your sense of the dramatic is overtaking your judgment."

The grip grew tighter. "You will not be baffling me as you have him."

"Then I go. I came, did I not?"

Boyett shuddered. "I'm sorry."

"For what?" she asked, but he did not answer.

Then the woman led her up a gangplank of a fast packet named *Mute Swan*, which shuddered as its engines chuffed somewhere deep within the metal hull. Childress looked back when she reached the top. Boyett stared up after her.

"What did you tell him?" she asked her captor.

"The truth," the woman said. "As for you, you go below now."

Childress looked up at the brass curving in the evening sky, wondering if that poor, lost Hethor had found any reward to go with his success.